Broken Pieces

Eve Campbell

Chapter 1

Life doesn't give a shit about me. It never has.

Not when I was thrown into one fucked-up foster home after another, passed around by strangers with dead eyes and fake promises. Tossed into rooms reeking of mildew and disappointment. Treated like I was nothing more than a broken thing no one ever wanted to fix.

I stopped unpacking my bags when I was ten. Figured there was no fucking point.

What's the use of pretending you belong when every door you walk through slams shut before you've even learned their names?

You learn fast. Hope fades. Words dry up. Survival means vanishing before anyone notices you're there.

Every place promising it was safe ended up being its own brand of hell. Some were cold and cruel. Some were quiet, and that was worse. Silence scraping against your ribs. Rules shifting with the mood of whatever fucker was in charge.

There's no safety in this world. Just different ways of being torn apart.

The only family I've ever had are these other fucked-up foster kids they dumped me with. All of us cracked down the middle, barely holding it together with secrets and whatever rage we hadn't burned through yet.

None of us chose this shit. We were only the unlucky ones. Shoved into the same sinking boat, throwing our pain at each other like it might help keep us afloat. All screaming into the dark, hoping someone might hear us before we all go under.

So I started building walls. Thick ones. Cold, unbreakable fucking things. Brick by bitter brick. I laid them with every lie I was told, every slap I was given, every time someone looked at me and saw nothing worth keeping.

Now they're so goddamn high, I don't even know what's on the other side anymore.

My mouth turned into a weapon. A blade I honed with every betrayal, every stare telling me I wasn't worth the trouble. I didn't speak to be heard. I spoke to wound. Every word a cut. Every sentence a warning. Sarcasm sharp enough to scar. Smirks cutting deeper than fists. I struck first, bled them out with language, and called it survival.

Because softness... it's blood in the water, and I've already drowned in it too many times.

My heart... that died a long time ago. If there's anything left of it.

It's buried so goddamn deep beneath shadows, regret, and everything I never said. I wouldn't recognize the fucker if it clawed its way out. It doesn't beat. Doesn't ache. Only festers, rotting slowly inside a body built to survive without it.

I'm not standing around waiting to be saved. Shit like that's a fairytale they tell kids to make them sleep through the night. I stopped believing in being rescued the first time someone looked me in the eye and walked away, anyway.

There's no knight in shining armor. No white horse. No hand reaching into the flames to drag me free. Only the smoke choking me and the burn that never goes away.

Right now, I'm slouched at the kitchen table in this godforsaken shithole the state has the balls to call a home. A thick, sour scent clings to everything, even my fucking skin. The linoleum's fucked, sticky in places, some spots ripped to hell. Every step reminds you exactly how little anyone gives a shit about the kids dumped here.

The walls are stained the color of piss, paint peeling, yellowed edges curling inward as if even the paint wants to escape. Faded handprints linger, ghosts of whoever came before.

Above me, a light buzzes and flickers, desperate to die but never quite making it. I watch it sputter and think, yeah, I'm the fucking same.

I drop my elbows onto the table's beat-to-shit surface, skin dragging across splinters and dried-up streaks of glue older than me. I don't flinch. Pain's familiar. It's there when I blink. When I breathe. When I fucking exist. It never fades. Only coils tighter, waiting to blow.

I don't want to carry it. Don't want to endure a fucking thing. Not the weight in my chest. Not the heat behind my eyes.

The door groans on its busted hinge, the same tired sound scraping through this place every fucking day, reminding me nothing in this place ever changes.

Another round of discarded kids drifts through the doorway. They move slowly, shuffling across the cracked linoleum, shoulders bent, eyes empty, faces drained of anything human. The ones who stopped asking questions because they knew the answers were always bullshit.

But they all wear the same forgotten face now.

They shuffle past me in a line, one after the other, skin drained pale beneath the harsh flicker of the light overhead. Their eyes are glazed, their steps mechanical, bodies moving on instinct alone.

The door slams shut behind them. Something shifts inside me, as if a fault line has split open beneath my ribs.

I feel him before I lift my head. Heat rolling off him, weight dragging at the edges of the room, a dangerous pull coiling low and refusing to let go.

Zane fucking Rivera.

He doesn't walk in. He fucking arrives, the air shifting the second his shadow fills the doorway. He carries himself with the force of a storm tearing through a sky already surrendered, every step a reminder nothing in his path gets out untouched.

He stands in the doorway with his arms loose at his sides, posture easy but charged. A stance declaring he owns whatever space he steps into. The leather jacket tells the story without him saying a word, stinking of backseat fucks, bathroom quickies, and fights he never lost. It's chaos stitched into leather, bragging for him before he even opens his mouth. His mouth curves with the ghost of a grin, all arrogance and filth, a grin promising he'll ruin you or make you beg for it. Every line of him drips with untouchable confidence, every step a dare, reckless to the bone. He's chaos wrapped in swagger, the storm every girl swears she can handle until she's already too deep to crawl out. And you know it long before he opens his mouth.

His shoulders roll back as he steps into the room, warping the air and dragging it with him. Swagger clings to every movement, carved from the fights he walked away from grinning and the rules he never gave a shit about breaking. It should piss me off. Should make me scoff, roll my eyes, and turn the fuck away.

But it doesn't.

The heat sinks low in my gut, hot and wrong, too sharp to ignore and too right to resist.

Trouble doesn't need words. Trouble doesn't need fists. It moves the way he does, every step a reminder he was built to destroy. And every inch of me fucking feels it.

He doesn't utter a single word. His presence says enough.

The room shifts, the air turning heavy, silence stretching until it presses hard against my chest. Every inch of space bends, drawn tight to the gravity he carries without effort.

And I can't stop myself. I stare.

His hair falls in careless strands across his forehead, framing a face cut sharp enough to wound. High cheekbones. A jaw carved from stone, built to grit through pain without ever breaking. His mouth is pure temptation, curved in a way that pulls dangerous thoughts to the surface, the kind of curve making sin feel inevitable. He is beautiful, and he fucking knows it. Cocky awareness runs through every line of him, every inch of confidence he wears as easily as the leather on his back.

And then those fucking eyes.

Storm-gray, cold and unreadable until they lock on me. When they do, the rest of the world disappears. He doesn't simply look—he strips people bare.

His stare drags across my skin. There is no trace of innocence to mistake it for sweetness.

This isn't the shallow hunger I've seen in boys who only care about what's under your clothes.

This is something else. Something darker... heavier.

The kind of hunger that doesn't ask. It fucking takes.

A violation built from his stare scraping over my skin, cutting down to bone, prying at every place I've tried to bury. There is something twisted in it. Something broken.

And the worst part?

I don't look away. I fucking burn beneath it.

Whatever he's hiding in his stare cuts me open, sinking too deep, crawling beneath my skin.

One corner of his mouth lifts, dragging with it a dangerous kind of arrogance. It's cockiness born in blood and bruises.

He leans against the doorframe as if the room belongs to him, arms crossed, body loose but edged with restraint, every line of him radiating a challenge meant only for me. The silence stretches, thick with his smug dare, a question pulsing in the air neither of us speaks aloud. Who will break first? Who gives in? Who loses?

I hold his stare, refusing to flinch, even as the heat coils tighter between us.

I lift my chin and let my mouth curve into the coldest fucking smile I can summon. A smile meant to wound, meant to scream I've already won even if the inside of me is bleeding raw.

I want him to speak first. To blink. For him to taste the sting of standing in front of someone who won't fucking break.

His eyes stay locked on mine, unwavering. Confidence rolls off him, the kind sinking its teeth into soft skin and waiting for the bleed.

I meet it with everything I have. Spine straight. Muscles coiled. My heart thuds hard behind my ribs, but I don't flinch.

He wants to see what I'll do when I'm pushed.

So I give it to him.

"You lost?" I say, voice low, laced with venom. "Or just wandering through hell to see who's still breathing in this dump?"

The words hit their mark. He doesn't even blink. His mouth curves into something that isn't a smile. Something meant to slice skin and leave a mark.

And fuck, it does.

"I'm just here checking if the queen of sarcasm's still holding court," he says, voice dripping with lazy confidence. "Looks like I'm in luck."

His voice scrapes down my spine, gravel-edged and smooth all at once. The kind of sound turning every filthy thought into something inevitable. It doesn't fit here, not in this kitchen reeking of cheap coffee and failure. His voice belongs in the dark corners of the city, pressed up against walls, whispered through clenched teeth, dangerous enough to make you forget yourself.

I bite back the twitch of a smile and let a slow grin spread across my mouth instead. It's cold. Controlled. The kind that never reaches my eyes and doesn't need to. It carries a threat on its own.

His gaze lingers, and I catch the shift in it. The flicker of interest, the dark amusement telling me he likes the fight. Proof I'm not another girl ready to fold.

"Annoying... Cute," I say. "You've got five minutes before I make you regret setting foot in here."

He pushes off the doorframe and steps closer, closing the distance only enough for the air to thicken between us. Close enough for me to feel it. His laugh is low, curling through the room until it knots low in my stomach, twisting everything I don't want to admit.

"Is that a promise or a threat?" he asks, his voice edged with amusement. A sound cutting and caressing in the same breath. His eyes stay locked on mine, steady, daring me to answer, to play the game he already knows I can't walk away from.

"Depends if you're smart enough to survive it." My voice is steady, but the fire behind it burns bright and unashamed.

Something darker curls at the corners of his mouth, the spark in his eyes catching flame until it holds me in place.

For a single breath, the world strips itself bare.

There's no peeling paint, no flickering light, no chairs marked with burn marks. All of it fades beneath the pull between us.

We are two forces staring each other down, neither willing to bend, neither willing to break.

"Oh, I don't just survive," he says, voice low and certain. "I break the rules while I'm at it."

The way he says it is unapologetic, smug, daring. His words slam through me harder than I want to admit.

And fuck, I hate the part of me wanting to see which rules he would break for me. Worse, I hate the thought of which ones he could make me want to break for him.

That gets to me, and he knows it. The grin tugging at his mouth dares me to answer, dares me to keep playing.

This is my territory. My fucking table. The one place I sit where no one dares to touch me or piss me off. I carved my name into the wood to remind myself I was still here, proof I existed in a world determined to make me invisible. Every splinter, every crack in this scarred surface is mine, proof I've endured, proof I've claimed something in this place where nothing shakes me.

Until him.

One look and the ground tilts. One grin and the fire burns to life. I was fine before he showed up in this shitty place where his swagger fills the doorway and his eyes drag me under. Now I'm burning, furious at the way he can walk in here and make me feel everything at once.

And I hate the part of me that doesn't want him to stop.

I throw punches because it's easier than letting anyone get close. I've perfected the art of pushing people away before they think about reaching for me.

Being near him is dangerous in ways I don't want to admit. Not his body or his voice. Not even the grin slipping too easily into my bloodstream and threatening to tear something loose.

It's the way he looks at me. The way his eyes move past every wall I've spent years building, past the barbed wire I've wrapped around my skin just to keep the world from getting in.

And fuck, it terrifies me.

Because he hasn't touched me. Even so, I can feel it. The pull, an unraveling, a fault line shifting inside me beneath his stare. The ache of finally being seen.

He doesn't say a word, just stares. His gaze moves slowly across my face. Down over the line of my jaw. Lingering on the scar above my brow. The one I don't talk about, the one no one ever has the balls to ask about.

He sees it. Despite this, he doesn't look away.

His eyes refuse to rush. Every movement is precise. Intentional. A stare turned into touch. The kind you don't consent to but feel anyway, sinking under your skin, memorizing the parts of you no one's ever taken the time to know.

His gaze drops.

Lower.

Fixes on my mouth.

And everything stops.

The noise. The air. The world. It all collapses, suspended in a silence laced with want and warning.

My breath catches. My pulse skips. Every instinct inside me screams to move. To shove him back before this crosses a line I won't come back from.

But my body doesn't listen. I stay frozen, chest tight, skin humming like it's waiting to be touched.

He smirks. It's slow and fucking lethal. The kind of smirk knowing exactly what it's doing. A promise of everything, daring you to survive it.

The twist of his mouth is cocky, confident, filthy in a way that dares me to call him out. And he knows exactly what the fuck he is doing.

"Not tonight, sweetheart," he says, then turns.

The words land hard.

He laughs as he walks away, as if he didn't just tilt my entire world sideways and walk off with the match still smoldering in his hand.

I want to scream at him. I want to chase him down and rip that smug grin right off his face.

I'm furious. Furious with him. Furious with myself. With every broken piece of me that responded to him without permission. He didn't even touch me, not a single fucking finger, and still I am sitting here, exposed, shaken to the core of bones I have spent years burying under armor.

I hate him. Hate the way he walked in here as if he owned the air I was breathing. The way my skin still buzzes even though he is walking away. And now I cannot stop hearing his voice. *Not tonight, sweetheart.* The words keep looping through my head, coiled tight around that cocky grin he stamped into me before walking out.

"Careful, pretty boy," I say, turning in the chair to face him. "Guys who walk around as if they own the room are usually overcompensating for a dick that is not even worth unzipping."

It is petty and cruel, but for one fucked-up second it makes me breathe easier, as if I have taken something back, even if it is only a scrap of control I never really had. The relief doesn't last.

He stops, turns, and his eyes find mine again, his grin tugging wider as if he has been waiting for me to snap.

"Oh, sweetheart."

That fucking word again. Soaked in mock sympathy, dipped in sin.

"You might be the first to call me out, but you will be the last to see what I am really packing."

And then he's gone, leaving me here, half furious and half fucked up in the worst way imaginable, pretending I'm not already drowning in the aftermath.

My whole body feels wrong, wired too tight, skin pulled thin over bones that no longer hold steady. My pulse refuses to settle. It pounds fast and fucked-up, chasing the echo of his stare still stamped across my skin. That cocky fucker walked in and detonated something inside me, and now I am the one choking on the dust, left to sift through the wreckage while he disappears as if he didn't set the whole fucking room on fire.

He got under my skin, burrowing deep, spreading through me as if he were a fucking virus I never saw coming. One smirk was all it took. One look. One fucking line, and suddenly he was everywhere I did not want him to be.

And I fucking hate it.

I hate the way my body sparks when he gets close, all heat and nerves and hunger I never gave it permission to feel.

But what I hate most is that for one impossible, goddamn moment, I wanted him to stay.

Chapter 2

ZANE

The kitchen door slams shut behind me, the crack of it loud enough to rattle the glass in the window. I don't turn around. Don't slow my pace. I don't give a single fuck if that cold, bitter bitch who runs this place caught me walking out again. Let her scream herself hoarse because I'm not fucking listening.

Her voice cuts through the walls anyway, high and jagged, barking orders at kids too small and too beaten down to push back. They nod quick, scatter faster, keeping their eyes down as if ignoring her could make her less of a monster stuffed into a cheap cardigan.

She isn't a foster mother. She's a fucking prison warden. A woman who cashes the state's money and calls it care. Nothing more.

None of us matter to her. We never have.

We are nothing more than numbers on her roster, broken bodies she trades in for government funding and the half-hearted praise she collects at church. It is all a game to her, and she plays it well. She keeps the place clean enough to pass inspections, keeps her threats quiet enough to avoid a report.

But I see it.

I see everything.

I don't owe her a damn thing. She will keep doing what she does best, collecting damaged kids and cashing in on our pain.

And we will all continue to do what we do best.

Surviving. That's all I've been doing. Two more months and I'm out of this shithole. Eighteen. Free. No more foster bullshit. No more rules. No more government assholes acting like they own me. They can't tell me what to fucking do—not anymore. They've already threatened to ship me off to some boys' home, and said I was on my last warning. One more fuckup and I'm gone. But once I'm legal, they can't touch me. So I keep my head down, grit my teeth, and wait it out.

Skylar's doing the same in her own way. We're both seniors, in our last year of high school. No doubt she's counting down the days too.

I've seen the way guys at school watch her, how they try to talk to her, try to charm her so she'll let them fuck her. She shuts it down without blinking. Doesn't give them shit. A single glance, a scoff, sometimes nothing at all. She doesn't hand out pieces of herself for free.

I've got a part-time job after school. Shit hours, shittier pay. But it's something. I've been saving every cent I can, scraping together whatever it takes so when I hit eighteen, I can walk out and never look back. I'm not expecting it to be much better than this shithole I'm stuck in now. Probably some crumbling apartment, a mattress on the floor, a busted lock on the door. But at least it'll be mine.

Not this old bitch's house with the stale cigarette stink and the way she watches me as if I'm a loaded gun ready to go off.

I just need to hold out. Two more months. That's it.

And if I can survive that... I can survive anything.

I cut across the courtyard, boots grinding against dirt and gravel, hands buried deep in the pockets of my jacket. Every inch of this place is shit. The swing set is nothing but rusted chains and metal that groans when the wind cuts through. Silence hangs heavy once the doors shut and the screaming dies out, wrapping the house in something colder than night.

It's "home". Sweet fucking home.

I dig a hand into the inside pocket of my jacket and pull out the joint I've been saving all day. The shake in my fingers has nothing to do with the cold. It's this place. It's what it does to me. The longer I stay, the harder it is to breathe.

The walls press in. The air is stale, heavy with smoke and rot that never fades. I fucking hate it here.

Lighting up is the only thing that keeps me from tearing this whole place apart.

A hit or two, and the static in my head quiets down enough to think straight. At least Skylar keeps me distracted.

A fucked-up distraction, but one I can't shake. Even when she isn't around, she crawls into my head, her voice chewing through my thoughts with the edge of a switchblade. She's a storm I never saw coming, and now she's everywhere. In every silence. Every corner of this shitty house. In every breath I drag into my lungs.

Her sarcasm burns hotter than wildfire, and her stare only pours gasoline over it.

And I'm the fucking idiot holding the match, knowing I should put it out but wanting to see how far the flames can spread.

I've seen plenty of girls try to act tough. They raise their voices, roll their eyes, push back hard enough to seem untouchable. Skylar is different. She doesn't pretend. She doesn't need to. The armor she wears isn't for show; it clings to her as if she was born in it, forged out of the same sharp edges she throws at the world.

And still, she pulls at me in ways I can't shake. A smirk that cuts too deep. An insult that lands harder than a fist. Even the way she spits the word "prick" at me, her voice dripping heat and venom, leaves a mark I can't ignore.

She's under my skin, buried in my blood, and it pisses me off more than anything.

I shouldn't be thinking about her, not when I know better.

Every time I close my eyes, I picture her mouth falling open, her body trembling while I fuck her, her eyes still throwing sparks even when she's breathless as she comes undone. She isn't the kind of girl you hold onto. She doesn't follow rules–not mine, not anyone's, not even her own.

But fuck, here I am, hard up over a girl who could burn me alive and make me thank her for it.

I sink to the ground behind the shed, dropping my ass onto the cracked concrete still holding the last of the sun's heat. Nobody comes here. This space is mine. My hideout. My escape.

I lean back, shoulders pressed hard against the warped boards, knees bent, boots scuffing loose gravel beneath me. Out here, the silence is mine. So is the distance from the eyes that never stop judging.

I slide the joint between my lips and flick the lighter, shielding the flame with my hand until it catches. The tip glows hot, a deep red pulse in the fading light, and the first drag hits hard. Smoke sears down my throat, sharp and familiar, burying itself in my lungs until the pressure turns to pain. I hold it there, let it sting, let it burn through the hollow space inside me. I exhale slowly, watching the smoke rise in twisting ribbons before the wind steals it.

I close my eyes and sink into the quiet.

For one stolen moment, everything fades. The weight pressing on my ribs eases. The voices lose their edge. The ache in my head slips to the background.

But peace never stays long.

When I open my eyes, she's there.

Skylar.

She moves across the street with her phone clutched to her ear, jaw tight and shoulders squared like she's ready to go to war. There's something in the way she walks that grabs you by the throat and doesn't let go. Every step is a warning. Every glance, a fucking challenge. She doesn't try to be seen. She doesn't care who's looking.

But I see her. And fuck, do I want her.

Those jeans cling to her hips, shredded at the knees, teasing enough skin to short-circuit the part of my brain that usually keeps me in check. My cock stirs, hard and aching, as if it already knows the shape of her mouth and how she'd taste moaning under me. One glance, and I'm gone. Again. I don't just think about her... I fucking obsess.

She's not the first girl I've wanted.

But she's the only one I've ever had to talk myself out of chasing.

And I'm losing that fight.

Every fucking time she storms past, all bite and fire, it guts me a little more. I want to ruin her composure. I want to hear her say my name when she's too far gone to pretend she doesn't want me back.

My eyes shift down over that tank top as it clings to her chest. The way the loose strap keeps slipping off one shoulder, teasing the sharp line of her collarbone and daring my gaze lower.

I shift against the cracked concrete, jeans tugging tight where I don't need them to. My cock is hard and unashamed, reacting before I can even get a handle on the thoughts detonating in my head. I grip the joint tighter, fingers white-knuckled, jaw clenched, trying to drag the heat back down. But it's no use. She's already in too deep.

Skylar fucking owns me.

Even when she's not around, she's under my skin. She lives in the shadows of my thoughts, in every breath I take. Every time I close my eyes, there she is on her knees, mouth parted, eyes locked on mine, full of that same defiance she wears like armor. That look she gives me, the one that dares me to break her, to see if I'll actually do it this time.

She thinks she's strong. Untouchable. But I see the cracks.

I don't just want to fuck her. I want to ruin her before anyone else does.

I want to see how far she'll let me go. How close I can get before she cracks. I want to taste that moment when she stops pretending she's unaffected and starts begging me with her eyes, with her mouth, with the sound of her voice breaking on my name.

I want to be the one who makes her lose.

Because no one makes Skylar bend, no one breaks through those walls she hides behind. But I want every goddamn inch of that.

And that's what makes this so fucked up.

She's still on the phone, pacing the sidewalk like the world owes her something. And maybe it does.

Whoever's on the other end has her pacing like a caged animal, trapped in a fight she can't punch her way out of. Her hand flexes at her side, fingers twitching like she's holding back something sharp. A scream. A sob. A curse that could cut glass.

I watch the way she shifts her weight, heel grinding into the pavement, foot tapping in quick, angry bursts before she snaps, kicking hard at a loose rock like it insulted her. It shoots across the road and smashes against the gutter with a sharp crack.

That's the Skylar I know.

Not some polished, perfect girl with a fake smile and a soft voice.

No. She's rough around the edges, stitched together with spit and survival.

The kind of girl who doesn't care if the world thinks she's too much.

She doesn't hide the rage boiling just beneath the surface. She lets it bleed through in the way she moves, the way she glares, the way her whole body vibrates as if it's seconds from going nuclear.

And fuck if that doesn't make me want her more.

She slips her phone into her back pocket and stares down the road, lips moving with words I can't make out. Then she throws her middle finger into the air, cursing the sky like it's personally fucked her over one too many times, and she's finally done pretending she can swallow it.

I grin around the joint, the smoke catching in my throat as I take another drag.

She's pissed.

Wound tight and close to breaking. Holding the kind of weight that crushes you slow, bone by bone, until you forget how to stand without shaking.

I've been there. Too many fucking times. And that's probably why she gets to me more than she should. Why my eyes stay locked on her even when I tell myself to walk away. Even when I grit my teeth and remind myself she's nothing more than another girl. Another distraction. A mistake I can't afford to make.

She pulls at the part of me that needs to be in control.

I drag another hit from my joint, holding it in until the burn claws its way up my chest. It scorches through me, a slow, crawling fire that does nothing to dull the pull she has on me. She runs a hand through her hair, yanking it into that messy knot she always wears. A few strands fall loose around her neck, sticking to the sweat at her collarbone, and I can't look away.

I run a hand down my face, trying to force her out of my fucking head.

I've had girls.

Names that meant nothing. Bodies that meant even less. Fake moans echoing in the dark because they thought that's what they were supposed to do. Mouths spilling promises they assumed I wanted, desperate to be wanted back.

But none of it ever fucking mattered. They came to me chasing danger. Wanting the thrill, not the pain. The edge, not the fall. They'd beg. Scratch. Moan my name and take every filthy thing I gave them.

But Skylar is different. It's the flash of her eyes that turns my chest into a fucking vice.

One glance and I'm drowning in it, ready to tear the world apart to hear the sound she makes when she breaks.

And the worst part... She doesn't even know she's doing it.

It doesn't scare me getting close to her.

It should. Any sane person would be running the other way by now, trying to carve her out before she digs any deeper. But I'm not sane when it comes to her. I never fucking have been.

It only makes me hungrier.

Fuck this. I'm not the kind of guy who waits around, bleeding in silence for a girl who doesn't even realize she's gutting me with every breath she takes. Every second she stands there, all unaware and untouchable, she carves a little deeper. And I fucking let her.

I shove myself off the ground, boots scraping loud against the concrete. My spine cracks as I straighten, every joint stiff from sitting too long in the shadows. Too long wanting something I've got no business wanting. The stretch pulls at my muscles, chest tight, arms heavy, blood still thrumming with that slow, dangerous pulse she dragged out of me the second she showed up to this dump.

I flick the joint across the gravel, watch it spark, skip, and die in a curl of smoke. All burned out. Same as me.

I move toward her. Every step soaked in intent. Gravel shifts beneath my boots, crunching under the weight of restraint I'm barely holding onto. She hasn't seen me yet. Her chin is tilted with that same don't-fuck-with-me defiance, shoulders squared like she's ready to throw punches at the next person who breathes too loud.

I take in all of it.

She's chaos wrapped in calm. Fury masked as silence.

The world around her dulls, edges fading out like even it knows better than to get too close. She doesn't need to do anything to steal the scene. She just stands there, unknowingly dragging gravity with her, warping everything in reach.

She's got no idea I'm watching. No clue that she looks like a fucking masterpiece, built from bruises, bite marks and broken rules from here. The kind of girl they write songs about but never survive.

Unless someone knows exactly where to press, and I do.

I don't speed up. There's no need to. She isn't some quick fix, some easy thrill you chase down in the dark just to feel alive. She's not a girl you rush. She's the kind you earn, slowly, painfully, one step at a time, if she even lets you.

Even if I don't deserve her. Even if getting close to her means I'm the one left bleeding.

She's vibrating. Full of fury. All wound-up tension and sharp silence. Every part of her coiled so tight it looks like the next wrong breath might set her off. And fuck, I want to be the one to do it.

When I get closer, my boots strike the gravel, each step cutting through the silence like a warning. I don't hide the sound. Don't soften my approach. I want her to hear me. To register it in her spine. Let it crawl under her skin and settle there, the way she's been living under mine.

The air between us turns electric, humming with something that burns too close to want and too heavy to ignore. It's still. Waiting. So thick I can almost chew through it, every breath laced with the weight of everything we've never said and all the fucked-up glances we've thrown when the days got too sharp. It settles in my mouth, bitter and charged. She doesn't move. Doesn't flinch. She stands there breathing harder, chest rising too fast, as if some part of her already senses it's me behind her—already bracing for what's coming.

I'm close now.

Close enough to thread my fingers through that wild, reckless knot in her hair and yank her head back to hear what kind of sound she makes. Close enough to press my chest to her spine and let my mouth brush her ear, whisper every filthy thing I've been biting back.

But I don't.

I hold the space between us, keep it taut, keep it dangerous, to see if she'll break first. To see if she'll turn around and fucking dare me.

My smirk curls slowly as I drop my voice, low.

"You standing there waiting for a hero... or just someone to fuck your shit up?"

She whips around fast, eyes flashing. Her jaw's set. That mouth, already half open. "You wanna fuck off, cocky prick?"

Her tone slams into me, and all it does is make the heat coil lower in my gut.

I take another step. I don't touch her. Not yet. I let the weight of me settle too close, breathing too steady, grinning as if the ending's already written.

"Careful, trouble. You keep talking like that, I might think you want me to ruin you."

She doesn't blink. Doesn't back off. She tips her chin higher instead, fire catching in her eyes like she's daring me to do it.

Fuck, she's perfect.

I laugh, and it's real. Deep and rough, torn straight from somewhere buried under all the shit I've had to choke down. A sound I haven't heard from myself in years.

"Careful," I murmur, my gaze dragging slow over her mouth. "I might take that as a fucking challenge."

She steps closer, head high, daring me to strike first. "What? You gonna fuck me up?"

God, that mouth. That tone. That fury.

She doesn't flinch. Doesn't even blink. Just stares straight through me.

I move in slow, eating the space between us with that kind of swagger that makes girls step back and beg. But she holds firm. Breath sharp. Chest tight. Shoulders locked. Braced for impact and refusing to back down.

I'm close enough now to smell her shampoo. Vanilla and sweat and danger. Close enough to feel the tremble she's trying so fucking hard to hide.

"Depends," I say. "You asking me to or warning me not to?"

Her lip curls. Her eyes narrow. "I'm warning you, asshole. I'm trouble you don't wanna fuck with."

I grin, eyes locked on hers. "Oh, sweetheart. I'm the king of fucking trouble." I lean in. "But I'm guessing you want a little chaos," I say, voice rough, daring.

Skylar doesn't fucking break.

The corner of her mouth pulls up with a kind of cruel grace, wicked and slow, sharp enough to slice skin if I got too close. The way she stares at me? It's pure fucking challenge. Brazen. Dangerous. Dripping with everything I should walk away from and already can't.

She's not just standing her ground. She's daring me to shove against it, to see how far I'll go.

And fuck, I want to.

She holds my gaze, letting the tension thicken until it settles in my gut, low and dangerous. Every second she keeps her mouth shut makes me want her more.

My blood's thumping harder. My cock's already aching with the image of her pressed to the wall, her hands in my hair, her teeth in my neck.

But I stay still. For now.

We're both staring, both waiting, both pretending we're not already ten steps past the line.

And then I move, because I fucking have to.

I turn away. My boots grind into the pavement with every step, each one a warning she won't forget.

I don't rush. I move in a way that makes damn sure she senses the weight of me leaving. I don't need to turn around to be certain her eyes are on me. Their heat drills straight through my spine.

The airs still charged. Her heat crawls up the back of my neck, and fuck, it makes my cock twitch all over again.

Finally, after giving her just enough time to stew in it, to think maybe I'm done, I glance back over my shoulder. Grin still there. Sharp. Cocky.

"Are you coming?"

She folds her arms tight across her chest, rolls her eyes hard enough to make a priest flinch, and fires back, "Where?"

It's clipped. Drenched in sarcasm. But buried under the bite is something else. A pause. A pulse. That soft edge of hesitation she hates me seeing.

I nod toward the alley. The one behind the fence. Cracked concrete, rusted bins, graffiti bleeding through years of paint. It's where I go when the walls press too hard. When breathing comes at a cost.

"Away from this shitshow," I say, voice low. "Somewhere quiet enough to piss off the neighborhood."

She snorts. One of those short, sharp sounds she doesn't mean to let slip. "Real tempting."

I shrug, let my grin stretch just enough to tease. "Thought you'd appreciate the view."

Her brow lifts, eyes trailing down my body slow enough to make it count. "Not bad," she mutters. "Shame about the mouth."

That smirk again. Crooked, dangerous, and carved from trouble. It's sharp enough to leave scars if I get too close.

I laugh. Low and dirty, the kind that scrapes up from somewhere dark. "Are you sure about that? Most girls can't get enough of it."

She rolls her eyes, but her boots move. One step. Then another. She remains silent and falls into step beside me with her hands buried deep in her pockets.

There's a shift in the air. Hot. Unsteady. As if we're both one breath away from doing something stupid.

She doesn't look at me, but I feel her presence. She's close enough that my cock's already twitching with every second of silence she feeds me.

But fuck, the space between us is alive.

My pulse won't settle. Not for a fucking second. Every step's a fuse lit under my skin, every breath edged with the kind of tension that begs for a fight or a fuck. She's too close. Close enough that if I reached out, I'd drag her in and wreck us both without thinking twice.

We don't speak.

Not because we've got nothing to say. But because everything we're holding back is louder than words. Her energy sparks next to mine, humming with heat neither of us has the balls to name.

I don't look at her. I fucking can't.

If I do, I'll say something I shouldn't. I'll bait her and she'll bite.

I keep my eyes on the alley, on the cracked pavement, and the shadows that don't ask questions.

And she's right there beside me. Silent. Tense. Following me straight into the storm.

I tune into the noise. Engines. Horns. The low hum of the city trying to swallow me whole. It's the only thing keeping my head on straight. Then her scent cuts through it, warm skin, heat, that fucking vanilla scent she always wears.

My hands ball inside my jacket pockets. Tight enough my knuckles pop.

We hit the corner and turn left. My eyes move to the brick walls tagged in angry colors. To the dumpsters kicked in and bleeding rust. Glass catching the streetlight like it's trying to show off.

It's a dump. There's no denying that.

Skylar stops dead in the middle of the alley, arms crossed, jaw locked.

When I look at her she's already watching me. There's no fear in her. Just that steady, razor-sharp challenge simmering in her eyes.

"Where the fuck are you taking me?" she asks, voice low and edged in steel.

She doesn't trust me.

I can see it in every tight line of her stance. But that's fine. I don't trust anyone either.

I watch the way the strands of her loose hair, sway in the cool breeze. She doesn't fix it. She stands there, stubborn as hell.

"You can come if you want," I say. "Or crawl back to that shithole. But you'll miss the view. Sun's about to hit at the perfect angle."

She stares at me like she's trying to figure out if I'm worth the risk.

"You planning on stabbing me?" she asks, voice flat.

"Not yet," I mutter.

I step up to the side door, fingers curling around the rusted handle. It's fucked. Bent halfway out of the frame. Paint's peeled clean off, flaking under my grip. I brace a boot against the wall and haul it open with a grunt.

The metal screams. High and sharp. A dying animal howl that echoes off the alley walls.

The smell hits next. Damp wood, old smoke, piss maybe. Years of stories no one wanted to hear.

I glance back at her.

"Ladies first," I say, gesturing for her to enter.

She moves slowly. Her boots crunch glass, hesitation loud in every step.

That stare hasn't softened. She's still watching me with the eyes of a hawk, like I might fuck her over the second she blinks.

I let the door groan shut behind us, metal dragging against metal. The sound bounces off the walls.

Inside, it's all shadows and rot. Dust hanging in the air, thick enough to choke on. A mattress slumped in the corner. Spray paint tagging every surface. The place stinks of old beer and burnt-out joints.

I nod toward the ladder bolted to the far wall. Rusted steel. Narrow as hell. It crawls up into an endless darkness.

"Come on," I say, already moving. "The best part's up top."

She doesn't follow right away. Just stares at the ladder, arms still crossed, one brow lifting.

"You always take girls to abandoned buildings and drag them onto rooftops? Real smooth."

I grin. "Only the ones worth the view."

She doesn't say a word, but I catch it. That twitch of her mouth trying not to grin.

Then she falls into step behind me.

I take the lead, climbing slow enough so she can keep up. Slow enough she sees where to step. But not too slow. I know damn well what this angle gives her.

Metal groans beneath my boots. Her breath hitches behind me. Then a muttered "fuck" when her foot slips and she catches the rung, knuckles white.

I smirk and keep going.

At the top, I haul myself over and sprawl across the roof, arms behind my head. The tin roof burns straight through my jeans, heat biting into my skin. My leather jacket keeps the worst of it off my back, but it's still hot enough to make me sweat.

The tin creaks under my weight. It's dented, sun-baked, half-collapsing in places.

But it holds. And so do I. Waiting for her to show up, for whatever comes next.

I tilt my head to watch her as she climbs over the ledge. That busted grace of hers, all fight and no trust, trying not to let on that she doesn't know what the hell we're doing up here.

From this height, the foster house shrinks into something far away and pointless. Just trees and rooftops and a town that couldn't care less if we burned or disappeared entirely.

She tucks her knees up, wraps her arms around them. Watching the edge of the world like it might blink first.

"Didn't take you for the romantic rooftop type," she says.

I laugh under my breath, shift onto my elbows. "I'm not."

She turns just enough to meet my eyes, expression guarded. "Then why bring me here?"

I stare past her. Past everything.

"Because up here," I say, "no one's watching. No one's waiting to fuck us over."

I glance at her. Her lips are parted just enough to fuck with my head. Her shirt's fallen off her shoulder again—always that fucking shoulder, and my eyes follow the curve down to the dip of her collarbone. I should look away. I don't.

"I don't know," I mutter. "Figured maybe you'd shut up long enough to enjoy the view."

She shrugs. "Still waiting to be impressed."

I shift onto my side, propping myself on one elbow. "What, you want fireworks? A fucking string quartet?"

Her smirk tugs sharp at the corner of her mouth. "Wouldn't hurt."

I laugh. "All I've got is rust and a half-collapsed roof. Take it or leave it."

She doesn't answer right away. Just shifts her weight, stretching her legs out and leaning back on her palms.

"Guess it'll do," she murmurs.

"Is that a compliment?"

She smirks, eyes flicking to mine. "Don't get ahead of yourself."

"Too late," I say, and this time when I look at her, I don't bother hiding that I'm checking out her tits. "You ever feel like the world just decided who you were before you even had a fucking chance?" I ask.

"Every fucking day."

The silence stretches. She picks at a flake of rust near her thigh, more interested in peeling metal than looking at me. She doesn't rush to fill the quiet. That's what makes her different. Most people panic when it gets too still. Not Skylar. She breathes it in.

After a while, I mutter, "You ever wonder what she does with all the money?"

She snorts. "Yeah. The government pays her to "care," but instead she spends it on holy threats and hooker perfume."

I bark out a laugh. "She's probably got a stash of cash buried under the floorboards. Saving up for a one-way ticket to hell."

Skylar pulls her knees in tighter. There's more she wants to say, but she swallows it down.

I shift closer, not touching, just close enough to feel the heat roll off her skin.

"How long you been there?" I ask.

She leans back on her hands. Head tipped to the sky. Her throat bare, too easy to get caught staring at it so I drag my eyes away before they settle.

"Four years." She shrugs. "What about you? How many foster homes have you crashed through?"

I lean back beside her, eyes on the sky. "Thirteen."

"Damn."

"Yeah. First one had a dog that pissed in my bed. Second was worse. The guy had a thing for locked doors and bullshit excuses."

She turns toward me, and I keep going. No point stopping now.

"Third one was alright. Fourth, I made it a month. Fifth? A week. Sixth had Bible verses taped to the fridge. 'He who spares the rod' kind of house."

She hums. "Nice."

"Didn't make it to the 'love thy neighbor' part."

Her mouth lifts, barely. Not a smile. More a crack in the wall. The kind of expression you give someone who's been stabbed in the same spot too many times.

"Got kicked out of the last few for fighting. And, you know... being me."

She cuts me a look. "So, being an asshole?"

I grin, slow and unapologetic. "A charming, fuckable asshole."

She snorts. "You really think that's a selling point?"

"Depends who's buying." I stretch out on the tin, heat still clinging to my jeans.

"Christ," she groans. "Do you ever shut the fuck up?"

"Only when my mouth's busy doing better things."

She snaps her head around, with a glare that's sharp enough to cut through bone. But her cheeks betray her. There's heat rising. That soft pink that says more than she wants it to.

"You're a fucking pig."

I grin slowly. "And yet, here you are."

She flips me off without a word, but she stays right where she is.

I nudge her foot. Just enough to make contact. "You ever try to run?"

"Twice," she mutters. "Got caught both times."

"Same. Made it all the way to a gas station once. Thought I was free. Got tackled by some guy outside 7-Eleven wearing camo and fucking crocs."

She laughs, head tipped back, eyes squeezed shut. Sound bursting out of her chest like it hasn't had permission in years.

That sound cuts through all the shit. Makes the weight in my chest feel a little less heavy.

Her smile lingers, slower now. She's watching me, really watching, and it's not pity. It's this quiet kind of seeing that undoes me. She looks at me like I'm not broken glass, like maybe I was never sharp enough to hurt anyone in the first place.

I don't say a word. I won't risk shattering whatever this is.

The sun drops low behind us. Everything turns gold. The roof. The rust. Her face. It hits her cheekbones first, then her lips. That mouth I can't stop staring at. That mouth I want on mine.

"I'll be out soon," I say, staring out across the rooftops. "Two months. I turn eighteen on November fifth. After that, they can't touch me."

She shifts, pulling her knees tighter. "November fifth?"

I nod. "Why?"

Her mouth tugs into something that almost resembles a smile. "Mine's the eighth."

I blink at her. "No shit."

She shrugs, eyes on the horizon. "Guess we're both on borrowed time."

"You know this doesn't mean we're friends now," I say, my voice low.

Skylar doesn't even flinch. "God, I fucking hope not."

"Good. I hate that shit."

"Same."

Neither of us moves. We just sit there, shoulders nearly touching, the sky bleeding orange and violet above us.

For once, it doesn't seem like the world is trying to crush me. And maybe we're still both fucked in different ways. Still angry, guarded, waiting for someone to give up on us.

But right now, sitting on this rooftop with her, nothing about it seems impossible.

Chapter 3

SKYLAR

The ceiling's cracked again.

The plaster's torn across the surface, a fault line carved by years of silence and bad decisions. This place isn't held together by bricks or hope. It's stitched shut with spit and shame. The kind of glue they slap on broken girls and dare them to hold.

I lie here, eyes locked on that crack, barely blinking. I'm not tired. Not really. But everything presses down heavier than it should. My body sinks into the mattress as if gravity's had enough of pretending to be gentle. This isn't sleep pulling me under. It's something else. Something quieter. Meaner. The kind of weight that doesn't rest. It waits.

Stillness is easier than thinking. Easier than carrying the full force of what last night did to me.

Zane fucking Rivera.

Even his name punches me in the gut. I keep seeing his face.

That smirk with teeth.

That grin that doesn't just promise destruction, it promises pleasure. The kind that lights a match, tosses it into your world, and whistles while everything burns.

And what's worse is that he made me laugh.

Not one of those hollow things I hand out to keep people from looking too closely. It was real. One stupid laugh on one even stupider rooftop, and somehow it cracked something open. And now I can't shove it back in.

The bed creaks when I shift. My body feels like it's made of cement. My shoulder hits the edge of the bunk rail, but I don't care. I just stare. That crack in the ceiling could split open and swallow me whole, and I'd probably thank it.

The fan clicks in the corner, trying to keep rhythm with my thoughts. But all I can think about is him.

That crooked smile. The voice that crawls under your skin and stays there. The way he smells, and those hands.

I saw the scars. Healed over by time but still there. Faint lines slashing across his knuckles, quiet confessions of every fight he's walked into and every one he didn't walk out of clean.

I wanted to ask him about them.

But I didn't.

I know what it's like to hate a question like that. To have someone's eyes linger too long on the scar above your eyebrow, as if it tells your whole fucking life story.

I never let anyone ask me about mine. So I wasn't about to ask him about his. He deserves to keep his secrets. Even if I can't stop thinking about them.

There are three other girls in this room.

One cries in her sleep, the kind of soft, broken sobs that make you feel like a monster for not caring.

One whispers to the ceiling after lights out. Things no one wants to hear. Secrets she buries in the dark because there's no one else to give them to.

And the last one's already half-dead. Her body breathes, her eyes blink, but whatever made her alive left a long time ago.

We're all ghosts in this place. Drifting past each other, pretending we're not desperate for someone to notice we're still breathing.

I pull the thin blanket tighter around my body, even though the room's already too warm. It's not the cold I'm fighting. It's the emptiness. I need something to wrap around me. Something to hold me still. Even if it's just fabric and lies.

Zane's grin flashes again in my mind.

Fuck him. He slipped under my skin. One night on a rooftop. That's all it took. One laugh that shouldn't have happened, one moment I didn't guard hard enough. And now I'm splitting at the seams, cracking open in places I swore I'd welded shut.

I roll onto my stomach, shove my face into the pillow, and scream until my throat's raw.

I want to forget the way he looked at me. The way his voice dipped soft when he asked that dumb question about the stars. The way my fingers almost brushed his.

I want to forget all of it.

But I can't.

And that makes me want to lash out and punch something.

I've seen him at school. He moves through the halls as if the place was built for him alone. The girls orbit him, always giggling too loud, tilting their heads at the exact angle they hope will catch his attention.

He isn't the golden boy with a football in hand, the kind teachers worship and parents parade around. He's the bad idea that pulls you in anyway. The dare you take even when you know it will end in tragedy. The mistake that leaves bruises you don't regret.

I could pretend I've never watched him, never noticed, never let my eyes catch on his shoulders or that grin.

But that would be a goddamn lie.

I've seen him lean against lockers, talking to girls who have no idea what the fuck they're doing. I've watched him pull that smirk he threw at me a dozen times on other girls. And I hate that it worked on them too. Hate that some part of me wonders if I'm nothing more than another piece in whatever fucked-up game he's playing.

As if one glance, one cocky comment, could be enough to make me spread my legs. That isn't me. It has never been me. Not once. Not when boys whispered promises they could never keep, not when men in my mother's orbit looked at me with the same hunger they wasted on her. I've never given anyone that power, and I sure as shit am not about to hand it over now.

The men I grew up around taught me early what it means to be used. They showed me how it looks when someone takes until there's nothing left but scraps. They taught me how to spot it coming, how to slam doors before hands could reach in, how to make sure it would never happen to me.

My mother never learned that lesson. She let men grind her down until she was dust, until her body was just another stop for someone else's hunger. She let them treat her as if she was disposable, leaving pieces of herself in every fucking ashtray, in every half-empty bottle, in every bed she should have walked away from. I watched her hollow out, piece by piece, until there was nothing left but skin wrapped around regret. It was then, I swore I would never let anyone turn me into the same kind of nothing. So I keep people out. It is not hard.

At school I wear the don't-fuck-with-me mask. I build it every morning, layering cold eyes over tired ones, sharpening my words into blades, tilting my shoulders just enough to make even the bravest boys think twice before stepping too close. It works. They keep their distance, but the girls still hate me for it. They whisper, they laugh, they spit the same names into the air as if saying them makes them true. Slut. Easy fuck. Whore. They see confidence where there is only armor and assume I am opening my legs behind closed doors.

The truth is that no one has ever touched me.

Not once. Not the way they imagine.

I am still a virgin, though I hate the word because it sounds soft and delicate and breakable. I am none of those things. I am iron welded shut. Every time a guy tries—and they always try—I slam the door in his face. They flirt, they push, they think persistence will melt me, but I shut them down until they finally walk away, muttering insults to save face. I make it look easy, but it isn't. It's just survival.

Because needing people only ever gets you hurt. That is the first lesson I learned, and the one I keep relearning every time I forget myself. It is the reason I ended up here in the first place. I needed my mother. I trusted her when I should have known better. And in the end she made her choice, and it was never me. She picked the needle, every single time, and left me holding the empty space where a mother was supposed to be.

Now I am here. In this fucking dump that pretends to be a home, surrounded by shadows who shuffle through the same hallways, and breathe the same air.

Morning creeps in, dragging its feet through the cracks in the blinds. The light cuts across the room in slanted stripes. I groan, every sound weighted, and force myself upright even though my body fights me. It feels heavier than it did yesterday, which is impressive when I think about how far down I already was.

Every bone protests, every muscle aches, and my head is thick with the hangover of thoughts I never wanted.

Today is going to be shit. I already know it. It sits heavy in my chest, drags through my limbs, sours the taste of the air.

The room stinks of morning breath and half-washed hair. That sticky blend of sweat and cheap detergent suffocating the room. I sit up slowly, every muscle aching like I ran a marathon in my sleep.

I hear Alyssa whimper again in her bed, that same soft, broken sound she makes every night. Marnie's already up, sitting cross-legged on her mattress, staring at the wall with her blank, empty expression like someone hit pause on her brain three years ago. The third girl, Kelly, I think, but it could be Kara who knows, mumbles to herself from the bunk below mine, words slurring in a whisper I'm too tired to decipher.

I reach for the end of the bed where my jeans are bunched in a knot. Same pair as yesterday. The knees are ripped open, threads curling like wounds that never healed. There's a faint burn mark on the thigh from when someone's cigarette slipped too close. I stretch out flat on the mattress, shove my legs into them, and lift my hips to drag the fabric over my skin.

My jacket's on the chair, sleeves inside out from when I stripped it off last night. It's frayed along the edges, worn through at the elbows, and the zipper only works if I hold my breath and pray. I don't give a fuck about trends or fashion. Those things belong to kids with clean closets and parents who still pay attention. They are luxuries for people who aren't clawing just to survive, people who don't measure their worth in how long they can keep breathing in a place that wants to choke them out. My clothes aren't about style. They are about endurance.

I don't bother with breakfast. There is nothing to eat here. There never fucking is. Hunger has become background noise, a constant hum I carry with me.

I sling my bag over one shoulder and move between the beds, careful with every step. My eyes stay low, locked on the floorboards instead of the faces around me.

The hallway smells like mildew and teenage despair. I pass the chipped mirror by the front door without glancing at it. I don't want to see my face. Not today. Not when I already know I look like shit.

Outside, the sun is too bright for the way I feel. It slams against my eyes and turns the world harsh, a spotlight I never asked for.

Cassie waits at the gate. She leans against the chain-link fence with her hips cocked and her head tilted, the picture of someone daring the world to try her. The lollipop juts out of her mouth, bright red against her smudged lipstick, the stick resting between fingers stained with ink from drawing on herself. Her eyeliner is thick, smeared at the corners, more war paint than makeup.

Her hoodie hangs open, showing the black tank top underneath, the faded name of her obsession stretched across it. Broken Oasis. The four guys she never shuts up about, the only band she claims actually gets it, the ones she swears saved her life one song at a time. Black combat boots on her feet are scuffed to hell, laces trailing loose, threatening to trip her but never quite daring.

She has been my friend since I was ten. We met in a different foster home, one where fists spoke louder than words. The walls there carried bruises the same way we did. We learned early that survival meant silence.

We have been through enough shit together to skip the small talk. We don't do it. We don't talk about feelings either. That is our rule. We keep it sharp, keep it shallow, because going deeper means bleeding and neither of us can afford more scars.

But she is here every morning, waiting at the gate, lollipop between her teeth and eyes scanning the world for trouble. That is her version of love, and it is worth more than every empty promise I have ever been handed.

"You look like shit," she says, the words muffled around the candy stick. She pushes off the fence and falls into step beside me.

"I feel worse," I mutter, tugging my sleeves down over my hands until only my fingertips show.

"Late night?" she asks, her voice flat, no judgment in it, just curiosity.

I shrug. I don't give her anything else, and she doesn't press. She never does. That is part of why she is still here.

We pass the liquor store. The metal grate is halfway down, the sign in the window still buzzing weakly. An old man is slumped against a wall, a bottle in his hand, chin resting on his chest. He isn't dead, not yet, but the smell rolling off him says he's close enough to dream about it.

We keep walking, past the corner where two girls we know used to turn tricks until one of them didn't come back.

Cassie tucks her hands into the pocket of her jeans, shoulders hunched against the morning air. "I saw Rivera last night."

My spine stiffens before I can stop it. I keep my eyes fixed straight ahead on the cracked pavement. "Yeah?"

"Yeah," she says again, drawing it out this time. "On Main. With that Samantha bitch who still thinks I give a shit about her opinions."

My mouth goes sour, a bitter taste coating the back of my throat. I try to swallow it down, force it into silence the way I do with everything else, but it sticks and refuses to move. He was with someone else. After talking to me on that rooftop. After the laugh I swore I wouldn't let matter.

I don't know why I let myself believe it meant anything. One scrap of honesty under the stars. That's all it was. Nothing more.

He probably does that with every girl. He talks just enough to make them think they matter, drops a grin sharp enough to convince them they're special. That is Zane Rivera. Always chasing something he will never keep, always restless, always reaching for the next warm body to distract him from whatever ghosts won't let him sleep.

Still, it stings.

It shouldn't. But it burns straight through me all the same.

"Don't worry," Cassie adds, her tone dry, the words rolling out slow as if they might soften the blow. "He looked bored."

I grunt. The sound barely passing for a response. My eyes stay locked on the cracked sidewalk. A weed has forced its way up through the concrete. I press my boot down on it until the stem snaps and the leaves crumple.

She changes the subject without warning, steering us away from danger as if it never existed. We trade cheap shots at Mr. Dalton's teeth, the way they are stained the color of old paper. We roll our eyes at the fact that Liza still drenches herself in perfume so strong it lingers in the hallway long after she is gone. We bitch about the vending machines that never stock what they promise, spitting out stale Cheezels and disappointment in equal measure.

It is better this way. The petty complaints. The pointless noise that keeps the real shit buried where it belongs.

By the time we reach the school gates, my chest is tight and my heart is beating like a fucking war drum.

We pass the cliques one by one, each group locked into their little kingdoms. The cheerleaders cluster together with their glossy lips and sharper eyes, their whispers curling through the air sweet as poison. The drama kids sprawl across benches in thrift-store jackets and scarves even though it is warm, reciting lines no one asked to hear, pretending every gesture is profound.

No one says a word to us. Their eyes do the talking, sliding over us with that mix of judgment and curiosity that never changes. We walk straight through the middle of them, our heads high. Every step is its own middle finger, even if we never lift our hands.

Inside, the school hums with life.

The fluorescent lights buzz overhead, a high-pitched whine that worms into your skull until it feels like static under your skin. Lockers slam shut with the subtlety of gunfire, metal on metal rattling down the hall.

And then I see him.

Zane.

He is slouched against the vending machine. His arms are crossed, shoulders loose, head tilted just enough to show he does not give a shit about anyone passing by. A smirk is already forming on his mouth that promises trouble before he even opens it. He doesn't need an audience. The room bends toward him anyway, pulled in by gravity that no one can explain.

His eyes find mine across the crowded hallway. He just stares straight through me as if he already knows where the cracks are.

I shoot him a glare so sharp it could peel the skin from his bones. My eyes narrow, every ounce of fury sharpened, meant to cut him down.

He doesn't flinch. The bastard drinks it in, savoring the way I burn, twisting my fury to fuel the smirk of his getting wider.

I lift my middle finger high enough for him to see it clear and keep walking without breaking stride.

Cassie snorts beside me. "You two gonna make out or murder each other?"

We slide into our usual seats in the middle of the room, Cassie beside me, always closest to the door. She says it is for the view, but I know the truth. Cassie always chooses the exit, always lines herself up with the fastest escape.

The desks around us are relics, covered in the ghosts of kids who probably don't even walk these halls anymore. Initials are carved into the wood in sloppy hearts with declarations of forever that probably ended the next week. Black marker scars the surface too, one desk proudly screaming "suck it" in uneven letters, the ink faded but still legible. Another has a crude dick sketched in blue biro, balls lopsided, lines overlapping as if the artist was laughing too hard to steady their hand.

Cassie drops her bag on the floor, slouching so far in her chair it looks like her spine gave up. She blows a strand of hair from her face and digs a pen out of her boot. It's chewed and leaking ink. It leaves smudges on her fingers. She doesn't care.

I pretend to organize my shit, dragging it out like a ritual that might make me invisible. I pull my books from my bag and set them in a neat stack, the edges lined up with obsessive precision, as if order can disguise the chaos in my head. I pick up my pen and click it three times, the hollow sound filling the space where thought should be.

He is not here.

Not yet.

Maybe he is skipping this class today. Maybe Samantha texted him and he is busy getting off with her, chasing the same easy distraction he always does.

I try not to care. That he is just another boy with a smirk and fists scarred from bad decisions.

But denial only gets me so far. Because I feel him before I see him. The air shifts and my pulse betrays me. My body knows he has arrived before my eyes confirm it.

I lower my eyes to my notebook as if it holds the answer to something important. The page is blank, but I stare at it anyway. Staring is easier than looking up at him. Plus it's safer.

He stops in front of our table. His shadow falls over my desk, stretching across the empty page, but I keep my head down.

The toe of his boot nudges the leg of my chair. Then again. A little harder this time, as if he is daring me to acknowledge him.

Still, I pretend not to register it. I let my pen hover above the paper.

Cassie stills for a moment beside me. Then her pen scratches across the margin of her notebook, but it is nothing more than a performance. She's pretending to doodle, lines and swirls looping over one another. She lives for this kind of theater, the quiet chaos before the explosion.

Zane leans forward, invading my space without hesitation. His voice drops low, carrying that weight that coils straight down my spine. His breath ghosts against my ear.

"Are you always this cold in the morning, or is it just me?" he murmurs.

A chill slides across my skin, raising goosebumps I try to ignore. I hate that he has that effect on me. Hate that a single sentence from his mouth can slip under my defenses and curl inside my chest. His words move the way smoke does, finding cracks I did not even know were there, seeping through until the air feels heavy and poisoned. I should push him out. I should shut him down. But instead I sit here, every nerve wired tight, furious that he can get past my walls at all.

I keep my eyes down. My pen scratches nothing across the page, my hand steady only because I force it to be. "You talking again, or is that the sound of your ego trying to unzip its own pants?"

Cassie snorts so loud she nearly chokes on her laughter, pressing her pen harder into the paper as if she can hide it there.

Zane laughs too, buried under his breath. "Feisty," he says, like he's proud of me, as if I am not a girl telling him to fuck off but some wild animal he has cornered. He sounds like he wants to poke me with a stick just to watch me snap.

He slides into the seat in front of me, the scrape of the chair loud enough to drag every eye in the room for half a second. It is the first time he has chosen this spot. Usually he plants himself at the back, half hidden, all attitude, while he does whatever the fuck Zane Rivera does when he is not busy getting suspended.

Now here he is.

Too fucking close for comfort.

He drapes one arm over the back of his chair with lazy confidence, the other spread across his desk, his whole body turned toward me as if I am the only thing worth looking at. His posture is loose, almost careless, but the weight of his attention presses against me.

I force myself to look busy. I flip through pages I have already seen a dozen times, pretending to search for something important. I click my pen again and again, and shift my books into a new stack, then another, arranging and rearranging as if the order of paper and ink could mean something.

But none of it fucking matters.

Because he is watching me.

"Didn't know I had that kind of effect on you," he says, voice smooth, every word dipped in arrogance.

I finally meet his eyes and aim the best death glare I have. It is the one I use when I want someone to back the fuck off.

"You don't," I snap.

The words land too fast. Too defensive.

His smirk only deepens, spreading slow across his face as if I just handed him proof of something he already suspected. His gaze flickers down to my mouth and lingers there for a half second too long, deliberate enough to make my stomach twist.

Fuck.

Zane Rivera is dangerous. Not in the casual way people throw that word around when they talk about boys with motorcycles or tattoos. Not the kind of danger that fades when the lights come on.

I force my attention to the front of the room. Mr. Harvey is at the whiteboard, uncapping markers and scrawling the outline of a lesson we haven't started yet. Grammar bullshit no one in here will bother to care about.

Then the sound in the room shifts. The air itself changes. The noise floods in, cutting across the low hum that had settled before. Laughter slices through it— too smug, entitled in the way only certain voices can be.

Footsteps follow. Every step dripping with that cheap confidence bought with money and last names, the kind of confidence that tells them the world will bend just because they showed up. It is in their walk, all chest and shoulders. It is in the tilt of their heads, the practiced roll of their smirks as they scan the room. Every move says the same thing: applaud us, worship us, hate us if you want, but do not look away.

Three of them.

Football jerseys stretched across their shoulders. Expensive haircuts, paid for by fathers who solve their problems with cash and lawyers.

They move as a pack, feeding on each other's noise, amplifying it until it fills every corner of the room.

Alone, they would be just boys in shoes too clean, they wouldn't matter. Together, they wear invincibility like a crown.

Zane doesn't turn to look. His body stays slouched in that lazy way of his, but I can feel his attention fixed on me. His eyes don't leave, not even for a second, as every muscle in my body coils tight. I know what's coming. The script never changes, only the volume.

Liam doesn't waste time. He spots me the second he crosses the threshold, his grin already plastered across his face, stretched too wide, too sure of itself.

He makes a beeline straight for our table, carving through the rows of desks, weaving between bodies without breaking stride. People move for him even when they don't mean to, pulled out of his way by sheer force of arrogance. His swagger isn't earned. It never is with boys like him. It's inherited, handed down with the letterman jacket and the empty praise that cushions every fall.

He stops right beside us, staking his ground as if the floor was marked with his name. His stance is wide, feet planted apart in that ridiculous show of dominance boys of his kind believe makes them men. His hands rest on his hips, fingers splayed, elbows out, his chest puffed up for maximum effect.

"Shit," he says, dragging the word out, making sure every single person within earshot hears it. His voice carries that mocking tone, drawn out as if the syllable itself is the punchline to a joke only he finds funny. He tilts his head toward me, eyes cutting sharp. "Didn't know the cafeteria was handing out strays this early."

I freeze. Not completely, but enough for it to show in the smallest ways. My fingers clamp down on the edge of the desk until my knuckles ache, white and bloodless.

Because I know this game.

I have played it too many times in too many rooms that reeked of sweat and cheap power. I know exactly what they want. They want the reaction, the spark that turns into fire. They want the snap, the flinch, the proof they can get under my skin.

"Aw, don't be bitter, foster girl," one of the other assholes says as he steps closer. "You can sit with us if you want. Rivera doesn't need to hog all the broken toys."

Zane shifts in his chair, the movement small but enough to drag the air tighter around us. He doesn't bother to look at them. His posture doesn't change, still loose, still lazy, but there is a coil beneath it, a wire pulled taut and ready to snap.

His voice cuts through the noise, stripped of anything human. Deadly in its calm. "Go sit the fuck somewhere else."

They ignore him. That is how this game always plays out. Guys like Liam are built to push, their grins plastered on as if mockery is oxygen. They never stop. They prod, they taunt, because they believe no one can touch them. They believe their jerseys are armor and their fathers' names are shields.

And Zane is a loaded gun sitting right in front of them, safety long gone, trigger begging to be pulled. They are too stupid, too cocky, too entitled to see it.

"You sharing this one, Rivera?" Liam says, his voice rising, feeding off the audience that has begun to form. He is louder now, braver under the weight of attention, mistaking their silence for approval. He leans into it, letting the words drip filth into the air. "Or keeping her to yourself? Bit greedy, don't you think? Thought your type liked to pass it around."

Laughter bursts out from a few desks away.

Zane's chair scrapes back against the tile. He rises in one smooth motion, every inch of him a threat.

The whole room goes still. Conversations die mid-sentence.

Liam's shoulders stiffen, but his shit eating grin doesn't falter. His mouth keeps moving, desperate to prove he isn't rattled. "What, you fucking her already, Rivera? I hear she's easy. Figured we'd have our fun."

That is all it takes. One sentence too far and Zane lunges forward, the calm stripped away in an instant. His fist arcs through the air and slams into Liam's jaw with brutal precision. The crack rings out, echoing through the room with a sound that is equal parts violence and satisfaction. For a heartbeat, it is the only noise that exists.

Liam stumbles back, head snapping to the side, his body crashing into the desk behind him. The impact rattles through the room as chairs topple, clattering against the floor. His friends scatter, all that swagger leaking out of them as they scramble, nearly tripping over each other in their rush to get out of the way. Their bravado dissolves into panic the second fists turn real.

One girl shrieks. Someone knocks their water bottle off the table and it rolls across the floor, unnoticed. Cassie shoots to her feet, wide-eyed, but I don't move.

I sit there. Frozen.

My hands stay clenched around the edge of the desk, nails biting into the wood, but I don't move. I can't. My body won't let me. All I can do is watch.

Zane doesn't stop. He hauls Liam up by the collar, fisting the front of his jersey.

Liam tries to fight back, arms flailing, legs kicking against the floor, but he isn't fast enough. Zane has been waiting for this. You can see it in the way his movements are sharp, in the way his fists land with precision.

A split lip blooms red across Liam's mouth. A bruise darkens over his left cheekbone, swelling beneath Zane's knuckles. Blood splatters the floor, tiny drops scattering across the white tile. The sight roots itself in my chest.

Mr. Harvey rushes forward, his face already flushed, his tie swinging loose as he shoves past desks and bodies.

"Rivera!" he roars, pushing through the wall of students as though the crowd itself is an enemy he has to fight through. He looks less like a teacher and more like a man barely holding himself together.

Zane doesn't flinch.

He stands over Liam, looming, chest heaving with each ragged breath. His jaw is locked tight, muscles straining beneath his skin. His fists are still raised, trembling with the urge to keep moving. His breathing is uneven, rough, as if every inhale is dragging nails through his lungs. He looks unstoppable, as if he could keep pounding Liam into the tile for hours if no one dragged him off.

Harvey's voice booms again, desperate this time. "I said that's enough! Office. Now."

Zane shoves Liam away with a hard push, releasing him as if he is nothing but dead weight.

Liam crashes back to the ground, shoulders slamming against the tile. Blood runs from the corner of his mouth, staining his chin and collar. His chest rises unevenly, but his eyes are steady, gleaming under the fluorescent lights. They burn with smugness, as if he believes he has claimed a victory in this mess.

Zane bends down, and grabs his bag off the floor.

Then he turns, and our eyes meet.

In that single second, I see all of it. The fury burning under his skin, the weight pressing into his shoulders. The years of rage carved into every muscle. I see the silence he has carried, the fists he has thrown in dark corners where no one bothered to watch. The battles he fought just to keep breathing. I see the boy he used to be, the one who learned to fight because no one ever fought for him. The one who has never had anyone to protect, until now.

He walks out. The door swings shut behind him, cutting him from the room, but the storm he left behind keeps raging in my chest.

Phones are still up.

Some are pointed at Liam, still sprawled across the floor like a broken puppet. Others are aimed at me. They're recording my face, my reaction, my everything.

Some people are whispering, some don't bother at all.

Their voices bleed together in waves.

"I bet she spreads her legs for him behind the gym," someone chimes in, louder, eager to feed the crowd. "Wouldn't take much. Bet she begged for it."

Another voice cuts through, meaner than the rest. "Look at her. She'd open her legs for anyone who gave her a second glance. Trash never says no."

Liam wipes his mouth with the sleeve of his jersey, smearing blood across it like war paint. He looks like hell and he looks proud of it.

Cassie leans closer, her shoulder brushing mine, her voice low but edged with steel.

"He's a fucking dick," she mutters, eyes locked on Liam still sprawled on the floor.

One of his asshole friends finally lowers his hand and reaches down, hauling Liam up by the arm. Liam staggers but stays on his feet, his grin twisted and wet. Blood drips from his split lip, smeared across his chin, glistening under the harsh lights.

"Guess she's a good fuck if Rivera's willing to throw hands over her," he mutters, his voice thick, lips shining red as he spits the words out for everyone to hear.

I turn toward him before I can stop myself, my body betraying me.

My gaze lands hard on his face, sharp enough to cut, but instead of shrinking, he feeds on it.

That's what this is for him—provocation, power, proof that he can still get a rise out of me even with blood dripping from his mouth.

"Didn't think street rats cared who they fucked," he adds.

His eyes glint with challenge, daring me to break my silence, daring me to let him win.

I hold his stare, locking onto it until the rest of the room fades away.

Heat pulses through me, demanding an outlet.

I want to grab the edge of my chair and hurl it into his smug face. I want to scream until my throat is raw. Scream that I am not what they think.

But I don't owe any of them the truth.

"Fuck you," I say.

Heads turn.

Desks creak as people lean in, hungry for the spectacle.

Liam doesn't blink. His sneer cuts across his face, blood still on his lip.

"Don't worry, foster girl," he spits. "If you ever get tired of the street rat fucking you, I'll show you what a real man feels like."

Every muscle in my body coils tight, but I keep my expression carved in stone.

I have heard shit like this before. In houses where the doors never locked, where shadows lingered in the hall. In kitchens where men stared too long over half-empty bottles.

That is why I ran from those foster homes and stopped letting anyone get close. That is why I learned how to make my glare a weapon sharp enough to cut.

I lean forward, only a fraction, enough to show I am not afraid.

"I'd rather fuck a cactus with teeth than touch you," I say, my tone surgical. "At least it wouldn't ask if I came when it barely lasted thirty seconds."

Gasps ripple through the class, sharp little intakes of breath that bounce off the walls. A few people cough into their hands, trying to bury laughter they can't quite swallow.

Cassie exhales beside me, and it sounds suspiciously like pride. Her smirk is hidden behind her notebook, but the pride radiates off her all the same.

Liam's jaw locks so tight I can see the muscle twitching, his teeth grinding down on whatever comeback he wants to spit but can't find. He blinks hard, twice, then narrows his eyes in a glare he thinks still has power.

"Bitch," he spits.

I raise an eyebrow.

"That's the best you've got?" I ask, tilting my head. "Jesus. No wonder your girlfriend's always crying in the bathroom."

Before Liam can say a single word, another voice cuts through the room.

"Miss James."

Mr. Harvey.

The vein in his forehead ticks, pulsing with irritation. He points at the door. A lazy, silent dismissal that says everything his mouth doesn't bother to form. He is done.

I stare at his finger. For a moment, the fight claws at my throat, begging to be let out. But I swallow it whole.

The assholes never get in trouble. They are the chosen ones, grins painted on, all teeth and charm, and somehow the world keeps mistaking it for goodness. The school protects them, funds them, builds banners with their names in bold black letters, monuments to boys who will never be held accountable.

They are untouchable.

But girls like me? We are disposable. Warning labels. The easy blame. The dirt swept under the rug so their shine never dulls.

I should be used to it by now.

But today, it crawls deeper than usual, reminding me that no matter how hard I fight, no matter how sharp my edges become, I am still proof that some people are born without value.

Chapter 4

The principal's office reeks of bleach and bullshit. It's all scrubbed walls and dirty truths.

I'm slouched in the chair outside his door, leg bouncing hard enough to rattle the floor, trying to shake the fury clawing at my skin. The anger sticks. It always does. Doesn't matter how many times I try to peel it off.

My knuckles are split again. Red. Throbbing. A mess of old scars torn back open. My jaw aches from how tight I've been clenching it, every muscle straining to keep the scream buried.

And fuck, I'll never learn.

Always fight or flight. But I never run, so I swing. Every goddamn time, because that's all I've ever been taught.

My whole life's been one long fucking brawl. Me against the world, fists up, breath short, waiting to be hit so I can hit back harder. It's instinct, more like muscle memory now. They come for me, and I burn the whole thing down.

Part of me wishes I didn't always end up bleeding and broken in someone else's hallway. But wishing only gets you so far. And no one ever taught me how to walk away.

The door groans open, dragging silence into the room. Mr. Granger fills the frame, face screwed up so tight it seems painful. As if he's been chewing on bitterness his whole life and still hasn't learned to swallow it. His eyes cut through me, dismissive—the same expression people give to roadkill they wish someone had cleared before they had to drive past.

His expression says everything.

I'm the mistake he wishes had been erased before landing in this school. The stain he'll never scrub out of it's shiny floors, no matter how much bleach he drowns the halls in.

"Inside," he snaps, voice flat and clipped, already done with me before I've even moved.

I push up from the chair, every muscle dragging, weighted with the kind of heaviness that never leaves. My shoulders square out of habit. My body moves like it's been trained for this routine. Dragged into offices, lined up for lectures, another adult waiting to carve their disappointment into my skin.

I don't meet his eyes. I refuse. His gaze is a trap, hungry for weakness. He won't get a damn thing from me. Instead, my focus stays locked on the wall past his shoulder, where the paint's chipped, a thin crack snaking upward, as if even this place can't hold itself together. That crack becomes my anchor, something solid to keep me from drowning in the weight of his stare.

The door clicks shut behind me, a clean, final sound. A lock without a key.

My teeth grind until I taste the copper of old blood.

"Sit."

The word lands sharp. A command, not a request. The kind of order they've been shoving at me my whole damn life. All I can think about is how much I want to ignore him. How much I want to stand there and watch him squirm when I don't fold into his rules.

I don't. Not straight away.

I stay on my feet, letting the silence stretch. The weight presses down, fills the room, drags against my skin. He waits for me to fold, but I won't... not yet.

I've seen how this plays out. Lived through it too many times to count. The script never changes. Troubled kid. The one with the fucked-up past stamped across his record. The one with fists for hands and anger for a spine. The walking cautionary tale everyone warns their sons not to become and their daughters to avoid.

Every glance, every sigh, every note scribbled in that fucking folder with my name on it says enough. They've already written me off. Waiting for me to prove them right again.

Eventually, I drop into the chair. Not because I've surrendered, but because my legs are heavy with a lifetime of this bullshit. I'm tired of this game, the labels, of pretending I'm not exactly what they've made me out to be.

I sit there with my arms folded tight across my chest, the kind of posture that says *fuck you* without a sound. Because if I'm going to give them what they expect, I'll do it on my own terms.

Granger folds his hands on the desk. His glasses slide down the bridge of his nose and he pushes them back up with one finger, as if the gesture alone makes him important.

He stares. Not the casual kind you forget after a second. The kind that drags, peeling me apart without ever touching me. It's quiet, calculating. His elbows sink into the desk, fingers laced, chin tilted forward to show he's in control. As if he's more than a bureaucrat who signs suspension slips the way most people sign checks. A man who plays God before breakfast, scribbling out futures with the flick of his pen.

I don't give him anything. Not a blink, a breath or even the satisfaction of a flinch. My eyes glaze over, locking on a spot past his shoulder until he's nothing but a blur I refuse to focus on.

If he wants me to squirm, he'll have to keep waiting.

Because the only thing worse than being their failure is giving them the show they came for.

He exhales, long and loaded, the kind of breath that carries judgment in the weight. This isn't air leaving his lungs... it's disappointment. A sound that tells me he's written the ending before I've even opened my mouth.

"Zane."

My name falls out of him like it's too heavy to hold.

"Wanna tell me what happened?"

I don't. I won't.

I sit in that chair, still as stone, arms clamped tight across my chest, my body nothing but a barricade. Because the second I open my mouth, it's over. They'll twist every word, spin the story, use the truth against me until even that starts to feel false. So I stay silent. Let the weight settle. Let him choke on the silence.

He picks up the manila folder with my name on the cover, corners bent and edges frayed from being dragged out too many times. Thicker than it has any right to be. A history of everything I've ever done wrong. Every late bell. Every detention. Every time I breathed in a way they didn't approve of. Documented. Stamped. Filed away until I'm nothing more than paper cuts and ink.

He flips through it slow, like he's savoring each page. But I know he isn't reading. He doesn't need to. The story's memorized by now.

His finger lands on the newest entry. He doesn't even blink when he says it. "Today: Violence."

The word hangs in the room, heavy as stone.

He clicks his pen against the folder. Once. Twice. Three times. Tap. Tap. Tap. The sound digs into my skull until I want to snap that fucking pen in half. Then he stills it with a sharp press, as if to underline the point.

"Do you want to tell me why you hit him?"

A single shake of my head. The answer's no, but I don't waste the breath on words.

His mouth tightens. "You're not helping yourself."

Good. Didn't walk into this office to save myself.

"Zane."

He says my name again, his patience now wearing thin. He leans forward, eyes hard, tone snapping against my ears.

"This is your third suspension. In three weeks."

His gaze pins me to the chair, while his voice carries the final blow.

"You're on your last leg, Mister. You so much as breathe the wrong way and I've got every right to suspend you. Permanently."

The word *permanently* drags across the desk, thick and final, like a coffin lid slamming shut.

I nod once. Nothing more.

He lets the silence hang long enough to see if I'll flinch, break or fill the air with some pathetic plea to keep myself from drowning.

I don't. Fuck these pathetic people and their judgements.

I sit still as stone, my pulse hammering in my ears. My knee bounces under the desk, but not a single crack shows on my face. If he wants weakness, he can go find someone else.

He finally drags the suspension slip across the desk. The pen scratches loud against the paper.

"Three days," he says, voice clipped, cold. "Effective immediately. You're not allowed back on campus until Monday." He pauses, jaw tight, eyes narrowing with one last swing of authority. "And if you come near that boy again—"

"I won't." It slips out low, scraped from the back of my throat, barely more than a growl.

Granger rises, then opens the door with that finality that tells me I'm nothing more than paperwork now. A signature and a problem shuffled out of his office.

I sling my bag over my shoulder, the strap digging into my palm, and step into the hallway. Every footstep pounds against the tiles, echoing too loud, reminding me what I am. Trouble. Noise. A warning carved into the echo.

By the time I shove the front doors open, I know I'm fucked. The sunlight is too bright. It makes everything feel rawer, every nerve ending exposed.

That fucker Liam deserved it.

He opened his mouth and ran it around the wrong girl. Thought he was clever. Thought he was untouchable. His words crawled under my skin. Calling her a fucking broken toy with that arrogance. The kind of shit that turns people into property instead of human.

The fuckers never get it. We didn't ask for this life. We didn't choose to be shoved into these cages and labeled defective. And I'll be damned if I sit quietly while some asshole treats Skylar as if she's nothing more than something to use and throw away.

So I swung.

And now the world wants me to fucking pay for it.

I keep walking. Past the gates. Down the road. No destination, just forward motion. The buzz in my bones won't quit, the heat in my fists still burning holes under my skin.

Third suspension. That was the nail in the coffin last time.

The Jeffersons hadn't been perfect, but they weren't bad. Not saints, but decent. Hot meals on the table. A garage that smelled of oil and gasoline, where I learned how to pull apart an engine without the world crashing down around me. The kind of quiet that didn't cut too deep. For a second, I almost believed I could stay.

Then I fucked it up. One fight. One detention slip and they didn't hesitate. Handed me the trash bag full of my things and sent me packing. Just a shrug and a "we tried."

Now I've got Dorlores, who is a whole different breed of bitter. The woman never hides the fact that I'm nothing but an easy pay check. Every word from her mouth tastes of resentment.

The thermostat's locked at freezing, her way of reminding me comfort costs extra. She counts the cereal down to the crumbs, sharpie-marks her name on the milk, bolts the bathroom door after ten as if I'd break in and steal the fucking toilet. Every rule is a knife, and she twists them daily just to watch me bleed.

Now I've got to walk into that fucking house and tell her I've been suspended again. Another failure stamped across my forehead, another reason for her to remind me I'm a burden she never wanted.

See if she lasts longer than the last one.

And I hate needing any of them. Hate being passed around from one door to the next, shuffled like a playing card in a rigged game. Strangers collecting kids the way people collect tax deductions, then patting themselves on the back and calling it charity.

But the truth is heavier. I'm seventeen and I'm exhausted. My bones ache with it. Survival isn't strength anymore. It's just repetition. And it's killing me slower than anything else could.

I'm two months away from freedom, but it drags out in front of me as if it's years. Every day stretches thin, a sentence I can't appeal. I can see the end, taste it, almost touch it, but it still feels out of reach. I can't outrun the name stamped on me at birth or the hands that taught me violence before they ever taught me love. That shit clings. It brands you, burns you, follows you into every fucking room.

I kick a rock down the sidewalk. It skips once, twice, then rattles hard against the gutter before vanishing into the drain. Gone without a sound. No explanation. No fight. Just erased.

Lucky bastard.

Some days I think about running. Getting out. My own life. No caseworkers, no locked thermostats. Just me, no leash, no one waiting to drag me back.

I picture it sometimes. Walking until the streets blur into highways, until the houses thin out into dirt roads and sky. Finding a place where no one knows my name, where I don't have to explain the bruises on my knuckles or the fire in my chest.

Freedom. It sounds cheap when I say it in my head, but fuck, I crave it.

Two months might as well be two years. But I keep walking towards that fucking house instead.

It sits at the end of the street, ugly and slumped, peeling paint flaking off in strips, half-dead lawn patchy and yellow. The screen door dangles off one hinge, groaning every time the wind pushes it, a sound that says nobody here gives a shit. The porch sags under nothing but air, still tired, still defeated, like even the wood gave up on holding itself up.

Dolores's car is parked crooked in the driveway. The passenger mirror clings on with duct tape and spite. That car's her, in a way—broken, patched with cheap solutions, too stubborn to die.

I stop when I reach the front gate, and just stand here, letting the house stare back at me. I know what waits inside. I don't need to step through the door to see it.

She'll be on her throne. That busted recliner sagging into the floorboards, the armrest patched with gray tape that sticks to her skin when she shifts. The paperback will be clutched in one hand, her pink highlighter in the other, ready to drag neon lines across the filthiest parts. Always the sex scenes. Always those moments, as if the words could open a door into a life she never had.

Trashy romance novels with covers that scream cheap fantasy, more bare skin than story, men painted to look powerful enough to carry someone out of misery. She devours them, page after page, her lips pressed tight, eyes glazed over. Addicted to a world that was never hers.

She eats them up the way starved kids tear through candy, desperate, greedy. And when the book closes, when the highlighter cap clicks shut, she sinks deeper into the chair, drunk on the fantasy, whispering to herself that she deserved better. That she could've had it. That the world robbed her.

And every time her eyes flick to one of the many kids in that house, I know she's found her thief.

She'll already know by now that I'm suspended again. The school would have called the second the ink dried on that slip. The phone's probably still warm from her hand, her fake sympathy voice still echoing through the receiver.

The lecture will be waiting, loaded like a bullet. She'll tell me I embarrassed her, that I dragged her name through the dirt, that every mistake of mine reflects on her. That she stuck her neck out for me. That she's tired. As if I'm the weight breaking her back instead of the reason her bills get paid on time.

I don't need to hear it again. So I keep walking.

Past the front steps, past the peeling door daring me to come inside. Around the house and down the alley.

Down past the old buildings where someone tagged the back wall of a shed with *dead kids don't talk* in red spray paint. It's faded now, cracked from years of weather, but I still read it every time I pass.

I don't know why it sticks.

The river waits ahead, if you can even call it that. More mud than water, slow and sluggish, a vein clogged with filth no one bothers to clean. A place bloated with the things everyone wants to ignore. It suits me.

I drop down near the bank. Not too close. The ground's soft, the kind that swallows your shoes whole if you're dumb enough to test it. I hunch forward, elbows digging into my knees, bury my face in my hands.

Three days off school. They think they're punishing me. But school's a shitty thing I don't want to deal with anyway. They basically did me a favour. I don't care about the classes, the teachers, the constant noise. None of it matters.

It's the consequences that come with it.

The threat of a group home.

I've been there once before, for a short time when I was eleven, when they couldn't find a placement and dumped me in with the rest of the kids nobody wanted. And if Dolores wants me out, I just gave her the perfect reason to hand me back.

Group homes don't hand out second chances. Back to dorms that stink of sweat, back to shared bathrooms with locks that never worked. Metal beds that froze your bones. Cinderblock walls that pressed in until you couldn't breathe. Boys who watched you too long, eyes crawling over your skin, waiting for weakness. Kids who tested your patience with every word, every look, just to see how far they could push before you snapped.

They wanted to see what you were made of. And you either proved it, or you got crushed.

I learned quickly. Came out colder.

Because when you're the angry kid, it doesn't matter what pushed you. They don't care about the match. Only the fire.

Chapter 5

Skylar

The final bell rings, and the whole building exhales in one desperate rush. Desks screech against the floor as bodies shoot up, every kid convinced freedom belongs to whoever gets out first.

The noise doubles once they spill into the corridor. Sneakers squeak across the tiles. Someone slams a locker so hard the sound ricochets through the ceiling. Laughter spikes, too loud, more hysteria than joy. And in the corner, a freshman is already crying, face crumpled, because high school is a fucking nightmare no one prepares you for, and the cruel truth is it only gets worse from here.

I clutch my books to my chest, pressing them so tight it feels as if they might splinter. The noise chases me anyway, impossible to outrun.

Cassie finds me outside the science wing, my back against the wall, trying to make myself smaller. She is wrist-deep in her bag, dragging out scraps of paper, discarded gum wrappers, and what might be a granola bar so ancient it deserves a memorial service.

"You coming?" she asks without looking up. Her feet are already moving, confident I'll follow.

I nod and fall into step beside her. The noise and rush of footsteps chase us through the doors, spilling into the open air as if the halls could not contain the chaos. Above us the sky hangs heavy, smeared in pale clouds that look soft from a distance but carry the weight of a storm.

Cassie tears open her gum wrapper and chews with the kind of spite you save for an ex-boyfriend's voicemail. Earlier we had pulled that beatdown apart piece by piece, dissecting every swing between Liam and Zane, dragging the asshole teacher into it too, the one who tossed me out of the classroom, pretending it was a solution instead of a punishment. I ended up in the library, pretending to read while every page blurred to nothing, my head replaying Zane's fury in high definition.

Liam never stood a chance. Zane's fists moved faster than thought, each strike carrying the weight of scars carved into his knuckles, proof they were not accidents but a history written in blood and bone. Those scars finally make sense. He is a storm when he moves, all muscle and violence, the kind of force that tears through anything in its path. Yet not once has it ever turned on me, not even when I ran my mouth, needling him, shoving at him just to see how far I could push before he snapped.

And maybe I should stop. Maybe what I saw today should have been enough to scare me off, to make me pull back before I get caught in something I can't control. But it didn't. Not once has Zane made me feel small, and even after watching him break someone apart, that hasn't changed. If anything, it only burned hotter, setting something inside me I don't want to name on fire.

Cassie blows a bubble with her gum, tugging at my arm so I'll pay attention as if it is the highlight of her day. It bursts across her chin, and she groans, peeling the sticky mess away with a scowl. A beat passes. Then another crawls by before she finally speaks.

"You sure there's nothing going on with you and Zane?"

"For the hundredth time today," I groan. "Cassie, I've already told you, there's nothing."

"It didn't look like nothing to me." Her smirk curls slow. "You sure he hasn't crept into your room in the middle of the night? You know, just to—"

"Yeah, right." I roll my eyes so hard it hurts. "All those bunk beds. Real romantic. Nothing screams foreplay more than rusty springs and some kid ripping one in his sleep."

"But you've thought about it, right?" she presses, eyes glinting with that smugness that makes me want to shove her into traffic.

I stay quiet. Because admitting the truth means admitting I've pictured it—him only a few doors down, stretched across his mattress, the silence between our rooms carrying more weight than it should. And I don't want her to know that. I don't want anyone to know.

Cassie cackles, head thrown back. "I wouldn't blame you if you did. He's fucking hot. If he looked my way, I'd climb him faster than a monkey on stolen bananas."

"Wow." My tone is flat, dry enough to cut glass. "Real classy. And for what? Just to be another girl he fucks and forgets?"

"At least I'd know what it's like to have his attention," she fires back, grin flashing.

"Trust me," I say, shaking my head, "he doesn't give anyone attention."

"Except you." Her voice slips into a sing-song, every note dragged out, sweet and cruel at the same time, just to watch me twitch.

I shake my head and lengthen my stride, but she falls in beside me without effort, her steps syncing with mine like muscle memory. By the time we hit the sidewalk, the rhythm feels rehearsed, two shadows moving in tandem. Cassie tears open another stick of gum and shoves it between her teeth, chewing hard, working it as if she has a personal grudge to settle.

"You know one day you'll choke on that shit if you keep stuffing your mouth the way you do," I mutter.

Cassie acts as if she didn't hear me, her gaze drifting to the cars that blur past, her jaw working slower now, just enough to show she did. Then she turns back, one eyebrow arched, eyes sharp with the kind of curiosity that never lets go. "You know you can't change the subject. He almost knocked that guy's teeth out."

A knot forms in my gut, because she's right. I have no fucking idea why Zane lost it, why his fury went nuclear in the span of a single breath. Especially when it was over me.

"Cass..."

She doesn't stop.

"Jesus, Sky. When a guy starts throwing hands over you, that usually means something."

I halt mid-step, the weight of her words pinning me in place. The street keeps moving around us, alive with its own noise and rhythm—cars tearing past, dogs barking from behind fences. I turn and face her head-on, pulse climbing.

"Don't."

Her eyebrows arch high. "Don't what?"

"Don't twist it into something it's not. Don't make it sound pretty. It's not cute, Cass. It's not some fucked-up fairytale. He's not a broody hero fighting for the girl. He's... he's Zane."

She studies me in silence, lips pressed so tight they turn pale. When she finally speaks, her voice is softer, but it cuts sharper. "And you're acting like that's not exactly why you're spiraling."

I don't answer. I can't. My throat locks around every word. So I shove my gaze forward instead, eyes on the cracks splitting apart the sidewalk, praying Zane's name will fade out of my head if I just keep staring hard enough.

Cassie sighs, dramatic as always, then flicks her gum into a drain with a flourish only she could make look intentional. "For someone who insists it's nothing, you sure talk about him a lot."

"I don't talk about him."

Her smirk blooms, slow and merciless. "You breathe him."

She stays smug in her silence, wearing it like a crown. Because she knows she's won. She always does. And even though I hate her being right, she's my best friend. The only person who can throw shit like that in my face and still walk away.

The worst part... she's not wrong. Zane isn't just someone I think about. He's something I feel, a bruise I can't stop pressing, gravity I never signed up to orbit.

"Can you just drop it, Cass, for fuck sake."

Her grin only widens, stretching until it's all teeth. She pulls me into a quick hug, her whisper brushing my ear. "One day you'll open up and tell me the things you're too scared to fucking say."

"Not today."

"Love you, girl." She waves, peeling off two streets before mine, her figure darting across the road.

I plaster on a fake smile and watch her go, her hair snapping in the wind, her body shrinking against the sprawl of houses that all blur into the same tired shape. Only when she vanishes on the far side do my feet start moving again.

And the problem is Cassie's right. She is always fucking right.

The closer I get to the house, the slower my steps drag. That familiar weight starts sinking in my stomach long before I reach the gate. I already know what waits for me on the other side.

The front door gapes open, same as always. Privacy doesn't live here. It never has. I force myself up the steps and shove through, shoulders braced, lungs locked, waiting for the hit.

And it comes.

A kid is screaming about wanting cereal from the kitchen. Someone else is crying near the entrance, a high-pitched wail that scratches against my nerves. Down the hall, the older boys are locked in another argument, this one over who fucked with the batteries in the remote. Their voices spike, sharp enough that I know punches will fly if Dolores doesn't step in. Which she won't. Not soon enough anyway.

The air is thick with the stench of dirty socks, stale spaghetti, and the sour tang of too many bodies pressed into a space never meant to hold them. A sock flies across the hall and lands at my feet, damp and reeking. On the wall to my right, a streak of tomato sauce is splattered like blood, drying into cracks that will never be scrubbed clean. Muddy footprints trail across the boards, proof no one cares about wiping shoes. One of the twins barrels past me, butter knife raised, chasing his brother down the hallway with murder in his eyes.

No one bothers to say hi to me. That's the rule here. The less you interact, the safer you are.

My bag slides down my shoulder as I take the stairs two at a time, ignoring the shouting that echoes up from below. The walls are too thin to hold any secrets. Every slammed door is another reminder that there is no such thing as peace.

My room waits at the end of the hall, though calling it mine is a stretch. The door doesn't lock and the roof leaks every time the sky decides to cry.

I drop my bag onto my mattress. The noise from the house seeps through the walls, every shout and slam bleeding into the room until it feels as if the chaos has followed me here on purpose. I last less than a minute before it crushes me.

I shove back through the door and slip out without a sound.

No one looks up.

No one notices. No one fucking cares.

I head down the back steps, past garbage bins spilling over, sour rot leaking from bags knotted too loose, flies swarming like they own the place. The fence groans when I shove through, splinters biting into my palm as the wood gives way.

My feet carry me without thought, each step pulled by something deeper than choice. The rooftop.

The one place in this entire fucked-up town that doesn't smell like despair. Where no one needs me to play a part I never auditioned for.

The fire escape ladder bites into my palms as I climb. My heart pounds with every rung, beating harder as I near the top.

When my fingers curl around the ledge, I haul myself up... then freeze.

He is already there.

Zane.

Sitting where he was yesterday. His hands are braced behind him, long legs stretched out, hair catching the light in a way that turns him into something half-boy, half-myth. His backpack beside him, unzipped, books spilling out because he clearly couldn't be bothered to close it.

And just like that, my breath falters, caught in my throat.

No matter how many times I see him, it still knocks the air out of me. Zane is chaos and calm tangled into one body, a hurricane stitched into skin. Beautiful in a way that shouldn't be seen, dangerous in a way that makes turning away impossible. And I hate that he is here.

Not because I don't want him here. Because I fucking do. And that is what terrifies me most.

He hasn't said a word. Neither have I. But his eyes lock on mine, and the world shifts under me. My chest knots tight, my pulse stutters out of rhythm. I lower myself onto the rooftop, legs folding beneath me, careful with every move.

His fingers tap against his leg, restless. His hair moves in the breeze, catching light in golden streaks. I steal a look at him anyway, and fuck me. Even from this angle he is infuriating. His hair is always tousled, the sandy strands a mess that somehow looks deliberate. His jaw sharp, clenched in thought. The crooked curve of his nose, proof of some fight that only made him more dangerous.

And then there is his mouth. That goddamn mouth. Smirking when he's being cocky. Sharp when he's pissed. Quiet now, but no less distracting.

He gets under my skin without trying. My body notices. That magnetic, destructive pull that Cassie warned me about. The one I can't shake, no matter how hard I try.

I blink hard, forcing the memory back, but Cassie's words slip in anyway. *"He was with Samantha last night."*

I never asked her for details. I didn't want them. The jealousy carved itself in anyway, branding me with marks I can't scrub clean, no matter how much I pretend I don't care.

And now he is here. A poem ruined before it was finished, built from broken shit no one could fix. He is a hymn and a curse in the same breath, beauty twisted into chaos. And I am the idiot sitting too close, letting it burn through me.

Zane doesn't move when I sit. The air shifts around him, in a way that makes it impossible not to notice every detail. His profile cuts sharp against the sunlight, the kind of sight that reduces the sky to nothing more than a backdrop. His lashes throw shadows I shouldn't be caught staring at. His mouth stays still, curved in that way that makes it seem he is keeping secrets no one else is allowed to hear.

I tell myself not to stare, but my body betrays me. My eyes drag down to his hands, knuckles split, bruises blooming across skin that should scream violence but doesn't. Even battered, they remain steady. Gentle enough to pull someone in, gentle enough to make her believe she mattered.

Something sharp turns low in my stomach at the thought. Samantha.

The name slices through me before I can stop it.

Now here he is, every inch of him reminding me that he could have touched her less than twenty-four hours ago. Those bruised hands, that mouth on her. His body pressed against hers in the way mine has only ever dared to imagine. The thought is poison, and yet I drink it down anyway.

Because no matter how many girls fall into his lap, I'm the one sitting here, heart unraveling just from watching him breathe.

God, I'm so fucking stupid.

He shifts, leaning back on one elbow, turning slightly so the last light catches the line of his jaw. His lashes are too long, unfair on a boy who doesn't deserve anything soft. His eyes are storm clouds when they flick toward me. Dangerous. Pulling.

He drags his tongue across his bottom lip, slow enough to wreck me. My breath stumbles, chest flaring hot, heat coiling where I don't want it. I drive my nails into my palms, pressing until the sting cuts through. Pain is the only anchor I have, because if I let go for even a second, I will do something reckless.

Then his voice sounds through the silence.

"I didn't realize you hung around rooftops now."

Cocky. Casual. As if the air belongs to him and I am just trespassing in it.

I shrug and turn my head, forcing my eyes to stay on the horizon. "I didn't think you would be here, that's all."

"Guess we're both full of surprises," he says with that shit eating grin

He always does this. Always manages to make it sound as if he knows more than he ever says, two steps ahead while I am still struggling to catch my breath.

I risk another glance, telling myself it is quick enough not to count.

It isn't. I fail before I even try.

His eyes are already on me.

"What?" I snap, heat clawing up my neck.

"Nothing." He draws it out. "Just wondering what it's like to be up here with me."

"Don't flatter yourself."

He leans back, head tilting, eyes narrowing with that lazy calm that drives me insane. "C'mon, Sky, you were practically staring."

"Was not."

"You were." His smirk widens, smug and unshakable. "But it's fine. I get it. I'm hot."

The arrogance sparks through me, sharp and unignorable. "Congratulations. Want me to get you a medal, or should I buy you a bigger mirror?"

His laugh rolls out low and satisfied, the sound of someone who knows exactly where to pull the strings. He is having the time of his fucking life watching me come apart.

The memory of Samantha slams into me, souring the heat in my chest until it curdles. Jealousy, the kind I refuse to admit to, but it rises anyway.

"So…" I mutter, tugging at a loose thread on my sleeve, refusing to meet his eyes. "You and Samantha. That's a thing now?"

He doesn't answer right away. His mouth curves at the corner, almost cruel, before a slow laugh drips out.

"That why you're really up here?"

"No." The word rips out too quick, too defensive.

He arches a brow, smirk sharpening, the swagger rolling off him in waves. "You jealous, Sweetheart?"

I bite back before I can stop myself. "The day I get jealous over you is the day I throw every shred of self-respect I've got straight in the gutter."

"Sure you're not." His voice dips low, certain he has already won.

I turn toward him fully, anger burning hotter than I can contain. "She's not your type."

The regret is instant. I don't hand people pieces of me or let anyone crawl under my skin. But Zane... he doesn't even have to fucking try.

He tilts his head, eyes dragging over me slowly, every second stretched just to make me squirm.

"Then what is my type, Sky?"

"Someone who doesn't know better," I snap.

His smirk curves deeper. "So that makes you what? Smarter than the rest of them?"

"Smarter. Meaner. Harder to impress." My chin lifts, daring him to argue.

He leans closer, bad boy swagger dripping from every word. "Harder to impress? Sweetheart, you've been staring at me for five minutes straight."

"Only because somebody has to keep track of all the bullshit coming out of your mouth."

His chuckle rumbles. "Careful. Keep talking and I might start thinking you actually enjoy this."

"Keep dreaming," I bite out, though the heat forming in my chest betrays me.

And he knows it. He always fucking knows it.

"Sharp words, Sky. Makes me wonder how your mouth would feel doing something else."

"Try that line on someone desperate enough to fall for it." I turn my head away, refusing to give him the satisfaction of seeing my face.

I fix my eyes on the birds cutting through the sky, wings sharp against the fading light. Still, his stare burns into me.

The silence stretches, and then he moves, slowly.

His hand lifts, fingers brushing along my jaw, light and careful, too gentle for who he is. My body jolts at the contact, and before I can stop myself, I turn my head toward him, nerves sparking, but I don't push him away. I can't.

And when I don't, his mouth crashes against mine.

It isn't soft or careful. It is wildfire pressed to my mouth, raw heat flooding straight into my chest, tearing through every wall I thought would keep me safe. His lips are hungry, edged in danger, the kind that carries warning and promise in the same breath.

I shove at his chest, my hands fisting in the fabric of his shirt, meaning to break the moment, meaning to stop it. But my body betrays me. Instead of pushing, I clutch tighter, caught in the pull I swore I would never allow. My heart hammers so hard it aches, each beat ricocheting through me until there is nothing else.

The world disappears.

The street below. The breeze cutting over the rooftop. Even my own thoughts. All of it drowned under the rush of him, the weight of his mouth, the way this kiss hits less as a choice and more as something inevitable.

His hand cups my jaw, firm enough to tilt my face exactly where he wants it. The other tangles in my hair, grip tight, dragging me closer until there is nothing left but heat and hunger. It is possession masked in tenderness, and I am drowning under the weight of it.

I should remember that this is Zane, the boy who ruins anything stupid enough to fall into his orbit. But my body doesn't give a fuck about logic. My chest presses into his, my mouth parts against his, my lungs refusing to work unless it is through him.

His teeth catch my bottom lip and I gasp, the sound swallowed by him.

"Zane," I whisper against his mouth, breathless, shaking. The word slips out before I can swallow it back.

He pulls back, just barely, his forehead pressing to mine. His breath is rough, uneven, proof that I am not the only one caught in this storm. His eyes stay closed, lashes brushing against his skin, his hand still cradling my face as if I might vanish if he lets go too soon.

"You want to tell me you didn't feel that?" He says, opening his eyes, every edge of him still cocky but cracked underneath.

I can't answer. My throat closes up. My chest is a war zone, torn between the need to deny it and the truth that already blazes in every nerve. I can't even fucking breathe.

He searches my face, and for a second I think he might kiss me again, might finish what he started. But he lets go. His hand slips from my hair. The other drops from my jaw.

He leans back, runs a hand through his messy curls, and that fucking smirk slides back into place, smug as hell.

"Didn't think so," he says.

And then he is on his feet. He yanks his backpack up, slinging it over his shoulder with careless ease, every movement casual enough to gut me. As if the kiss never happened. That he hadn't torn through me and left the pieces scattered.

He heads for the ladder, each step clanging against the metal, ringing louder than my own pulse, until the sound fades and he is gone. Swallowed whole by the shadows below.

I sit there, frozen, lips still tingling, pulse thrashing so hard it rattles through my ribs. My head is nothing but static, my chest cracked wide open, because that kiss wasn't some passing thing. It was a brand seared into me, burned too deep to ever scrub clean.

My fingers lift to my mouth, trembling. My first kiss, stolen by the one boy I swore I'd never let get close.

And fuck my traitorous, desperate body? It wanted it more than it has ever wanted air.

Chapter 6

ZANE

Fuck me, that was a stupid thing to do. My head won't let the memory go, and my body sure as hell won't either. I'm still hard from that fucking kiss, and no amount of pacing, no number of angry thoughts will untangle what that moment left behind. My pulse won't calm down either. My body is wound tight, coiled with a need that ignores every command I throw its way.

I shove my fists deep into my pockets, jaw locked so hard it aches, every step heavy with a weight I can't shake. The pavement stretches ahead, cracked and uneven, but I keep moving, pretending I am steady, that I am not seconds away from turning back around just to have another taste.

I tell myself to breathe, to drag my mind anywhere else but there. To shake her loose from the hold she has over me. But it doesn't work. Because the second she stepped onto that rooftop, the second her mouth brushed mine, the whole world cracked wide open, and I can't shove the pieces back together no matter how hard I try.

I've kissed girls before. Too many. Some were a blur I barely remember, bodies pressed together in a corner at some party. Others I wish I didn't remember, their hands clutching at me, their mouths hungry in a way that left me empty. But none of them ever tasted like her. None of them ever made me feel this way before. Made me want to close my eyes and keep that single moment nailed to the inside of my skull so I could replay it again and again.

And fuck, I hate that I crave another hit of her.

My hand drags down my face, fingers scraping over stubble. I should have pulled away sooner. Should have shut that shit down before I let things go that far. Not with the one girl in this whole fucked-up town I shouldn't be touching. She sleeps down the hall, close enough that her presence is a constant fucking torment. Her bed only a door away, her hair spilling across the pillow, and I've pictured her there more times than I'll ever admit. The curve of her body twisted in sheets, the soft sound of her breathing in the dark. Every night she's close enough to turn sleep into torture. She's the temptation I can't shake, the one that wrecks me without ever lifting a finger.

But the second her lips pressed into mine, every reason not to vanished.

She's always been beautiful. I knew from the second I walked into that hellhole we call a home a year ago and fucking saw her. One glance and I already hated myself for wanting her.

Girls at school trip over themselves to get close, chasing that bad-boy story, convinced they can fix the mess or brag about the scars. They blur together, nothing worth remembering. But Skylar... fuck, she's different. She doesn't fall at my feet. She stands her ground, spits fire back in my face. I watch her when I fucking shouldn't. I've memorized the sound of her laugh, the way it bursts out when she finally lets herself laugh for real. The way her eyes linger on me when she believes I'm not looking.

Only, I am always paying attention.

She makes me want things I swore I never wanted.

Things I don't let myself even picture. I am ruined by a girl I haven't even touched yet. A girl who should never get tangled up with someone like me. Because if she does, she burns. And I will be the one who sets the match. Because I know I am not good.

People have hammered that into me for years. Screw-up. Lost cause. Broken beyond fixing. But I don't want that for her.

I should have told her Samantha is my cousin. Set the record straight before she could twist the story into something else. But then I saw her face, the jealousy in her eyes, and the hit landed harder than it should have. The whole thing was fucked-up. Selfish. Wrong. And I liked every second of it. I liked that she cared enough to hate the idea of me with someone else.

Not many people at school realize Sam and I are related.

I do not hand out details about my life, and Sam sure as hell does not either.

The only time our worlds collide is when my mother shows up like a storm no one invited, knocking on Sam's door, begging her Dad (my Uncle) for money. That is how my mother works. Always needing. Always taking. Never stopping.

I don't tell people about my mother. About the way she grinds me down until nothing's left. Even with Sam, the truth stays unspoken. Some things are too ugly to put into words. But the weight gnaws at me anyway.

If my mother ever found out I had cash hidden, if she knew about the money stuffed in my bag from the shifts I grind through, she'd rip it out of my hands without thinking twice. She'd bleed me dry and still tell me I owed her more.

That money is all I've got. My shot. My way out. Proof that I don't have to rot here forever. A place that's mine. Walls that don't watch me. Air I can finally breathe without choking on it.

I make my way back to the house. Every step feels heavier, dragging me closer to the bullshit waiting on the other side of those walls. My pulse has finally eased from Skylar, but now it shifts into something else, anticipation, dread, the kind of burn you get when you know you are about to be torn apart again.

Dolores. She will be waiting. She always is. That woman could sniff out a mistake faster than anyone I have ever known. And me, I am her favorite punching bag.

My shoulders brush the fence as I slip through the slat in the back. The boards snag against my shirt, catching, pulling.

I blow out a breath and edge toward the back door. My hand trembles against the handle. I tell myself the shake comes from the cold.

Inside, the house is loud, a storm that never passes. Three young boys throw a football across the room, the ball smacking against the wall with a hollow thud.

"Outside!" Dolores's voice booms from somewhere in the house. The kids freeze for half a second before one of them catches the ball, rolling his eyes as if he already knows better than to test her. The other two follow, dragging their feet toward the door. The last one lingers, smaller than the rest, his eyes darting up at me.

"She's been looking for you," he says.

Of course she fucking has. She always is. The words settle like a weight across my shoulders.

I nod at the kid, not saying a word, and start down the hall, keeping my steps light, careful, hoping I can reach my room without her catching me. My room is the only place I can breathe, even if the air inside feels as poisoned as the rest of this house.

But I am not that lucky. I never am.

Her voice slices through the air the moment I'm about to make my escape.

"You got something to tell me?"

I freeze. One foot in the hall, one foot out.

"No."

"So nothing?" she prompts again, sharper now. "You just stroll in here, head held high, like the school didn't call me earlier to tell me you cracked some kid's nose?"

My shoulders go rigid. I turn to face her because pretending I didn't hear her will only make it worse.

She stands there in the doorway, hands on her hips, curlers still in her hair. A bathrobe hangs half-open, sagging off her body, the sight of it making bile crawl up the back of my throat. Her tits spill out through the lace she probably thinks makes her look like one of those heroines in the steamy romance novels she devours. The whole picture makes me want to set the house on fire just to erase it.

"You think I'm made of time, Zane?" she snaps, voice climbing with every word. "You think I enjoy getting calls from the school? Do you like embarrassing me?"

I say nothing. Because there is no winning here. There never is.

Her sigh is long, theatrical, a hand pressed to her chest as if I just wounded her with my silence alone. "I told them you were trying. Told them you'd been better lately. That you were calming down. And then this."

"Well, I didn't ask you to." My voice is low, but it lands like gasoline.

Her eyes narrow, her mouth pulling into that bitter twist I know too well. "I should have known," she mutters, shaking her head, each word sharp enough to cut. "You're just another screw-up no one can fix."

My nails dig deep into the fabric lining my pocket. Rage curls hot in my gut, boiling up into my throat. I want to scream. I want to slam my fist into the wall until the plaster cracks and my knuckles split more. To prove I am not the fuck-up she says I am, but the only proof I have is history, and history says she is right.

I clamp my teeth together until my jaw throbs. Because yelling won't change shit. Exploding won't fix it.

All it will do is prove her point.

"I don't know how much more I can take of yo-"

A crash of footsteps cuts through her rant. A couple of kids bolt through the hall, nearly colliding with her. One of them freezes when she snaps her gaze on him, a box of cereal clutched tight against his chest.

"Where the hell did you get that?" she screeches, snatching it from his hands so fast the cardboard dents beneath her grip. "If you've gotten into that damn cupboard again, I swear to God!"

The boy's lip trembles, his eyes wide as he stumbles back. She doesn't wait for an answer. She spins, storming off toward the kitchen, muttering curses under her breath about food and money and kids who don't listen.

And just like that, I am dismissed.

I don't care about the way she tosses me aside mid-argument. I welcome it. Every time she turns her rage on someone else, it gives me room to breathe. I take off, pivot down the hall, chest still tight, her words clinging to me like smoke I can't cough out.

My room stinks. The window only opens halfway, rusted into place. The mattress on the floor is mine. Beside it, the bunk bed rattles every time Johnny shifts underneath. I won't touch the top bunk. It's a hazard, it feels like it could give way at any moment. And when it does, it won't matter that it's old and falling apart. They'll blame me. They always do.

In the corner, my clothes sit stacked, each pile neat, folded the exact way I learned back in the group home. Discipline drilled into me in a place where you survived by keeping your head down and your shit organized. I carry that habit with me, the laundromat trips, the clean stacks, because I don't trust Dolores' busted washer. The thing rattles so hard it sounds like it is going to explode. If it breaks on my watch, I will carry the blame for that too.

I drop my bag beside the mattress and yank the thin blanket from my bed, tossing it over the top. So no one will touch it. The last kid stupid enough to go through my things walked around with a busted lip and swollen eye for a week.

Word spread quick after that. Still, I don't take chances. I cover the bag, tucking it away beneath folds of fabric.

I move into the bathroom and twist the tap until the pipes scream. Cold water blasts over my knuckles, burning as it hits the open cuts. Blood blooms into the stream, clouding it pink, swirling down the drain as if it belongs there. I grit my teeth and let it sting. I don't bother wrapping them. What's the fucking point? By tomorrow they'll be split open again. There is always another fight waiting, always another asshole who wants me to prove I'm harder, meaner, willing to bleed just to shut them up.

I glance at the mirror and freeze. The face staring back doesn't feel like mine. The eyes are too dark, shadows carved so deep they may as well be permanent. My shoulders sag forward, my jaw clenched, hair hanging into my face. I look swallowed whole by this house, this system, this shit life. A boy who stopped fighting to be anything else.

I shut the bathroom light off and stand in the dark longer than I need to, breathing in the silence. A cough sounds through the hall, heavy enough to crawl under my skin. It doesn't sound right.

I push off the wall and follow the sound, another cough ripping through the silence. It drags me to a door halfway down the hall. I stop and lean in, pushing it open just enough to look inside. A kid is curled on the bottom bunk, pale, swallowed up by a blanket that does nothing to hide how small he looks. His eyes track me as I step closer, wide and cautious, waiting to see if I'm trouble.

"You want me to tell Dolores you're sick?" I ask,

Caleb shakes his head weakly. "She knows."

My eyes catch on the empty glass on the floor beside his bed. I bend down, pick it up, and straighten.

"I'll get you some water," I mutter, already turning for the door.

I walk to the bathroom, carrying the glass. The tap groans when I twist it, coughing out rust before the water finally runs clear. I hold the glass under, filling it to the rim.

The glass is cold as I carry it back down the hall. The boy sits up when I step inside. His eyes look too big for his pale face. He takes the glass with both hands, his fingers shaking around it. He drinks fast, the water sliding down his throat as if it is the only good thing he has had all day.

"Thank you, Zane," he whispers, handing it back.

I set the glass back beside his bed.

"If anyone gives you shit, you come find me, Caleb," I tell him. My voice is low, steady, carrying a weight I'm certain he'll hear.

He nods, eyes wide, and something in my chest tightens.

"If you get worse, you come to me, not Dolores. I mean it." I tell him. If I have to take him to emergency, I'll fucking do it. Whether Dolores likes it or not.

He nods again. His lids droop heavy, exhaustion pulling him back under. When he closes his eyes, I stand there longer than I should, listening to his breathing even out.

The thought chews at me. How easy it would be to expose her. To let the government see her for what she really is. To strip away the act she puts on every time a social worker steps into this house. She fools them all, wrapping her venom in a practiced smile, feeding them the lines they want to hear. Meanwhile, the cupboards are locked, the kids hungry, the sickness ignored.

I turn and walk out, shutting the door softly behind me.

Back in my room, I drop down onto the mattress. I lie back, staring up at the ceiling and turn my thoughts toward the future that seems too distant to ever reach.

I think about the job at the workshop, about Rainer, the only person who has ever given me a real shot. He doesn't ask questions. Never looked at me like I am a problem waiting to happen. He lets me work, and in that, there is a kind of freedom I have never had before.

Maybe when I finally get out of here, when I've got a place that's mine, I'll ask him for more hours. No more school. No more fuckers waiting for me to snap. Just work, sweat, and something that finally gives me a sense of control for the first time in my life.

Planning futures that still feel too far away, promises I am not sure I can keep.

But that is all I fucking have.

Chapter 7

SKYLAR

It's been four weeks of fucking silence.

Twenty-Eight days since Zane kissed me—almost a full month. Not that I'm counting.

Except I fucking am. Every day. Every breath. It's carved deep into me, ticking like a goddamn clock I can't shut off.

Every fucking second, it loops in my head. His mouth crashing into mine. It tore through the rules about never letting anyone too close. And now... Now he's keeping his distance. As if it meant nothing. As if I'm the idiot still carrying the scorch of it across my mouth.

I haven't seen him around the house. He's become a ghost, vanished into shadows that don't leave footprints. Truth is, I can't even tell if he's still there. For all I know, he's already packed up and disappeared, left nothing behind but silence and the taste of that kiss still burning through me.

At school, he avoids me. Eyes fixed on the wall, the floor, the fucking clouds—anywhere but me. Most days he doesn't even show, and no one asks why. Not the students. Not the teachers. That's what happens when you're a foster kid—your absence isn't noticed, it's expected. Fucked if I know where he disappears to. But every time I walk in and see that empty seat, something sharp twists deeper under my skin. It pisses me off more than I'll ever admit, because boys aren't supposed to haunt me. They're supposed to pass through, be forgettable.

But Zane? He lingers.

What... if he thinks I'm just another girl to keep him company? Fuck that and fuck him. I'm not some name he forgets by morning, not some throwaway moment he files with all the others.

Still, I do the one thing I swore I wouldn't. I wait. I drag myself up to the rooftop after Cassie dumps me back at that hellhole, and sit on the cold tin until my legs go numb, pretending the view is enough. But I always find myself listening. Waiting for footsteps, waiting for him. But he never comes.

Guess he's too busy getting off with Sam or whoever was easy enough that day.

And yet, on the rare days he actually shows up at school, Cassie swears he watches me. Says she catches him staring when I'm not looking. But she could be full of shit. Cassie wants there to be something between Zane and I. She wants it to be messy, dramatic, fucked up in all the ways that make sense in her head.

I never told her about the kiss because Cassie would ask the kind of questions I'm not ready to answer. So I keep my mouth shut. Pretend it didn't happen. That I don't care. Even though I do. Too fucking much.

Today, I'm stuck in the counselor's office again. My fortnightly dose of bullshit. Some caseworker decided I need regular check-ins, as if thirty minutes of soft voices and generic advice is going to stitch me back together. Like I'm a school project someone's trying to salvage with dollar store glue and fake empathy.

She sits across from me, her face stretched into that practiced expression, concern just warm enough to be patronizing. Thin-framed glasses slipping down her nose. Hands folded in some fake display of calm, the kind meant to trick me into trusting her.

She blinks slowly, dragging it out, convinced the silence will make me crack wide open and I'll spill everything.

"Skylar," she says, all gentle and rehearsed, "do you want to talk about your outburst last week?"

Fuck no. I want to slam the door so hard the frame cracks and never step foot in this office again.

But instead, I sit here. Arms folded tight across my chest. Chewing the inside of my cheek until I catch the tang of blood.

The woman across from me doesn't get that. She never will. To her, I'm another case file with a temper problem. Another foster kid with bruises no one bothers to ask about. A red folder stamped with "trauma" and shoved to the bottom of the stack. She doesn't see me, she only sees a warning label.

"Why don't you just go find something else to fix?" I mutter. "There's enough broken shit in this place more fucked up than me."

Her lips twitch in some half-assed attempt at patience. It lands somewhere between awkward and pathetic.

"You're not in trouble, Skylar. This is a safe space," she says, all soft and soothing.

Safe. That word tastes like ash. What a fucking joke.

What she really wants is to poke around, peel back the layers until she's sure I'm not seconds away from burning the place down. But she's looking in the wrong direction.

The thing chewing me alive isn't school. It's not Dolores. It's not the mountain of bullshit stacked on top of me every damn day.

She tries again. Switches tactics, voice soft like that'll make a difference.

"I understand Zane lives in the same foster home. Skylar, if he's bullying you—"

There it is. Straight to the assumption. Of course she assumes it's him. The boy with bruises for knuckles and a record of fights behind him. They always blame him. Never the bastards who put us there.

"Seriously," I snap. "Don't."

If she says one more thing about him, I'll lose it. I'll tell her to fuck off, take the suspension, whatever. Anything to get her to shut her mouth.

"Then tell me what's going on," she presses.

"Maybe this meeting is what's getting me down," I say, picking at a frayed thread on my jumper, eyes locked on the floor.

She sighs. Patient. Pretending again. "Skylar, you're supposed to open up here. Next time, I can invite Dolores if that makes you more comfortable."

I let out a laugh. Fucking stupid bitch. She doesn't have a clue.

"If you do that, I won't be here."

The clock ticks. Five minutes down. Twenty-five more of this suffocating silence. Her eyes on me, her fake concern while she waits for me to snap.

I force a smile. All teeth, no warmth. A trick. Two can play this game.

"I've just got a lot of work due," I say, voice tight with fake worry. "I'm stressing about getting it done."

Her face softens, eyes going all gentle. She thinks she's cracked something open.

"Would you like me to ask your teachers for an extension?"

"No." I cut in too fast. "I can handle it. I just need somewhere quiet. Somewhere now. Dolores's place isn't exactly built for peace and focus."

She nods, all knowing and smug. "With all the kids there."

"Exactly." I let the smile stretch, feed her the version of me she wants. Let her believe I'm opening up. "Even the next twenty minutes could help me get something done."

She hesitates. Just for a second. But she's already hooked.

And every part of me screams I've won.

She studies me, trying to decide if I'm full of shit. Perhaps I'm wrong and she can see straight through it. But I keep my face steady, let the fake smile sit just soft enough to pass. That's all adults ever want. The illusion of effort. The lie that you're trying.

She sighs, then leans back in her chair. "All right, Skylar. Go on, get some work done. I'll write it down as time used productively."

Bingo.

I fake a grateful smile, throw my bag over my shoulder, and get the hell out before she changes her mind. The door clicks shut behind me, her stale office air traded for the noise and stink of the hallway.

I don't head for the library. Screw that.

I take the long corridor, cut down the stairs, slip out the back until I'm behind the building, tucked against the brick wall by the old incinerator.

No one comes here. Not teachers. Not kids.

I sink down against the wall, put my knees up, and lock my arms around them. The bricks dig into my back and I don't care.

My birthday is coming and I don't want it.

Eighteen.

Every time the thought surfaces, it stings. What happens when my birthday hits. It comes off more like a death sentence than freedom. Do they throw me out the second the clock hits midnight? Dump my clothes in a trash bag, hand it to me and call it a fresh start?

No one has said a word.

Not Dolores. Not the ghost of a social worker who only shows up when a form needs signing.

Cassie still has six months before this becomes her problem. She still believes someone will catch her when she falls.

I already know the truth. No one will.

I have an uncle somewhere across the state. Or there was. He might have moved or changed his number. Might not even remember I exist.

The truth is, no one comes for girls like me. No one stays.

You turn eighteen and the world stops pretending to care. There's no warning, no goodbye, not even a door left open behind you. One day you exist on their clipboard. The next, you're gone.

I close my eyes and let my head fall against the brick. It's rough, but the scrape feels real.

For a breath, I slip somewhere else. A place where birthdays mean cake instead of dread. Where someone notices if you don't make it home. But reality's a cruel bitch.

The bell rings, cutting through my thoughts. The sound snaps me back into my body.

Lunch.

I push off the wall, getting up onto my feet. Dirt clings to the back of my skirt, and I brush it away with my hands. I grab my bag and move back towards the noise.

When I step through the doors, it hits all at once. The sharp tang of burnt oil from the cafeteria clings to everything. Bodies press past one another in slow waves, the scent of cheap deodorant choking out whatever oxygen's left.

The fluorescent lights hum above, too bright, too unforgiving.

Then I see him.

Zane.

He leans against the lockers with that lazy kind of confidence that dares you to look twice. Loose black hoodie, hood half-up, shadows falling across his jaw and throat. That mouth pulls into a slow smirk while he talks to some girl I don't recognize. Every movement is practiced, effortless, but there's still this tension under it, the kind that says he could explode at any moment.

Behind me, two girls dissolve into breathless giggles, voices syrup-thick with want.

"If he so much as blinked in my direction, I'd crawl into his lap and beg him to wreck me."

"He could spit in my mouth and I'd moan a thank you."

They laugh louder, drunk on the idea of him.

I hear it all the time.

The bad boy fantasy they all worship, sold on the smirk and the hoodie without ever seeing the person underneath.

My fingers tighten around the straps of my bag. Nails dig into the fabric. I keep my eyes forward and pretend my chest isn't already burning.

Cassie steps in beside me, shoulder brushing mine. She nudges my ribs, her voice low and teasing. "Jealous?"

I scoff, way too fast. "He can fuck whoever he wants. I don't give a shit."

Cassie snorts. "Please. You care so loud I could hear it from the science block. You're one eye twitch away from ripping her extensions out."

I roll my eyes, but she's not done.

"Honestly, if looks could kill, that girl would be ashes and Zane would already be shirtless in front of your locker."

A laugh slips out before I can stop it. It catches me off guard.

"That's not even funny," I mutter, trying to bite down the smile.

Cassie grins. "It's hilarious. You're acting all cool while your soul is trying to crawl out of your body and mount him."

I smack her arm, but the smile won't leave my face.

That's the thing about Cassie. She always knows where to press, always finds the one thread that unravels the tension just enough to make me laugh.

But the second the laughter fades, it's there again.

The truth. Ugly. Unavoidable. I don't want to laugh or joke. I want him to want me.

The rest of the day crawls by.

Teachers drone on, and every tick of the clock sounds louder than the last. My notes are a mess and my head is somewhere else entirely.

By the time the final bell rings, I'm exhausted. There were lectures I didn't hear, questions I didn't answer, and eyes I refused to meet. My pen barely touched the page. I stared out the window while the clock dragged its feet, each second stretching just long enough to remind me I don't belong here.

On the walk home, Cassie talks the whole way, filling the space with gossip, teacher complaints, some story about a guy who tried to cheat off her math test and called her "hostile" when she told him to fuck off.

I laugh when I'm supposed to. Nod when it fits. But my mind's somewhere else.

She doesn't notice. Or maybe she does, but lets it slide. That's always been our deal.

When we reach the corner where Cassie and I split, I don't move. I watch her cross the road, her braid swinging as she throws me a wave. When she disappears down the street I turn around and go in the opposite direction. I'm not ready to go home just yet.

I drift past store windows filled with clothes that will never be mine. Crop tops, ripped jeans, leather jackets standing stiff on faceless mannequins.

The park feels easier. I drop onto a metal bench, my eyes moving towards the duck skimming across the pond. Kids laugh hard enough to echo, handfuls of bread, parents snapping photos like they can trap joy in a frame.

I stay there, the minutes slipping by with the ripples on the pond and the squeals of kids that eventually fade as their parents drag them home. The park empties until it's just me. I stay long enough for the sky to shift, for the world to sink into shadow. Streetlights buzz to life, throwing pale halos across the pavement as I walk home.

The second I push through the door, it slams into me. Noise everywhere. Someone's losing their shit over socks. Another kid bawls because they got slammed into the wall. A toddler shrieks like the world's ending while the TV hammers football commentary loud enough to rattle the windows.

Dolores doesn't move. She's sunk into the couch, two wine coolers down, eyes glued to the game. She yells at the screen, slurring curses like the players might actually hear her through the glass.

I dump my bag on the bed and head for the window. Dinner doesn't even cross my mind. Dolores would lose her shit if she caught me climbing out, threaten the social workers, call me a runaway again. She pulled that stunt when I was fourteen, when all I'd done was sit in the backyard staring at the stars. I hadn't even left.

Didn't matter. She twisted it, turned me into the problem because that's what she does best.

The rooftop pulls at me louder than anything else. It's more mine now than Zane's, since he can't be bothered to show up anymore.

I cut through the alley. The moon spills silver across the pavement, lighting everything up in a way that's too bright, too exposing. My steps fall into rhythm, quick, carrying me straight to the ladder.

I climb without hesitation. Except tonight it isn't empty.

Zane. Hood pulled low, cigarette burning between his fingers, his body slouched against the tin as if the whole roof belongs to him.

He turns his head, and our eyes collide. The hit is immediate. My chest caves around the slam of my heart, pounding a rhythm I do not recognize. It's too fast. Too frantic.

I know what it means. I'm in fucking trouble, because I'm falling for the boy carved from fists and fury. The boy made of bricks and bruises. And I can't stop.

I wonder what he's doing here. If he still comes to this rooftop and waits me out, hiding in the dark until I leave. The notion burns. Because if that is true, then he has been haunting this place the whole time, letting me cling to the lie it was mine.

The roof creaks under my steps, each sound carrying in the quiet. My skirt moves against my legs in the breeze.

Zane takes a drag from his cigarette, chest rising slowly before he tips his head back toward the sky. Smoke spills past his lips, drawn out, controlled, the kind of move meant to hold my attention.

He stays quiet. The burn of his silence wrapping tighter around me than anything he could say.

His eyes lock on mine. Heavy. Unreadable. Heat coils low in my stomach. Whatever it is burning there, it's dangerous. And it has me.

I lower myself onto the roof beside him. Not close enough to brush against him, but near enough that the warmth radiating from his body slips under my skin. It teases, taunts, makes me restless.

His gaze cuts sideways, one brow lifting with that careless edge, as if the last four weeks of silence never touched him.

"Thought you wouldn't want to be here with me."

I shrug, my voice flat, steady. "You think too much of yourself. I came here for the rooftop, not for you."

The corner of his mouth twitches.

A long pause stretches between us, too long. Then I move without asking. I reach out and pluck the cigarette straight from his lips.

The filter is warm against my fingers. It still carries the taste of him.

I take a drag. The smoke burns on the way down, scraping my throat until my lungs ache. I do not cough. I do not break.

I hold his stare as the smoke settles inside me and let it spread until it's burning me alive.

His mouth quirks again, but there is no humor in it. "Did not peg you for a smoker."

"There are a lot of things you do not know about me," I answer, flicking the ash from the end with a steady hand, as if I have been doing this my whole life. I let the smoke slip slow from my lips, eyes locked on his. "You bring out the worst in me."

That earns me a smirk. A real one this time. For half a second, I feel like I've won something. Then it's gone, his face hardening again, like it cost him too much to let that slip. He leans over and takes the cigarette from my fingers.

I tilt my head back, eyes tracing the sky. Stars scatter above us, sharp as broken glass, glittering in patterns that pretend to mean something. They shimmer with the shine of promises no one ever keeps. Fragile. Untouchable.

The words hesitate at my throat, but the need for answers drags them out anyway. "Why have you been ignoring me?"

Zane freezes. His whole body goes still, like the truth is a gun pointed at his chest.

The cigarette hangs between his lips, forgotten, smoke curling up into the dark.

When he finally speaks, his voice is low, rough around the edges. "You mess with my head."

My breath falters. "What?"

This time he turns. The hood cuts shadows across his face, but his eyes pin me in place, burning hot and unflinching.

"You get under my skin, Sky. And I don't know what the fuck to do with that."

My chest caves, breath catching somewhere between disbelief and something I can't name.

He drags a hand through his hair, fingers rough, frustration carved into every line of him. "I have been through a lot of fucked-up shit."

"Yeah, and who hasn't," I shoot back.

His silence answers louder than words, stretching until it hurts.

Finally, he mutters, "You'll be rid of me in a month."

The words land like a punch. "What if I don't want to be rid of you?"

That cracks him. His head snaps toward me, his eyes wide, the fight clear in them.

"I have had girls. I've had chaos. I have set fire to everything I touch. But you..." His jaw locks, his eyes never leaving mine. "You make me want things I shouldn't want. And that," his voice drops to a whisper, "that terrifies the fuck out of me."

He turns away, pulling smoke deep into his lungs, holding it there until his chest strains before letting it bleed out slow, as if the release could steady him. Then, with a sharp flick of his fingers, he sends the cigarette arcing off the roof into the night.

"Say something," he mutters. The words are rough, scraping the space between us.

I swallow, my throat raw, pulse thrashing against my ribs. "People don't stay. Not for me. I learned that a long time ago." My voice drops, softer, even though I hate that it does. "So if I want you to want me, that's because I don't know what the hell it feels like to be wanted."

His breath punches out, sharp enough to sting.

"Sky..." The crack in his voice ruins me.

I drag in air, desperate and shaking. "You have no fucking idea how much I want you to want me."

His jaw locks, muscles twitching as if he is holding himself together by force. "You don't get it. I am no good for anyone. Least of all you."

"Then tell me why you've been ignoring me." My voice shakes at the edges, but the demand cuts through. "I want the truth, Zane."

He drags his gaze away, throat working hard, the silence stretching before he glances back my way. His eyes flick to my mouth, then away again, like he is fighting a losing battle.

"You think I've been ignoring you," he mutters at last, his voice rough.

"I don't think," I bite out. "I know."

When he doesn't answer, the silence gnaws at me until the words slip free. "Don't act like I imagined it," I whisper.

His eyes snap to mine, blazing.

"I'm not," he rasps. "I'm fucking trying, Skylar."

"Trying what?"

His laugh is sharp and broken, scraping the air between us. "To keep my distance. To stop wanting you so bad I can't fucking breathe."

The rooftop tilts under me, my heart pounding hard enough to split my chest.

"Then don't."

The fight snaps in him and he surges forward, his mouth landing against mine.

The kiss is not cautious. It's desperate. Hungry. Reckless. His lips tear the air from my lungs, taking everything I thought I had left. He kisses me as if he has been drowning, and I am the first breath he has had in years.

His hands are everywhere. Cupping my face, tangling in my hair, gripping hard enough to pin me to the roof. Heat pours through me, flooding fast, searing down to my bones.

Then he pulls back, abrupt and ragged, breath tearing from him in violent bursts.

I blink, reeling. "What—"

He sits hunched, chest heaving, jaw tight, as if holding himself together costs him everything. "You don't get it, Sky. You make me forget all the shit. Where I come from. What I am. What everyone sees when they look at me."

"I don't see what they see."

His voice drops. "Then what do you see?"

I do not hesitate. "You."

And I mean it. I see him. The boy who sits alone at lunch because people are never safe. The boy who looks ready to break your jaw if you get too close, yet stays still when you lean into him. The boy who kissed me as if it mattered, then ran because he didn't know how to stay.

He cannot hold my stare. His jaw flexes hard as he looks away, as if turning from me could hide the way my words cut into him.

I reach for him. His hand snaps up, catching mine midair, stopping me cold. His grip is rough, his skin hot against mine, and for a breath it comes off less as rejection and more as a warning.

"Don't pull away from me, Zane."

His jaw locks. "Fuck. You're gonna kill me."

His eyes close, head tipping back as if it physically hurts him to look at me. "You think I don't fucking want you?" His voice cracks.

He drags my hand down until it lands on his hard cock against his jeans. My breath stumbles, my pulse thrashing as I curl my fingers around him through the denim. I stroke him, hesitant at first, then firmer.

His breath tears out in stutters, curses spilling from his lips, voice breaking apart. "Fucking hell, Skylar—"

His head tips back hard, eyes squeezed shut, mouth parting as a moan rips from deep in his chest. The sound spurs me on, drives me past the shaking in my fingers.

I rise onto my knees, pushing gently until his back sinks against the tin. His chest rises hard, his breath stills as I hover over him.

My fingers fumble at the button, clumsy and unsteady, trembling with nerves I can't shake. The metal fights me, slipping each time I think I've got it, frustration clawing its way through my chest. My pulse hammers harder, my breath uneven, but I don't stop. I can't. His eyes pin me in place, dark and burning, watching every single move I make, stripping me bare without a word.

This is the first time I've ever touched someone like this, and the weight of it presses down until my skin prickles, every nerve lit and screaming. My whole body buzzes, breath stuttering as I force my fingers to keep working, knowing exactly what waits on the other side of that zipper.

His jaw flexes, a muscle jumping as his eyes stay locked on me. His chest heaves, every rise sharp, as if he's fighting to keep himself from snapping apart.

The button pops, the zipper rasping down. My hand slides inside, over the rough fabric, brushing the waistband of his boxers before I push lower. My fingers curl around him. My lungs forget how to work.

He's hard. So fucking hard in my hand, every twitch against my grip proof of how bad he wants it.

A hiss tears from him the second I touch his cock. His head tips back, throat bare, and a curse rips out of him.

"Fuck—"

His hips jerk up into my fist, chasing it, demanding more. I stroke him slow, then tighter, dragging my hand along his shaft, feeling the weight, the size, the ache of him. Precum smears over the tip, making every slide dirtier, filthier.

His breath shudders, broken sounds spilling from his mouth. His chest heaves, every line of him straining.

"Fucking hell." The sound tears out of him.

There's no mistaking what he wants. His eyes crack open, dark and burning.

"Get your fucking mouth on me," he rasps, voice shredded, jaw flexing as his cock jerks in my hand. His chest heaves, every muscle pulled tight. "Suck my cock, Skylar."

Chapter 8

ZANE

Her hand stays on my cock, stroking slow, unsteady, enough to rip a growl from my throat as my head tips back. Every nerve is burning, my blood pounding so hard it deafens me.

I have wanted this. Wanted her more than I ever fucking should. More than I will ever admit. And now she is here, on her knees, her fingers tight around my cock, and I swear I could die right now and it would be enough.

I reach up, fingers tangling in her hair, wrapping tight until I feel the gasp break free from her throat. Fuck, that sound... it shoots through me like a live wire, makes my cock throb harder.

I pull, it's rough, guiding her down until her lips hover right there. The tip of my cock brushes her mouth, and the sight of it—her, on her knees, mouth inches from where I need her—nearly fucking undoes me.

Another curse rips from my throat. My jaw locks, teeth grinding, trying to hold it together. But I'm right on the edge.

"Open," I growl. My voice is all wreckage and need, no space for mercy. "Now."

She hesitates. Her breath hits the head of my cock, and that pause cuts deeper than anything. My chest heaves. Every muscle is wired tight, caught between restraint and the brutal urge to shove her mouth open and take what I need. She has no fucking clue what she does to me.

I'm trembling. Fucked with it. This needing, wanting, ready to lose control. Then her lips part.

The first brush of her lips hits hard.

Soft heat on the tip of my cock, and my vision flashes white. A hiss tears from my throat.

"Fuck, Skylar," I grind out, voice wrecked. "Do it. Suck me."

Her lips close around me and the fucking world slips sideways. Heat slams through me, and for a second I forget how to breathe. My hand fists harder in her hair, holding her still, watching her mouth stretch around my cock.

It's too much. Too good. The sight brands itself into me, a collision of filth and beauty I'll never scrub out.

She's hesitant. Careful. Her mouth moves slowly, tongue sweeping over the head before sinking lower. Every second of it destroys me. My body jerks, broken sounds tearing from my throat, nothing controlled about the way I groan her name.

"Skylar..."

It comes out full of hunger I can't hide.

My hips shift into her, desperate for more, chasing the edge even as I try to hold back. She gags softly, and her eyes flick up to meet mine. That shine in her eyes is all it takes. Heat crawls under my skin. My grip in her hair turns possessive. Because in that moon-lit moment, with my cock buried in her mouth and her stare locked on mine, she fucking owns me.

Because this is not just about getting off. It's her. How her mouth around my cock feels like drowning and being dragged back to life in the same fucking breath. I'm too far gone to pretend this is casual. Too fucked to stop now.

"Yeah," I rasp, chest heaving. "Take it. You're doing so good." The words tear out of me, half praise, half command. I want to shove deeper, to feel her throat tighten around every inch, but I hold back.

Her hand wraps around what her mouth can't take, stroking me slow, matching the pull of her lips. The friction is fucking perfect. It's too much and not enough. My stomach twists tight, muscles coiled, every nerve pulled to the edge.

"Jesus, Skylar." My voice breaks. My head falls back. Eyes slam shut. "You're gonna fucking ruin me."

I drag my gaze down again, needing to see her. She's between my legs, mouth stretched around my cock, spit glistening on her lips in the pale light.

The stars blur above me. Tin cold against my back. Her warmth burning into my skin.

She is filth and beauty twisted into something holy. Her hair spills over her shoulders, her focus locked on me, her mouth wrecking every last shred of control I had left.

And I know I'm already lost.

The longer she works me, the harder it is to hold back.

My grip tightens in her hair, dragging her closer. My hips jerk up into her mouth before I can stop it. She chokes, a wet, broken sound that rips a curse from my throat.

"Fuck… yeah, that's it." My voice scrapes out of me, hoarse and shredded. My chest heaves, every breath sharp, my control fraying with each second.

The sight of her, knees pressed to cold tin, mouth stretched around my cock, burns itself into my brain. Her throat working, hands steady. She's giving me everything, and it's too much.

I'm seconds from the fucking edge, jaw clenched, body tight, every muscle straining not to fall apart already.

Her hand keeps working me, twisting just enough to make my thighs tighten. Her mouth sinks lower, tongue dragging along the underside of my cock, and my body jerks hard. The need is brutal. It claws through my chest, settles in my gut, makes me shake with how bad I want it.

"Take me deeper," I rasp, my voice low and strained, every word clawing its way through grit.

I tug her forward. She chokes, throat tightening around me. My eyes slam shut, jaw clenched, every part of me on the verge of snapping.

"That's it. Fuck, Skylar. You feel so fucking good."

She pushes down further, swallowing me, and I can't hold back the filthy sound that spills from my throat. My hand guides her, setting the pace, rougher now, harder. I can feel every twitch of her mouth, every scrape of her teeth when she slips, every wet drag of her tongue.

I look down and nearly lose it. Her cheeks hollow, my cock vanishing between her lips, her eyes locked on mine. There's heat in them. Hunger. Challenge. It's the dirtiest, most fucked-up beautiful thing I've ever seen.

"Good girl," I groan, voice splitting at the seams, sweat rolling slow down my spine. "Suck it deeper. Show me how bad you want this."

Her tongue works me, dragging along the vein. Her lips stay sealed tight, sucking harder with every pass, and I can't stop the curses spilling from my mouth. My thrusts turn rougher, messier. I'm past the point of restraint. I'm desperate now.

"I'm close," I rasp, voice raw and torn to pieces. "Don't stop. Don't you fucking stop."

The pressure coils low, twisting hard in my gut. Every muscle locks. My hips jerk into her mouth, chasing that edge, a broken rhythm that's all instinct and no control. My cock pulses against her tongue, twitch after twitch dragging me closer, wrecking me with every second she doesn't let up.

"Fuck, Skylar—" My voice is shot, nothing but desperation now. "You're gonna make me come."

I yank her down one last time, my cock buried deep in her throat, and the world shatters. Everything goes white.

"Fuck, yes..." The words tear out of me, a growl I can't hold back.

I spill hard, my release flooding her mouth, hot and unrelenting. My hips jerk, nerves firing all at once, my grip locking in her hair, holding her there, forcing her to take every last drop. She gags, a soft choke against the pressure, but she doesn't pull away. She stays right there, swallowing me down, her lips stretched tight, mouth wet and ruined.

She looks up at me through that mess, and fuck, she's the most beautiful thing I've ever seen.

I ride it out, every pulse dragging another ragged groan out of me, until I'm emptied and trembling, my chest heaving, my cock still twitching in her mouth.

Slowly, my grip loosens in her hair. My hand falls useless to my side.

I'm completely fucking wrecked.

Silence slams down around us. My chest won't calm, breath tearing in and out heavy and uneven.

Skylar's still on her knees, spit shining on her lips, her hands hanging at her sides.

I drag my eyes off her.

What the fuck did I just do.

This wasn't just about her mouth on my cock under the night sky. It was more. A step I didn't think about until it was already done, the heat of her dragging me past the point of stopping.

I wanted it. I wanted her. That's the fucking truth.

I should've pulled back. Stopped before this turned into something I can't walk away from. But I didn't. And now I'm stuck in it, caught in the mess of wanting her so fucking bad my body still aches for her.

She's in my breath, in the fire running through my veins. The thought of stepping off this rooftop and pretending that this never happened is fucked.

But if I don't put distance here and shut this down, then I'll be hers. I'll chase her. I'll drown in her until I can't see straight.

And I can't let that fucking happen.

She doesn't deserve this.

I know exactly what I am. A fucking wrecking ball. Nothing steady, nothing safe. Just destruction. I fucking destroy until there's nothing left but pieces, then I walk away without a second glance. That's the pattern. The only thing I've ever been good at.

And I never wanted her on that list.

Skylar's been through hell already. Foster homes, scars no one sees, a life that's taken more from her than it's ever given. She doesn't need me tearing at those seams. She doesn't need the kind of hurt I bring. She deserves something steady, not the destruction I leave behind.

Because that's all I fucking know how to do.

I shove my cock back into my jeans, zip the fly, fingers clumsy. I keep my eyes on anything but her. The tin under my boots. The shadows swallowing the edges of the roof. Anything that keeps me from locking on to her eyes and undoing every bit of distance I'm clawing for.

The wind lashes the rooftop as I rise. The ladder stands there, rusty metal fading into the night.

"Zane." Her voice cuts through the quiet. "Where are you going?"

I don't turn. My jaw locks, teeth grinding hard enough to send pain up the side of my skull. The ladder waits in front of me, steel fading into the dark, and I fix on it like it's the only thing keeping me steady.

When I finally speak, I make my voice sharp enough to cut. "Does it matter?"

"Yes, it fucking matters." She pushes to her feet, tin rattling under her steps as she comes at me. She plants herself in front of the ladder, forcing me to see her. Moonlight cuts across her face, eyes blazing even through the streak of tears in her eyes. "You don't get to walk away and treat me like I'm nothing."

She's beautiful with that fire in her eyes and spit still on her lips. I've never wanted anything more than I want her at this moment.

But wanting and keeping aren't the same. I've never kept a damn thing in my life.

"Skylar..." My voice cracks. I swallow it down, force it flat, make it sound mean. If I don't kill this now, I never will. "You think this meant something? You think sucking my cock made you special?"

She flinches, but I keep going.

"You were on your knees. That's all it was. A good mouth and a tight throat." I step back, cold spreading through me, even as my cock still throbs from the way she took me. "Don't confuse sucking my cock with something real."

I watch the hit land.

"You were just a mouth, Skylar. A good one. But still just a mouth."

Her lips part. Hurt flashes in her eyes.

Good. I need her to hate me.

"Next time, don't act so fucking needy."

I watch her breathe it in. No tears. Just silence.

Her face hardens. "Fuck you," she spits. Her voice shakes, but her eyes burn straight through me.

"You wish, sweetheart." The words drip off my tongue, cruel and easy, even though something in my chest tears wide open. I shove the pieces back together, forcing myself into the only armor I've ever had.

I move past her, step onto the ladder, and climb down into the dark, leaving her standing on the roof.

My boots slam the ground, the impact rattling up through me, and whatever was still human in me stays behind on that roof with her. I bury it before it has the chance to breathe.

The darkness surrounds me, but the fire under my skin refuses to die. Walking away isn't mercy. Skylar deserves a world that doesn't cage her, a life where she can breathe, fight, and actually win. She deserves more than a mess of a man dragging her down into his shadows. If I stay, that future vanishes. I won't be the reason she never escapes.

Every step on the cracked pavement tastes bitter. My hands bury deeper in my pockets. I force my eyes forward, clinging to the dark ahead so I don't have to think about her on that roof, tears drying on her cheeks, staring after me. The thought alone tears me open. I push on anyway, one foot, then the next, pretending movement can drown the guilt clawing its way up my throat.

The streets are dead. The only sound is the echo of my boots and the low hum of traffic bleeding in from somewhere two blocks away. Dolores's place isn't far, and the thought of heading back into that house twists my gut. I fucking hate it there.

Each step drags heavier than the last. My feet don't want to carry me back. They want to run until the night swallows me whole.

Reality cuts deep. Less than twenty-five days and the system's grip will be gone for good. Twenty-five days until my name slides off their books and I can vanish wherever the fuck I want. But now, how the hell am I supposed to stay in that house with Skylar down the hall, knowing she had her mouth around my cock. The thought shreds me, fucks with my head until I can't breathe straight. I can't stay there. Not another night.

By the time I cut across the empty lot to Dolores's house, my head is already sprinting ahead of my body. Pack up my shit. Get out. Don't wait for the clock to run down. The state won't give a fuck about me now, not with only a few weeks left on the leash. They'll shrug and move on. That's the only plan left worth holding onto, walk out, and burn the whole place from my memory. Whatever comes next, I'll figure it out once I'm gone.

The front gate sags, hinges shrieking when I shove it open. The sound crawls up my spine and dares me to turn back. Just ahead, the house sits in the dark, porch light dead for months. Windows blank. I walk the short path and climb the steps, each one groaning under my boots, loud in the quiet.

The back door sticks. It always has. I lean my shoulder into it, trying not to make a sound, but it still drags loud through the frame, a scraping sound that always gives me away.

I freeze.

Wait.

Any second now I expect to hear her voice tear through the house. That sharp, cracked yell that carries from one end to the other, dragging your name through it like you're filth for daring to breathe too loud.

But nothing comes.

Which means Dolores is done for the night. Probably screamed herself hoarse at the little ones, slammed a few doors, then shoved them into their rooms whether they'd eaten or not. Right now, she's either crashed on the couch or in her bedroom with one of those trashy paperbacks and a drink in her hand, her version of peace.

The kids are always quiet once the yelling's over.

I don't bother shutting the door. I won't be here long enough for it to matter. Just grab my shit and get out before the walls remember I was ever part of them.

I move down the hallway, past the frames Dolores keeps nailed to the walls. Photos meant to convince the system this place is something it's not. All those kids from years ago, frozen in time, their names probably long gone from her memory. Smiles stretched too wide, faces pressed behind glass like that makes them real. Smiling hard enough to make your teeth ache.

My room's at the end of the hall. Door shut, same as always. I push it open. Smells of old sweat and dirty socks, something sour shoved under a bed and forgotten about.

One kid's curled in the corner, legs folded underneath him, a book cracked open in his lap. He doesn't look up, just keeps reading, eyes locked on the page as if maybe if he stares hard enough, the words will crack open a trapdoor and take him some place better. He's smart. Too fucking smart to rot in a place like this. If he was anywhere with clean floors and real meals and someone who gave a shit, he'd be the kind of kid who makes it. But here... He'll get swallowed. Forgotten. Just another file in a drawer no one opens.

The other two are sitting on the bottom bunk, shoulders pressed together. A cracked phone screen glows between them. One earbud each. Some video playing.

They look up when I walk in, eyes blank, then drop their gazes like I was never here. That's the rule. Don't ask. Don't talk. Don't fucking look too long. Around here, survival's a quiet game, heads down, mouths shut, pretend no one bleeds.

I drop to the mattress and rip off the blanket to get to my backpack. I drag it closer and pull the zipper open. One side's torn, the teeth don't close properly, but I force it open anyway.

I grab the jeans crumpled by the wall and shove them into the bag. The black hoodie goes next, then the socks at the end of the mattress, one balled, the other inside out. I lean down and scoop up the two shirts from the floor, shove them in until the seams bulge.

The blanket waits at my feet. Thin. Frayed. Mine. I roll it tight and cram it into the top of the backpack, and push down with both hands. The zipper fights me the whole way, but I drag it closed, teeth grinding, until it zips shut.

I cross the room to the wardrobe. My dirty laundry sack hangs off the hook. I yank it down and twist the strings tight around my wrist. Then move back over and lift the pack off the mattress. The straps digging deep into my shoulder.

This is it. Every fucked-up, used-up piece of my life, shoved into bags that barely hold. Everything I can carry. Everything I have. And it still doesn't feel like enough to outrun this place.

I turn to see the kid with his face in the book is now watching me. I look past him. Past all of this, I don't give him anything. I shift the bag higher on my shoulder and turn to the door.

I don't say goodbye.

I just keep moving, slipping down the hall, shoulders brushing cracked plaster, and step through the open door without so much as a pause. I don't bother closing it. I leave it wide open, a final fuck-you to a place that never gave a shit about me.

Gravel crunches beneath my boots as I cut across the yard. I reach the fence, find the hole I tore months ago in a rage, and push through, the jagged wire snagging my sleeve as if even this place doesn't want to let go.

I have nowhere to go. No one waiting. Just a backpack that digs into my spine and a night dark enough to swallow me whole.

But that's always been the story, hasn't it?

I was born disposable.

Shoved between broken walls and cracked floors. Handed off, passed around, forgotten. I learned early how to fight. How to stop asking. The world never opened its arms to me. It opened its jaws.

So I keep moving. Just me and this pack full of fuck-all, dragging my shadow down streets that don't give a shit who I am. If survival's all I've got, then I'll take it. I've been doing that since I was a kid. No backup. No safety net. Just fists, scars, and whatever the hell gets me through the next day.

Chapter 9

ZANE

The sun's already up when I jerk awake.

The bench under me is hard as shit, my spines twisted wrong, neck aching from slumping too long against the rusted pole. The bus stop's dead quiet, nothing but the groan of traffic bleeding through the distance. There's a bottle cap under my boot, a smear of old gum dried on the concrete by my hand. A trash corner of the world, and somehow it fits.

Perfect place for a guy like me.

My mouth is sour, stale from sleep and the storm that ripped through me last night. Every swallow tastes like rust. I drag my hands down my face, palms scraping over grit that never leaves. My shirt hangs heavy on me, creased and stiff from wearing it too long. The bench digs into my back, unforgiving, but I don't move. Moving feels worse. Moving means thinking.

Both bags are still with me. The pack with my money is practically glued to my side, every strap pulled tight, every zipper checked more than once. The other sits at my feet, cords wrapped around my boots so no one can touch it without taking me too.

My body's stiff, legs numb, but the ache in my chest drowns it all out. I breathe through it, forcing the air to scrape past the knot in my throat. Out here, I'm not trapped in their walls.

Out here, there's no one watching me, no one pulling at the parts of me I can't keep locked down.

Morning traffic groans, rolling past without ever slowing down. Somewhere, people are dragging themselves out of bed, pouring coffee, getting ready to face the day. Their lives keep moving, simple and steady, while mine sits stalled on a busted bench.

I didn't even make it to the workshop. Just sat here and let the night bleed into morning, watching the world drift past me.

Great start to this new fucking life.

I'd told myself I'd go straight there, find Rainer, ask if I could start my job full time now instead of waiting three weeks. But somewhere between Dolores and the corner past the liquor store, my feet stopped dead. I dropped onto this bench under the busted glass of the bus shelter and stayed.

I couldn't drag myself through that door yet. I needed to sit in the cold, to understand what it means to have nothing over my head.

My eyes burn.

Sleep, guilt, her—all of it grinding behind my lids until they're raw. Skylar's face wouldn't leave my head last night. The way she stared at me, as if I was worth something. How it shattered when I threw the cruel words at her, told her she was nothing but a mouth around my cock.

I swallow hard, bile clawing up my throat until it scorches. The taste sits there, bitter and permanent. There's no taking that back. No way to touch her without causing her more pain.

I shove myself upright, every muscle stiff from the night. My spine cracks, knees creak, and a low groan slips out before I can choke it back. What I need is a shower, a coffee, maybe a new soul. Two out of three might be possible.

The workshop's a twenty-minute walk from here. I drag the backpack strap over one shoulder, fist tight on the laundry bag so it doesn't slip, and start moving. The streets buzz around me with early workers, delivery vans, kids in uniforms shoving past each other, all of them with places to be. I keep my head down and keep walking.

The mirror in the corner shop window catches me, and I almost don't recognize the wreck staring back. Bloodshot eyes, face hollow, jaw rough with stubble. Hair sticking out in every wrong direction. Shirt creased, stained, clinging to the proof I spent the night on a bench instead of a bed.

I keep walking.

His place sits at the edge of the industrial strip, brick faded, roller door scarred, a peeling sign that still manages to shout *Rainer's Custom Restorations*.

The smell hits before I even touch the door. Oil. Steel. Dust. It sinks into your skin, into your lungs, and tells you this is real work, not bullshit.

I stop outside, hand tight on the strap of my bag, every ounce of weight pressing down harder than the canvas on my shoulder. This is it. No turning back. No Dolores. No classrooms. No Skylar.

Just this.

I press my palm to the metal door and shove it open. Light slants in through high windows, cutting across the shop floor in sharp bands. Machines line the walls, hulks of rusted frames waiting to be torn apart and built back again. The air is humming with heat, and the faint sting of burnt metal.

Rainer is at the back, bent over his bench, torch flaring blue, sparks bursting off the steel in showers of fire against the concrete. The sight makes me breathe better—it's work, it's purpose, it's the kind of place a man can bury himself and not be dragged out.

When the door shuts behind me with a thud, he looks up. Torch clicks off, goggles shoved to his forehead. He studies me in the kind of silence that makes your skin itch. His eyes sweep slowly, from my face to the crumpled shirt, the backpack strap, down to the laundry bag at my side.

"Shit, kid." His voice carries across the space, rough as gravel. He sets the tool down, wipes his hands across a grease-stained rag. "You sleep in a gutter?"

"Close enough." My voice comes out raw, throat scraped from the night. "Bench by the bus stop."

Rainer studies me for a beat longer, then jerks his chin toward the back wall. "There's a room upstairs if you want it."

I nod once. "Thanks, that would be great."

He doesn't ask anything. No why, no how, no if I've thought this through. He heads for the small office at the side of the shop. The air in there is different, a mix of coffee gone bitter and old paper. Hooks line the wall above the desk, keys dangling from them like scraps of freedom waiting to be claimed.

He reaches up, grabs one and tosses it across the space. I catch it one-handed. The metal hits my palm, edges biting into my skin. It isn't just a key. It's a lifeline.

"Upstairs, back corner." His voice is flat, all business. "Mattress isn't much, but it's clean. Shower's through the steel door. Fridge works, but I'm not sure for how long."

The words land like a checklist, but they feel like more than that. A door cracked open. A place to stand.

"Thanks." The word comes out thin, not nearly enough for what he just handed me. I pause too long.

Rainer tilts his head, eyes narrowing the way they do when he's measuring up a piece of metal. "What's on your mind, kid?"

I swallow, forcing the words out. "Can I start early?"

His brow lifts. "How early are we talking?"

"Now."

"Unload your shit. Get cleaned up. Then come back down." He turns toward his bench, voice flat but solid. "Got some parts that need sorting. Could use your eye on it."

I grip the key tighter, metal digging into my palm, and head for the narrow stairs at the back of the workshop. My boots echo against the steel with every step, the sound too loud in the quiet above.

The room is bigger than I expected. One window set high in the wall, glass smeared with dust but still letting in enough light. A single bed shoved against the far corner, mattress thin but flat. A crooked chair sits hunched in the opposite corner. On the sill, a chipped mug, left behind by someone who probably walked out and never looked back.

That's it. Empty space and bare walls. But it's mine.

For the first time, the room is mine. No bunks stacked three high, no kids fighting over space that never belonged to us. Just four walls and a door that shuts.

It's almost clean compared to everything I've known. I drop the backpack in the corner, no blanket needed to hide it, no hands waiting to pry it open and steal what's inside. The laundry bag thuds down beside it.

The silence presses in, but it doesn't feel empty. It's solid. It's a fucking chance.

Dolores won't notice as long as the check keeps showing up. The state won't care. School never gave me anything but hours to kill and rules to break. This is my shot, if I can keep my head down and make it stick.

But behind all of it sits Skylar. The first girl who ever made me feel something I couldn't shut off. She doesn't know I'm gone yet. When she figures it out, she'll think I used her. She'll hate me, and that's the way it has to be. Hate will keep her out of reach.

I move towards the bathroom with the steel door. Inside, a bare fluorescent tube hums above, spilling hard white light over cracked tiles and rust-stained sinks.

I twist the tap. Cold water gushes out. I lean in and splash it over my face. The chill bites into my skin, slides down my neck, and soaks into the collar of my shirt. For a second, it shocks me awake. I cup my hands, take a quick drink.

Rainer's workshop waits below, the clink of tools pulling me forward.

Downstairs, the workshop hums with low music from a radio buried somewhere in the back. Rainer's at the bench, torch lit, sparks spitting as he fuses metal.

I hang back a few feet, waiting him out.

A moment later, the torch dies with a hiss. He pushes the goggles up, eyes shifting to me.

"Room okay?"

"Yeah," I say. "Better than okay."

He wipes his hands on a rag and nods once. "Good. You look like you haven't slept."

"I haven't."

Rainer leans back against the bench, arms crossing over his chest. "What's on your mind, kid?"

The air thick with oil and heat is heavy in my throat when I drag in a breath. "The apprenticeship you talked about. You said it starts when I'm eighteen."

"That's the deal."

"What if I start now?" The words are out before I can stop them. "I'm done with school. Been done for a long time. I just need a reason to stay out."

Rainer studies me without a word. His gaze is steady, weighing me, no pity in it, no disgust either. Nothing but measuring. "You're still on the books. State won't let you quit before you're eighteen unless you've got a job lined up."

"I'm standing in a workshop with a job lined up." My teeth grind together. "I'll work. I'll be here every day. I'll learn whatever you throw at me. You won't have to babysit me. Just give me a shot."

His mouth twitches, a ghost of a smile. "You in trouble?"

"No." My eyes flick away, then back to his. "I'm done. That's it."

He shifts his weight, rag twisting in his hands. "You'll have to work your ass off. This isn't a charity gig. You'll be on your feet all day. No whining. No excuses."

"I don't make excuses." My voice hardens. "I just need a way out. Out of that house. Out of that school. Out of all of it."

He exhales through his nose, slow. "Fine. You start now. No pay until the books say you're legal, but I'll feed you and keep a roof over your head. You'll shadow me, clean up, learn the basics. When you hit eighteen, the real apprenticeship starts. You screw up before then, you're gone."

Relief crashes through me so hard my knees almost give. "I won't screw up."

"Good." He drops the rag on the bench. "There's a stack of parts in the corner that need sorting. Start there. Wash your hands first. You look like you crawled out of a ditch."

"Bus stop."

He snorts. "Then wash twice."

I nod and head for the sink tucked against the far wall. The tap groans before water spills out, running brown until it clears. I scrub hard, knuckles raw, watching the dirt peel off in dark streaks that swirl down the drain.

For the first time in longer than I can remember, something inside me eases—only a fraction, but enough to feel it.

I dry my hands on a rag, grab the first part from the pile, and get to work.

Hours pass in a grind of bolts, rust, and grease. My fingers ache, my shoulders burn, but I keep going. Piece after piece, I sort, wipe down, stack. The rhythm steadies me in a way nothing else does. Metal in, metal out.

At some point, Rainer steps in beside me, checks my progress without a word. He doesn't hand out praise, but he doesn't correct me either. That's enough.

Before he leaves for the night, he tosses me a couple of hot pockets from the mini freezer and tells me to lock the door behind him, saying he'll see me in the morning. When he's gone, it's me alone with the machines.

The workshop settles into silence once he's gone. The only sounds left are the scrape of metal in my hands and the rasp of my breath. I keep working.

My back knots, shoulders tight, fingers burning from the grind, but I don't stop. Not yet. The ache is better than the thoughts waiting to tear through me if I slow down. Every piece I wipe down, every bolt I line up, keeps my head steady.

By the time I drop the last piece onto the stack, the clock on the wall creeps past midnight. My hands are raw, grease carved deep into the cracks of my skin, nails blackened. My stomach growls, dragging my eyes to the two frozen hot pockets Rainer tossed me.

I peel one open and shove it in the microwave tucked near the back wall. The machine buzzes loudly in the quiet; the smell of pastry and meat fills the workshop. When the bell rings, I wrap both hot pockets in paper towels, and head for the stairs.

The climb upstairs is slow, every step dragging me lower with exhaustion, but I don't fight it. For once the ache feels earned. My arms throb, my back screams, my legs are heavy beneath me, but when I glance back at the sorted piles, something inside me settles. Order where there was none. Proof I didn't waste the hours. Proof I can do this.

In the room, I set the hot pockets down on the bed, heat seeping through the paper towels. I strip down to my underwear, tossing my clothes in a heap on the floor, too drained to care where they land. I duck into the bathroom and scrub my hands under the cold tap until the sting bites at my skin.

When I come back, I drop onto the mattress and tear into the first hot pocket. The pastry flakes, the filling burns my tongue, but I don't care. I finish it fast. By the time I finish the second one, my eyes are already shutting.

I fall back against the pillow, stomach warm, body wrecked. Sleep takes me before I can even breathe out.

Chapter 10

SKYLAR

The corridor smells of cheap perfume, and something fried drifting in from the cafeteria. Fluorescent lights buzz overhead, casting everything in a sickly glow. Lockers slam open and shut. The noise presses in, squeezing the air from my lungs, turning every breath into a battle.

Cassie moves beside me, her voice low, talking about something we're supposed to hand in for English. I nod at the right places but don't really hear her.

My fingers clamp the strap of my bag, nails biting into the canvas. I keep my eyes on the tiles, counting the cracks instead of looking at the faces that turn when I walk past.

They're not saying anything. Not yet. But the itch between my shoulder blades is already there. The way whispers travel faster than footsteps in this place. Something in the air's shifted, sharp around the edges, and I can't tell if the change is crawling under my skin or hanging in the air around them.

Cassie stops at her locker, twisting the dial. "Did you do the reading?"

"Yeah," I lie.

She side-eyes me. "You okay?"

"Fine."

She doesn't buy it, but she doesn't press.

It's been a week since I last saw him. Zane's seat in homeroom stays empty. His boots don't drag across the floor. His hoodie or that black leather jacket aren't slung over the back of his chair. He's gone, and no one even mentions him. Teachers still call his name, pause for half a beat, then move on.

I tell myself I don't care. That I'm glad he's not here. That what happened on that rooftop was a mistake and I'm better off without him.

But the memory keeps clawing back with those fucking words he threw at me before he left.

Cassie's locker swings open with a screech. She mutters something about forgetting her gym shirt again, but I'm watching the hallway.

Cassie leans in, spritzing way too much perfume over her neck. The sweetness hits hard, thick enough to taste. It clings to the back of my throat.

I cough, waving it away. "Jesus, you trying to kill someone?"

She smirks. "Boys like girls who smell good."

"Boys like tits and trauma," I mutter, waving the cloud away.

She pulls out her notebook and slams the locker shut, then turns. "You're off today. Weird off."

"Just tired." I shrug.

"You've been tired all week."

I don't answer. I can't.

We start walking, dodging groups of boys yelling about some game, pass girls reapplying lip gloss in mirrors, teachers barking about passes. Everything is too loud. Too close.

My eyes dart to the far doors again, but he's not there.

Cassie stops in front of the drinking fountain, pressing the button and taking a sip, before she squints up at me. "Okay, what's with the murder face?"

"I don't have a murder face."

"You do. Your eye's twitching. Pretty sure you scared that scrawny kid into dropping his juice box out of fear."

"For fuck's sake, Cassie, I'm fine."

She plants herself in front of me, arms crossed, that trademark Cassie death-glare locked and loaded.

"Girl, you just lied to my face. NASA's probably tracking your bullshit from space."

I almost crack, but I hold it in. Barely.

"You wanna tell me, or should I start guessing?" She doesn't wait. "Okay, first guess—you finally snapped and buried Dolores in the backyard."

My lip twitches.

"Second—you found your birth certificate and your real name's... wait for it... Dorcas Moonshine."

That gets a snort out of me.

"Three: you joined a TikTok cult that drinks neon sludge, sobs to sad-girl edits, and thinks burning sage cures childhood trauma."

I choke on a laugh. "You're such a dick."

She smirks victoriously. "There she is. I fucking told myself you hadn't disappeared." She hooks her arm through mine. "Let's go, Dorcas Moonshine. We're skipping class."

"Cass."

"Don't Cass me. I'm being a supportive friend. Against my better judgment."

"Where are we going?"

"Somewhere sacred."

She pushes open the side door, and we head down the back path behind the cafeteria. A guy I don't recognize is leaning against the wall, hoodie up, cigarette in hand.

He spots us and smirks. "Yo, Skylar. Wanna ditch your babysitter and come sit on my face?"

I don't even blink. "How about you go fuck yourself? Should be easy. You've had enough practice."

He coughs on his smoke.

Cassie bursts out laughing beside me. "Jesus, warn me next time you go full castration with words."

She pulls my arm and drags me off the path.

"Where are we going now?" I mutter, heels skidding in the gravel.

"To the sacred wall of bad decisions and emotional breakthroughs," she says, yanking me down the hill behind the gym.

We duck behind the old incinerator, a brick wall cracked with graffiti. Cassie drops her bag and slides down with a grunt, legs sprawled out in front of her.

She digs into her hoodie pocket and pulls out a joint, holding it up like it's holy.

I squint at her.

"Where the hell did you get that?"

Cassie sticks it between her lips and lights it, taking a long, practiced drag before grinning around the smoke. "Gave Tyler Finch a blowjob behind the music room."

My jaw drops.

She passes me the joint.

"And before you judge, his cock is actually impressive. I'm talking ruin-your-standards, question-everything-you-knew-about-size impressive."

I shake my head, snorting as I sit beside her. "You're unbelievable."

Cassie exhales, smoke curling around her smile. "Thank you. I try."

She takes another hit, leans her head back against the wall, and looks over at me.

"What the fuck is wrong with you, Sky?"

I blink. "Jesus. Subtle."

"Don't give me that bullshit answer either. I know you better than anyone. Spill."

I stare at the gravel between my shoes, toeing a broken bottle cap like it might hold the answer.

Part of me wants to say it. Spill the whole messy truth to her. Zane, the rooftop, the way he looked at me right before he walked away like I was something he regretted touching. The way it sits inside me now. Hollow. Dumb. Used. Even though I swore I wouldn't let anyone do that to me again.

But the words get stuck.

Plus there's the other thing. The louder thing. Eighteen in two weeks. No more roof over my head unless I find one myself. And I have no fucking clue where I'm supposed to go when the clock runs out.

I scratch at the frayed knee of my jeans and say nothing.

Cassie sighs. "You're doing that thing again. Where you shut down and pretend you're fine until you explode or ghost me for two weeks."

I lift a shoulder, still not looking at her.

She bumps my arm. "Sky. Talk to me."

I take the joint from her fingers and breathe it in, trying to stall. But the burn in my throat doesn't drown the panic rising in my chest.

Cassie watches me, eyes narrowed like she's already decided she's not letting this slide.

"You gonna tell me what's going on or am I gonna have to pull a full FBI sting? Because I swear to God, I will waterboard your ass with Mountain Dew."

I huff a laugh. "You're so dramatic."

"Uh-huh." She takes the joint back, blows smoke up toward the crumbling brick above us. "And you're so full of shit. Seriously, Sky, you're scaring me. What happened?"

I lean back against the wall, the warmth seeping through my shirt, and let my head fall back.

"I did something stupid," I say finally.

Cassie goes still.

"Like... dye-your-hair-with-food-coloring stupid or..." Her eyes widen. "Oh my god, did you get matching tattoos with someone?"

"No," I snap. My voice drops. "Worse."

She blinks. "How much worse?"

"I... It was Zane."

Cassie chokes. "Zane... As in, tall, broody, emotionally unavailable Zane?"

I nod, jaw tight. "We were on the roof of this abandoned building. It was intense. And then I..." My voice trails off, heat crawling up my neck.

Cassie stares. "Wait. Did you blow him?"

I squeeze my eyes shut. "Don't."

"Oh my god. You did."

"Cass—"

"Holy shit."

"I said don't."

Cassie exhales a curl of smoke and grins at me through the haze. "So... what was his cock like?"

I choke on air. "Are you serious right now?"

"Dead serious. I've always wondered. Zane's got that silent-storm energy. I bet he's big. No way a guy with hands like that isn't hiding a fucking monster."

I shake my head but can't stop the heat crawling up my throat. "Yeah, he's big. And no, I'm not giving you inches."

Cassie leans in, wide-eyed. "Oh come on, throw a girl a bone. Preferably his." She laughs.

I stare at the cracked concrete under our feet. "After that, he fucking walked away. Didn't say a word. Left me there as if I was some piece of shit he used to get off."

"Fucker."

I nod, jaw clenched. "And there's that other thing."

Cassie narrows her eyes. "What thing?"

"I turn eighteen in two weeks. You get what that means. What if I have to sleep on the fucking street, Cass?"

She doesn't blink. "I won't let that happen. I promise."

"You can't promise that?" My voice cracks on the last word. "You gonna pull a spare bedroom out of your ass?"

She blows out smoke, flicks ash against the wall, after that shifts closer, nudges her shoulder against mine. "I don't have a place either, Sky. You get that. But if you end up on the street, we'll be fucking roommates under a bridge."

"Great," I mutter. "We'll start a girl gang. Fight raccoons for snacks."

"Exactly. You, me, and a sharp stick. We'll survive."

I laugh, my shoulders easing a little. Trust Cass to drag me out of the dark with zero effort.

She chews the inside of her cheek before exhaling hard. "You're gonna hate me."

I tense. "What now?"

She won't look at me. Keeps picking at a crack in the brick wall instead. "I heard where he went."

Heat pulses under my skin. "Who... Zane?"

She nods once. "He's not coming back to school."

I blink. "What do you mean?"

"I heard he's working full-time down at that grimy mechanic place on Harris Street."

I stare at her. "And you're just telling me now?"

Cassie lifts her eyes. "I wasn't sure if it was true. But I saw him yesterday."

"What?"

"He looked... rough. Tired. But free." Her gaze softens. "He got out, Sky."

"Right. Good for him." I laugh, bitter.

"No," she says, grabbing my arm. "You don't get it. If he got out, we can too. You don't have to end up couch-surfing. There's still a way."

I huff out a laugh. "I don't even know anyone with a fucking couch."

Her grip tightens, and for a second, I think she's gonna hit me with some speech about hope. About how things get better if you just want it bad enough. But she doesn't. She sits there watching me.

"You've got me, ride-or-die, you know that."

"You live with the Romeros, Cass. Ten kids in that place and a curfew stricter than prison. Where exactly do I go? The floor under your bunk?"

"Then we find something together," she says. "A squat. A busted caravan. A sugar daddy with a limp and low standards."

I snort, but my throat still burns. "Cool. Can't wait to trade blowjobs for power outlets."

Cassie passes me the joint again. "At least charge your phone first. No one wants to suck dick in the dark."

I laugh, but it scrapes at my throat. "Yeah. Gotta keep the lights on while they remind me I'm nothing but a warm body."

I take a drag, hold it until my lungs sting, exhale slowly. Smoke curls between us.

"I wish I could hate him, Cass," I say, voice breaking around the words. "God, I wish I could. It would make it fucking easier."

Cassie leans back against the wall, one knee bent, eyes never leaving me.

"Then don't fucking hate him," she says softly. "Don't waste the energy. Just... survive him."

The word hits like a bruise. Survive. I'm always surviving. Always fucking crawling out from under someone else's wreckage. I shut my eyes and press my head back against the brick. I'm so tired of feeling like this was all I was born for.

The joint trembles in my fingers. Cassie snatches it, takes a hit as if it'll silence the truth between us.

"It'll work out," she says, the words flat, unconvincing.

I side-eye her. "You don't know that."

"No," she says. "But I'm saying it anyway. Because someone fucking has to."

I look at her, jaw clenched.

She shrugs. "You just need to trust me."

The words hang there.

I want to believe her.

"I've trusted people before."

Cassie doesn't blink. "Yeah, well, none of them were me."

She holds the joint out again, a quiet kind of promise. And maybe that's enough.

We sit in silence, passing it back and forth until the day frays at the edges. The concrete holds the last of the sun, warm under us, that only lasts until the bell from the main building sounds, dragging us back to reality.

Cassie sighs.

We don't say anything for a beat.

Cassie nudges me with her foot. "Come on. Before they send a search party and find out their perfect little foster girl's have been getting high by the incinerator."

I stand, brush the dirt off my jeans. "Pretty sure they already assume we're a lost cause."

"Good. Saves time." She shoulders her bag and starts walking.

I follow.

By fourth period, my head is already pounding.

The classroom reeks of sweat, too many bodies crammed into chairs that were never built for comfort. The windows are sealed shut, dust caked thick along the ledges. I sit in the back, where no one looks twice if I zone out, but today, even that doesn't help. Everything presses in. The scrape of chairs. The tap of pens. The endless hum of voices that all sound the same.

Cassie's next to me, chewing the hell out of her pen cap, eyes pinned to the clock like it owes her something. She hasn't said a word since I opened my mouth, and honestly, I don't blame her. I don't talk about that kind of shit. Not out loud. The second Zane's name slipped out, I wanted to shove it right back down my throat.

The teacher drops a worksheet on my desk. I don't bother looking at it. My pen's in my hand, but it doesn't move. Neither do I.

Two rows up, one of the dickheads from this morning twists in his seat. His eyes land on me. That smirk creeps back, all teeth and ego, and I catch it—that flicker of something foul gearing up in his brain. A punchline. A power move. Something he thinks will make him feel bigger.

I hold his stare. Cold. Unmoving. Daring him to open his mouth and choke on whatever shit he's dying to spit.

Cassie leans in, voice all silk and threat. "You want me to shank him?"

He's the one who breaks first, eyes slicing away like the stare never happened. All bark and no fucking teeth.

Cassie grins like she won something. "Fucking coward."

Up front, one of the jocks hurls a crumpled worksheet at Rebecca's head the second the teacher turns. It clips her shoulder. Laughter spills out, the kind that sticks to weakness and waits for someone to flinch.

I like Rebecca. She's one of the few who actually says hi when I walk past, eyes meeting mine instead of darting away. That small thing matters. She doesn't belong here, not really. She's too kind. Easy prey for assholes who get off on weakness.

The dickhead rolls another sheet of paper tight and whips it straight at her back. It lands with a dull smack and drops to the floor. His friends lose it, snorting, elbowing each other, proud of the show they're putting on. It's fucking stupid how cruelty gets the applause. How being a prick makes you somebody.

Rebecca flinches but doesn't turn around or say a word.

He grins, already rolling up another sheet, as if being a piece of shit is a full-time job he's proud to show up for.

I shove my chair back. It screeches across the floor, a sound that cuts clean through the noise.

Heads turn.

He freezes just as he's about to throw, eyes dragging to me.

"What the hell is wrong with you?"

I don't yell. I don't have to.

He blinks. Smug still clings to his face.

"What, you got a thing for the freaks now?" He says.

I step out from behind my desk.

"Oh, shit." Cassie mutters under her breath.

"You think that's funny?" I say, to the dickhead. "Picking on the quiet girl because you know she won't fight back? Real tough of you." I step forward. "Bet your mommy's real proud knowing her son turned out to be a pathetic little bitch who gets off on making girls cry."

A few students gasp. One laughs.

"Skylar," the teacher snaps, finally noticing. "Sit down. Now."

I don't move.

"Last warning."

I keep my eyes on him. "I'm not done staring at stupid," I tell her.

"That's it," she barks. "Out. Get out of my classroom."

I grab my bag without a word and sling it over my shoulder. Every step down the aisle burns up my spine. My pulse thuds so loud it might as well be a war drum. No one laughs now. Not even the prick who started it.

At the door, I stop. Face the teacher.

"Good job, Miss," I say. "Real solid message, kick out the girl who called out the bully, and let the asshole stay seated."

I hold her gaze just long enough to make her uncomfortable.

Then I walk out, letting the silence eat up the space I leave behind.

Chapter 11

ZANE

The shop hums around me.

Not loud. Not quiet. Just steady as if it's got a heartbeat of its own.

Sparks spit from the torch. Steel groans under the grinder. And that smell... the burnt oil and hot metal, gets into your clothes, your skin, your fucking bones.

Rainer trusts me with jobs that matter now, no longer sweeping floors or stacking parts.

Now, it's real work.

Engines torn down to their guts. Welds that burn hot enough to blister. Tasks that leave my muscles screaming and my shoulders aching in the best possible way.

This is the kind of pain that proves I still exist.

That I'm still here, and that maybe I'm worth something after all.

Rainer's decent in a way that doesn't need to be loud. He doesn't hover or question every move I make. Just tosses me a job and waits to see if I can handle the pressure.

And I do. Because here, I'm not the wreck everyone looks at with guilt in their eyes. I've got a purpose. I count.

The days fall into a rhythm. Start early. Work hard. Go home with every muscle screaming for rest.

My hands stay busy enough to keep the noise out. While my body is tired enough to sleep through the dark.

And for once, that's enough.

So, I keep my hands busy. Wrench in one, torch in the other. Sweat dripping down my spine.

But still... Skylar is still here with me. In every bolt I twist. Every grind of steel. She's even in the goddamn fucking air.

I tried to fuck her out of my system last night, with a girl whose name vanished with the night. She smiled too easily, dropped to her knees like she'd done the whole routine a hundred times. I told myself the release would help. That closing my eyes would make Skylar vanish.

But the second her lips wrapped around my cock, everything in me screamed this wouldn't work.

It wasn't right. It didn't feel at all like the way Skylar touched me.

All I wanted was Skylar. On her knees. Mouth slick. Eyes burning. That wild fucking fire in her stare before I snuffed it out.

I came hard, in the chick's mouth, she swallowed everything I gave her, but there was no victory in it. Just a hollow kind of ache that settled deep and stayed.

She laughed, wiped her mouth, and asked if I wanted to grab a drink.

I walked away and didn't even glance over my shoulder.

No one gets close to what Skylar carved into me.

And I fucking hate that. Almost as much as I need the fire she lit in me.

Rainer gave me permission to make the apartment mine. Said the apprenticeship was official now, which is good because the money I had saved is already gone. I've tried to build something real. Little by little, it's started to feel that way.

There's a blanket on the bed now. Thick enough to bury myself in when the nights turn mean. Weights stacked in the corner that I lift until my arms shake and my abs burn. Until the pain silences everything else.

But nothing drowns her out. Not completely.

I lie there some nights and tell myself I'm safe, that I made it out. And for a minute, I believe it.

But then the dark crawls in and all I can think about is her.

I don't get why the fuck she's still in my head. She doesn't belong in my world. It's been four goddamn weeks—gone, out of her orbit, out of her life—and I still can't fucking shake the pull.

That alone pisses me off more than anything.

The sun cuts hard through the windows, a blinding strip of light slicing across the concrete. My hands are slick with grease, shirt clinging to my back, soaked from the heat. I kill the torch, peel the goggles off, and squint into the glare.

That's when I see her.

A blur of movement. Sneakers on cracked asphalt. Eyes too familiar.

Cassie. Skylar's friend.

The one who always watched too much. Who knows shit she shouldn't.

No one moves the way she does. Chin high, like the world can go fuck itself for staring. She's small, sure, smaller than most of the kids at school, but carries that kind of fire that grabs you by the throat. That kind of spark you don't mean to notice but can't ignore. She walks ready to fight. If you knock her down, she'll bleed on your shoes and come back swinging.

She's not soft. Not beautiful in the way Skylar is. There's nothing delicate about her, but she's fucking tough and all edges.

She storms straight across the floor, sneakers squeaking against the concrete. Eyes locked on me.

I catch it in the corner of my eye. Pretend I don't. My hands stay busy with the torch, twisting the valve that doesn't need adjusting.

I don't give her the satisfaction.

Not yet.

Her shadow slides over the floor, until it's brushing my boots. She doesn't say shit, just stands in it, letting the silence cut.

Then comes the cough. Short. Sharp. Designed to get my attention.

I let the silence drag a little longer than I need to before I turn.

Cassie waits, arms crossed, chin lifted. The girl's got more backbone than half the assholes I've met. I'll give her that.

"What the fuck do you want?" My voice is flat. Dry. Scraped of anything that might give her the wrong idea like I give a shit.

Her eyes narrow, arms still crossed. "Well, that's just fucking rude."

I turn back to the bench, grab the rag, wipe grease from my palms. "I'm working. Spit it out or leave."

Cassie takes a step closer. "It's Skylar."

I freeze. Only for a second. Barely long enough to count. I keep my expression bored, detached.

"What about her?"

"She's not okay," Cassie snaps. "Four days until she leaves Dolores, and she's got nowhere to go."

I keep my eyes on the bench, toss the rag aside, and reach for the socket set. "Not my fucking problem."

"You're such a heartless asshole."

"Keep your voice down." My tone is steel, final.

But she holds her ground. "I know what you did. And yeah, that was some next-level asshole shit, even by your standards."

Fuck.

I wonder what she told her. If the memory still burns. Whether the hurt still hits.

I turn slow, my stare cutting into hers. "You done?"

Cassie doesn't flinch. Her chin tips higher. "Not even close."

That's it. I drop the socket set with a sharp clang and close the distance.

My hand clamps around her arm. Not enough to bruise. Just enough to jolt her.

She stumbles when I yank her toward the door.

"We're not doing this in here," I mutter, dragging her across the floor.

Cassie twists hard. "Oh, fuck you. You think hauling me outside makes you some kind of big man?"

I shove the door open with my shoulder, sunlight crashing down on us as it slams shut behind. I drop her arm but plant myself between her and the door. No fucking way she's going back in there.

Cassie spins, her eyes blazing. "I came to you because I don't know what the fuck to do."

Her voice cracks. Tears bite at her lashes, and for a second, I catch everything. The way she cares. The way Skylar means something real to her.

She softens but only for a breath.

"I'm scared she's gonna end up sleeping on the street."

Then she catches the way I'm looking at her.

Her jaw sets. Her spine straightens. "Not that you'd fucking care anyway, asshole."

I smirk. I can't help myself. She's grit and steel and every kind of stubborn. Walked into a place she didn't want to be to fight for someone else.

Skylar's lucky she's got someone like that in her corner.

Cassie jabs her finger into my chest. "She's fucking drowning in all the worry, Zane. And you're standing here, not giving a shit. I figured you'd understand, me showing up here, being one of us."

I get what she means. An unwanted foster kid, surviving on our own. But I don't let her off easy.

I fold my arms over my chest, lean back on my heels, and let the silence stretch until it hurts.

"So are you gonna say why you came here..." I ask, voice low. "Or keep circling around it like a coward?"

Her jaw clenches. Good, let her fucking squirm, because stepping back into Skylar's world... that'll wreck fucking everything.

It will rip me open.

Bleed me out.

If I can avoid it, I will.

But fuck me, Cassie is making that difficult.

Her mouth twists. She looks away for half a second, chewing the inside of her cheek like it might keep the words in. Then she shoves her hands into the pockets of her jacket.

"I don't want to be here," she says through gritted teeth.

I don't respond. Just wait.

She drags in a breath. "I fucking hate this, okay? Hate you. Hate that I'm standing here asking you for something."

Still, I say nothing.

Her head snaps up, eyes burning. "But I need your help."

"Give me your phone," I say, extending my hand.

She doesn't move, only lifts a brow. "What for? You wanna scroll through all the dick pics and rate them out of ten?"

I grunt. "Yeah. Figured I'd kill time while you finish running your mouth." I flick my fingers. "Do you want my help or not, for fuck sake?"

She huffs, digs her phone out of her back pocket, and slaps it into my palm.

I punch in my number, fast, then hand the phone back. "There. Don't call unless she's in real shit and you're desperate. And don't fucking give that number to anyone."

She stares at the screen, before lifting her eyes to mine. Her glare could flay skin.

"You really are an asshole," she mutters, snatching the phone as if it's tainted and then storms off.

I stand frozen, hands clenched, wondering what the fuck I've done, letting Skylar back into my world.

I shove off the wall and head back into the workshop, grabbing the first thing I see on the bench. Steel in my palm. Work. That's the answer. It always has been. Keep my head down, my hands moving. Bury the past so deep it forgets how to crawl out.

I tell myself I gave Cassie my number for Skylar. In case the shit gets too real. Not because I care or that I want to get involved.

I tell myself I'll keep my distance. That I can. That I fucking will.

But by the time the sun sinks and the shop's gone quiet, I already know I'm lying.

And still... Cassie's voice plays on repeat. *"She's drowning."*

And I haven't got a fucking clue what to do with that, let alone how to be the guy who saves her.

Chapter 12

SKYLAR

Morning crawls through the curtains, gray and washed out, the kind that doesn't belong to birthdays. The light hits the walls faintly, as if even the sun knows this day isn't worth showing up for.

Last year's birthday balloon is still here. It's half-dead, half-alive. Cassie's gift, not Dolores's.

It floats by the dresser, sagging at the edges, holding on to the last breath of air it doesn't deserve. The ribbon's crusted with dust, curled in on itself the way everything in this house eventually does.

This is what birthdays look like here.

No candles. No cake. Just the same tired walls, the same fucking ache in my chest.

Eighteen… And it already feels too old to matter.

I lie on my back, staring at the water stain on the ceiling. It's getting bigger, spreading across the plaster in uneven circles.

They say eighteen is the age when everything begins. Freedom. Adulthood. The world waiting for you with open fucking arms.

It sure as shit doesn't feel that way.

The room seems smaller, the air heavier, every breath a little harder to take.

I'm not free. I'm just… empty. Used up before I got the chance to spread my wings and fly.

A knock cuts through the quiet. Three dull thuds that hit. Dolores never waits. The door creaks open, hinges crying out in protest.

"Are you awake?" Her voice is rough, morning-thick, with no trace of softness in it.

I push myself up, hair sticking to my face, sheets twisted around my legs. "Yeah."

She stands in the doorway in her robe, hair pinned, coffee in hand. Her face is unreadable, wearing that same empty expression she saves for bills and bad news.

"You realize what day it is."

"Yeah." I pull the blanket over my legs. "Hard to forget."

She lets out a sigh that sounds too heavy for the morning. "Then you already know what comes next."

I've seen this coming, the colder tone, the shampoo she stopped buying for me.

"Dolores."

"You're eighteen now." Her tone doesn't rise, but it doesn't soften either. "That means the checks stop. And when the checks stop, so do you staying here. I can't keep you for free."

"But I have nowhere to go." My throat aches, but I keep my voice flat. I won't give her the sound of me breaking.

"That's not my problem." Her eyes drift across the room, landing on everything except me. "You had plenty of time to get ready. You knew this was coming."

I let out a small laugh. It sounds wrong. Empty. "Yeah. Because people are just dying to rent a place to some broke kid with nothing but a garbage bag full of clothes."

She shrugs, the movement lazy, uncaring. "I'm not running a charity. You age out, you move out. That's how it works."

She crosses the room; the floor creaking under her slippers. A small box hits the dresser, wrapped in cheap paper that's already tearing at the corners.

"Happy birthday."

Two words. No smile. No pause. And she's gone.

The door clicks shut, and the quiet that follows is worse than anything she could've said.

It seeps into the walls, pressing into my chest until breathing feels like an effort.

I glance at the dresser. The box sits there, waiting. Small. Useless but still trying to pretend it matters.

I shove the blanket off and climb down from the top bunk. My feet hit the floor hard.

The paper's wrinkled, taped unevenly, covered in those stupid cartoon candles that seem more like a joke than a celebration.

I tear it open, and a keychain drops into my palm. Plastic. Pink. A little heart that reads Dream Big. The words catch the light for half a second before fading back into nothing.

The irony stings. Dream big, when the only dream I've got is finding somewhere to sleep tonight.

It's cheap. Hollow. Exactly what this house has always been.

I want to hurl it against the wall to watch it split open, plastic heart snapping in two. I want to scream that she could've at least pretended I was worth the effort.

But I don't.

I stare at it, the words Dream Big staring back, all fake shine and cheap promises. My vision burns until everything goes fuzzy.

In my head, I hear her voice. The same line she feeds every kid who ever passes through that front door. Don't get comfortable. This isn't forever.

I grab a clean shirt from the chair and pull it on. Jeans next, followed by socks that don't match because none of it matters.

When I'm done, I glance around the room, ignoring the other girls watching me. My eyes land on the keychain sitting on the dresser, pink and pathetic, still telling me to Dream Big.

For some stupid reason I can't explain, I slip it into my pocket.

Then, I pack up my shit.

There isn't much to take. A few shirts. Two pairs of jeans, a skirt. The photo of me and Cassie from her fifteenth birthday. We're both grinning, sunburnt, mid-laugh. The kind of smile you only wear when you still think the world's gonna be kind.

That was the last time I believed in happy endings.

By the time I zip the bag shut, my chest is hollow. I catch my reflection in the cracked mirror. My face appears older somehow, sharper around the edges. It's what happens when you finally stop hoping someone will choose you.

I sling my backpack over one shoulder, the duffel bag over the other.

Outside my bedroom door, Dolores stands in the kitchen stirring coffee, back turned, shoulders stiff. She doesn't lift her head, but I'm certain she heard me. She's got ears sharp enough to catch a whisper from three rooms away.

I stop in the hallway, fingers tightening on the strap of my bag. The words crawl up my throat. I so desperately want to tell her she's a shitty foster parent, tell her we're just kids who didn't choose this fucking life, who still ended up in this shithole where no one gives a fuck.

But what's the point? She's probably already lined up the next kid to fill my bed, the next face she won't care about.

I shift my bag higher on my shoulder and keep walking.

The front door opens without a sound. I step out without looking back.

The sky is gray, thick with rain that hasn't fallen. The kind of morning that feels hungover.

I stand on the porch, fingers tight around my bags. The world spreads wide and empty, stretching out in every direction with nowhere to land.

I'm eighteen. Free. And nowhere to fucking go.

It's too early for Cassie, so I walk alone. The street's empty, the only sound is my footsteps and the dull hit of the duffel against my leg.

By the time I reach the school gates, my shoulders burn.

People stare as I walk through. The difference is, today I don't have the energy to glare back.

I spot Liam leaning against the fence, surrounded by his pack of brainless followers. He clocks me instantly, that shit-eating grin spreading across his face.

"Damn, Sky," he calls out. "Are you wearing those jeans for class or to get the attention of my cock?"

The boys erupt into laughter, one letting out a drawn-out "fuuuck."

Liam, the asshole doesn't know when to quit. "Bet that mouth's good for more than mouthing off, Sky."

More laughter.

One of them mutters something about bending me over.

I keep walking. Most days, I'd say something sharp enough to make his balls shrivel. But not today.

Today, I've got too much weight on my back and not enough fucks left to give. He's just noise. Ugly, empty noise.

The hallway reeks of floor cleaner and something stale trapped in the vents.

Most of the students are still outside, crowding around Liam and his pack of dickheads, hoping if they laugh loud enough, he'll look their way.

I slip into the seat under the stairwell and drop my bags at my feet. It's quieter here, if only for a second.

The quiet doesn't last.

Lockers slam. Voices blur. The hallway fills with sound. Laughter, footsteps, someone yelling about a test.

I stare at the tiles. One's chipped, right at the edge of my shoe. I count the cracks. Try to think. Try to breathe, rack my brain for a plan that doesn't end with me curled up sleeping behind a dumpster tonight.

"There you are," Cassie says, all bright and grinning like the world isn't falling apart. "Happy birthday, bitch. Where were you this morning?"

She slides into the seat beside me, all ease and habit, as if this were another day. Her arm slips through mine.

She doesn't see the second bag. Not yet.

"We're doing something tonight," she says. "Pizza. Cake. A movie. You're not saying no."

Her smile is wide, waiting for the version of me she expects to show up. But I'm not sure that girl still exists.

I shake her off. "Can't."

Cassie's smile falters. Her eyes drop to the duffel at my feet. "What's that?"

"All my stuff." My voice catches. "Dolores kicked me out."

She blinks, the words not landing yet. "What?"

"She said I'm eighteen now. The government stops paying, so I have to go. Said she's not running a charity."

Cassie's mouth opens, but nothing comes out. Her face looks as if she's just been slapped. Finally, she manages, "She can't... she can't do that."

"She can." I force my voice to steady. "And she did. It's fine. I'll figure something out."

Cassie grabs my arm.

"No, it's not fine. Where are you gonna stay?"

"I said I'll figure it out." I yank my arm back, harder than I mean to.

"Sky, stop acting like this is normal—"

"It is normal." The words come fast, sharp, too loud. "You think I haven't seen this shit before? You think Dolores didn't do the same thing to the last three kids? This is what she does. It's my turn now."

Cassie flinches, and I hate how much I notice it.

"I'm just trying to help." Her voice drops, soft and breaking.

"I don't need your help Cass. I've got to start doing things on my own now."

And that's the biggest lie I've ever told.

The bell rings but it barely cuts through. The sound's there, but it feels far away, like it's coming from underwater. School's over. People move, scraping chairs, laughing too loud, but it all washes past me.

I couldn't tell you what happened between first period and now if you put a gun to my head. I have no idea who sat next to me, no clue what assignments were due. It's all a smear of voices and faces, static that crawls under my skin.

The only thing in my head all day has been where the fuck I'm going to sleep tonight. A weight sitting in my chest, as if I'm walking through someone else's day while mine's already over.

I've let every asshole in this place take shots at me all day. Liam and his pack, throwing words like stones. Some girls near the lockers whispering about how I love the attention. On any other day I'd slice them open with my mouth, leave them red-faced and wishing they'd never tried.

But today I just took it.

Every jab, every laugh. Every set of eyes crawling over me.

Maybe they can see the crack in my armor. Maybe my shoulders are broadcasting defeat. Or my silence is louder than any comeback I could spit. Whatever it is, I wore my weakness like an exposed nerve, and every glance grazed it.

Cassie's been on my back since third period.

Hovering. Watching. Talking as if saying it out loud solves anything. Throwing out ideas I can't use and names I don't trust. Listing off shelters and hotlines and other things she's probably Googled in the middle of class while I sat there pretending the floor could open up and swallow me whole.

She means well. I know she does. Even so, that doesn't stop her from pissing me off.

Every word she says piles on top of me, heavier than the last. Every offer drags me further under.

I've told her. Over and over again that this isn't her fucking problem. That I'm not some stray she needs to look after.

We push through the school doors and down the front steps. Cassie's right next to me, rattling off another list of ideas, her voice tumbling over itself, desperate and fast. I don't even know what she's saying anymore. I stopped listening a while ago.

There's no couch to crash on. No shelter I trust. No family waiting at the end of the street.

Just the bag digging into my shoulder.

I keep walking, eyes fixed ahead, hoping that if I move fast enough, the world will blur and she'll stop trying to save me.

I haven't told her where I'm going, and she hasn't asked. But I can feel her eyes on me, weighing every step, waiting for me to crack.

I keep my head down and finally make the choice I've been circling all day. I'll sleep at the town library.

There's a corner near the front entrance tucked out of sight, wedged between the columns and the brick wall. Half-covered. Quiet.

Not safe. But safer than a park bench.

Cassie slows the moment the library comes into view.

I sense it in the drag of her steps, the space opening up between us, the way her shoulder stops brushing mine. She keeps glancing at me, at the building, and back again.

She knows.

I keep my eyes on the pavement. One foot in front of the other. Pretend I'm just walking, anywhere, everywhere. Not scoping out a corner to sleep in. Not deciding where I'm going to disappear tonight.

"Sky," she says.

I don't answer her. I just keep moving forward.

She catches up with me. "What the fuck are we doing here?"

I stop at the edge of the stone steps, right in front of the alcove. The spot's tucked away enough. Mostly hidden, out of view unless someone's looking too hard.

I drop my bag. My shoulders cave the second it hits the ground.

Cassie stops cold beside me. Her eyes flick from the duffel to the brick wall then back to my face.

"No," she says, already shaking her head. "No. You're not sleeping here."

I drop down onto the step and lean back against the stone. It's cold enough to bite through my shirt, grounding in a way that almost feels good.

"I told you," I say. "I've got it handled."

Cassie's standing over me, arms crossed. "This isn't handled."

"It's temporary."

She laughs once. "You're sitting outside a fucking library, Sky."

"Just go home," I say. My voice comes out flat, but my hands won't stop shaking.

She doesn't move. "You think I'm gonna fucking leave you here?"

"You don't have a choice."

"That's bullshit." Her voice rises. "You're not staying here. I'll call someone, we'll find somewhere for you to stay tonight, and we'll figure it out in the morning."

"I said no."

"Why not?"

"Because I said so."

"That's not a reason." Cassie's breathing is fast now, chest rising and falling. Her voice drops, barely a whisper. "You don't deserve this."

I glance away.

"You don't," she says again, voice trembling now. "You're not some throw-away, Sky. "

"I am."

"You're not."

"You should go." I pull my bag closer.

Cassie doesn't move.

"Go home," I say. "You've done enough."

"But I haven't done anything."

"Just go home, Cassie," I whisper. "You can't fix this. Just... please. Go home. I'll see you tomorrow."

Traffic hums in the distance. A light drizzle starts to fall.

Her shoulders sink, but she still stands there, staring at me like she can hold me together just by staying.

I give her a glare that tells her not to fuck with me right now. The one that means I'm hanging by a thread.

She blinks hard, nods once. "Okay."

She turns and starts walking toward the corner, each step slower than the last, as if she doesn't want to leave me here alone.

I watch her go, every step pulling her further out of my reach.

When she reaches the corner, I watch her pull her phone from her pocket, tap the screen, and lift it to her ear.

I don't need to hear the words to know she's not done trying to save me.

Chapter 13

ZANE

Rainer's still talking when my phone buzzes in my pocket.

I pull it out, thumb slick with oil, streaking black across the glass until her name cuts through it.

Cassie.

I answer.

Her voice hits through the static, fast and shaking. "She's at the library. Says she's got nowhere to go."

Nowhere.

The word slides under my skin and stays there. Everything in me goes tight.

Rainer's still talking, but those words are just noise now. All I can hear is that one word burning through the rest.

The words rip out before I can swallow them. "What the fuck do you mean nowhere?"

"She aged out," Cassie rushes. "Dolores told her to leave this morning. She's been sitting out front of the library since school ended. I tried to stay, but she told me to go. Zane, she won't let me help her. Skylar says she's fine, but she's not fine."

Her voice cracks on fine and the sound goes straight through me. All the places I thought were numb start bleeding again.

The world dulls. The compressor hums somewhere behind me, metal hits metal, but the rest is just static now.

I press the phone harder to my ear, oil slicking down my wrist.

Skylar. The sound of her name burns. Always has.

"You sure she's still there?" My voice isn't steady. Never is when she's involved.

"She hasn't moved since I left. Please, just—"

The line dies.

Silence.

It hits hard, heavy enough to bend my knees and settle in my chest.

"Zane?" Rainer's voice cuts through the fog, distant, like he's calling me from another world. "You good?"

No, not even fucking close.

I drag in a breath and grab a rag off the bench, smearing the grease deeper into my palms instead of wiping it away.

"I gotta deal with something," I mutter. My voice sounds wrong. Hollow. "I'll finish this when I get back."

He stares at me a second too long, eyes narrowing like he knows I'm walking straight into trouble. Then he nods. "Be careful, kid."

There's nothing careful left in me.

I toss the rag onto the bench, and push through the door.

The door swings shut behind me, and the air hits— that spring kind of chill that hides under the sunlight and waits for night to fall. I shove my hands into my pockets and start walking. The sky's soft, pale blue bleeding into dusk.

Cassie's words keep looping in my head. *"She's got nowhere."*

Skylar. Fuck.

Today's her birthday. I remembered this morning. Eighteen now, probably rolling her eyes at anyone dumb enough to make it a big deal. I told myself not to reach out, not to make things weird.

Now she's sitting outside a goddamn library with a bag and nowhere to go.

I pass the 7-Eleven on Fifth. The two closed down shopfronts and the cracked bus stop where I stayed the night. Kids yell a few streets over. The pavement's uneven. I pass the laundromat that always smells like damp clothes and burnt lint. My hands stay deep in my pockets. My jaw won't unclench.

I see her before she sees me.

Out front of the library, folded in on herself, a bag by her feet. Her head's down, forehead to her knees. From a distance, she looks small. Too small for someone who always bites first.

But it's the quiet that gets me because Skylar isn't quiet. She spits fire, starts fights she can't finish, walks into a room like she owns the oxygen. This version of her, hunched, shaking, pretending the world can't see her, hurts to fucking look at.

I tell myself to walk away. This isn't my fucking problem, it never was. But my feet don't listen. My body never fucking listens when it comes to her.

I keep my head down and walk faster. Every step makes the anger worse. The burn that sits right behind my ribs and won't fuck off.

I don't even know Skylar, not really. Just the edges. The sharp parts. The pieces that don't belong to anyone. And still, something in me won't let it go.

This isn't pity or duty, not because we came from the same foster home. This is something else. Something I don't have a name for, and I don't fucking want one.

I tell myself it's nothing. But my hands are already in fists, my jaw already locked, my heart already fucking there.

Lying to yourself gets easier the more you do it. Feeling something when you're not supposed to, that's the part that kills you.

I cross the street, lean against the pole in front of the steps, metal cold through my shirt.

"You always hang out in the cold for fun?"

Her head snaps up. Those beautiful fucking eyes find mine — glassy but still fierce. The burn's still there, buried under everything else.

"You stalking me now?" she says, voice rough.

I shrug. "Cassie told me you were here."

She huffs a bitter sound. "Did she also tell you to come play hero?"

"No one's playing anything."

"Good," she mutters. "Because I don't need saving."

"Didn't say you did."

"Then why are you here, Zane?"

I give her half a grin that doesn't reach my eyes. "Guess I'm bad at minding my own business."

She looks away, lips pressed tight. The silence that follows isn't awkward. It's heavy — the kind that has its own weight.

"Go home, Zane."

"Can't."

That earns me a glare, weak but still there. She unzips her bag, pulls out a thin sweater, and slides it on. Her hands tremble when she tugs at the sleeves.

"Are you planning to stay out here all night?" I ask.

She shrugs.

"You'll freeze."

"Then I freeze." Her voice is steady but soft and it hits harder than I expect.

The wind cuts through the street, carrying the scent of rain. Her hair whips across her face. She pushes strands aside with a shaking hand, trying to stay composed, but the cracks start to show.

I move closer. Not too close. Enough to force her eyes to mine.

"Come on," I say quietly.

"Where?"

"My place. You can crash there. One night. Nothing more."

She shakes her head. "No."

"Sky—"

"I said no. I don't need your pity."

"Not pity. It's fucking common sense."

"I'm fine. You'll probably want something in return anyway."

That one lands. I feel it hit deep, a clean shot straight to the gut.

I want to tell her I hate myself for what happened that night. That I'd take everything back if I could. That I've thought about that night more than I should, not because of what she did, but because of how wrong it was to let her believe she was nothing but an object to get off with.

But I don't say any of it.

"Yeah," I snap. "You look real fucking fine. Sitting on concrete with a bag for a pillow. Real picture of happiness."

Her jaw tightens. "You don't get to talk to me like that."

"Then stop making me watch this shit."

She looks away again, stubborn to the core.

"Cassie shouldn't have called you," she mutters. "She doesn't know when to quit."

"Yeah, she gets that from you."

Her head snaps up, glare sharp enough to flay skin. "Don't."

"What? Tell you the truth?"

"Act like this is your business."

"It is now."

Her mouth opens, pauses, then shuts again. She's out of comebacks, and that's how I can tell she's tired. The kind of tiredness that sits in your bones and won't wash off.

I drop down beside her on the cold step. "Fine. We'll sit here. I've got nothing but time."

She shoots me a look. "You're serious?"

"Dead."

The streetlights turn on, throwing yellow over cracked pavement. A bus rolls past, windows glowing, people staring out but not seeing anything.

"Why do you even care?" she asks finally, voice low, almost a whisper.

I stare at the street ahead. The truth sits heavy in my chest, begging to be said out loud.

Because you're the only person who ever made me want to be better, and that scares the fuck out of me.

But I keep it buried.

"Guess I'm just wired wrong," I say.

She exhales, shaky, the fight draining from her face.

She pulls her knees in tighter. "Go home, Zane."

I ignore her.

A car passes, headlights sliding across her features. In that quick flash, I see all of it — the red eyes, the cracked bravado, the girl who's been told she's temporary her whole damn life.

I look away before she catches me staring.

I lean back, arms folded. "You know I'll only stay here and annoy the shit out of you all night if you don't come with me."

She glares, lips pressed tight. The kind of stare that's meant to scare me off, but it does the complete fucking opposite.

A long beat passes before she exhales hard, shoulders dropping.

"Fine," she mutters, pushing herself to her feet. "One night. After that, you leave me the fuck alone."

I grin.

Skylar grabs her bags with force, rough movements hiding the shake in her hands. I catch it anyway.

"Which way?" she asks.

"This way."

"Well, lead the way," she says, tone clipped, but there's a tiny tremor at the edge of it that tells me what she refuses to. She's scared.

I shove my hands in my pockets and start walking.

We walk in silence. The town hums around us. Our steps fall out of sync, only to fall back together again, without meaning to.

Skylar keeps her head down, bag strap cutting into her shoulder. Every few seconds, she adjusts it, rolling her shoulder to take the pressure off. The streetlights hit her hair and turn it gold for half a second before the shadows take it back.

I force my hands to stay shoved in my pockets, nails carving crescents into my palms. If I pull them out, I'll reach for her. I fucking know it.

She cuts me a side glance. "Why did you come?"

I let a slow grin crawl across my face. "Wanted to see if you're still making terrible decisions without my help."

Her mouth curves, not quite a smile. "What are you, my babysitter now?"

"Babysitters get paid."

That earns a quiet huff that could almost be mistaken as a laugh.

We pass the 7-Eleven, the flicker of the half-dead sign throwing light across her face. There's a bruise forming along her temple I didn't notice before.

"Who did that?" I ask.

Her eyes narrow. "No one."

"Bullshit."

She speeds up. "Drop it."

I catch up, voice low. "You know I won't."

"You think I owe you an explanation now?"

"No. I just want to find out if I should break someone's jaw."

That gets me a glare. "You always need a reason to fight somebody?"

"Only when it's worth fighting for."

She shakes her head, muttering something under her breath. I don't push it. Not tonight.

We turn down the back street that runs along the side of the workshop.

She stops walking for a second, the strap of her bag slipping lower.

"Give me that," I say.

She shakes her head. "No."

"Skylar—"

"I said no."

She's stubborn to the fucking core. Still the only girl I've ever met who could fold a smile into a fuck-you.

The workshop comes into view, steel siding dull under the streetlight. Upstairs, a single window glows. I forgot to switch off the light this morning.

She slows down before I move over to the large door, her eyes moving over the place. "Is this it?"

"Yeah." I nod. "I crash on the top floor. It's not much, but it's warm. You hungry?"

She crosses her arms. "You always take in strays, or am I just special?"

"Only the ones who bite." I grin.

She shifts her bag again and side-eyes me. "So what's the catch?"

"No catch," I say.

"Bullshit."

I shrug. "You're not that interesting, Sky."

Her mouth quirks into almost a smile. "You sure know how to make a girl feel special, Rivera."

I open the door and gesture for her to enter. She steps through, dragging her bags through the narrow doorway. And my eyes check her out.

I can't fucking help it.

Her ass in those jeans? Fuck me.

The kind of curve that makes you forget your name. Makes your hands twitch with the memory of gripping it once, too long ago. There's exhaustion in the way she moves, but all I see is how fucking hot she is.

Too hot for me to be standing this close without doing something stupid.

I want to fucking touch her. I want to tell her she's safe. That she can sleep without looking over her shoulder. That I'll make damn sure no one ever lays a hand on her.

But I don't.

I brush past her instead, moving across the workshop, heading for the stairs as if she's not every goddamn temptation I've ever fought off.

Rainer doesn't glance up. He's elbows-deep under the hood of a beat-up Dodge, radio low, engine ticking. The place could be burning down and he wouldn't notice.

Good. Last thing I need is for him clocking the way my eyes drag over her like she's mine.

The stairs sound under my boots as I take them two at a time. I keep my hands in my pockets and my mouth shut.

Keep your fucking hands to yourself, Rivera.

She's not yours.

No matter how much she feels like it.

Chapter 14

SKYLAR

The place smells of oil and cigarettes. It's the kind of smell that latches onto the back of your throat and refuses to let go.

The apartment is small. One room divided by a worn-out couch that sags in the middle. A punching bag hangs in the corner, a stack of weights scattered near its base. A bed sits made against the far wall, low to the floor. Bare bulbs swing from the ceiling. The tiles near the kitchen sink are cracked and dirty, the grout worn thin. Shadows crawl along the edges of the room, clinging to the places the light refuses to touch.

I stand there, hands still clutched around my heavy bags, pretending I don't notice the thin film of dust on the counter or the plate sitting in the sink. Everything in this place hums with the weight of him. Rough. Unpolished. Real.

"It's not much," he says, raking a hand through his hair.

"It's fine," I lie. It's his place. His mess. His bed. At least he has something to come back to. I don't even have that.

He moves past me and heads for the kitchen bench, tossing his jacket onto a nearby chair without looking. The fridge door groans as it swings open. Inside, there's almost nothing. A few beers, a half loaf of bread. A block of cheese and a jar of mustard scraped nearly clean.

He grabs the bread and cheese, then closes the fridge door with his foot. He sets everything down on the counter, his movements steady. Unhurried.

I drop my bag beside the couch and sit. The cushion sinks under my weight; the springs creaking loud enough to cut through the quiet. The walls press closer with every breath.

He grabs a pan and sets it on the stove. The burner clicks, then catches. Butter hits the pan with a hiss, the sound cutting through the quiet.

I shift on the couch, pulling my knees in, trying not to watch the way his shoulders move beneath his shirt. He never glances my way, but every action comes off as deliberate. Controlled. There's no softness in him. He's always been hot. Infuriatingly so. Even when I hated myself for noticing.

I listen to the soft crackle of bread toasting in the pan. A moment later he flips the sandwich, checks the edges, presses it flat with the back of a spatula. My stomach clenches without warning. I hadn't realized how long I'd gone without food that didn't come from a vending machine.

I watch him slide the toast onto a plate, then turn toward me.

He doesn't ask whether I want it. Just walks over and holds out the plate, the grilled cheese still steaming. Melted cheese spills from the edges, thick and golden where it seeps through the crust. The bread's burnt around the corners.

I look up.

His eyes meet mine, and something shifts low in my stomach. That stare doesn't waver or soften. The weight of it pins me in place, dragging heat through my chest and down between my thighs. My body twitches with the urge to move, to do something, anything, before I drown under the pressure. I reach out and take the plate, using the motion to break whatever the hell is happening between us.

"Thanks," I say too quickly, dropping my gaze to the food.

The first bite scalds my tongue. I chew slowly. It's good. Greasy. Heavy. The kind of warmth that sticks to your ribs. Better than anything Dolores ever ruined in her kitchen.

Zane leans against the counter, arms folded. His eyes stay on me, steady and unreadable.

"You feed everyone who shows up at your door?" My voice catches in the middle. I hate that he hears the crack.

His brow lifts. "Why? You planning on moving in?"

"I didn't say that."

I take another bite, chewing slowly, doing anything to buy time. The bread's gone soft at the edges, but the taste still beats anything I've had in weeks.

"So," he says, "turning eighteen. Not all it's hyped up to be, huh?"

I glance up at him. "Didn't expect you to remember."

He shrugs. "Hard not to. It's the kind of day people either celebrate or run from."

"Guess I'm the second kind."

"Yeah. Me too."

I go back to chewing, the warmth of the sandwich sitting heavy in my chest. I'm too aware of him standing there, not looking away. The quiet stretches, not quite uncomfortable. Just full.

I nod toward the room. "So what's the deal with this place? Doesn't really scream long-term."

He pushes off the counter and rinses his hands under the tap. "Rainer lets me stay here. He owns the building. Said if I showed up in the garage on time and didn't trash the place, I could crash here for now."

"So... foster care, but with tools and engine grease."

"Pretty much. No caseworker though, which is a plus."

I smirk, before taking another bite. The last one. I chew slower, letting it linger.

"And the grilled cheese? That your way of saying happy birthday?"

"Don't get used to it."

"Too late. I'm already rating it five stars."

"You're not the first girl to say that to me." He gives me that bad boy grin that makes the heat sear between my thighs.

"You mean about your cooking?"

"No... about the overall experience."

I shake my head, but the smile slips through before I can stop it.

When I finish the sandwich, Zane pushes off the counter. He moves slowly, eyes on me as he crosses the room. The plate rests on my lap, my fingers curled tighter around the edge than they need to be. Something snags in my chest when his eyes find mine and hold, because there's nothing soft in them.

The way he looks at me tears through clothing and scrapes straight to skin. This isn't curiosity. This is possession. He drags his stare across my mouth, down my throat, then lower, his attention sweeping over my body as if he's already memorized every place he plans to touch. Heat builds under my skin, spills through my chest, coils tight and induces the throbbing between my thighs. I fight the urge to squirm. I don't want him to see the effect he has on me. But my body betrays me anyway. Wet. Wanting. And I hate myself for feeling every single second of it.

He takes the plate from my hands, fingers grazing mine on the way. The contact is barely anything, but it sets me off. Heat settles deep in my pussy. I feel the clench hit hard, sudden and aching, my thighs pressing together to chase the pressure. I sit pretending I'm not unraveling under the weight of his touch. Pretending he hasn't already pulled every reaction from my body without even trying.

Then he smirks. A slow, filthy twist of his mouth, smug and knowing. The kind of smirk that says he caught the way my thighs pressed together. That he knows exactly where my mind went, because he's the one who dragged it there.

He turns and walks to the sink. The water hits steel, it's loud, but that's not what keeps me frozen. His shirt pulls across his back, every muscle shifting beneath the fabric. My eyes drop lower. His ass fills out those jeans in a way that should come with a warning label. Firm. Perfect. Built to be grabbed.

What the hell was I thinking, staying here? Alone. With him. Looking the way he does. Every inch of me is on fire and he hasn't laid a hand on me. Please God, don't let me do something fucking stupid.

He shuts off the tap and grabs a towel from the bench, wiping his hands. The fabric's rough and stained, the kind of thing that's been used too many times and washed too few. He doesn't rush. Doesn't look at me until he's done.

"I've got shit to finish in the workshop," he says. "I'll be back later." He nods toward a door on the left. "Shower's through there." His eyes drag across the room, landing on the mattress. "You can take the bed."

"I'm fine on the couch."

His jaw flexes. "It wasn't a fucking suggestion, Sky."

"Why do you care where I sleep?"

"Because that couch will fuck your back up worse than I ever could."

My breath stutters, but I can't pull my eyes off him. I shift without meaning to.

His eyes watch me.

Tracking the way my chest lifts. The way I swallow like it might kill me.

Every inch of me burns. I try to mask it, force my body still, but the damage is already done.

I hold his stare. "Then take the bed."

"I don't need it," he says.

"You think I do?"

He steps forward. Not enough to touch me, but enough that I feel it. That shift in the air, the heat that spikes between us.

"You're exhausted," he says. "Don't pretend you're not."

"I'm not pretending anything."

His jaw ticks, and I can see that I'm getting to him.

"Just take the fucking bed, Skylar."

He holds the stare for one breath too long. Before turning and walking out the door.

The mattress dips beneath me as I sit cross-legged on top of the blanket, pages of math homework stretched out across my thighs. Calculus. Useless numbers swimming in and out of focus. What the hell is the point of solving X when I can't solve where I'll be sleeping tomorrow night? I've got no address. No plan. School ends, and then what the fuck do I do?

My thoughts splinter. Algebra fades. The lines on the page blur. I haven't solved a single problem in fifteen minutes. Maybe longer. Not since Zane stepped into the shower and took every rational thought with him.

I shouldn't be thinking about him.

But I am.

Zane. Naked under that stream. Hands dragging through his hair. Head tipped back. Water pouring over every inch of him. Soap gliding over the ridges of his stomach. Steam curling around his chest. His skin slick, veins flexing with every movement. I picture it all. My lips part, and I don't realize it until I drag my teeth across the bottom one.

I press my thighs together; the ache blooms fast.

The water stops.

I should pretend I'm asleep when he comes out here.

But the bed smells too much of him. It's in the pillow, in the blanket. That grease and grit smell that clings to his skin after a full day under the hood of some busted engine. It crawls under my skin and settles there. And because of that, I can't fucking focus.

All I want is to bury my face in his pillow and breathe him in until my head stops spinning. Until something inside me quiets and I remember who the fuck I was before he cracked something open in me.

But I can't. If I do that, I might not come up for air.

This is totally a fucked-up situation, and I've got no clue what the hell I'm doing here. My body's a mess of want and warning signs. I can't tell if I should bolt for the door or curl deeper into these sheets and lose myself in the way they still smell of him.

Zane gave me a place to land tonight, and yeah, I'm grateful. I am. But it doesn't fix shit. Tomorrow, I'm back in freefall.

And Cassie... fuck, Cassie should've stayed out of it. She should've kept her damn mouth shut.

She had no fucking right to go behind my back. To call Zane. Acting like I'm too broken to handle my own mess as if I need saving.

How the hell did she even get his number? Jesus.

My eyes drop back to the numbers on the page. I stare until they blur, until my mind stops spinning. I tell myself to focus.

Zane walks out, dragging a hand through his damp hair, water still tracking down his chest. Grey sweatpants hang low on his hips, clinging to him in all the worst ways. His shoulders roll loose, that slow, dangerous swagger stamped into every inch of him. Bad boy without trying. Trouble without effort.

And then I see it.

The ink on his body. The way it twists down from one shoulder, sliding over the curve of his chest, black against golden skin.

My eyes follow it before I can stop them. I wonder if it's new or if it's always been there. All I know is I can't stop looking.

He moves into the kitchen, and I track every step, pulse climbing with every shift of muscle under his skin. He grabs a glass from the sink and fills it with water from the tap. His movements are slow and unhurried. He has no idea of the effect he has on me seeing him like this. Or maybe the asshole fucking does. Maybe he always has.

He's beautiful in the worst way. The kind of beautiful that carves you open from the inside out. That leaves bruises in places no one else can see. He smells of danger and something darker. Something that pulls even when you know better. The beautiful you fall into with no warning and no way out.

A girl could lose herself in him without even meaning to. And I'm already halfway there.

Zane drinks, water dripping from his fingers. He tips the glass upside down on the sink, then turns. His eyes catch mine from across the room, and I feel it everywhere.

That stare drags. It doesn't skim. It lands. Lingers. Tracks over my face, down my neck, until it hits my chest. My tank top is too tight, too thin, doing nothing to hide how hard my nipples have gone under the fabric. His eyes don't move. Just stares for one heartbeat too long before moving across the room.

I try to breathe through it, but it's useless. My mouth has gone dry. My skin burns. Every nerve hums under the weight of him. And through it all, one truth keeps pulsing in my head. I am so fucked.

Zane crosses the room, the floorboards creaking under his bare feet. He opens the cupboard on the back wall, reaches in, and pulls out a spare pillow. Every inch of him is coiled with that restless energy he wears like a second skin.

He tosses the pillow onto the couch, then turns and walks back over, dropping down onto it. One arm hooks lazily over the backrest; the other drapes across his stomach. His legs spread wide. His head tips back, eyes slipping closed. He's a storm pretending to be still. But every part of him thrums with tension. Ready to break.

The room falls quiet. Only the soft hum of the fridge breaks the silence, paired with the slow, rhythmic tick of the clock by the window. Every second drags, stretched thin by the weight in the air. Even my breathing sounds too loud, too obvious, as if it might give me away.

Zane shifts, the couch groaning beneath him as he adjusts. His body moves slowly, weighed down by the kind of exhaustion that seeps into your bones.

"Are you planning to stay up all night?" His voice cuts through the silence. A breath slips out of him. It's almost a sigh, like the day's finally caught up to him and there's no fight left to hold it back.

I gather up the papers and set them on the floor. My hand finds the old lamp beside the bed. With one click, the light vanishes, throwing the room into shadows.

I lower myself onto the mattress, the springs groaning beneath my weight. The blanket comes next. I drag it up and clutch it close, his scent bleeding into my skin. It crowds my lungs and fogs my head, curling around every thought until my chest starts to ache.

I glance across the room. His silhouette shifts on the couch. He's lying down now, one arm tucked behind his head. The other resting across his stomach. I can't tell whether his eyes are closed or if he's watching me the way I'm watching him. But my skin burns at the thought of it.

God help me if he says my name right now, because I'm on the verge of doing something stupid.

Chapter 15

ZANE

Morning slips through the window, slicing pale stripes across the ceiling. Dust drifts in the light, slow and aimless, the only thing moving in the room. The couch digs into my ribs, springs pressing into skin, and my neck's fucked from the way I passed out. I should move, but I don't. Not yet. The air still holds her scent—warm, faintly sweet, threaded through the quiet.

She's still here.

Skylar. Sprawled across my mattress, curled into herself, one leg bare where the blanket is tangled low around her thigh. Her light brown hair's a fucking mess, wild across my pillow, strands catching the morning light in golds and chestnuts. She's still out cold, breaths soft, lips parted. And for once, I don't have to pretend I'm not watching her.

My eyes catch on that scar. Just above her brow. Small, almost nothing, unless you're looking. And I was. On that rooftop, pretending I didn't give a shit when every part of me wanted to ask her how she got it. Wanted to know what hurt her. Who?

But I held back because I didn't want her to see how much space she'd already taken up in my chest.

Even now, it fucks with me. That tiny flaw pulling at something buried deep, something I don't have a name for. The part of me that wants to trace that scar with my thumb. The part that wants to kiss it.

She's not all gloss and bullshit. She doesn't mask the things she's been through or try to pretty them up for anyone else. She doesn't cake on fake smiles or hide behind layers of make-up pretending she's never been touched by the world. She wears it all. Quiet. Unapologetic. Real.

And fuck, that's what makes her perfect.

I told myself last night it'd be gone. After I dragged my fucked-up tired body into the shower and wrapped my hand around my cock, jerking off to the memory of her scent, her mouth on me up on that rooftop.

I swore that'd be enough. That getting off would clear her out of my fucking system. But fuck, that was a lie.

I came fast, and this morning I'm still hard. Still strung tight. That same brutal want's right there, clawing under my skin, begging to be fed.

She fucking undoes me. Every look, every breath, every fucking inch of her makes me forget who I am. This girl could ruin me without even trying... and the worst part... I want her to.

I push up from the couch before she opens those eyes and catches me staring. My steps are slow as I walk barefoot to the kitchen, the floor cold beneath me. I fill the kettle and flip it on. One of the few things I've bought in some half-assed attempt to make this place a home. It still feels empty.

The cold bites at my skin.

I should throw on a shirt. A hoodie. But I don't. The cold is easier to deal with than the heat pulsing low in my gut. It's better than the hard cock I've been trying to ignore since I opened my eyes.

I reach into the cupboard and pull out two chipped mugs. They're mismatched and rough around the edges, same as everything else in this place.

Behind me, I feel it... that shift in the air. That quiet pause that says she's awake.

I don't turn around.

"You own any shirts?" Her voice is rough from sleep, but still edged with that attitude that I love.

I smirk at the counter. "Why? You jealous the couch got more action than you did?"

"Please. I've seen stray dogs with better manners."

I glance over my shoulder, just in time to catch her eyes dragging over my body before she snaps them away.

"You sure about that?" I ask with a smirk on my face. "Because you've been staring at me for a solid three seconds."

She snorts. "I was checking for lice."

I grin. "Nah, you were checking out the goods. Don't worry. It happens a lot."

She rolls her eyes so hard I swear I hear it.

"Jesus. Your ego must need its own fucking postcode."

The kettle clicks off. I pour the coffees and grab hers from the counter, carrying it over without asking if she wants one. Pure hospitality, right? Or maybe it's just that doing shit for her doesn't feel as fucked as it should. Not that I'd ever tell her that. She'd never let me live it down.

Skylar sits up in the bed, legs folding beneath her, hair messy and falling into her face. She takes the mug from my hand without looking at me, fingers curling tight around the ceramic.

While her eyes are on the coffee, mine are somewhere they shouldn't be.

Her strap slips off her shoulder, turning skin into temptation and cotton into a fucking weapon. Her nipples are hard against the fabric, twin triggers wired straight to my cock.

Fucking hell.

I shift my weight, jaw tight, trying to think about anything else. Barbed wire. Broken teeth. But she's sitting there in my bed, wrapped in sleep and heat and everything I shouldn't want, and my cock's already got its own fucking plans.

I turn back to my cup, eyes on the counter, trying not to look at her. I tell myself she's just passing through, just some fucked-up detour I got dragged into. I repeat it like a fucking prayer. That she doesn't matter. But my body's calling bullshit on that, because every fucked-up part of me is tuned to her.

The mattress creaks behind me. I grab my coffee from the counter, turn around, and lean back against it.

She pushes the blankets down and swings her legs over the side of the bed. Miles of fucking skin, smooth and bare. My eyes drop without permission. Those long legs, that make a man forget how to breathe. The kind of legs you want around your waist, around your throat that could squeeze the fucking life out of me.

My eyes track every step as she crosses the room, hips swaying just enough to make it hurt. She moves to the wooden table I dragged in off the curb last week and sets her coffee cup down.

She grabs my hoodie from the back of the chair.

My fucking hoodie.

Pulls it on without asking, the hem brushing her thighs, sleeves hanging past her fingertips like she's trying to hide inside it. She tugs the hood up and burrows in, disappears into it as if it belongs to her.

I don't know why the fuck seeing her in it hits me the way it does.

But it does. Hard. Right in that place I pretend doesn't exist.

She sits down and picks up her coffee, both palms wrapped around the cup like she needs the warmth. She brings it to her mouth, takes a slow sip, eyes on nothing.

We sit in silence for a few minutes. It's thick, loaded, crawling with shit I can't quite name.

If she were anyone else, I'd have already made a move. I would've had her up against the wall, her moans in my mouth and her legs around my waist.

But she isn't just anyone.

She scares the shit out of me. Not because she's mouthy and hard to read, but because she makes me feel, and I spent my whole life not feeling a fucking thing.

And I don't know what the fuck to do with that.

"Thanks for the bed," she says finally.

"Didn't figure you'd want the floor."

She snorts, but it's short-lived. Her gaze flicks across the room, landing on the mess, the chaos I call home.

"This place... it's not what I pictured."

I arch a brow. "Yeah? What did you picture?"

She takes a slow sip from her mug, eyes skating over the couch, the counter, the stained wall near the door.

"I don't know. Something filthier. More empty bottles, less furniture. Maybe a thong hanging off a ceiling fan. A pile of lace and bad decisions on the floor."

I huff out a breath through a crooked grin. "Harsh assessment."

She meets my gaze, steady. "Tell me I'm wrong."

"Well, you're the first chick that's been here."

Her brows lift. "Bullshit."

"Swear on my shitty furniture."

She studies me for a second, searching for the lie. "Guess that explains why the place doesn't reek of cheap perfume and regret."

I can't help it. My mouth curves. "Give it time."

She rolls her eyes and brings the mug to her lips, hiding the smirk she doesn't want me to see.

And fuck, it's almost a smile.

I finish my coffee in one long swallow and set the mug down. Then I pull on my jeans, drag on my boots, and reach for my shirt.

I pause when I feel her eyes on me.

I turn slowly and catch her watching.

Her eyes drop fast, pretending she wasn't just checking me out.

She can hide her eyes all she wants, but I know what I saw. And fuck, I like that she was checking me out more than I should.

"You need somewhere to crash, this place will do," I say, keeping my voice as casual as I can. "Just until you get your shit sorted."

Her brow lifts, that teasing glint back in her eyes. "Are you offering me a home, Zane?"

I scoff, tugging my shirt over my head. "Don't get misty-eyed. You snore, you're gone."

She smiles and for a second, I forget what fucking day it is.

"I mean it," I say, "You can stay as long as you need."

She nods, and I move for the door. Just before I step out, I glance back over my shoulder.

"But don't burn the place down."

Her smile tilts. "No promises."

I shut the door behind me and take the stairs fast, feet heavy, breath tighter than it should be. The air shifts as I step into the workshop. It's quiet, too quiet. Rainer's not even in yet.

I'm never here this early. But I couldn't stay up there. Not with her in my hoodie, looking at me like I'm something worth trusting.

I needed to get out before I did something fucking reckless. The kind of mistake I'd taste on her mouth and feel in my bones.

I drag a hand through my hair, jaw clenched, muttering curses under my breath, every one of them aimed at myself.

I'm in trouble. Real fucking trouble. And every part of me knows it.

And I just told her to stay with no fucking clue what that's going to do to me.

Fuck me. What the hell was I thinking?

· • • ● ● • ● ● • • ·

My body moves on autopilot, hands buried in grease and busted engine parts, but my mind is still stuck in that apartment, on her.

Skylar.

I told myself not to look when she left for school. But I saw her go.

One bag slung over her shoulder. The school one. Which means the other one with all her shit is still upstairs.

Every time I spoke to Rainer, she was the only thing on my mind. My focus was fucking shot, and I knew it. I wasn't present, not with the tools in my hands or the job in front of me.

Rainer noticed, I know he did. He saw her leave this morning. Watched her walk out while I stood there, pretending I wasn't watching too.

I waited for him to say something. To call me out and remind me that hook-ups aren't supposed to be crashing in the room he gave me.

But he didn't say a fucking word. Just wiped his hands and slid back under the old Chevy he dragged into the workshop this morning.

He slides out from under the car, grease streaked up his forearm, a rag already in hand. The concrete under him is stained from years of engines bleeding out.

"Give me a hand with this," he says, voice rough from age or smoke or both.

I move toward him.

The metal frame is rusted to shit, but there's a curve to it. That kind of old-school shape that's more muscle than shine.

"Who owns it?" I ask, running my hand along the edge. "It's rough, but it's got that vintage thing going on. The kind I've always had a soft spot for."

He snorts under his breath. "This old guy was cleaning out his shed. Said it hadn't been touched in over twenty years. I gave him a hundred bucks and towed it in this morning."

"You planning to flip it?"

He wipes his hands and shrugs. "Nope. Do you want it?"

I don't even think. "Yeah."

Rainer nods, as if he knew I'd say that. "Keep it here if you want. Tinker with it in your spare time."

Most people see me as a fuck-up first and never look past it. But Rainer never has. He doesn't treat me as some fucked-up foster kid. He just sees me. And for once, it feels like I'm not being measured against all the shit I came from.

I brush my hands off on my jeans and hold out a hand. "Appreciate it."

Rainer grips it and gives a solid handshake.

He moves across the workshop and grabs his water bottle from the bench. Takes a long drink, then caps the lid.

"The girl who left this morning. She yours?"

The word sticks. "Yours."

The thought hits hard. Too hard but I shake it off before it settles.

"Nah," I say, clearing my throat. "Just helping out a friend."

He doesn't say anything, just waits. Steady and patient, giving me room to either speak or walk away.

"Her name's Skylar," I say eventually. "She aged out yesterday. Foster home kicked her out." I rub a hand over the back of my neck. "I told her she could crash with me just for a bit. Until she gets her shit together."

Rainer watches me for a beat. Then he nods once. "That's fine."

We work in silence, both of us buried in our own tasks. Rainer sticks to the Chevy, grumbling under his breath about bolts that won't budge. I'm at the bench, stripping down a busted alternator, hands deep in grease.

By the time I drag myself up the stairs for lunch, my shoulders ache and my stomach's already growling. I haven't eaten anything, and it's catching up to me.

I always eat the same thing. Grilled cheese, cheap bread, whatever slices of cheese are left in the fridge. The same one I made for Skylar yesterday.

I shove open the apartment door, ready to zone out for ten minutes.

Then I stop.

The apartment is clean.

Not just clean. Fucking spotless.

The coffee table's wiped down. The dishes I left in the sink are washed, dried, and stacked with military precision. The ratty throw blanket I used last night, the one I left half off the couch, is now folded tight over the armrest. My boots are lined up by the door, straight and even, which is already weird as shit.

The floor's been swept. The counter's been wiped down. The garbage is gone. She even scrubbed the grime off the stovetop, the same shit I've ignored for weeks.

I blink.

She's not here, but the air still holds her. That soft, sweet scent I caught last night. The one that stuck in my head and hasn't let go since.

I step inside. The space feels quieter somehow, not in a hollow way, but settled. Warmer. Lived-in. Touched by someone who gave a shit. Someone who didn't have to, but still took the time anyway.

There's a note on the kitchen counter. Torn paper, edges uneven, the corner curled up slightly, looped writing in black ink.

You live like a raccoon. You're welcome.

I stare at it for a long time.

Then I laugh.

I fold the note slowly, pressing the crease hard with my thumb. I slide it into my wallet and tuck it behind the card I never use.

I close the wallet shut and shove it back into my pocket, then move to the stove to make lunch.

Chapter 16

SKYLAR

The sun hangs low, throwing gold across the stairwell by the time I reach the top step.

Below, metal clangs, tools scrape, along with a muttered curse I can't quite make out.

I tell myself not to turn. Not to glance at him. But it's Zane. And somehow, he's the one I keep searching for without meaning to.

He looks happy under the hood of some beat-up car, sleeves shoved past his elbows, arms deep in the guts of the engine. Grease smears the inside of his forearm, a dark mark against skin that always runs too hot.

His mouth moves, lips forming curses I can't hear from here, probably aimed at a bolt that won't budge or a hose that refuses to line up. Yet his movements stay calm, steady, and focused. Rooted in something that holds. He looks happy.

I turn back to the door before he catches me staring. My fingers wrap around the handle, and I slip inside. The door clicking shut behind me.

I drop my bag at the end of the bed and stand still for a second, frozen in the quiet. I let out a breath I swear I've been holding since I woke up. The air leaves my chest slow and shaky, too heavy to carry any longer.

This isn't home. It's worn-down floorboards and second-hand furniture. A borrowed place with borrowed warmth. A just-for-now.

But, fuck, it's something.

And right now, that's more than I had yesterday.

I close my eyes and let the stillness settle. No one watching, waiting, or pressing.

For once, I don't have to be anything but me.

Cassie was already waiting out the front of the school this morning, arms folded tight across her chest, foot tapping like she'd been rehearsing the lecture all night. Her face said everything before she opened her mouth.

She was pissed.

Pissed I'd ignored every single one of her texts. Let my phone blow up for hours last night and never once picked it up. She had no idea where I was, and that alone would've been enough to set her off.

She gave the same energy back. Loud, relentless, not giving a shit who heard. She told me I was reckless, that I shut people out when shit gets hard, that I never let anyone help until everything's already gone to hell.

I tried to tell her she had no right to make that call or to go to Zane behind my back. But somewhere between all the shouting, I also told her thank you.

Because as much as I wanted to be angry, I knew the truth. She did it because she cares. Even if her brand of loyalty comes armed with fireworks and a middle finger.

I grab my homework from my bag, mostly out of boredom, and carry the pile to the kitchen table. My books thud against the wood as they drop. The table shifts under the weight, one leg shorter than the others, the whole thing leaning toward the wall as if trying to escape.

I sink into the uneven chair, spine aching, and start working through the pile. Math, mostly. Numbers that blur if I stare too long.

Time slips. The light changes through the window, stretching across the table until it hits the edge of my paper. Sheets are scattered everywhere, my pen smudging across the margin.

I reach for my phone and fire off a text to Cassie.

Skylar: WTF is question 9 even asking? did she say we had to do all of it?

Cassie replies within seconds.

Cassie: Absolutely not the point right now.

Cassie: Are you staring at Mr tall, dark and angry?

Cassie: Tell me he doesn't always walk around shirtless because that should be illegal.

I stare at the screen, thumb hovering.

Then I lock the phone and set the screen face down on the table.

Nope. No fucking way am I touching that.

I let out a sigh and pick my phone back up. I unlock it again, thumb hesitating for half a second before I open the job listings.

I scroll slowly.

Barista. Waitress. Shelf stacker. Anything with a pay check to keep me from being someone else's responsibility.

I need my own money. My own space, my own way out.

Zane didn't ask for this. And I don't want to be another mess he has to clean up.

The door swings open, and Zane strolls in with that slow, loose-hipped walk that shouldn't make my chest tight but it fucking does. Grease smudged on his jaw. T-shirt clinging to his shoulders like it's part of his skin. Jeans riding low on his hips.

He doesn't say shit as he walks to the table, and drops a crumpled brown bag beside my notebook. He grabs two forks from the drawer.

I keep my head down. But every damn step, every shift in the air, pulls at me. And fuck, I hate being this fucking aware of him.

He comes back over and drops into the chair opposite mine and pulls two containers out of the bag. Noodles. The greasy hot kind. The smell of soy and garlic hits hard. He puts one container in front of me on top of my papers.

"Eat," he mutters finally.

"You bringing me dinner now?" I mutter, phone still in my hand.

"Didn't do it for you. I was just tired of hearing your stomach bitch louder than you do."

I finally glance up. His eyes are already on mine, his arm stretched out, holding a fork towards me. Mouth twitching like he's enjoying himself way too much.

"You didn't have to spend money on me."

His gaze drops to my mouth before dragging slowly back up to my eyes. "Relax. I didn't pay."

I hesitate, before putting my phone back down on the table.

"Guy at the shop owed me a favor. Don't ask."

"Legal favor?" My eyes narrow.

He shrugs with a grin slowly spreading across his mouth. "Define legal."

Our fingers brush as I take the fork. Heat jumps straight to my throat. I hate the way he doesn't even have to try and I'm already short circuiting.

For a while, we eat in silence. The quiet isn't awkward. It never is with him.

My eyes flick up, and I catch him watching me.

Shit.

I shove a forkful of noodles into my mouth, chew too fast, and stare back down at my homework, pretending question six is the most fascinating thing I've ever seen. The silence stretches until I can feel it scrape against my skin.

"You finished that?" he asks, nodding toward the shitty old book written by some dead guy we are forced to read because it is a "classic".

"Nah... Don't have to. It's not due till the end of the week."

"Still, slacking I see."

I arch a brow, lift my gaze slow. "Didn't know you cared about my grades."

"I don't. Just didn't picture you the type to leave things half done." His mouth curves, lazy and smug. "Thought you'd be the kind who finishes what she starts."

Heat coils low in my gut, hating that his words sound filthy even when they aren't.

"Not everything's worth finishing," I say, the edge in my voice sharper than I intend.

"Guess that depends on what you're starting," he says, leaning back in the chair.

The air shifts. Thick. Charged. Neither of us moves.

I force myself to look back at my notebook, even though the words blur on the page. My pulse doesn't settle. His eyes are still on me—I can feel them, tracing, testing, daring.

And fuck, I hate how much I want him to keep looking.

The noodles go cold in their containers, but neither of us cares. I push mine around absently, swirling the soy-stained strands into a lazy spiral.

I glance up and catch him staring at me. Not in a weird way. Just... observing.

"What?" I mutter.

He shrugs again, the corner of his mouth lifting. "Nothing. You've got sauce on your chin."

I swipe at it and glare at him when he grins.

"I want to show you something I found when I moved in," he says, pushing his barely eaten noodles away, then he stands.

"Let me guess. This is the part where you tell me it isn't sketchy, and I wind up in a true crime documentary?"

"It's on the roof."

I blink. "Yeah, no thanks. Last time we were on a roof together, I sucked your dick. I'm not doing that again."

He freezes for a beat, head half turned as if he didn't expect me to say that out loud.

"Noted," he says, turning his gaze back to me. "Fucking disappointed... but no. That's not what I want to show you."

I stare at him. He holds my gaze without flinching.

Goddamn. Those fucking eyes. The ones that see through every defense I pretend to have. He waits. Calm and steady. Already so sure I'll say yes.

I let out a sharp breath, shove my chair back, and snatch my jacket off the end of the bed.

"Fine. But if I fall and die, I'm haunting you."

His mouth lifts at one corner, smug as sin. "Fair enough."

His eyes drop to my chest, then trail down over my short skirt. Heat coils in the pit of my stomach. He knows exactly what he's doing.

"Wouldn't be the worst thing," he says. "I could use a ghost with legs like yours."

"Jesus, you're a pervert."

He shrugs, no shame. "Never said I wasn't."

I shoot him a glare as I pass him and head for the door. I don't even know if we're meant to take the stairs or go out the window or through some fucked-up secret passage he found, Narnia-style, behind a wall panel. None of that matters. I can't stay in that room with him staring at me the way he is. The kind of stare that peels me open and destroys every wall I spent years learning how to build. Because no matter how many times I swear I won't fold, no matter how fucking hard I fight to keep my guard up, Zane always finds a way through.

Every single fucking time.

I move down the steps, the thud of my shoes echoing in the quiet workshop. There's that pull in my spine again that tells me he's watching.

Halfway down, I stop and glance over my shoulder.

"Am I going the right way?"

His eyes drag up slow. Not rushed. Not even pretending to hide the fact that he was staring at my ass.

"Were you—" I narrow my eyes. "Were you checking out my ass?"

Zane smirks. "If you're gonna wear a skirt that short, you can't be mad when someone appreciates the view."

Heat prickles across my chest. I turn back, gripping the rail tighter. "Are you always this cocky, or is this special performance just for me?"

"Sweetheart, you bring it out in me."

I move down another step, like putting space between us might save me from the heat crawling up my spine.

"You're such a dick," I mutter, gripping the railing until my knuckles turn white.

His laugh follows me down the steps.

"You say that like it's news."

"So," I bite out. "Which way? Or are we just gonna stand here while you eye-fuck me to death?"

He brushes past me, his shoulder grazing mine. I catch the smell of him and it fucks with my head.

"Head to the front door," he says over his shoulder. "Metal steps are to the right. Hope you're not afraid of heights."

Zane flicks on the workshop lights. The overheads buzzing to life with a low electric hum. The room spills into a warm amber glow, casting shadows against the far wall where a metal ladder climbs straight through a square cut-out in the ceiling.

I spot it immediately.

No fucking way I'm going first and giving him a front-row seat to my ass.

He strides to the base of the ladder and stops, turning slightly toward me. One hand curls around the rail. He waits.

"It's steep," he says. "I'll help you up."

"I'm not helpless. And I'm not giving you a full view of my ass on a silver platter so you can jerk off to it later."

He barks out a laugh, head dropping back for a second before he looks at me, grin crooked. "Sky, if I was gonna do that, I wouldn't need the view. Your ass has been living rent-free in my head for weeks."

"Asshole," I mutter.

He plants a foot on the rung and glances over his shoulder. "But if you want an excuse to stare at my ass, Sky, all you had to do is ask."

Sky.

He says it like it's his to use.

Not the way Cassie does, where she tosses it into conversations without a second thought. This is different. This is drawn out in a way that curls around my ribs and squeezes.

Fuck him.

He's almost through the hatch when I blink, heart hammering way harder than it should. I set my foot on the first rung and start climbing after him. My palms sting where I grip the metal, breath catching when I reach the top.

His hand shoots down. Fingers curling around mine, slipping slightly before they catch and hold. He hauls me up, easy, as if I weigh nothing. The second my feet hit the roof, I suck in a breath.

This is not what I expected at all.

The roof's pitched, slanted at just enough of an angle to make my steps careful. Tin roof beneath my shoes. It's quiet, dark, nothing but moonlight bleeding down over us.

Zane jerks his chin. "Come on, it's over here."

I follow him, taking my time, careful not to slip.

I look up when his steps falter, and he turns back towards me. He holds out his hand to me again. "You'll slide in those shoes," he says, eyes flicking down.

I hesitate for a second before sliding my hand into his. Last time, it was quick. I was too distracted making sure I didn't fall to notice anything else. But this...

This is different. This time when I touch his hand, I feel everything.

The rough edges of his skin. The callouses built from hours in the workshop, the way he drags his thumb across the back of my hand.

"This spot's better," he mutters, carefully guiding me toward the section where the roof levels out.

When we reach the spot, he drops my hand and lowers himself onto the roof, legs stretched out in front.

But the second his skin leaves mine, I fucking notice the change. I stand in place for a beat, trying to shake the reaction off, pretending this doesn't matter, before I sit beside him.

My knees brush his for a second too long before I shift back.

Even so, my heart's thumping. From the climb. From his touch... from whatever the fuck this is turning into. But his knee nudges mine again. This time, he doesn't move away. Neither do I.

We don't speak. We simply breathe. Moonlight drips over the rooftops in silver puddles. The town looks asleep. Porch lights glow softly in the dark. Streetlights flicker across the town. The world is a little quieter up here. A little farther away. A little less cruel.

Zane shifts beside me.

I turn my head, and the flick of his lighter cuts through the dark. It clicks once, twice, before the flame flares to life, catching on the end of a joint. The ember glows orange, bright against the line of his jaw and the mess of his hair. He is trouble dressed in shadows, that stupid hot mouth tugged into a smirk as if he already knows I'll take whatever he gives me.

He drags in a slow, cocky as fuck breath. Eyes half-closed, chest rising with that first hit, as though the smoke is the only thing keeping him breathing. He exhales, thick smoke drifting up into the night, and holds the joint out towards me without a word.

His fingers graze mine as I take it from him. Slow. Intentional. A tease.

Zane lies back on the roof, arms folded behind his head, his shirt riding up enough to expose a sliver of skin and an old scar slicing across his hip. My eyes catch both. And suddenly, my mouth's dry and everything inside me is burning.

I bring the joint to my lips and inhale deeply. The burn trails down my throat, heat curling low in my stomach.

I pass it back. Our fingers brush. He holds on a second too long. Heat sparks in the space between us. My skin hums, every nerve awake and aching for more.

I lie beside him, my shoulder brushing his. The stars burn above us, but all I sense is him. The shift of his arm — the heat he left on my skin. One fucking touch and my whole body's rewired, every breath out of rhythm. He's chaos in a slow burn, the kind of fuck-up your body aches for even when your head's screaming no. And I'm already too far gone to pretend I'm not falling.

The world quiets. For the first time in days, the silence doesn't choke. It seeps into my bones, and finally... finally I can fucking breathe.

Zane takes another hit, the tip flaring red as he drags in deep. Smoke curls from his lips as he exhales, then holds the joint out without a word.

We fall into a rhythm. Passing it back and forth, no rush, no pressure, just silence.

The sharp edges of everything melt, bleeding into each other until nothing feels real. The stars smear into silver streaks above us, dancing across the sky that won't stay still. They sway and breathe and blur. My limbs go heavy, loosening them until I'm nothing but heat and haze, stretched out beside Zane with no will to move. There's no need to. I could stay here forever and forget the world ever hurt me.

When Zane holds out the joint again, I lift my hand, palm up. "I'm good."

He nods once, then takes one last hit before snuffing it out between his fingers

He exhales slowly. "Rainer got me a car today."

I turn my head toward him. "A car?"

He nods. "Nothing fancy. Rusted to shit. But it's mine."

There's something in the way he says it that guts me. Like it's no big deal. Just another step forward. A car. Freedom. Proof he's clawing his way out of the wreckage and building something that almost resembles a life.

Meanwhile, I'm stuck in the same busted loop. No fucking clue where I'm going. No plan. A borrowed roof and a string of bruises I keep hidden under a fake smile. We both came out of the same system, both dragged through the same shit. But he's moving. Evolving. While I'm still spinning my wheels in the mud.

Maybe that's what fucks me up the most. He's not stuck in the mess anymore, like I still am. I need to figure out a way to pull myself out, get some kind of plan together before the weight of it buries me.

"That's good, Zane," I say. "Are you related to him or something?"

Zane shifts onto his side, propping himself up on one elbow. "Nah. He's some guy who looks out for me, I guess. I was digging through the skip out the side of the workshop, trying to find shit I could clean up and sell. Old tools, scrap metal, whatever I could get my hands on. He came out, stood there watching me. I thought I was fucked. Figured he was gonna call the cops, maybe come out swinging. Figured that was it. That I'd have another night in a holding cell... another mark on my record.

I blink, trying to picture that version of him. "He didn't though."

Zane shakes his head. "Nah. He asked if I'd eaten. Took me inside, gave me a sandwich, asked if I wanted to sweep the floor. Said if I didn't steal anything, I could keep coming back."

A gust of wind cuts across the rooftop. It lifts the edge of my skirt and I reach down fast, pressing it back to my thighs. But not fast enough. Zane's gaze dips, catches on the movement, tracks across the tops of my leg slowly before he looks away.

I glance over at him. "He sounds decent."

"Yeah, he is. He doesn't ask questions and most of all he doesn't treat me like a lost cause. That's fucking rare." Zane pauses again, dragging a hand through his hair. "Rainer lost his wife years ago. He has no kids or any family. There's just him and that workshop. It's the only thing he's got."

"You're lucky you found someone who gave a shit."

Zane doesn't answer at first. His fingers toy with the tin, his nails scratching over it like he's thinking too hard. "I didn't find him," he says. "He found me."

Zane turns his head, eyes finding mine through the dark. There's something quieter in him now. Something focused. Every part of him tuned in, as if the rest of the world has dropped away.

"I've wanted to ask you..." His voice is low. "That scar. The one above your eyebrow. How'd it happen?"

I wasn't expecting that. No one ever asks. Most people glance away, pretend it's not there. They smile, talk over it, act like if they ignore the scar, they won't have to ask what made it.

But not Zane. He just puts it out there.

The breath I take feels sharp in my chest.

"When I was seven, my mother threw a beer bottle at me. I told her I was hungry."

Zane's jaw ticks. His knuckles curl against the tin.

"She was drunk," I add, not to excuse it but because it's the only explanation I've ever had. "Missed the wall. Got me instead."

I remember the crack of the bottle. The way it spun through the air, catching the light before it shattered against my face. The sting hit first. Then the heat. Blood spilling fast, hot, into my lashes until I couldn't see. It burned my eyes, but I didn't cry. Not then. Not in front of her because I knew it would piss her off even more. I just stood there, stunned, and dinner was still out of reach.

"Split my skin open," I finally say. "There was blood everywhere. I remember the floor being red."

"I figured it wasn't from something small," he says, voice low. "But that... fuck."

"Yeah." I nod.

A beat passes before he speaks.

"She ever get done for it?" His voice is steady, but there's something buried under it. The kind of anger that sits in your gut when you hear something you can't unhear.

"Nah," I say, shaking my head. "No one ever knew. When people asked, she said I fell off my bike." I pause, eyes flicking to his face before dragging back up to the sky. "I didn't even own a fucking bike."

"Fuck," he mutters.

"Yeah... You know I used to think if I stayed quiet, kept my head down, it would get better." I laugh, but there's no humor in it. "Turns out silence just makes it easier for people to pretend nothing's wrong."

"Have you ever told anyone?" he asks.

"No," I say. "What's the point?" I shift my head and look at him again. "No one wants the broken kid with the scar and the fucked-up story."

"Maybe they're just not the right people," he says.

Zane clears his throat. "I got my first scar stealing a can of ravioli."

That pulls my gaze back to him. "You're kidding."

He shakes his head, a grin tugging at the corner of his mouth. "Owner had this ancient mutt out back. It looked half-dead, all ribs and attitude. Bit my arm straight through my hoodie. Little fucker was faster than I thought."

"What kind of dog was it?"

"A fucking Hellhound. I swear on it."

My laugh bursts out before I can stop it. The sound is rough, rusty from disuse, but it's real. The kind that burns through your chest because you didn't know how badly you needed it until it was there.

When I glance over at him, he's smiling. A real one. Not that cocky half-grin he throws around when he's being a smartass or trying to charm his way into someone's pants. This one's softer. It turns my insides to fucking mush. It makes him look younger... almost innocent. But there's nothing innocent about the way I ache just looking at him. He's so fucking beautiful it hurts, and the worst part is he doesn't know what that smile does to me.

"What happened after?" I ask. "Did you get the ravioli at least?"

"Course I fucking did," he says, like it should've been obvious. "Bled all over the damn can, but it still tasted like victory."

"You're such an idiot."

His grin widens. "You say that like it's a bad thing."

"Have you ever thought about going back?" I ask, voice low, almost afraid to break whatever fragile thread holds us together in this moment.

His smile fades. Wiped clean in an instant. "To where?"

"Wherever you were before the homes."

Zane shrugs. It's a move meant to look casual but it's loaded with things he won't say out loud. "There's no point. I've been in enough places to know the only person who gives a shit if I eat or breathe is me."

I press my lips together. Swallow the sharp edge in my throat. "I've always been a burden. That's what people saw when they looked at me. A problem to be dealt with. Something they were desperate to shake off."

His jaw clenches. For a second, I think he's gonna leave it. But he leans forward.

"You're strong, Skylar," he says.

I shake my head, the words landing heavy. "I don't feel strong."

His hand moves before I can even think. He reaches across the space between us and brushes his thumb over the scar above my brow. The touch is soft, gentle. The pad of his thumb catches against the raised skin, and it wakes up something buried under layers of hurt.

It shouldn't matter. It's just a touch. But fuck, it matters.

His eyes stay locked on mine. "You don't get a scar like this from being weak," he says. "That shit stays because you fucking survived it. That scar says you kept breathing when she wanted to break you."

I can't find my voice. My chest is tight. That memory, the one I shove down every time it gets too close, it's hovering just under my skin now.

"You really think that's what it means?"

His hand doesn't leave me. If anything, it settles firmer against my skin, trailing down to the edge of my jaw. Heat flares beneath it. My entire body goes still, caught in that place between wanting to move closer and not knowing how.

His eyes never waver. "I know it is. You survived her, Skylar. That's the whole fucking point. You lived through it. You didn't let her finish you."

The world quiets. It's just the two of us, suspended in something that is too big to name.

His fingers drag along the curve of my jaw, as if he's memorizing every line of me. My breath stutters again. This time, it has nothing to do with fear and everything to do with him. With the way he looks at me like I matter. That I'm not broken in the ways I thought I was.

He leans in.

The look in his eyes says he's already made up his mind. He's going to kiss me. And I'm going to let him.

I feel his mouth getting closer to mine, his breath catching the edge of my lips.

And I let him come the rest of the way.

His mouth brushes mine. A tease at first, barely there. But it lights a fuse under my skin and makes every nerve stand at attention. I go still, breath caught in my throat, my heart hammering. The taste of him sinks into me before I realise I've closed the distance. His hand fists in my hair, dragging a gasp out of me as his lips slam into mine, all heat and fury and want.

He doesn't kiss soft or sweet. He kisses like he's starving and I'm the only thing that's ever satisfied him. Tongue, teeth, the scrape of his stubble against my chin. There's no pretending anymore. His kiss is brutal, filled with everything he's never said out loud. He kisses the way I've imagined he fucks. Deep. Dirty. Possessive. The kind of kiss that ruins you for anyone else. The kind you never come back from.

He cages me in with his body, chest brushing mine with every desperate breath, as if he needs every inch of me. His other hand moves fast, sliding down onto my hip, gripping tight, fingers digging in through the fabric. He yanks me closer until there's no space left between us. Every inch of him presses against every inch of me and still it's not enough. I want more. I want him.

His teeth catch my bottom lip and he pulls, hard enough to sting, just enough to make my body shake. I moan into his mouth, a needy sound that I couldn't fucking stop if I tried.

Then I feel it.

His cock. Hard. Thick. Straining against his jeans. Pressed right into the heat between my legs. A sound breaks in my throat, one I've never made before. It's need and ache fusing together in something I have never let myself feel before. He grinds against me, slow at first, then rougher.

His name stumbles out of me, broken and breathless. There's no coming back from this. No pretending I don't want him, fucking crave him... not after this.

His mouth finds the edge of my jaw, heat trailing heat across my skin. Down to my neck. His tongue flicks over the spot below my ear before he sucks, hard enough to leave a mark. My hands are in his hair now, tugging, anchoring myself as his hips roll again, dragging a broken sound from my chest.

His hand slips beneath the hem of my skirt, fingers dragging up my thigh, taking his time. My breath hitches. Every nerve is buzzing, my blood pounding so hard in my ears I can't hear a damn thing except the rush of want crashing through me.

He doesn't rush, just keeps going, one inch at a time. Fingers brushing bare skin, teasing the edge of my panties. His fingertips find the seam and glide along it, right over where I'm soaked and aching. My hips jerk without permission, and a helpless moan spills out of me.

"Fuck," he growls, eyes locked on mine. "You're dripping for me, baby." His finger presses harder, rubbing slow circles over the soaked fabric. "All that attitude and this pussy's been begging for me the whole fucking time, hasn't it?"

I can barely breathe. My legs are shaking. His mouth curls into a smirk, dangerous and hungry, as if he knows exactly what he's doing,

"You walk around all tough, talking shit, but under this skirt? You're just a needy little thing, fuckin' soaked and waiting to be ruined."

He leans in, lips brushing my jaw as his fingers slide under the fabric. His fingers graze my slit. Then his middle finger finds me, slick and throbbing, and he groans against my throat. "Fuck, you're perfect."

I gasp, grabbing his wrist without thinking. My voice comes out broken. "I need to tell you something."

His eyes flash to mine, but his fingers don't stop. "Tell me, baby."

"I've never..." I swallow hard. "I'm a virgin."

He stills. But it's enough.

Enough to feel everything shift.

The heat. The hunger. The way his hand tightens on my thigh as if he's anchoring himself, holding back a storm that was raging only seconds ago.

And in that pause, I know everything's about to change.

Chapter 17

ZANE

F uck.

Her words slam into my skull before anything else, before I can even think straight. That one word, and everything else just shuts down.

She's a virgin.

Everything inside me grinds to a halt.

My fingers are still pressed against the soaked lace between her thighs, heat radiating into my skin, but I can't fucking move. I'm suspended in this moment, pulse hammering, lungs locked up, caught between wanting her so fucking bad and knowing I can't have her.

I pull in a slow breath, trying to calm the storm inside me. My hand stays where it is, not moving, not pushing, just holding her.

I've had sex before. Too many times to count. But they were quick, rough, and meaningless. But this isn't that. This is her.

Skylar.

The girl who's clawed her way through shit most people wouldn't survive. The girl with smartass comebacks and sad eyes. The one who walked into my world without asking and flipped it on its fucking head.

And now she's here. Laid out. Thighs trembling. Mouth parted. Staring up at me with wide eyes and that soft pant falling from her lips.

The kind of look that hits me dead in the chest.

That I-trust-you-with-every-piece-of-me look. I should run. I don't do virgins or delicate things. Fuck... I don't do this.

But I stay.

My hand's still under her skirt, fingers pressed against lace soaked through with her need, still pulsing, still begging.

"Say it again," I breathe. Thumb dragging over that damp heat. Barely any pressure, but enough to tease her, to watch her hips twitch because of my fingers.

She breathes in sharp. Eyes dipping away with a flicker of panic. This is the first time I've ever seen fear on her face. The girl with teeth and fire, who I've never seen flinch, not once.

"I've never been with anyone," she says, barely a whisper.

Fuck me.

I lean in. Lips barely brushing the corner of her mouth. My breath thick against her cheek. Voice low, tight, on edge.

"You mean to tell me you've been walking around all this time with no one tasting this pretty pussy?" I drag my mouth to her jaw, breathing her in. "Because that's a fucking crime."

My fingers press harder against the soaked heat. She gasps. Her hips lift, chasing more. That sound hits me low. Straight to my cock, making it throb.

I drag my mouth to her ear, my voice rough, filthy.

"No one's ever spread these thighs wide and made this pussy come apart?" My thumb circles, right over that swollen clit, her breath hitching as if I've just cracked her open.

"No one has ever got on their knees and worshiped this cunt with their mouth? Tongue-fucked you until your legs shook. Sucked on this pretty little clit until you were dripping all over their face."

Her thighs twitch again. My cock jerks behind my zipper, it's hard and ready, dying to sink into that wet heat.

"No," she says, breath stuttering.

My fingers keep working, slower now, teasing, coaxing. She's so damn responsive.

My teeth graze her jaw, then I whisper it right against her skin, "Baby, I'd spend all fucking night down there. Mouth full of you. Cock hard. Just to hear how you sound when you come for me."

She moans, head tipped back, throat exposed like she's offering it up just for me. My mouth drags along the line of it, tongue slow, tasting every inch of that soft skin while she trembles beneath me. I suck just beneath her jaw, let my teeth scrape before I bite down hard enough to make her gasp. Then I soothe it with a slow lick, lips brushing her pulse, cock aching at how fucking sweet she sounds.

"Fuck, baby," I breathe against her skin, voice rough, wrecked, and hungry. "You've got no fucking idea the shit I wanna do to you. Got no clue how long I've wanted my mouth on you."

I move back on my knees, eyes dragging over every inch of her. Her chest rising fast, nipples hard under her shirt.

"Relax," I growl, sliding my hands up the inside of her thighs. "I'm gonna take care of you, now. Give you every filthy fucking second you've earned."

She whimpers, legs falling open wider. And fuck, if that's not the most beautiful thing I've ever seen.

"All you've gotta do is lie there and take it, Sky. Let me fucking ruin you."

My fingers hook into the lace at her hips and I drag her panties down in a slow, fucked-up worship. I'm not rushing shit. I want to see every fucking inch of her as I strip her bare. Her thighs tense under my hands, soft skin brushing mine, and then that perfect little pussy is right there in front of me.

Fuck.

Pink, glimmering, and already wet for me.

It's not some dainty thing. It's the kind of cunt that haunts a man. The kind that makes you drop to your knees and forget every reason you told yourself you weren't gonna fall.

I tug the panties the rest of the way off her legs, ball them in my fist, and shove them straight into my pocket. They're mine now. I'll keep them for later, fist wrapped tight around my cock as I jerk off, while I replay every second of this. That smell, the taste. That fuck-me look in her eyes when I touch her.

And fuck, she's already fucking wrecking me.

I shift back onto my knees, eyes locked on her cunt. It's flushed, slick, clit swollen. I want to drag my tongue through that mess and make her sob. Make her fall apart on my face. I want her squirming. Desperate. Needing me so bad she forgets how to speak.

I trail my fingers up her inner thigh, just a breath away from where she wants me the most. Her breath catches. Her eyes are glassy, locked on my face like she's begging me to put her out of her misery.

"You feel that?" I mutter, voice gravel and smoke. "That ache in your gut... that need. You think that's bad, wait till I make you come so hard you forget your fucking name."

My fingers ghost over her slit, slick already clinging to my skin, and I grin, cock twitching so fucking hard it's painful.

Fuck, I'll bury my mouth between her legs until she's crying from it. Because this, her spread out in front of me is the only high I've ever wanted to overdose on.

I've never done this before. Never fucking wanted to. Eating pussy always seemed pointless to me. Just another thing guys talked up to sound better in locker rooms. I am the type to fuck fast and leave faster. Get my cock sucked, blow my load, and move the fuck on. No meaning. No connection. Just release.

I run my tongue over my bottom lip, slow. Drawing out the moment. My fingers trail over the soft outer edges of her folds. Slick as hell. My throat goes tight just from the feel of her. Fuck, I'm already addicted. I want to spend hours here. Days even... no forget that my entire fucking life.

When I drag a single finger through her slit, catching just the barest graze of her clit, her whole body jolts.

"So wet," I mutter, my voice thick. "This all for me, baby?"

She nods. Her lips part, her chest rising too fast. She's wrecked already and I haven't even fucking tasted her.

I press my thumb to her clit, real gentle at first, circling in a slow rhythm that makes her whimper and rock her hips. My other hand grips her thigh, holding her in place so I can see every twitch and pulse.

She moans again. It's all soft and breathy. Her hips lift, chasing my touch.

"You ever touch yourself here?" I ask, my thumb pressing a little harder, dragging in lazy, messy circles now.

She nods again, eyes glassy. "Yeah," she whispers.

My grin's pure filth as I picture her in bed alone, fingers buried deep in that sweet little pussy, hips grinding into her hand while she whispers my name in the dark. I imagine her biting her lip to keep from moaning too loud, eyes closed. "You think about me when you touch yourself?" I murmur, voice thick with heat. My thumb drags over her clit, again... teasing her just enough to watch her squirm. "Ever wished your fingers were my cock?"

Her breath catches, that soft little gasp spilling from her mouth like a fucking prayer.

"Tell me, Sky."

She swallows hard. Her chest heaves.

"Yes," she whispers. "Fuck… yes."

And fuck me, I almost lose it.

The sound that tears from my throat is guttural, something deep and animalistic. I lean forward and the second my breath hits her clit, she jolts, but I don't stop. I hold her hips down as I flatten my tongue and lick her pussy claiming every inch of her like I've been starving for it.

She tastes sweet and so fucking addictive it punches the air from my lungs.

My tongue drags through her folds again, slower this time, soaking her taste into me. I swirl over her clit, just once, and her entire body shudders. Her fingers bury in my hair, tugging tight as if she needs something to hold on to.

"Shit," she gasps. "Zane—fuck—"

I groan into her pussy, the sound vibrating through her, and she cries out again, hips rising into my face. My hands grip her thighs, keeping her right where I want her while I devour her like she's the only thing I'll ever need.

She tastes so fucking good I could drown in her. Every flick of my tongue sends heat rolling through my body, makes my cock throb. Nothing prepared me for this. Not the way her pussy pulses against my mouth, or the way her breath catches every time I hit that spot.

Nothing warned me that licking her would short-circuit every thought in my head.

I take my time. Lick after slow, deep lick. Her whole body jolts. A strangled sound tears from her throat. She arches, spine lifting. She's not used to this. Has no idea how to handle being worshipped with a mouth.

Good. This is mine to teach her how good it can feel.

My tongue circles her clit. I don't settle into a pattern. I tease… flick… roll the tip around the swollen nub, then drag lower, tasting all the way down, before coming back to that perfect spot and flattening my tongue against it. Her hands reach for something and fail to find it.

I glance up.

Her head's thrown back, hair splayed across the tin, mouth open, eyes glazed over. Her chest rises fast, breaths shallow and desperate. She's somewhere only I can take her.

I hum against her clit, let the vibration roll through her. She cries out. Her hips buck. She tries to close her legs again but I snarl against her pussy and force her open, tongue dragging in slow, cruel strokes that make her squirm and whimper.

Not yet.

I want her to beg. I want her to break.

I slide two fingers inside her. She's so fucking tight I have to curl them just to ease the pressure. Every small movement draws me deeper, until my hand is shaking from how good she feels wrapped around my fingers. Her pussy clenches down hard, the slick sounds obscene as I fuck her slowly, my mouth still working her clit.

I find a rhythm. Fingers deep, tongue teasing, and every time I flick against that spot, her whole body jerks. Her hand gets tighter in my hair, pulling me closer, dragging my mouth harder into her cunt. She doesn't care if I suffocate.

"Zane," she whispers. It's broken, almost like a plea and a confession at once.

That's when I know, she's right fucking there. I feel it. The tension in her thighs. The way her pussy squeezes around my fingers. Her whole body locks up, breath catching, then it hits.

She comes hard.

A shudder. A cry. Her voice splits in half as she breaks apart on my tongue. Her pussy pulses, spasming around my fingers, wetness soaking my hand and chin. Her back bows off the tin, legs shaking so hard. Her head falls back, mouth open, a sound ripped from her throat that could fucking ruin me.

I don't stop. I keep licking. Keep tasting her as the orgasm tears through her, wave after wave, until she's gone weightless. Until her grip loosens in my hair and the tremors fade into soft, wrecked breaths.

I bet she's never come like that before.

And fuck, no one else is ever gonna make her come like that again.

When I finally pull back, I don't go far. Just hover there, breathing her in, the taste of her still thick on my tongue and I just stare at her.

She's never looked more beautiful.

I rest my palm flat on her stomach, needing the weight of it, the contact. She's still trembling.

"You're fucking perfect," I say. It's not some throwaway line, but the truth, scraped straight from somewhere I didn't know existed in me.

Because she is.

I slide up, press my mouth to hers in a kiss that's all tongue and fucking desperation. It's messy. Deep. Hot. I kiss her like I'm drowning in her.

Her legs are still open under me. I could take her right now. Slide in slow, stretch her around my cock and fuck her until she forgets her own name.

God, I want to push inside and fuck her slow, then fuck her rough, have her whole body shaking, begging me not to stop. I want to be her first, her only, her fucking last.

But I don't move.

I hold myself there, panting hard, jaw clenched so tight it hurts. My cock is throbbing. My hands are shaking. I'm right there, on the edge of losing control. And it takes everything in me to pull back just enough to follow through.

I drag my fingers gently down the side of her face. "I'm not gonna fuck you tonight."

I can't believe in a million years that those words are coming out of my mouth.

Her brows knit together, confused. "Why not?"

I grit my teeth and stare at her, every cell in my body screaming to take what she's offering.

"Because I want your first time to mean something," I say. "Not here like this. Not with your back against a tin roof and your ass going numb from the cold."

I drag my thumb over her bottom lip, put that cocky smirk on my face, the one I know the girls love. "But if you want to give me something tonight?" I smirk. "Then be a good girl and suck my cock. Because if I don't bury myself in something soon, I'm gonna lose my fucking mind."

I don't push her. I wait even though waiting has never been my thing.

She smirks, as if hearing me lose my fucking mind is funny to her.

"You want my mouth?" she whispers. "Then take off your jeans."

Jesus fuck.

I sit up fast, fingers flying to the button of my jeans, heart hammering in my chest. My cock's hurting, desperate to be touched. I drag my zipper down, shove the denim past my hips, and pull myself free.

Her eyes drop to my cock, thick, hard and leaking. She licks her lips, dragging her tongue across them like she can't wait to tase me.

Then her hand wraps around me.

I hiss through my teeth, the sound ripped straight from my chest. Her fingers curl around the base of my cock and she gives it a stroke and I'm already fucking gone.

My hips jerk, cock throbbing in her grip, leaking against her palm. She doesn't stop. Just watches me while she pumps me again, a little tighter this time, wrist twisting just enough to make my whole body clench.

"Fuck, baby…" I groan, breath catching hard in my throat.

She leans in, mouth parting, hot breath teasing the tip. Her tongue flicks out and catches the drop of precum, eyes locked on mine the whole fucking time.

"Such a filthy little mouth," I murmur.

And then she takes me.

Warm lips stretching over my cock as she slides down inch by inch. I groan, my hand flying to her hair, not to force, just to hold on. She takes me deeper, tongue pressed flat against the underside, her throat tightening around the head when I hit the back.

"Shit… Skylar," I choke out, voice shredded, thighs drawn tight, every muscle locked down.

She pulls back, lips wet and glistening, a string of spit connecting her mouth to the tip of my cock. Her eyes are dark, blown wide with heat, and fuck, there's something dangerous in them.

Then she takes me again. Harder this time.

Her mouth slides down fast, hot and greedy, sucking with purpose. She sets a rhythm that tears through me. Her hand wraps around the base, pumping what her lips can't reach, her wrist twisting with every pass. I can't fucking breathe.

Every time she swallows around the head, my cock jerks. My hips buck.

I'm close. So fucking close I can feel the pressure building, burning through every nerve.

"You want me to come down your throat?" I growl, jaw clenched.

She moans around me, and the vibration tears through my cock, hot and sharp, setting every nerve on fire. It's filthy. Perfect. The sound, the pressure, the way her mouth grips me and pushes me right to the fucking edge.

One more second of this and I'll be fucking gone.

I try to hold back. Bite down on the inside of my cheek. Think of anything else. Cold showers. Chain-link fences. My fucking laundry.

But all of it is useless.

She sucks me deeper, throat flexing, hand still pumping the base with that slick, perfect rhythm, and my control snaps.

"Shit... don't stop," I groan, voice breaking, hips jerking forward as my fist tightens in her hair.

I want this to last. Fuck, I need it to. Because this is going to be over fast. Too fucking fast.

She's barely started, and I'm already there,

This is gonna be the quickest I've ever come. Not since I was a teenager, getting my first awkward hand job behind the lockers. And even that felt easier to hold back than this.

I fucking come... hard. No way to slow it down. My cock twitches between her lips, pulsing, spilling down her throat in messy, relentless bursts. My head tips back as I groan. The kind of sound I've never made in my life.

She doesn't pull back.

She takes it all.

Her mouth stays on me, tongue still working my cock, milking every drop while I lose my fucking mind. My hips jerk, chasing the last of the high.

"Fuck," I pant, voice rough, hand still buried in her hair. My thighs tremble with the aftershocks, the pleasure so intense it almost hurts. I'm gasping, wrecked, the release crashing through me in waves that won't stop.

She pulls back slowly, her mouth slick, lips flushed. There's a glint in her eye that says she knows exactly what she's done.

I'm still breathing heavily. Still trying to recover. My legs feel weak. My chest is tight. I've never come that fast, never come that hard, and it's never felt at all like this before. It's not just a release. It's total obliteration.

And all I can do is stare down at her... completely fucked, completely hers, knowing that nothing will ever compare to this again. Knowing that in this moment I'll never be the fucking same again.

Chapter 18

It's been a week.

Seven endless days since we were on that roof. Since his mouth ruined me, and I came undone under the stars while he worshipped me.

He hasn't touched me since.

Not once.

I sit on the bed, cross-legged, pretending to study. The page in front of me is nothing but blurred ink, numbers turning to nonsense as my pen taps against the edge of the notebook. I keep telling myself to focus. To care about algebra. But he's here.

Across the room. Shirtless. Gloriously fucking distracting.

The weights clink softly as he lifts, muscles coiling and flexing with every rep. His chest glistens under the light, skin flushed from the effort, veins standing out across his forearms. That jaw is locked tight, his expression unreadable, all focus and control.

He's too much... too close. Too goddamn beautiful.

I tell myself not to look, but my eyes betray me. They trail over the slope of his abs, the sheen of sweat slipping across his stomach, the dark waistband of his sweatpants that hang low enough to make my breath hitch.

My gaze moves past the tight line of muscles to where they disappear beneath the waistband of his sweats.

The soft fabric clings in all the right places, and I swear he's doing it on purpose. Every time he exhales, the muscles along his stomach tighten, and my pulse goes with it.

I try to avert my eyes. Try to act normal.

It doesn't work.

He hasn't said a single word about that night. Not one mention of how he had me shaking, begging, soaked in the sound of his voice while he devoured me under the stars.

But he still makes me grilled cheese melts. Always two pieces cut diagonally, the way I didn't know I liked until he started doing it. He still brings me takeout.

It's become routine now, the way we move through this space. Somewhere in the blur of days and cheap instant coffee, this place stopped feeling temporary.

It feels settled. He still sleeps on the couch.

Every night, without fail, he tosses a pillow down, drags a blanket over himself, and stretches out as if it's nothing. He never asks for the bed or tries to crawl in beside me, even though I want him to.

But he looks.

When he thinks I'm not paying attention, I catch him watching me. Eyes dark. His expression unreadable, but his body is tense as if he's fighting something hard. Maybe he's just wired that way.

Zane isn't sweet.

He's all bite and swagger. Smokes too much. Talks too little. Walks around like the world owes him a fight.

But then he tosses my favorite chocolate bar on the bed without saying a word, and it fucks with me.

Because I don't know what that means.

Perhaps it is nothing.

Maybe I want it to mean something.

But it's hard to tell with him.

Some nights he's quiet, stretched out on the couch in just his sweats, arm over his face, jaw slack with exhaustion. Other nights he's wired, pacing the floor or working the weights hard, sweat dripping down his back, shoulders tense as if he's trying to outrun something in his head.

But no matter what version of him I get, there's always something there between us.

When he walks into the room, his eyes flick to me for half a second, long enough to make sure I'm still here. The way he keeps making sure I have what I need without ever asking what that is. The way he doesn't talk about anything real, doesn't offer explanations or promises, but still leaves the heater on when it gets cold. Still makes enough food for two and makes space for me without ever saying the words.

And that's what fucks me up the most.

The way this place feels more like home than anywhere I've ever been. Even when he's being an emotionally unavailable asshole.

I want him. All of him this time. But I have no idea if he wants me back. And I sure as shit aren't going to be the one to say it.

I glance up again and catch the flex of his biceps as he curls the weight, the way his mouth drops open slightly as he exhales. My thighs press together. I turn back to my homework, trying to blink it away.

"You keep staring like that," he says suddenly, voice rough, breathless from the set, "and I'll start thinking you want something."

I snap my head up. He's watching me now, weight hanging loose in one hand, smirk tugging at the corner of his mouth. That cocky, dangerous, stupidly hot smirk that drives me insane.

"You wish," I fire back, though my voice sounds thinner than I want it to.

He drops the weight with a dull thud, his eyes never leaving mine. "Yeah. I fucking do."

The words hang in the air. Thicker than the silence that follows. I don't know what to say. My cheeks flush, burning hot, and I glance down at my notebook, suddenly aware that my hands are shaking. I grip the pen tighter, but it doesn't help.

I hear him move—slow footsteps across the room. I don't look up.

Not until his hands grip the edge of the mattress.

My gaze lifts, and he's standing right in front of me. His expression isn't playful now. It's serious. Hungry. His eyes are darker than I've ever seen them.

"I haven't touched you," he says, voice low, "because I didn't know if I could fucking stop."

My mouth goes dry.

His hand lifts, knuckles grazing my cheek. "I've been trying to be good, Sky. Trying to give you space. But fuck... since I tasted you on the roof that night it's been fucking with my head. Every time I close my eyes, I see you. Spread out for me. Moaning my name. Fucking shaking on my mouth."

I can't breathe. I can't move.

"I fucking want you," he says, fingers dragging down my jaw, thumb brushing the corner of my lips. "I want to fuck you slow. Deep. Until you're begging me not to stop. I want to feel your pussy wrapped around my cock while you lose your mind under me."

Zane's filthy mouth does something to me. Every word drips heat, dragging across my skin like a physical touch.

I can't hide it. My body betrays me before my head can catch up. It hits my chest, coils in my stomach, burns in the slick ache between my legs.

I want him.

God, I fucking want him. My lips part, but my voice is gone.

So I nod.

His eyes lock on mine, searching my face—the muscles in his jaw flex.

"You sure?" he asks, voice rough as gravel, the words curling through me, dragging every ounce of sanity I've got left to the edge.

"Yes," I whisper.

And then he's on me.

His mouth crashes into mine, all tongue and heat, no hesitation. It's not sweet. It's filthy. Desperate. Full of fuck-you heat that's been building for weeks. His hands grip my waist hard, dragging me closer as if he needs me under him. I claw at his shoulders, fingers digging into hot skin, trying to get closer.

He growls into my mouth, that deep, feral sound that makes my cunt throb. My notebook and homework scatter to the floor with a sweep of his arm. Papers flutter, but he doesn't care. He lays me flat on the mattress and follows me down, his weight pressing into me, his sweat-slick chest against mine.

I wrap my legs around his waist, hips grinding up against his hard cock, greedy and aching. My pulse is a roar. Every breath feels stolen.

"Fuck," he mutters against my throat, kissing down to the hollow, biting just enough to make me gasp. "You drive me insane, you know that? Sitting there with that mouth and those fucking eyes. Pretending you're not soaking through your panties every time I walk in the room."

My shirt's shoved up, his hands rough as they push under it, thumbs brushing the underside of my tits, palms greedy and hot as he pulls it over my head.

He groans when he sees me.

"Fucking hell, Sky."

His mouth is on me again, licking a path over the swell of my breast before sucking hard around my nipple. I arch up, gasping his name, fingers tangling in his hair, dragging him closer.

He pulls back just enough to speak, his voice thick with need. "I'm gonna ruin you. Gonna fuck you so good you won't remember your own fucking name."

Then he's back on me, mouth everywhere, hands everywhere, tearing me open with touch alone. I've never wanted anything so fucking bad.

"Tell me if you want to stop," he murmurs, his lips dragging fire across my skin.

I don't.

Not now. Never.

His mouth keeps moving. Wet kisses. Open-mouthed. Slow. His tongue flicks over my nipple, sucking it between his lips until I arch into him.

I moan his name, and something in him snaps.

He freezes, and groans deep, the sound punched from his chest. "Fuck, baby. You moan my name like that, and it does something to me."

His hands trail lower, moving over my ribs, tracing the curve of my waist. His breath catches. He's trembling; it's in the tight pull of his jaw, in the way his fingers pause on the waistband of my shorts as if he's giving me one last chance to stop him.

I don't.

He drags my shorts down, and my panties go with them. His eyes don't leave my skin as more of me is revealed.

Hunger darkens his gaze, the muscles in his throat working as he swallows hard. He's still got that cocky, confident smirk. That rough, fucked-up swagger. But underneath it all, there's a softness that kills me. Destroys me.

When I'm bare, he tosses the shorts aside and grips my thighs, spreading them open until my pussy is completely exposed.

"Fuck," he mutters, his tongue coming out to wet his bottom lip. "You're fucking perfect." His voice is hoarse, wrecked, eyes locked between my legs. "So beautiful."

I freeze.

No one's ever said that to me before. I've always been a burden... the broken one. The girl you walk around to avoid. But Zane... he doesn't see any of that when he looks at me. He sees all the shit I carry around and still calls me beautiful.

He drops to his knees, grabbing my thighs again, this time firmer, dragging me closer to him. His fingers press into my flesh, and he leans in, breathing hot against my pussy. Every nerve lights up, every thought wiped clean. I sense him watching me, wanting me, holding back by a thread.

"Let me make it feel good, Sky," he says. "I'll take my time. Bring you to the edge. Get that sweet pussy ready for my cock."

"You sound really experienced in this whole virgin thing," I say.

He snorts, grinning as his hands push my legs further apart. "No, sweetheart. You're my first."

A shiver tears through me at hearing that he's never done this before with a virgin. There's something filthy and raw about that...how much he clearly wants me, how hard he's working to rein it in.

Heat throbs low in my belly, pulsing through me. My heart's pounding, and I can't breathe right, not with the way his gaze drops from my face to my pussy. There's a hunger in his eyes that makes me feel bare in a whole new way.

He blows gently across my cunt. The warm rush of air hits my clit, and my whole body jolts, a gasp ripping out of me. I feel exposed, raw, so fucking ready I could cry. He's not even touching me with his mouth yet, and I'm already losing it.

Then finally... finally, his fingers move, just a light graze skimming over my pussy in the lightest fucking touch I've ever known. It's maddening. My hips twitch, chasing it, wanting more, needing more. I squeeze my eyes shut, drowning in the sensation.

"Open your eyes," he says, voice low. "I want you to watch me taste your pussy. I want you to see what you fucking do to me."

When I open my eyes, his tongue dips down, and the moment he licks me, it's game over. My back arches, fingers gripping the sheets, his name a desperate moan on my lips.

And all I can think, through the haze of pleasure crashing down around me, is that no one's ever made me feel this wanted. No one's ever looked at me and seen anything but the mess I am.

But Zane... he looks at me and sees something else entirely.

He's the only person who has taken the time to truly see me.

Chapter 19

ZANE

The taste of her has my cock throbbing, hard and aching beneath my sweats. Skylar isn't just fucking hot, she's fire, softness and chaos wrapped in the tightest little body I've ever had between my hands. She moans, and it punches straight through my chest, the kind of sound that rewires something in my fucked-up head.

My tongue slides through her wetness, tasting every part of her. I press my mouth harder, tongue flicking, sucking like I need it to breathe. She gasps again, louder this time.

I don't stop. I double down. Suck harder. Lap at her as if I'm starved.

She tastes so fucking sweet. I watch her, eyes glazed, mouth parted, hair a mess on the pillow. She's the sexiest fucking thing I've ever seen. My mouth is soaked with her, and I'd stay between her thighs for as long as she'd let me.

"Fuck, you look amazing," I whisper against her pussy, tongue flicking over her clit. My hands spread her wider, holding her open, watching every bit of her unraveling for me.

"Zane," she moans, begging without even knowing it.

That sound... it sinks through every inch of me. Her body arches under my mouth, pussy soaked, clit begging for more. I lick her slow, then go harder, dragging my tongue through every drop of wetness she gives me. She whimpers. Her thighs shake. She's already losing it.

I slip a finger inside her tight little pussy, then another, stretching her open while my mouth keeps working her clit. Her sounds slip out, filthy and perfect. She's so fucking tight. My cock throbs at the thought of pushing into her, splitting her open on me. If she's this fucking wrecked from my fingers, what the fuck is she going to be like when I slip my cock into her?

I curl my fingers, hit that spot deep inside that makes her jolt. She's grinding herself against my hand, chasing every filthy stroke, her slick soaking my face. I growl, tongue moving faster, devouring her as she fucks my face like she owns it, and shit, I don't fucking care. I want her needy... begging.

My balls ache. My cock's about to explode in my sweats. Every fucking part of me is wound tight, focused on her pussy. On the way she gasps. The way her body shakes when I circle her clit with just enough pressure to keep her on edge.

"Oh God—" she cries out.

I look up at her, lips wet, breath ragged. "I'm not gonna make you come."

Her eyes snap open, dazed and needy.

"I want you worked up," I growl. "So when I fuck you, it won't hurt."

My gaze drags down the length of her body, slow and greedy, drinking in every inch. Her tits rise with every shaky breath, her nipples harden, begging to be touched. That soft flush across her chest is a dead giveaway she's worked up, even if she's trying to hold it together. She's laid out, skin flushed, legs parted, pussy wet and aching, and fuck if that doesn't make my cock ache with need.

Her eyes meet mine, and there's something burning there, something that grabs hold of my chest and twists. I should tell her how fucking beautiful she looks spread out like this, but I've already said it once, and that's not who I am. Handing out sweet talk is not my style. I don't do soft. I fuck. I use. I take.

But with her, I'm going to take my time. It will take everything in me to drag it out, tease her until she's begging.

I want her to tell me how fucking much she's been thinking about me. Tell me she wants to do every filthy thing I've ever fantasized about. Every dirty fucking thought I've had jerking off while thinking about her mouth, her tits, her pussy wrapped tight around my cock.

I suck that little nub until she's squirming, panting, right there on the edge, and then I pull back, my lips slick, my mouth aching to go back for more. Her body jerks, hips chasing the pressure I've stolen from her. That frustrated breath escapes her throat.

With a smirk, I run my tongue slow along my bottom lip, tasting her. Then I give her a wink, it's cocky I know, but I don't fucking care.

"You're such an asshole, you know that," she grits out, eyes heavy.

I laugh. She's the only one who can draw that out of me.

"You can only come when I have my cock buried inside you," I growl,

"Well, I'm waiting," she says, and I can see she's clearly frustrated that I never let her come.

I grin, the kind of grin that always gets me in trouble. "You're a pushy little thing, aren't you? Patience, baby. You'll get what you're waiting for," I say, giving her pussy an open-mouthed kiss, tasting her all over again.

She hisses, and fuck, that sound… I could listen to that all fucking day.

For half a second, I imagine having that sound on repeat, saved somewhere I can hear it at any time. My own personal fucking addiction. But the thought of anyone else hearing her like this, anyone knowing how she sounds when she's falling apart for me, has something dark twisting in my gut.

That possessive, fucked-up part of me wakes up fast.

Those sounds are fucking mine. Her gasps, her whimpers, the way she moans my name when I'm between her legs. Every single one of them belongs to me. She doesn't know it yet, but she will. Because no one is ever gonna make her sound this way.

I pull back; her taste still on my tongue, and climb off the bed.

"Where are you going?" The desperation in her tone hits me straight in the chest. Fuck, it does something to me. The fact that she wants me, needs me, makes my blood run hotter.

I turn back to look at her. She's propped up on her elbows, eyes wide, lips swollen, chest rising and falling fast. Her hair's a mess, her skin flushed, and she looks so fucking perfect I almost forget what I was doing.

"I need a condom to fuck you," I say, voice low.

Her lips part, but she doesn't say a word. Just watches the way I grab the waistband of my sweats and shove them down, my cock springing free, thick and hard, the tip already slick. Her eyes drop to it, and she lets out the slightest sound; it's enough to make my cock twitch.

I head for the bathroom, each step heavy with the need to get back to her. My pulse is loud in my ears, the air thick with sex and heat. I grab a condom from the top drawer and move back toward the bedroom.

She's exactly where I left her.

Legs still spread wide, with that glistening pussy on full display, waiting for me.

I tear open the packet with my teeth.

My hands are shaking, a little, when I roll the condom down over my cock. The latex stretches tight over my skin, every drag of my hand adding pressure, grounding me, giving my body something to focus on before I lose control completely. The motion feels good. Too fucking good. My pulse hammers in my throat, my cock throbbing in my grip.

I've never been this turned on in my life. Not once.

A pussy spread open in front of me has never made me this crazy before. Usually, it's a means to an end — a wet hole to fuck until I'm done. No meaning. No heat that burns through me and leaves me feeling out of control. But Skylar... fuck. The sight of her spread out, breathing fast, waiting for me, has been haunting my fucking mind since the first time I saw her.

I look up and catch her staring, eyes fixed on me, pupils blown wide. Her gaze trails down my body, stopping at the way my fist moves over my cock one last time. She swallows hard, lips parted.

I climb back onto the mattress; the bed dips under my weight. My knees press against the sheets between her thighs. I let my hands slide up her legs, tracing the smooth skin of her calves, over her knees, along the soft insides of her thighs. Her skin's warm, and when I reach the top, my thumbs brush over the edges of her pussy, spreading her open.

She watches me as I lean forward, my thumb finding her clit again. I barely touch it at first, just enough to make her hips twitch. Fuck, she's sensitive, every breath coming out in soft, uneven sounds. I move slowly, working her clit, teasing her, keeping her relaxed.

My voice comes out rough, low. "I don't want to hurt you."

Her eyes flicker up to mine, wide and trusting.

"I want you to enjoy this as much as I fucking will," I tell her, my thumb still moving, her body trembling under my hand.

I glance down at my cock, standing hard and ready, aching for her.

I've been told I'm big before. Hell, most girls brag about it, but that never mattered. Not until now. Now it's not about ego. It's about her. About making sure this first time is good, that it's something she'll remember, not something that fucking hurts.

I position myself, my cock brushing against her entrance, and her breath catches, that perfect little sound escaping her lips again. My other hand grips her hip.

"Relax," I whisper, voice barely holding steady. "I've got you."

And fuck, I mean it.

"Take a breath, Sky," I whisper, voice rough, my thumb still moving in slow, steady strokes. "I won't move until you're ready."

I press my thumb harder against her clit, just enough to keep her distracted while I push forward.

The first inch is tight as fuck... hot, wet, gripping me so snug it almost hurts.

"Fuck," I breathe, closing my eyes for a second, fighting to keep it together. "You're so fucking tight."

I stop, forcing myself to breathe, close my eyes to the feeling, and tell my cock not to lose it. At this pace, I'll fucking come before I'm even halfway in. My whole body trembles from the effort of holding it together, my cock throbbing as I wait for her to adjust around me.

When I open my eyes, I look down, and fuck—only the tip's inside her, nothing but the head, and it's already too much.

She's wrapped around me; the sight of splitting her open is enough to make my control crack.

I drag my gaze up and catch her watching me. Her lips are parted, eyes heavy, chest rising and falling in quick bursts.

"Are you okay?" I ask, voice tight.

"M'mmmm." It's barely a sound, more of a sigh than a word. Her head tilts back, lashes fluttering, completely lost in what I'm doing to her clit. She's not even hearing me.

While she's caught in the pleasure, I inch forward again, slow as I can manage, her body stretching around me. A sharp hiss leaves her, muscles locking beneath me.

I freeze immediately, every muscle locked, my cock buried halfway, throbbing with the need to keep going.

"Easy," I murmur, keeping my voice low. "Just breathe, baby. Don't fight it."

I remain completely still, every muscle in my body strung tight. She stares up at me, wide-eyed and breathless, her lips parted, her chest rising and falling like she's trying to find air.

Her gaze doesn't leave mine. I brace one hand on the mattress beside her hip, and I slowly push in again. The pressure makes her suck in a breath, her legs tensing around my hips. I groan, the sound tearing from my chest with the sensation.

"Fuck," I mutter, my head dropping forward as I suck in air. She's so fucking tight, hot, gripping me like her body was made to fit mine. I blink, trying to focus, but her heat nearly knocks the air out of my lungs.

I glance up and swallow hard. She hasn't told me to stop yet. And shit, I think I might actually fall apart if she does.

"Does it hurt?" I ask.

I've never asked a chick that before, because I never cared as long as I was getting off. But everything now is different with her.

Her brows pull together slightly, lips pressing into a line before she whispers, "It feels weird."

Weird. Okay, not bad so far, or painful. Just different.

I pull out an inch and then slide back in, careful with every movement. Her body flexes around me, and it takes every ounce of strength I have not to slam the rest of the way home.

"Is this okay?" I ask.

She nods quickly, her voice soft but certain. "Yeah. It still feels kinda weird."

God, this is the best fuck I've ever had, and I haven't even started fucking her yet.

I move slowly, with shallow thrusts, letting her adjust, waiting until the tension in her muscles starts to fade. Every push in has me fighting for control; every pull out leaves me aching. Watching my cock slide in and out of her pussy has my balls tightening, ready to explode. If I go too fast, I'll blow before she's had the chance to enjoy it.

I reach up and cup her breast, thumb brushing her nipple, then I squeeze. She hisses, and fuck, that sound shoots straight to my cock. My hips jerk forward on instinct, burying myself to the hilt. She gasps beneath me, pussy stretching and tensing around my cock. I freeze there, deep inside her, giving her a second to breathe through the stretch, through the way I'm fucking claiming every inch of her from the inside out.

She's so fucking tight.

So warm.

So goddamn perfect it's almost unbearable.

I lean down, crushing my mouth to hers. Tongues tangling. Breaths stolen. I kiss her slow. My tongue sliding against hers, tasting her, devouring her. I want her to know what she's unlocked.

The kiss slows my pulse just enough to keep me from spilling inside her, but it doesn't make anything easier. My balls are already pulling tight, and we've barely started.

Then I move.

Slow. Deep. I pull nearly all the way out, until only the head of my cock sits inside her, then I ease back in, burying myself until I'm balls-deep again. With each thrust, her breath hitches. Her back arches. Her body meets mine, her hips rolling, fucking chasing every inch of me as I move.

"Fuck, you feel amazing," I whisper. My hips grind down, and I press my body tighter against hers, pausing. "Just give me a minute before I lose it and finish inside you like a horny teenager." I breathe the words into her mouth, my lips brushing hers.

Because if she keeps making those sexy fucking sounds, keeps pulling me in deeper with that greedy, dripping pussy, I know I won't last. And right now... I want to watch her come on my cock before I do that.

She bursts into a giggle at what I just said and hastily covers her mouth, eyes wide, breathless with amusement and desire.

I lift my head from her neck and give her a slow, cocky grin.

"Yeah, laugh all you want. Don't hold back, because it's the fucking truth. Your pussy is so fucking tight and I love it."

I breathe her in, her scent wrapping around me, sweet and dizzying. Slowly, I shift, sliding one arm beneath her hips and lifting her just enough to keep her shoulders flat, her ass tipped perfectly into me. So I can sink deeper.

She stares up at me, pupils blown, lips parted, as if she's trying to figure out what the fuck I'm about to do.

That's when I fuck her, one deep, slow thrust, and I find that sweet spot that makes her back arch and her mouth fall open in a moan that shreds me from the inside out.

"Oh God… please, don't stop," she pleads, voice cracked, breathless. Her nails dig into my arms as I roll my hips the way she needs, hitting that spot again and again, grinding into it. She moans louder this time, a filthy, helpless sound that goes straight to my balls.

"Good?" I ask, breath jagged, watching her unravel beneath me.

"Fuck, yeah," she cries out, before she moans again, high and desperate, and her whole body trembles.

Her thighs shake. And fuck if I'm not chasing that moment, chasing her release as if it's mine too. Because nothing comes close to fucking her right to the edge and watching her fall apart all over my cock.

I move my other hand down lower, over her stomach, before slipping between her thighs. I find her clit, my fingers working in tight, filthy strokes that make her body jerk beneath mine.

"Oh my fucking God, Zane," she cries out, her voice cracking as her hips lift to meet every stroke. Her eyes are locked on mine, her mouth parted as breathless moans spill out between gasps.

"Yeah," I growl, grinding deeper, cock buried to the hilt, still fucking her slow, while my fingers work her without mercy. "You feel that? How fucking perfect this is?"

She whimpers, thighs trembling around me.

"Fuck," I bite out, losing rhythm as her walls clench tighter around my cock. "Come for me, baby. Fucking come for me before I lose it and fill you up."

And she does.

Her pussy clenches, body locking tight as she cries out, her whole frame shuddering beneath mine.

She's still coming when I fuck her hard. No more slow, controlled strokes. This is desperate, I'm relentless.

"Zane! Fuck, fuck, don't stop—"

She's loud. Perfect. I thrust into her like I'm losing my fucking mind, the sound of skin on skin filling the room. My cock's so fucking hard it hurts, and everything in me is burning, on edge, seconds away from shattering.

"God, you feel so fucking good," I bite out, the pressure building fast, brutal, blinding.

Then it hits.

I groan as the orgasm rips through me, head dropping back, jaw slack, every muscle locking up as I shoot into the condom. My whole body jerks with every pulse of release, and I can't stop moving, can't stop grinding into her as I come, cock milked for everything I've got.

I fuck her slow through the aftershocks, both of us already over the edge. She twitches beneath me, overstimulated.

I lower myself gently, resting on my elbows, lips hovering above hers. I kiss her softly. My forehead presses against hers, our bodies tangled, skin hot and damp. And for the first time in what seems like fucking forever, I finally breathe.

"Are you okay?" I ask, my voice low, brushing her lips with another kiss as my eyes roam over her beautiful face.

She nods, lips parted, cheeks flushed, lashes heavy. She's still floating in that orgasm haze, her body loose, her breathing uneven.

"You're pretty good at that," she murmurs, a lazy smile tugging at her lips.

I give her my signature smirk.

The one that usually gets girls begging for round two.

"Did you expect anything less?"

She snorts, teasing, "Yeah, I suppose all those chicks you've fucked... you'd have to get good at it eventually."

I say nothing about that because none of them meant a damn thing, not like this.

I kiss her lips, tasting the warmth, drawing it out like I never want it to end. When I finally pull out, the abrupt absence is a cold shock, already missing the slick warmth and rhythmic pressure of her wrapped around my cock.

I take the condom off, tie it in a knot, and throw it in the trash can in the bathroom, not bothering to flip on the light.

I should leave it there, leave her.

That's what I always do. Fuck, finish, gone. No lingering. No clingy chicks wanting more. No room for softness.

But my feet don't take me toward the door.

They take me back to the bed.

She shifts slightly, eyes barely open, lids heavy. I slide in beside her, pulling her close without thinking. Skylar snuggles against me, like she belongs. She's warm and soft and fucking perfect in my arms.

And I just lay there.

Listening to her breathing, catching the rhythm of her chest rise and fall against mine. Her skin is warm, her legs tangled with mine, her hair brushing against my neck, and something about it feels almost... dangerous. Not because it's wrong. But because it hits too fucking real.

This isn't what I do. I don't stay or hold girls afterwards. But I can't bring myself to let go of her.

I watch the ceiling for a while, my hand drifting up and down her spine, trying not to think too hard, or name the thing clawing at my ribs. But it's there... loud and fucking obvious.

I'm falling for her.

For Skylar.

And that's the one thing I told myself I'd never do.

Love makes you soft. It makes you rely on someone. And when you rely on someone, they break you. They leave. They fucking destroy every part of you that you've worked so hard to protect. I've already lived through that shit. I swore I'd let no one get that close again.

But she's already there.

Wrapped up in my arms. Under my skin. All over my fucking heart.

And, fuck me—I don't know how to stop it or really... if I want to.

Chapter 20

ZANE

The morning creeps in slowly through the window, with that dull gray light that never quite touches everything. My eyes open, and then I feel her. Warm. Soft. Pressed against me.

Skylar.

Her thigh is draped over mine, skin smooth against my hip, her head resting under my chin. Her breath ghosts across my chest, each exhale hitting me harder than it should. My arm is already around her, hand splayed low on her back.

Fuck.

I can't breathe.

She fits against me too well. Too fucking natural. Every part of her molded to mine like she belongs there. My cock twitches, traitorous as hell, pressed against her thigh. But it's not just her body. It's the weight of her in my arms. The way her fingers curl against my stomach even in her sleep.

I stare at the ceiling, trying to steady the pounding in my chest. I should have gotten up already, pulled on my jeans and fucked off, pretending none of this had happened.

But here she is, curled into me, breathing against my skin, and I can't bring myself to pull away.

Fuck. I'm in trouble.

I don't fucking move. Not a twitch. I don't fucking breathe for a moment.

I lie there, staring at her like she's some dream I never deserved. Her lips are parted, breath real slow, lashes casting shadows across her cheeks. She looks peaceful in a way I've never been. In a way I've never seen her. Fuck, she looks soft, not in a weak way, but in an untouched-by-this-fucked-up-world way. That this world hasn't clawed at her skin or dragged her through broken glass just for daring to exist. As if no one's ever broken her, and I know that's bullshit, because I've seen her cracks. Hell, I've kissed half of them.

But right now... she's whole. And I'd burn the world down to keep her that way.

Fuck me. I wanna be the one who keeps the cold out. Make sure there's food in the fridge and my hoodie on her back. I want her to know what it feels like to be safe. Not because she can't handle shit. She's tough as hell. But because no one's ever protected her.

I'm already in too deep and I know it because I think I'm falling in love with her.

And that thought alone nearly fucking kills me.

It crawls up my throat, burns through my chest, and I can't swallow it back down. I don't want it. Don't need it. I've spent my whole goddamn life building walls high enough to keep this kind of shit out. Needing someone makes you soft. It fucks with your head. Makes you reckless... weak.

But she's sleeping beside me in one of my shirts, skin warm against my sheets. The collar's slipping off one shoulder, and the sight of her wearing something that's mine hits differently. It is dangerous and too fucking real.

That weakness presses into my chest until it hurts to breathe.

She digs up shit I poured concrete over and promised myself I'd never touch. Now all of those emotions are clawing to the surface, wild, messy and fully fucking alive.

I reach out before I can stop myself, brush a strand of hair from her face. My fingers move carefully, tracing the soft skin of her cheek. She stirs, her nose scrunching, then relaxes again. Her lips part, a quiet sigh leaving her.

I lean in and press a kiss to her cheek. Barely there. Barely a breath. But it hits too fucking big. Too honest.

That's when I know I need to get the fuck out of here.

I shift carefully not to wake her, peeling myself away even though every cell in my body protests it.

The moment her warmth is gone, my chest aches in a way I can't fucking name.

Sitting on the edge of the bed, I drag a hand over my face. I can't be here when she opens her eyes. I can't let her see me this raw, this close to losing the armor I've spent my whole fucking life building.

She stirs again, mumbling something, her voice soft and drowsy.

I lean down, keeping my tone steady, casual, even though my heart's still slamming against my ribs. "Rainer's expecting me."

She doesn't wake. I stand there for a second longer, watching her, fighting every fucked-up instinct screaming at me to stay.

Then I walk away.

Because that's what I do best.

It's a lie. Rainer's not waiting for me at all.

I throw on my jeans, boots, and the first shirt I find, fingers fumbling as if they forget how to work. Everything seems too big. My hands. My chest. The space between every breath. I move fast, down the stairs, two at a time, as if I don't stop, nothing will catch me. Not the guilt.

The workshop's dead quiet. Only me and the ghosts I dragged in.

I lift the hood of the car I was working on yesterday and get to it. Wrench in hand. Tighten a bolt. Loosen another. Pretend I'm doing something that matters. But my head's shot. All I see is her in my bed, in my shirt.

Every move reminds me of her. The press of her skin against mine. Those sounds she made when I touched her. The way she looked at me like I was worth saving.

If she stays, I'll burn. But, fuck if she leaves, it'll hurt just as much.

That's the truth of it.

I've got grease coating my knuckles, and a wrench clenched so tight it might snap. But it's not the busted alternator that's fucking with me.

It's Skylar.

I force my ears to stay tuned to the rhythm of the engine, but all I hear is the sound of her breath catching against my chest, the ghost of her lips brushing my jaw, soft, warm and fucking unforgettable.

I twist the bolt harder than I should. It snaps in my grip, the crack sharp as a gunshot.

"Fuck." I throw the broken piece across the concrete. It skitters, spins out near the wall.

"You always this charming in the morning?" Rainer's voice cuts through the haze.

I push off the engine and wipe my hands on a rag that's already soaked with grease. "Didn't hear you come in."

He strolls over to the bench, grabs his shitty black coffee from the corner where he hides that old-ass thermos.

Rainer leans back, watching me with that half-grin that says he knows too much.

"Got a new kid on trial," Rainer says, casual as ever.

I arch a brow. "Yeah?"

"Mason. Nineteen, maybe twenty. Couple priors. Petty shit. Foster kid." He shrugs.

My gaze drags to the far side of the shop.

There he is.

Crouched low, hands dunked in a tray of degreaser, scrubbing parts with practiced ease. Dark hair buzzed on the sides. Ink snaked down both forearms. Shoulders broad. Frame solid. He's got the build of a guy who's taken hits and thrown harder ones back.

I know the kind. I used to be the kind. I guess I still am.

His hands are busy, but his eyes tell the real story. He's not focused on the tray in front of him. He's clocking the exits, the tools, the layout. Me.

Every glance is calculated. Measured. Sizing up the shop and the people in it. Working out who are the threats and who aren't.

I know that look. Used to wear it every day. Still do, when it counts.

And right now, I'm the threat he hasn't figured out yet.

Good.

Keeps things interesting.

The stairs creak, cutting through the quiet hum of the shop.

Light footsteps.

Skylar, bag slung low on her shoulder, jeans painted on, hair a little messy from the morning rush. She steps into the workshop, and everything slows. My throat goes dry. My pulse forgets what steady means.

She's herself again—the girl who could cut you open with a look and make you thank her for it.

Her eyes find mine. Every time they do, it's a punch straight to the ribs. She smiles. That smile that strips the air from my lungs and reminds me how fucked up about her I really am.

I nod, pretending I'm not burning from the inside out. Pretending my cock isn't half-hard from a single fucking look. But my body's already betrayed me. It's wired. Buzzing. Begging.

She moves past the workbench, throws Rainer a quiet "Morning."

He starts to reply, but I don't hear him. Because that's when I fucking see it.

Mason.

The moment she appears, he looks at her. His hands stop moving. He openly and shamelessly checks her out. His jaw clenches. I see his head tilt. It's deliberate, like he's memorizing every inch of her. Before his stare drops to her ass, and it lingers.

Heat floods my chest. Heavy. Possessive as fuck.

The air feels thinner. My grip on the wrench tightens until my knuckles ache. I could bash it through the bench just to stop the urge to put it through his fucking head. He keeps watching her until the door swings shut and she's gone.

Then his eyes flick to me.

I stare back.

I slam the hood of the car harder than I need to. The bang echoes through the shop, and Mason flinches just enough to feed the fire already clawing at my chest.

"You eye-fucking her or are you just fucking dumb?" I ask, voice sharp enough to cut steel.

His head lifts. There's surprise in his eyes for half a second, before that fucking smirk slides across his face, slow and smug. "Didn't know she was yours."

Yeah. This prick and I? We're gonna get along real good.

"She's not." My voice stays calm, smooth as oil, but my hands are curling into fists. The kind that would have already broken jaws by now. The kind that wouldn't mind doing it again. "Doesn't mean you get to stare at her like she's yours to take."

He shrugs; it's casual, real fucking smug. "She doesn't seem like the kind that needs protecting."

I step toward him. Only one. It's enough to make the air shift.

"No one said she did. But if you wanna keep chewing your food with your own teeth, keep your fucking eyes off her."

Rainer doesn't say a word. He doesn't move, but I feel the weight of his eyes, steady and silent, watching every second.

I turn back to the bench, muscles tight, heart beating loud enough I can feel it in my fucking throat. My hands won't stop shaking. Not from rage. Not from whatever the fuck Mason stirred up.

It's from fear.

Because I'm not supposed to be this guy who wants to knock another guy's teeth down his throat just for looking at a girl.

But then again, she's not some random girl.

She's Skylar.

There's no version of this where I come out clean. No path I walk down this road that doesn't cut me open. Every step drags me deeper towards her, drowning in something I never wanted in the first place. And still, I keep fucking going.

Rainer's boots sound across the concrete behind me. He doesn't speak straight away, just stands there, his silence pressing against my back. That old-school kind of silence that cuts deeper than any words.

When he finally moves, he strolls up beside me, coffee in one hand, gaze sharp beneath the brim of his cap.

His eyes flick to Mason first. Quick. Measured as if he's calculating how bad this could get. Then they land on the tools scattered across the workbench, before they glance up to look at me.

"Kid," he says, voice rough from too many years of smoking. "You wanna lose everything?"

I don't meet his eyes. "What's that supposed to mean?"

"It means if you keep throwing punches at ghosts, you'll lose the few things worth holding on to."

"I'm not swinging at shit."

He lets out a slow breath, the kind that says he's seen this story play out too many times and never once with a happy ending. "Then learn to fight without your fists and start using your fucking head."

I grit my teeth. "That's what you think I'm doing?"

He takes a sip of his coffee. "That girl upstairs. The one you can't stop watching. Yeah, that's exactly what you're doing."

My throat locks up. Words build, but they don't come out.

Rainer's voice comes again. "You can't fix the shit that made you. None of us can. But you don't have to drag it into what's left of your life."

Then he walks off. Leaves me standing there in the quiet with too many truths.

I stare down at my hands.

"Learn to fight without your fists."

I know what he means.

And, fuck, I hate that he's right.

Chapter 21

SKYLAR

The first thing I register is the emptiness.

Not the silence or the cold sheets. It's the smell of him. It clings to my pillow, my skin, the fucking air.

He's gone.

I stare at the ceiling, eyes tracking the cracks that crawl through the plaster. My chest is tight. My throat is tighter, but I don't cry. Just sit with it… the hollow space where he should be.

He left before the sun came up. Before I could ask if any of it meant something.

Maybe that's the answer right there. It doesn't.

My thighs still ache, every throb a reminder of how he fucked me. How much I wanted him, how much I needed it, thinking it would fill something.

Instead, it's simply carved me out.

I pull the blanket in under my chin, not for the warmth, but for the cover as the shame creeps in.

All that's left now is the dent in the mattress and the sting between my legs. A memory I never asked for. But a night I'll never forget.

And the kind of silence that makes you realize how alone you really are in this world.

I shower fast.

Cold water hits my skin, sharp enough to make me gasp, but it doesn't do shit to wash him off. He's still there. In the bruises on my hips. In the ache, I can't scrub away, no matter how hard I try. Zane Rivera is everywhere. Under my skin. In my blood. And I fucking hate that I care. Hate that a part of me hoped he'd still be there when I woke up.

The apartment seems too quiet when I step out. It's too still, like it's waiting for me to break. I towel off, throw on a pair of jeans and a hoodie, and tie my hair up in a messy knot. It doesn't matter how I appear. No one sees past the front I put on, anyway. That tough-girl mask I wear like armor. If I look untouchable, they won't see how cracked I really am underneath.

I grab my bag and head down the stairs, and that's when I see him.

Zane.

He's bent over an engine, sleeves shoved up to his elbows, grease staining his forearms. His jaw's clenched tight, teeth grinding around whatever tension he won't say out loud. With a wrench in one hand, he's focused on the machine in front of him.

He doesn't look up.

Doesn't say a fucking word.

My chest squeezes, something sharp pressing beneath my ribs. I shift my weight, suddenly unsure what to do with my hands, or even how to stand without looking as if I'm falling apart.

The moment he looks up and sees me there, I do what any idiot girl with a broken heart does.

I smile.

Just a tiny one. I lift my hand, fingers twitching in a pathetic little wave.

Zane gives me a single nod. Nothing more.

And it fucking burns.

I glance away before the sting behind my eyes turns into something worse. My throat's tight, raw from everything I never said last night. The way I came apart while he was inside me. I force myself to keep moving, one step in front of the other, so he can't tell I'm breaking apart.

Rainer's by the tool cabinet. He's rough around the edges, but I like him. I always have. There's a kindness buried beneath the gruff exterior. And I'm glad Zane has someone watching out for him, even if he pretends he doesn't need it.

"Morning," I say as I pass him, forcing my voice steady.

He looks up, eyes crinkling at the corners. "Well, hey there, Skylar," he says. "You look like trouble."

"Always," I say with a smirk, though my stomach's still knotted.

I push open the door, the morning air biting as it hits my face. I don't stop walking or glance back. Because if I do, I might catch one last glance of Zane not giving a shit.

And I'm not sure I can handle that today.

The world doesn't slow down. Engines rumble, brakes squeal, someone yells across the street. Laughter from a group of guys floats past me. None of it lands. It's all background noise to the chaos in my head.

Every step I take pulls another memory to the surface. The way his hands gripped my waist. The sound of his voice, curling around my name, while he was buried inside me. The heat of his breath on my skin. The way I came apart for him.

And then the cold bed this morning.

That fucking ache in my chest when it dawned on me that even though I gave him my virginity, it meant nothing to him. That perhaps I was only a warm body he used to burn off whatever demons were clawing at him last night.

Maybe that's all I ever was to him.

By the time I push through the school gates, I'm already spiraling. My chest feels too tight, throat raw, stomach twisting. I don't paste on a smile. My face tells the truth today. I'm storm clouds and cracked bones and not in the mood to play nice. Let them fucking stare, whisper. I've got nothing left to give.

Cassie's waiting by the lockers, holding two coffees and bouncing on her toes. She waves one when she sees me coming. "Morning, Sunshine."

I grunt and take the cup from her hand. The heat seeps into my fingers, but it doesn't reach the cold sitting under my ribs.

"Wow," she mutters, watching me. "Someone's in a mood."

Then I hear them.

"Hey, Skylar," Liam calls out, that sleezy voice makes me sick. "Still got that pretty little moan? Thought maybe you'd saved a few for me."

Laughter follows. His pack's always around him. Bryce Anders, who walks like he owns the place because his dad's a hotshot lawyer who slips the cops enough cash to clean up his messes. Connor Vale, another rich asshole who thinks money permits him to treat people like trash. They feed off each other's filth.

I keep my eyes forward, steps steady. No reaction. No emotion. Just keep moving.

Cassie doesn't.

"Go fuck yourself, Liam," she snaps, her voice sharp through the hallway. "Actually, scratch that. I doubt your pathetic little cock could survive the trauma of your own hand."

There's a beat of silence.

Then the laughter starts. Not from his boys. They've gone dead quiet, but from everyone else crowding the lockers.

Liam's hands curl at his sides, his jaw grinding like he's chewing on broken glass. But he's not stupid enough to do anything. Not here. Not with this many witnesses.

He tries to recover, sneering through gritted teeth. "Fuck off. No guy with standards would ever fuck you, Cassie. They'd have to be blind or desperate to touch you."

She steps forward, smile stretching, all teeth and vengeance. "Good. I'd hate to contract your limp-dick disease. Pretty sure my pussy would dry up just hearing your voice."

More laughter.

Liam's face goes red, followed by that weird blotchy purple he gets when he's close to losing his shit. He mutters something about sluts and stalks off, his crew trailing behind him.

Cassie watches him go, shoulders squared, breathing a little hard. After a beat she turns to me.

"You okay?" I ask, hating that asshole even more for going after the one thing I know gets to her. Cassie hides it well, all loud confidence and sharp comebacks, but I know the truth. She hates how she looks, even though she has no reason to. She's pretty—fuck, she's more than that—but she never sees it.

Her mouth quirks into that fake-ass grin she always pulls out when someone hits too close. "I'm fucking fantastic. Nothing like emasculating an idiot in front of his own limp dick parade to make a girl's morning."

I don't say anything. I walk beside her, letting the silence settle.

"Alright, what the fuck is going on with you?" she demands, stepping in front of me as if she's about to stage an intervention. "You've been weird all morning. You didn't even laugh at my perfect dick joke. That shit was gold. Pulitzer-worthy."

I rub the back of my neck, let out a breath. "I lost my virginity last night."

Cassie's jaw hits the floor. "Shut the actual fuck up. Who?"

I don't say a word.

Her eyes nearly burst out of her skull. "No. No. Don't even play. Zane?"

I nod once.

"Fucking finally," she exhales. "I knew it. I fucking knew it. The tension between the two of you could power a city. Was it... Wait, no, don't tell me. Actually, do. No, don't. Shit." She fans herself dramatically. "Of course it was good. That boy has fuck-me energy for days. I'd be on my knees every night thanking the universe if I had a piece of that."

"Cass—"

She throws her coffee in the trash, eyes still bulging like I told her aliens landed in the quad. "Nope. I can't. I need a fucking minute to process this. You need to sit my ass down and walk me through every detail. I want timestamps. I want choreography. Hell, I want mood lighting and background music."

She grabs my arm, dragging me toward the bench as if it's a crime scene that needs investigating. "Was it the roof? Oh, tell me it was the fucking roof. Wait, no... don't tell me. Actually, fuck it, tell me. How was it? Did he have that fuck-all-night stamina or the I'll-ruin-you-in-ten-minutes kind? Wait. Did he go down on you? Of course he fucking did. That boy looks like he eats pussy for sport. And takes his damn time doing it."

I open my mouth to speak but she steamrolls right over me.

"God, I knew he'd be good. It's the quiet ones, you know. The ones with those hands. You know the ones." She wiggles her fingers for emphasis. "Those are not the hands of a man who's in a hurry. Those are the hands of a man who studies anatomy for fun."

She beams at me, completely unbothered, practically vibrating with second-hand orgasms. "Bitch, spill every filthy word."

I blush, which only makes her cackle harder.

"It was... incredible," I admit, voice low. "But now it's fucking weird."

Cassie stops laughing instantly. "Weird how? Did he pull some freaky shit? Chains... Mirror above the bed. Leave nothing out."

I shake my head. "No. It wasn't like that. He was... God, he was fucking perfect. But after that, he left early."

Her smile fades. "Wait. That's it... he walked out? No smug post-sex smirk?"

"No. He left before I woke up this morning."

She frowns. "Sky, it's always been weird between you two. This whole forbidden tension, loaded glances, don't-touch-me-but-fuck-me energy. But you've got to stop doing that thing."

"What thing?"

"That thing where you shut down. You disappear. You act like you don't give a shit, but you're already halfway in love and spiraling."

"I don't do that," I mutter.

"You do," she says flatly. "You get scared and you fucking run. And he's a guy. Which means he's probably overthinking everything, twisting it around in his head until he doesn't know if you regret it or if you're about to tell him to fuck off."

I cross my arms. "You sound way too invested."

"Someone has to be," she shoots back. "And also, bitch, you still haven't told me any details."

I blink. "I said it was incredible."

"That tells me jack shit," she scoffs. "Did he go down on you? Did he make you beg? How big is his cock? I need answers, Sky."

"You talk too much," I mutter.

"Lucky for you. Otherwise you'd still be locked in your own head, pretending you don't want him when it's written all over your fucking face."

I groan. "Jesus, Cass."

"Nope. Don't Jesus me. I want filthy. I want to know if he made you see stars or cry his name into the mattress."

I flip her off as I stand. "You're disgusting."

She grins. "And you're deflecting."

We fall into step; the hallway buzzing with the pre-class chaos. Slamming lockers. The sharp bark of laughter. Someone throws a crumpled worksheet across the corridor and gets a chorus of oohs when it hits a teacher's back.

Cass nudges me. "Tell me this? Was it rough?"

My throat works. "Yeah."

"Good rough or holy-shit-he's-gonna-ruin-me rough?"

I blink, heat coiling low. "Both, I guess."

Cass whistles. "Damn. So why the fuck are you walking around here like your puppy got shot?"

I shrug, chewing the inside of my cheek. "Because I let him touch me and then he vanished."

She stops walking. Right in the middle of the hallway traffic.

People shove past, someone curses, but she doesn't move. "Sky. You've been in love with that boy since the moment you saw him."

I flinch.

She lowers her voice, eyes on mine. "And he's been drowning in you the whole damn time. So whatever this is, it's not done."

I don't answer.

She bumps her shoulder against mine, softer now. "Come on. Let's go fail math together."

I bailed on the last period.

The walk home feels longer than usual, my chest heavy, my head loud with thoughts I don't want to face.

The apartment is too quiet when I open the door. The kind of silence that crawls under your skin and settles in your bones.

I drop my bag beside the couch and collapse onto the cushions. Pull my knees to my chest. My arms wrapped tight as if that's going to hold me together.

The clock ticks. The fridge hums. Hours crawl by, slow and cruel.

I don't eat or move. I sit there instead, chewing at the inside of my cheek until it stings. Every minute that passes beats against me, a steady reminder that he's downstairs in the workshop, choosing engines and pretending last night didn't happen after the way I gave him all of me.

Cassie's voice keeps circling through my skull, loud and relentless.

"Talk to him, Sky. Don't do that thing where you shut down."

Too late.

I've already sunk so far into the silence, I can't remember what it feels like to be seen.

By the time the last bit of daylight bleeds out of the sky, I've had enough. The waiting is a weight pressing into my ribs.

I move to the internal window that looks down into the workshop. Push the curtain aside. The glass is smudged, but I can still see him.

Zane, the only one left down there. Hair falling into his eyes. I watch the muscles as he wipes sweat from his neck.

I tell myself to stay upstairs. To leave him be. To pretend it doesn't matter.

But I can't.

My chest pulls too tight, thoughts crashing into each other, too loud to ignore. My pulse is a steady drum in my throat, and before I can stop myself, I'm moving.

One step. Then another.

Down the stairs.

Toward him.

I move closer, each step loud in the quiet.

"You think I'm a fucking joke?"

That gets his eyes on me. He straightens.

"What?" he says.

I swallow hard. "You think I can easily forget what happened? That it meant nothing to me? I'm not some broken charity case you pitied enough to touch for one night before tossing aside."

His mouth parts as if he's about to speak, but no words come. He stands there, arms stiff at his sides.

The silence afterwards feels louder than the words.

And I hate how my chest burns, how my throat feels like it's caving in. Hate the tears in my eyes, the way my voice cracked at the end. I blink fast, furious with myself, because I am not that girl. I don't cry over boys. I don't fall apart over someone who clearly doesn't want me.

But, fuck, I wanted to matter to him. Just once, I didn't want to be the girl people walk away from when the high wears off.

Chapter 22

ZANE

There are tears in her fucking eyes, and it cracks something in me I didn't know I was holding together.

She turns to go, and the second she moves, something inside me snaps.

"Sky."

She freezes, but doesn't turn to face me. She stands there, spine locked up as if she's bracing for another hit.

I step around the car until I'm in front of her. That's when I realize what I've done.

Her eyes are glassy. Shining with something more profound than pain. It's not only hurt. It's betrayal. And I fucking did that to her.

It hits harder than any punch I've ever taken.

I drag a hand through my hair. Every part of me wants to grab her face in my hands, press my forehead to hers, tell her I didn't mean to fuck this up. But I did. I always do. I fuck everything up. I break the only good things I get.

"You're not a broken charity case, Sky" I say, voice thick.

She doesn't react. Just stares up at me, and lets me stand there in the mess I made.

"You're not like the others."

"What others?"

I swallow hard. My jaw grinds.

"All of them." The words taste bitter, but I force myself to keep going. "The girls I've fucked and forgotten. The ones who don't mean shit once I pull my jeans back up. You're not that."

My throat burns because she's not some girl I found at a party. Not some name I'll forget tomorrow. And now she's standing in front of me with tears in her eyes because I let my own shit fuck it up again.

I take a step closer. My lungs are on fire, voice barely scraping out. "I woke up this morning and panicked."

Her eyes flick to mine.

"I didn't know what the fuck to do with the way you made me feel, Sky."

She exhales hard. "So you left?"

I nod. "Yeah. I fucking left. Because you're the only girl who's ever mattered, and that scares the shit out of me."

She doesn't move. Just watches me as if she's trying to figure out if I'm just another asshole with pretty words and dirty hands.

"You think I don't care?" My voice drops to a whisper. "You think I could fuck you, touch you like that, and walk away clean?"

She stays quiet. But I see it in her eyes. The cracks she's trying to hold together.

"I haven't stopped thinking about you since the first second I fucking saw you," I admit. "You came in with your walls up and your fists ready, all that fire and scars and the shit you don't let anyone see. And I was fucked from the start."

She takes a deep breath, the first one since I started talking.

"I tried to fight it, Sky. Told myself you were nothing more than a distraction. A body to take the edge off, something to help me forget the shit I carry around. But after that, you looked at me, saw through all of it, saw through me. For the first time in my fucked-up life, I didn't want to run."

My chest rises, breath coming hard.

"I've never had someone give a shit whether I stayed or left." I swallow hard. "I fucked it up, yeah. But not because you don't mean anything. It's because you mean too much. I don't know how to hold something that matters without breaking it. I don't know how to be the guy who gets to keep you."

I shift closer, close enough to feel the heat coming off her skin. "But, fuck, Sky, I want to be. For you, I'd try."

I reach for her now. My hands find her waist, fingers curling into the fabric of her hoodie like I need something to hold on to. She watches me, chest rising fast.

"I'm sorry," I say. "For this morning. For everything."

She blinks fast, and then she whispers, "I thought I meant nothing to you."

My heart fucking caves.

"No," I breathe. "Fuck, no."

She exhales, shaky and slow. Her hands come up, fingers brushing my chest, hesitant at first, finally curling into the fabric like she needs something to anchor her.

I can't take it anymore.

I grab her face and kiss her. It's not soft. I pour every jagged, fucking piece of myself into it. Every goddamn thing I've buried since the first time she looked at me and didn't see a fuck-up.

She melts into me. Fingers tugging my shirt. Her breath stutters against my lips, and I tighten my hold on her waist, dragging her into me until nothing fucking exists except her mouth, her body, the way she fits against me like she's always belonged there.

The kiss turns hungry. Messy. Tongues tangling.

My hand fists in her hair. I tip her head back and kiss her deeper, rougher. She moans into my mouth, and it tears something fucking open inside me.

I break from her lips just long enough to rasp, "You don't know what you fucking do to me."

She looks up at me, breath catching. "Show me."

Fuck. That word detonates inside my chest.

I walk her backwards until she's pressed up against a car. Her gasp cuts off against my mouth when I kiss her again, harder this time. My hands are everywhere. Her neck. Her waist. Her ass. I grab it, lift her. Her legs wrap around me, and I sit her on the hood of the car, cock pressed tight to her heat through our clothes.

I trail my lips down her throat, tasting her skin, biting hard enough to make her tremble.

"I need you," I growl into her skin. "Right fucking now."

"Then take me," she whispers, voice shaking. "I'm yours."

She's already tugging at my shirt, fingers frantic, breath shaky. I yank it over my head and toss it behind me. Her eyes drop to my chest. She pauses. Takes me in. Her lips part, and I swear I feel her gaze in my fucking bones.

I reach for her hoodie, pulling it up and over her head in one motion, her shirt going with it. She's left in a pale pink bra that barely covers her, and fuck, she's beautiful. Flushed skin. Wide eyes.

I don't give her time to second-guess it.

"Tell me you want this," I rasp against her skin, voice ragged, cock already straining in my jeans.

Her hands frame my jaw, pulling my face back to hers. "I've only ever wanted this."

I groan, and crash my mouth onto hers, harder now, hungrier, tongues fighting. She moans into me, and I swallow it, grinding against her until the heat of her burns through both layers of denim.

I need her more than I need fucking air.

My hands slide down her sides, gripping her hips, pulling her against me. I break the kiss long enough to drag her jeans down her thighs, kneeling to strip them off completely. My eyes travel up her legs, slow, worshipping. She's trembling. Breath coming in short, shaky bursts.

I toss her jeans aside, lean in, forehead pressed to hers. Her hands rest against my bare chest, fingers twitching, eyes wide and glassy.

"I'm gonna make you feel everything I don't know how to fucking say," I murmur. "Every fucking thought. Every ache and second I spent today thinking about you."

Her lips fall open on a shaky breath.

That's when I sink to my knees between her legs.

My hands grip her thighs and I kiss a line up the inside of one. She gasps again, one hand curling on the hood of the car, the other tangling in my hair.

I kiss higher. Breathe her in. She's already soaked through the thin cotton of her underwear, and it makes me fucking feral.

I pull her panties down slowly, watching her squirm. Watching the way her chest rises and falls, the way her lashes flutter. And when she's finally bare, I groan again.

"Fuck, Skylar…"

I grip her thighs, opening her up wider.

And I taste her.

My tongue flicks over her clit once.

She jolts, hips arching, a sharp gasp tearing from her throat.

I do it again. Slower this time, until I'm sucking her into my mouth and holding her there, groaning against her. She's trembling under my hands, thighs quaking as I keep her open, exposed, fucking adored.

Her fingers tighten in my hair, nails biting into my scalp, dragging me closer. "Fuck... Zane—"

I look up at her from between her thighs. "That's it. Say my fucking name again."

She whimpers, head dropping back, chest heaving. I dive in, tongue circling her clit, before flattening and dragging down through her soaked folds. I fuck her with my mouth, let her ride every filthy stroke.

She's a fucking mess above me, hips grinding, breath stuttering, hands desperate. I hold her down and keep going, relentless, my mouth wet, rough, and hungry. Her thighs try to close but I pin them apart, groaning as she bucks beneath me.

"Zane... I'm... shit... don't stop—" Her voice breaks. Her whole body bows. I feel it coming, the way she shakes, the way her thighs lock, the way her hips jerk up into my mouth.

I keep sucking. Keep licking and fucking worshipping her with my tongue until she comes hard with a strangled cry, thighs clamping around my head, body shaking as she's falling apart in my hands.

I kiss her inner thigh before dragging my mouth away, wiping my chin on the back of my hand as I rise to my feet.

She's gorgeous. Sprawled out, ready for me to take, her chest still rising in fast little jerks.

I stare down at her and unbutton my jeans, voice low and hungry.

"I'm not done with you yet."

Chapter 23

My whole body's still pulsing. Thighs trembling. Breath uneven. I can't fucking move.

Zane stands there, looming over me, eyes dark and full of something I don't know how to name. His chest rises and falls, lips still wet with me. He unbuttons his jeans slowly, as if he's giving me a second to catch my breath. But I don't want to catch up. I want all of it.

I push up onto my elbows, still dizzy from the high, but my body is already reaching for him. I can feel the heat rolling off him, see his cock straining against the denim.

"Take them off," I whisper, voice shot to hell.

He freezes for a breath, before shoving them down. My mouth goes dry. His cock's already hard, thick, flushed, so fucking perfect I ache from looking at him.

I sit up fully and reach for it. My fingers wrap around the base, and he lets out a sharp hiss through his teeth.

"Sky..."

I stroke him once, and then again. His whole body goes tight. I catch the pulse under my hand, see the way his head tips back for a second, jaw flexing as he tries to hold it together.

"Open that sweet fucking mouth for me," he grits out.

I don't hesitate. I sink down onto my knees in front of him and take the tip into my mouth.

His hand flies to the back of my head, not pushing, just keeping me there. I take him deeper, lips sliding down his length, one inch at a time. His whole body shudders. A low groan rips from his throat. I suck harder, hollowing my cheeks, letting him experience every inch.

I look up at him. He's braced with one hand on the hood of the car, the other holding my head in place.

His grip tightens.

"Fuck," he mutters, breath catching.

I pull back just enough so he can fuck my mouth.

And he does. Slow at first, like he's testing how deep he can go, how much I can take. Then deeper. Rougher. His hips jerk forward, cock sliding against my tongue, hitting the back of my throat.

I keep my lips tight and let him use me, and take what he needs. Saliva drips from the corner of my mouth, but I don't care. I want him wild and desperate.

His fingers tighten in my hair, pulling enough to sting.

"Fuck... Sky—"

His rhythm falters and his thrusts become erratic. He's close. I feel it in the way his cock twitches, the way his abs clench and flex with every movement. His voice breaks on a groan, hips stuttering.

Suddenly, he pulls out.

I look up at him, breathless, lips swollen, spit trailing down my chin.

"I need to be inside you," he growls, dragging me to my feet like he can't fucking stand to be apart for one more second. "I need to have you wrapped around my cock."

He spins me around and lifts me onto the hood of the car. His mouth crashes against mine, messy and frantic. His tongue finds mine, claiming me all over again.

He grabs his cock and drags the head along my slick folds before he stills.

"Fuck," he mutters, forehead dropping to my shoulder. "I don't have a condom."

I freeze too, chest heaving, heart pounding. My whole body is strung tight, throbbing, aching for him. I'm soaked, swollen, and fucking empty. All I can think about is him sliding into me, stretching me open. I crave it more than I crave my next breath.

"I'm on birth control," I whisper, dragging his mouth back to mine. "I swear. I've been on it for years."

His hands grip my thighs harder, holding me wide open.

His cock jerks against my pussy. His mouth brushes mine, teeth catching on my lip.

"Fuck, are you sure?" His voice is thick with restraint. He braces one hand against the hood of the car, the other digging into my thigh. His eyes are wild, chest heaving with each breath.

"I'm clean," he grits out. "I've fucked no one bare before."

He drags the head of his cock through my slick folds, groaning at the sensation. I can see the moment it hits him, how fucking wet I am. How ready and hungry.

"Shit, baby," he mutters. "You're dripping for me."

I grip the edge of the car. "Then fuck me."

He grabs the base of his cock, positions it, and pushes in. The stretch steals the air from my lungs. He sinks in slowly, cursing under his breath, his fingers gripping my thighs hard enough to leave marks.

"Fuck," he growls. "So fucking tight."

I whimper, head falling back. He doesn't stop until he's buried to the hilt, every thick inch of him inside me.

He leans forward, forehead pressed to mine.

"You feel so fucking good. I don't think I'm ever gonna get enough of this."

Then he moves.

He pulls back enough to drag his cock almost all the way out before driving in hard enough to knock a gasp from my throat. The car rocks beneath me. My back arches. He does it again. And again. Each thrust brutal and deep, the kind of fucking that leaves marks, that makes you forget your own name.

"Fuck," he growls. "It's like you were made for me."

His fingers grip my hips, bruising tight, dragging me down to meet every filthy thrust. He doesn't hold back. Not when I'm already unraveling under him.

I dig my heels into the car, trying to brace myself, but it's no use. He's everywhere. His cock buried inside me. His body pressing me down until I can't think, can't breathe, can't do anything except feel.

"You take me so fucking good," he says, each word rough with strain. "So tight around my cock. Shit, baby, look at you."

I drag my gaze to his, and the second our eyes meet, something inside me snaps wide open. His eyes are dark and wild, his lips parted like he can't catch his breath.

I wrap my legs around his waist and lock them there, heels digging into the small of his back to drive him deeper, harder.

"Don't stop," I moan, voice broken.

"I wasn't planning to," he says, before shifting his rhythm. It's rougher. Meaner. As if he's lost all control.

My body arches to meet every thrust. I feel every inch of him, every drag and push, every filthy promise etched into the way he fucks me like he can't help himself.

"Fuck," he growls against my mouth, lips brushing mine but not kissing. "You're gonna fucking ruin me."

He slams into me harder. Filthier. A savage rhythm that has my body clawing toward release. My nails scrape his back, my head drops forward, lips brushing his jaw as I moan his name.

He shifts the angle, hitting that spot that makes me see stars, and I cry out, clutching at him, lost in it. Every thrust pushes me closer to the edge, every breath I take is laced with him.

"Are you gonna come for me?" he rasps. "Gonna come all over my cock?"

I nod, too far gone to speak, too full of him to care how desperate I sound. My body's coiled tight, aching, shaking with the need for release.

"Then fucking come," he growls, snapping his hips once, twice, hard enough to punch the air from my lungs.

And I do.

Hard. Loud.

My head tips back, a strangled moan tearing from my throat as the orgasm crashes over me, violent and all-consuming. My spine bows, muscles locking tight, fingers clawing at anything as wave after wave drags me under. It's not gentle. It's not soft. It's a brutal kind of pleasure. Blistering heat licking through my veins, every nerve set alight, every thought burned away until there's nothing left but the blinding, soul-wrecking high of it.

"Fuck... Zane—" I cry out, voice breaking as my body jerks beneath him, completely undone.

My walls clamp down around his cock, pulsing around him, clenching so hard I catch the twitch of him inside me, sense the way he stutters, fights to hold on.

He groans low in his throat, eyes dark and locked on mine. But he doesn't let up or stop. He keeps fucking me through it, riding out every tremor that racks my body, chasing the explosion building in his own.

"Shit... Skylar... fucking hell," he says.

His thrusts turn frantic, deeper, harder, each one rougher than the last as he chases his release. His abs clench, every muscle in his body pulls tight like a wire about to snap. I feel it in the way he trembles, the way his hips jerk, every movement unhinged, primal.

His jaw locks, eyes squeezed shut for a second as he sucks in a sharp, broken breath. A sound rips from his throat, a half-moan, half-snarl and then I watch him shudder. Full-body, violent. His hands grip my thighs, holding me there.

"Fucking hell," he chokes out, voice catching as his body bucks once, twice, until he stills for a second.

He spills inside me—hot, thick, pulse after pulse—his cock twitching as he grinds again and again, lost in the release. His head drops to my shoulder, breaths ragged against my skin, chest heaving with every exhale as he fucks me slowly, riding out his orgasm.

When he stops, he doesn't pull out. He stays there, buried so deep it is like he's part of me now. His chest presses against mine, slick with sweat. Every breath is ragged, every muscle in his body still trembling.

His hand lifts, fingers threading through my hair. He brushes it back from my face with a touch so careful it makes my chest ache. His thumb grazes over the scar above my eyebrow. That tiny mark I've tried to forget, but the one he sees.

Then he leans in and kisses it.

His mouth lingers on the scar, his lips brushing over that mark as if it's something sacred.

He pulls back just enough to look at me. His gaze is fierce, dark, but there's something raw hiding underneath.

His thumb drags slowly across my cheek, over that damn scar, then down, following the shape of my face. That signature Zane edge is still there... cocky, dangerous, untouchable, but there's a softness to him now.

"I promise you," he says, voice low, breath still uneven from everything we just did. "This time, I'm not fucking running."

He leans in and kisses me.

I believe him.

Even if I shouldn't. Even if it's reckless, wild and stupid. Because right now, Zane doesn't feel like the boy I should run from.

Chapter 24

ZANE

Sweat clings to every inch of me as the heat pours through the corrugated roof, turning the whole place into a goddamn furnace. My shirt's somewhere behind me, tossed the second it started sticking. Grease stains my jeans. I don't stop. Not when the noise in my head only quiets when my hands are busy.

The compressor kicks in. The radio crackles, cuts out, comes back in with some shitty rock song from decades ago. I let it play. Anything's better than silence.

I wipe my hands on a rag and crouch by the engine bay, bolts half-loose. My knuckles ache. But it's honest work. The kind that gives you something back when everything else in your life doesn't.

Then I hear her.

That voice.

"Brought you lunch."

I lift my head and wipe the sweat from my forehead with the back of my wrist. Skylar is standing close now, too close, holding a plate with both hands. Her hair's twisted up, strands stuck to the side of her neck. That neck. Soft skin, flushed from the heat. She looks at me with those wide beautiful fucking eyes.

Behind me, Mason lets out a low whistle.

"Didn't know you brought food," he says, mouth curled into that smug grin he wears when he thinks he's got a shot. His gaze drops, lingering where it shouldn't. On her chest. Down her legs.

My fists tighten. It'd be too fucking easy to bury my knuckles in his face and call it a day.

I don't look at him. Don't give him that satisfaction.

"Ignore him," I tell her.

She shrugs like she doesn't care, but I see it. The way her fingers twitch at the edge of the plate. The tiny shift in her stance. The way her eyes don't meet mine.

"It's a cheese melt," she mutters.

She hands it over. I take it. Our fingers brush.

I lean against the car. She follows, settling beside me without a word. We both stare ahead, not talking, not touching, but every part of me is tuned to her.

I take a bite. The cheese burns my tongue, but I swallow anyway.

"You made this?"

She nods, brushing a loose strand of hair behind her ear. "It's not hard."

"No, but it's good."

That almost-smile flickers. Just a twitch of her mouth, as if she doesn't want me to see she's proud of it. But it's there.

Mason's still watching her. Arms crossed, leaning against the tool rack like he owns the place. His gaze drags over Skylar's body again, slow and obvious.

Every part of me screams to walk over and make him turn the fuck away. But I stay where I am, even though it fucking kills me.

I take another bite, eyes still on her. She's not looking at him now, but I see the way her shoulders stiffen, the way she steps a little closer to me without even thinking.

"You wanna see what I've been working on?" I ask. My voice comes out low. Less of an offer, more of a distraction.

She hesitates. Her eyes flick to the car, then back to me. Curiosity wins.

"Yeah."

I set the plate on the workbench and nod toward the open hood. She steps closer. I reach out before she can move past the jack.

"Watch your step," I murmur, fingers grazing her waist, steadying her without thinking.

She nods. There's oil on my hand. It smudges her shirt, but she doesn't say anything.

I lead her over to the car Rainer gave me, keeping close. Not touching, but still there. Every movement she makes pulls at something in me. Every breath she takes, I want to bottle it.

"This here," I point, forcing myself to focus, "is a piece of shit that hasn't run right in five years. But I'm getting there."

Her eyes skim over the wires, the grime, the tools.

She leans in, close enough for her shoulder to brush mine. Her voice is soft.

"How do you know what's wrong with it?"

I glance at her.

"I just do," I say. "You learn to listen."

I pick up the wrench and point to the joint near the coolant line, the one that's always been a bitch to thread clean.

"That bolt's loose," I say, moving under the hood.

She steps in close. Her arm brushes mine. Bare skin against sweat and grit.

I've had girls touch me before. I've had them press up close, flirt, ask for favors I never gave. But this is different. The contact burns slow. Crawls under my ribs. Settles in places that have never been touched.

I pass her the wrench without looking at her, because if I do, I'll stare.

She takes it, her fingers brushing mine. The fucking smallest touch and my pulse is hammering. I hate how easy it is for her to pull that out of me.

"You tighten it slow. Steady pressure," I say, keeping my voice even. "You rush it, it strips. Then the seal is fucked and coolant bleeds through the whole system."

She leans further in.

"Here?" she asks.

I nod, reach out, cover her hand with mine. I guide her hand to the bolt.

She watches, eyes narrowed with focus.

I could kiss her right now. Push her back against the hood and taste that smart mouth. Instead, I hold her hand steady, show her how to move, how to feel the bolt catch and settle.

"You don't force it," I murmur. "You listen for the catch."

She turns it, carefully. Her bottom lip caught between her teeth. The sound of the wrench turning is soft, almost drowned out by the crackle of the radio and the thrum of the heat brimming between us.

"Is this right?" she asks.

"Yeah," I mutter. "Just like that."

She turns her head to look at me, sunlight catching in her eyes. She's proud, even though it's something small. That tiny spark in her face makes the whole world slow down.

I've spent my whole life staying out of reach, keeping it easy, keeping it physical. But this isn't that.

I'm totally fucked and I know it. Because I don't feel shit like this. Not for anyone. Never have. I can feel something breaking loose inside me. The kind of thing you can't shake once it starts. The kind of thing that makes you want more.

Then Mason ruins it.

"Didn't know we were giving private lessons today."

I don't move. My hand stills on hers, fingers wrapped tight around the wrench. I stay there longer than I should, staring at where our skin touches, trying to pull back the part of me that just got exposed.

I let go. Straighten. Spine stiff. My neck cracks when I tilt my head and lock eyes with him.

"You got a problem, Mason?"

He grins. That slow, lazy one that makes you want to hit something. His gaze drops to her ass, drags up her legs, all casual like he doesn't give a shit that I'm right here. As if he thinks I won't do something about it.

"No problem at all," he says, voice thick with the kind of smug that's gotten his nose broken more than once.

I watch him eyeing her and everything in me goes still.

Every instinct I've spent years sharpening tells me to walk over there and knock the look off his face with a fist he won't forget.

"Get back to work," I say, voice flat and cold.

But he doesn't move.

He leans against the tool rack. Each second heavier than the last. My pulse thumps in my ears. I'm two seconds from closing the gap, no words, just blood.

Then I feel her hand. Light on my arm. Grounding me in a way nothing else ever has.

"Don't waste your breath on him," she mutters.

And for the first time I let someone pull me back from the edge.

Footsteps echo from the far side of the bay. Rainer steps into the light, squinting towards me.

"Zane."

"Yeah?"

He jerks his chin toward the lot. "Got a job outside. Old Mustang just pulled in. You wanna take the lead on this one?"

I stare at him, not sure I heard him right.

"Are you serious?"

He nods once. No hesitation. "You've earned it. Time you handle something from start to finish."

The words hit harder than they should. Rainer doesn't hand out trust like candy on Halloween.

I wipe the grease off my palms. "Yeah. I'll take it."

"Good," he says, stepping in close, clapping a hand on my shoulder. It's firm. Measured. The kind of gesture that means something. "You've come a long way, kid. Don't fuck it up."

I know exactly what he's referring to. My fists. My fuse. My history.

The way I was two seconds ago ready to drag Mason across the floor and remind him what real pain feels like.

I nod.

Behind us, Mason's still hovering, pretending to scrub down tools with the grace of a guy who's never worked a real day in his life. His eyes keep finding Skylar. Every time she shifts her weight, or crosses her arms, his gaze drags over her like he's entitled to it.

I see the tension in her jaw. She's trying not to let it get to her, but it is.

And I catch it. So does Rainer.

"Hey, Mason," Rainer calls out, sharp in that way that means don't fuck around.

Mason looks up. "Yeah?"

"Go strip down that old engine out the back. The one stacked near the scrap."

Mason frowns, pausing long enough to make a point without saying a word. Then he tosses the tool onto the workbench and mutters something under his breath about being a dick before walking across the workshop.

Rainer lets it slide. He has more fucking patience than I ever will.

I move toward the front open roller door where the Mustang waits. She's a beauty. Low, black, and mean. All engine and attitude. Exactly the kind of job I'd kill to take the lead on.

But then I hear it.

Rainer's voice.

"You're good for him, Skylar."

I freeze mid-step, everything grinds to a halt.

"You think so?" Skylar asks.

Rainer clears his throat. "I've seen him try to outrun himself for months. It doesn't work. But with you... He slows down."

Chapter 25

SKYLAR

I t's past midnight when I give up pretending to sleep.

The fan rattles over in the corner. Zane lies beside me, bare chest rising slow, the kind of rhythm that makes my insides ache. One arm's flung across me, fingers brushing the top of my thigh. Even unconscious, he's touching me. Always. It's instinct for him now. Possessive in a way that some part of him is terrified I'll vanish if he lets go.

I sit up slowly, careful not to wake him. The sheet slips down my chest, cool air dragging over my skin. The window's cracked open, moonlight spilling in and cutting across the floor, catching the edge of his jaw and the shadows between his abs.

It's been hours since he came home from the garage, exhaustion in every line of his body. But instead of crashing, he went straight for the weights in the corner.

I probably should have looked away, but I didn't. I sat there, without a trace of shame, watching his muscles working under that inked skin, the way his shirt clung to his back before he pulled it off and cast it aside. Every drop of sweat, every flex and bite of tension in his jaw. I took all of it in like a goddamn addict.

And now here I am, still staring.

He looks younger in sleep. Less worn down by the weight he never talks about. No scowl carved into his features. No bite behind his stare. Lips, soft, opened around his breath, lashes long and dark against his cheek. He looks so peaceful.

It's a breathtaking kind of beauty.

My eyes drift to the ink on his collarbone, the way it disappears beneath the sheet and curves around muscle. It makes me want to trace every line with my mouth. Kiss it slow until he wakes up, rolls me under him and fucks all the noise out of my head.

I should lie back down.

But I don't.

I stay sitting, watching the rise and fall of his chest. I could sit here all night staring at him and still not figure it out.

Why someone who doesn't let anyone in... let me. Or why a person who's all fists, fire and fuck-off attitude, kisses me so slowly some nights, I swear it'll break me.

I reach down, touch the edge of his wrist where his fingers still rest against my thigh. And I wonder how long before he realizes he's got my whole fucking heart in that hand.

I climb out of bed, careful not to wake him, the sheet dragging off my legs as I move. I cross the room in nothing but my underwear. Each stride is more weighty than usual.

I grab the first scrap of paper I can find. A crumpled receipt from the corner of the nightstand, bent and smeared with old ink. I smooth it against the wall, pressing my palm flat to hold it still. My fingers tremble. I bite the inside of my cheek until I taste blood.

Then, I write.

The pen scratches across the paper, rough and fast, as if I don't get it out now, I never will. My hand shakes. Not because I'm unsure. I know exactly what this is.

I'm not scared of you. I'm afraid of what I feel.

I'm shaking because it's the truth.

Every second with him chips away at the girl I used to be. The one who flinched at kindness. Who kept her guard up even in sleep. The one who let no one close enough to matter. Now I let him touch me, hold me. Breathe against my skin.

And what's left of me now freaks the hell out of me.

I fold the note, cross the room and tuck it into the back pocket of his jeans. He always leaves them hanging off the edge of the chair.

I slip back into bed, the mattress dipping under my weight, and curl in close. Chest to his side, head near his shoulder. His skin is now warm and familiar.

He shifts, breath catching, arm sliding around my waist without waking. His breath brushes the side of my face. It's soft. Barely there. I close my eyes and try to let that be enough.

But it still isn't enough.

My mouth wants to say it. My heart already has.

I love you.

It resides there, quiet, behind my lips. The truth that could either save me or destroy everything.

He stirs a moment later, muscles shifting beneath my cheek. I freeze.

The words sit heavy on my tongue, still burning from how close they came to leaving my mouth. Three fucking words that could change everything. I swallow them back because he's not ready for that kind of weight in the dark. Not yet. Perhaps never.

His voice breaks the silence, rough, thick with sleep. "You're awake."

I nod against his chest. "Couldn't sleep."

He hums in response, a deep sound that vibrates under my cheek. His lips brush the top of my head, his mouth lingering there for a beat longer than necessary. The kiss that says you're mine with no need for words.

"C'mon," he says, voice husky.

I pull back just enough to look at him. "What?"

His eyes crack open, still heavy with sleep, but there's something in them. A flicker of mischief. That spark I only ever catch in the quiet, when he lets his guard slip for half a second. He looks boyish for a moment. Not broken or guarded. Not the guy who's spent his whole life surviving instead of living. Just... him. Stripped down. Soft in a way he never lets the world see.

"Roof," he says again, like it's obvious.

I blink up at him. "It's the middle of the night."

"Exactly," he says, grinning slowly. "Best time."

He gets up, boxers hanging low on his hips, muscles flexing as he stretches. He goes across the room and gets the bottle of whiskey from the floor close to the desk, and pivots towards me.

His free hand reaches out.

I take it.

His fingers close around mine, and we move together toward the roof.

The tin roof creaks under our feet as we get to our usual spot. We sit side by side, legs stretched out, the whiskey bottle between us, catching the moonlight.

The city hums below. Lights blink. Somewhere, a siren cries out. But none of it touches us.

Up here, it feels as if the world doesn't exist beyond this rooftop. It's just us. Two fucked-up people holding onto something neither of us knows how to name.

He tilts the bottle toward me. I take it, sip once, let the burn slide down my throat. He watches me, mouth twitching at the corner.

Zane's head tilts back, eyes on the sky. "I used to come up here when I needed to think."

I hand him back the bottle and rest my hands behind me. "What about now?"

"Now I come up here to breathe."

For a while, we sit there in silence; the bottle moving between us.

"You ever think about what comes next?" He asks, breaking the stillness.

I glance at him, catching the way his thumb rolls over the glass, slow and distracted. "What do you mean?"

He shrugs. "Tomorrow. Next week. When this all goes to shit."

My heart loses its rhythm. The ease of the moment slips, and I feel the familiar pull of anxiety clawing at my ribs.

"You think it will?" I ask.

"Everything does eventually."

I shake my head. "You don't know that."

"I do," he says with no hesitation.

He takes another, longer drink before speaking again.

"People leave. Things break. That's the world, Sky. You get something good, and it slips through your fingers, no matter how tight you hold on. That's how it goes."

I study his profile. His words are meant to sting, but they come across as the words of someone who has weathered countless farewells and lost faith in permanence.

"Maybe," I say quietly, "but not everything that breaks stays broken."

That earns me a glance.

One of those long, unreadable ones that steals the air from my lungs. His eyes flick over my face, like he's trying to figure out what kind of fucked-up magic it takes for someone to have hope still even after the world's tried to rip it out of them.

He leans forward, elbows resting on his knees, the bottle hanging loose between his fingers.

"You talk like you still believe in shit."

"Maybe I do."

"Even after everything you've seen?"

"Maybe because of it."

His eyes don't leave mine. They narrow just enough that I know I've touched something he didn't want touched. A memory. A scar. Something that still bleeds even if he swears it doesn't.

After that, he laughs. It's simply a breath of sound that catches in his throat. A laugh that tastes more like pain than amusement.

"You're something else, you know that?" he murmurs.

"Yeah?"

"Yeah." His voice drops another octave, rough and soft all at once. "Fucking impossible."

He pauses, eyes still on me. The smirk fades, replaced by something quieter, something that hits deeper. "But you make everything seem easier. Even when it's not."

Then he adds, almost under his breath, "You make me want to stay."

It shouldn't make me smile. But it does.

Because despite all his walls, all the sharp edges and fuck-off energy he throws at the world, this—him saying that—is more intimate than any kiss he's ever given me.

Chapter 26

ZANE

It started when I ran into Griff.

I wasn't looking for him. I didn't even recognize him at first. Just saw a guy leaning against the side of a liquor store, hoodie up, jaw tight, smoke curling from his mouth. Then he turned his head, and it hit me. The twitch in his jaw. That scar near his temple. Eyes that always looked one wrong word away from snapping.

Griff. Only older. Meaner.

The fucker owes me from way back. We were in the same hellhole of a foster home when we were kids. Both angry. Both used to getting hit more than hugged. I took the fall for him once—busted nose, split lip, blamed for a fight I didn't fucking start. He never said thanks. Just gave me a nod and walked away as if that was enough.

We hadn't seen each other since we were fifteen. I figured he was either locked up or dead by now.

But that night, he looked at me as if no time had passed. Spit out my name and gave me that same crooked grin. We swapped numbers, not because I wanted to, but because there was something about seeing him again that dug up old shit I hadn't dealt with.

That was a week ago.

Now he's texted me. Said he wants to meet.

So here I am, standing on the corner outside some dive bar with a busted neon sign buzzing overhead, throwing pale blue light across the cracked sidewalk. The alley reeks of piss and old beer. Trash rustles behind a dumpster, probably a rat or something worse.

Then I see him.

Shitty leather jacket. Eyes bloodshot. The twitch in his jaw is still there.

"You wanna make some quick cash?" Griff asks, flicking his lighter open and shut in that twitchy rhythm he always had as a kid.

He used to do that all the time. Sit on the bunk across from me, flicking that damn lighter until the noise made you want to scream.

I shrug. "You know anyone giving it away?"

He laughs. "Not exactly giving it. But I got a place. They pay for fists."

That gets my attention. I glance over. "How much are we talking?"

His grin spreads slowly, teeth yellowed from smoke and bad choices.

He nods toward the alley. "Come on. You'll want to see it first."

We cut through alleys and backstreets, heading deeper into the industrial wasteland on the edge of the town. We stop in front of an old, long-abandoned meatpacking warehouse. The sign above the door is rusted. The windows are blacked out with tarps or sheet metal.

There's a guy at the door. Buzz-cut. Neck tattoo. Arms folded across his chest.

Griff steps up, mutters something low, too quick for me to catch. The guy grunts, gives him a once-over, and moves to the side, letting us pass without another word.

Inside, the air hits different.

Stinks of old sweat, fresh blood, and years of bad choices. The floor is sticky. In the center of the space, surrounded by rows of bodies packed shoulder to shoulder, is a cage.

Chain-link. Eight feet high. Rusted red in patches that sure as hell ain't just rust. Bare bulbs hang from wires above it, some flickering, some dead, all casting a sick yellow glow that turns everything into something uglier.

And fuck the crowd—it's a goddamn circus.

Men in tailored suits with Rolexes that cost more than rent. Rings thick with diamonds. Faces I've seen in the news. Women in thousand-dollar heels, lips red, expressions colder. Their dresses barely cover anything.

I clock it all fast. This is Griff's world. Not mine.

But I'm already inside.

We push closer to the cage, shoulder to shoulder with people who don't flinch when blood sprays. People who lean in when bones crack.

They came for the sound of fists on flesh. For the sight of a man crumpling under the weight of another. For pain, they don't have to feel themselves.

There's a fight on.

One guy's built like a tank, head shaved clean, veins bulging across his neck. Arms thick enough to snap bones without effort.

The other's lean. Quick. A blur of tension and twitching muscle. His face is a mess—nose smashed flat, one eye already swelling shut, blood dripping from a split across his cheek. There's something unhinged in the way he moves. Controlled chaos. He's not fighting for money. He's here for something else. Something darker.

There's no ref. No gloves. No one intervenes when things go too far. Just fists, feet, elbows, knees. Whatever it takes to end it fast and brutally.

The crowd is pressed tight against the cage, packed shoulder to shoulder, shouting over each other, fists raised with money clutched tight and betting on pain. On who bleeds first. On who doesn't get the fuck back up.

They're not here for sport.

They're here for blood.

I watch.

The big guy lunges, all brute force and bad intentions. His fist tears through the air, aimed straight for the wiry guy's skull. But he's too slow. The lean guy moves smoothly, slipping beneath the arm. Next comes the strike.

A vicious knee, driven up hard into the big bastard's ribs. The crack echoes across the cage, loud enough to sound over the crowd. The big man stumbles, arms sagging for just a second.

The smaller fighter closes in. No hesitation. Elbow to the temple—fast and savage. Bone meeting bone. The bigger man reels, eyes dull, legs already losing ground. Blood spits from his mouth.

A pivot kick to the head that snaps sideways. Spraying blood through the crowd before he goes down hard.

Shouts. Cheers. All of it drowned beneath the roar that follows.

His body hits the concrete with a dull thud. No twitch. No breath. Arms sprawled wide, mouth open, eyes glazed over. The crowd explodes, fists in the air, shoving each other, voices colliding as bets are cashed in and names are shouted across the ring.

A man from the back steps forward. No expression. No rush. Rubber gloves already on, apron streaked with dried blood. He moves into the cage, grabs the body by the ankles, and starts dragging him out.

No one stops him.

No one checks for a pulse.

The next fighter's already heading through the cage door, bare-chested, knuckles taped, eyes scanning the blood-slick floor.

Griff leans in. "Different breed in here, huh?"

"Did that fucking kill him?"

"Nah. He's still breathing. Barely."

"Jesus."

Griff chuckles. "Don't go soft on me now, Zane. You want fast cash. This is where it lives."

A man in a navy suit steps toward us. Italian cut. Tailored. Too clean for this place.

"Griff," he says, voice smooth and wrong. "Is this your guy?"

Griff nods. "Zane Rivera. Kid doesn't lose."

The man sizes me up. "You street fight?"

"Used to."

"Ever lose?"

I meet his eyes. "Never."

He nods once. "You fight for me, and I'll pay you."

"How much?"

He smiles slowly, a grin that stretches too wide, the kind that says he already thinks he owns me. "You win, first fight's five grand."

I feel a tightening in my chest. Five K. To them, it's pocket change. A number thrown around without thought. A drunk night out. A tip to a dealer.

But to me... It's more than survival. It's a step toward freedom, towards standing on my own without feeling as if I owe everyone.

"What's the catch?" I ask, eyes locked on the man in front of me.

He laughs, but there's no humor in it. "You lose, you don't get shit. Simple. You win I get 10% of the earnings" He takes a step closer, voice dropping low. "You throw a fight and I'll fucking come for you."

Then he looks back towards the cage, where another fighter steps inside.

"You win fair," the man says. "And you walk out with more cash than you've ever seen in your fucking life."

Griff slaps my shoulder. "Told you it was worth showing up."

I don't answer. My eyes stay fixed on the cage.

They don't wait for a bell. No count. No rules. Just charge.

A blur of fists, knees and pure fucking violence explodes inside the cage. The crowd loses its shit, pounding on the cage, screaming for more.

Maybe this is a bad idea. Or it's fucking suicide.

But five grand says I don't care. And there's something in me that's been aching to hit something for weeks.

"Yeah, alright." I say.

The second the words leave my mouth, everything shifts.

Griff's grin stretches wide. He mutters something to the guy in the suit, some wordless deal sealed between men who've seen too much. He jerks his chin for me to follow.

I do, even though my gut twists as if I've stepped into something I won't be climbing back out from.

We move through the crowd, pushing past the noise and the heat. Fists full of cash flash in the air, money changing hands faster than blood hits the floor. We pass women draped across the arms of men in suits.

The crowd fades behind us.

Giff stops at the third door on the left.

"This one," he says. "Don't fuck it up, Zane."

There's something in his voice that sounds almost like a warning.

"They remember faces here."

Chapter 27

SKYLAR

The pasta goes cold.

I cooked for him. I don't know why. Maybe I thought it would matter. Perhaps I just wanted to do one soft thing in a world that doesn't let me be soft. So I stirred the sauce until it clung to the wooden spoon, boiled the spaghetti until the steam filled the apartment, checked it twice to make sure it didn't turn to mush. I even plated it. Two servings. Forks crossed on chipped plates.

I even lit the tea light candle I found under the sink last week. Dust still on the bottom. Set it in the middle of the table.

Stupid. I know.

But I did it anyway.

Then I waited.

And waited.

The clock ticked loud in the quiet. Six. Then seven. By nine, the candle had burned out. The pasta was stiff, the sauce congealed, and my throat was too tight to swallow any of it down.

No messages. No calls.

Not that I expected one. Zane doesn't explain himself. He doesn't check in with me.

But tonight... nothing.

Finally, I scrape the plates into the bin, sauce sliding off in thick, cold clumps.

I wash everything as if it were personally offending me. Too much soap, scrubbing so hard I nearly strip the non-stick off the damn pan. The sponge tears. Doesn't matter. My skin turns red. The kitchen smells of garlic and regret, and still I scrub, chasing some fucked-up sense of control in suds and steel.

I don't cry.

Fuck him. I won't give it that power. I've cried for people who let me down, and Zane won't be one of them.

I turn off the tap. My palms sting, the heat from the water still trapped in my skin. I glance down at what I'm wearing—a short skirt, a tank top, lip gloss I applied for no goddamn reason other than I thought he'd be here.

The apartment's quiet, but not in a good way. It's that heavy silence that wraps around your chest and squeezes until you can't tell if it's hurt or shame.

Every shadow appears darker. Every creak of the floor is a sound I want to be him. My heart jumps at the slightest noise. A car passing. The wind at the window. The fridge humming to life.

But the door never opens.

I go to bed.

The sheets are cold when I crawl under them. The mattress feels too big without him. My legs tangle in the mess of blankets that still smell of him. I detest loving that scent so much.

I roll onto my side, fists tucked under my ribs, arms tight around myself as if the pressure can fix the ache. But it doesn't. It never has.

I stare at the wall and try to focus on anything but the emptiness beside me. But my mind drifts before I can stop it.

I try not to think about where he is.

But I do.

My head spins through the worst-case scenarios, every one darker than the last.

All the versions of Zane I've met.

The one with blood on his knuckles and no explanation.

The one who kisses me as if I'm the only thing keeping him alive.

The one built from scars and ash and all the shit he carries from a life that taught him not to trust softness.

The one I love.

I think about the promises I never asked him to make. The ones I wanted but never said out loud. The ones I know better than to hope for.

He could be out there right now doing something reckless. Something that ends with him curled up on the cold pavement, bleeding under a streetlight while I lie here, alone, in a bed where he's supposed to be.

I close my eyes, and pray for sleep to take me. But all I can feel is the space where he should be and the ache in my chest that won't shut the fuck up.

Finally, I hear the front door open.

It's so fucking late the numbers on the clock don't matter anymore.

I don't move. Not because I'm asleep. I don't want to give him the satisfaction of thinking I waited up, or that I sat at the chipped table like an idiot, hoping he'd walk through the door in time for dinner.

He moves through the dark without turning on a light.

Then the bathroom door clicks shut.

Water sputters from the pipes, the wheezing stream that always takes a minute to heat. The shower rattles through the wall behind my head.

I stare at the ceiling. Even so, my mind wanders.

Shower.

The thought creeps in before I can stop it. Something bitter and bruised and ugly.

Maybe he fucked someone else tonight.

This may be the reason for his showering. Scrubbing away perfume, sweat and her fucking hands off his skin before he slides in next to me like nothing happened.

That's the version of Zane from before we became whatever the fuck this is. The Zane who burned through girls the way he burned through cigarettes, always needing the next hit. But I know he has not touched anyone in months.

Still, that thought burrows in. Rotten and sharp. It coils low in my gut, heavy with the kind of jealousy that doesn't have teeth but still tears you up from the inside. I push it down, shove it into the dark corner of my brain where all the other ugly things live.

The water stops. The pipes give one last groan, echoing through the wall like they're exhausted too. Then silence. It stretches out until my skin prickles.

The door creaks open a minute later. I keep my back to him, face buried in the pillow, pretending to be asleep—something I haven't managed for hours.

The bed dips behind me. Sheets lift, and then he's there.

His chest presses against my back, all heat and muscle, his skin still damp from the shower. His arm snakes around my waist, fingers splaying wide over my stomach. He pulls me into him until my body curves into his on instinct.

His cock is hard against my ass, and it shouldn't do a damn thing to me. I'm too pissed for this, but I'm already coming undone.

His face tucks into the crook of my neck, breath grazing over my skin in warm, steady puffs. He doesn't kiss me. Doesn't whisper my name. Just breathes like I'm his anchor and he's been drowning all night.

But I'm the one trying not to fall apart.

I want to roll over, shove him back, ask him where the fuck he was, who he's fucked, and why he thinks he can walk in and press himself against me like this is still okay.

But then his thumb drags slowly across my hip, dragging heat in its wake. I fucking melt. All my tension is leaking into the sheets beneath me.

I hate how good it feels. I hate that even now, after everything, his touch breaks me open. He still has the power to make me safe and wrecked at the same time.

He holds me tighter, arm banded around my waist. Just him, solid and steady. Somewhere in that warmth, I let it go. A state of uncertainty. The fury. The fucking ache in my chest. I let it slip, piece by piece, off my skin and into the dark where it can't hurt me anymore.

I close my eyes and fall asleep in his arms.

The smell hits before anything else. Strong enough to claw me up out of whatever restless sleep I'd fallen into. It curls in the air, punching straight through the dull ache in my chest that hasn't eased since last night. Coffee.

I blink, the light through the curtains is soft and warm. Morning's wrapped in quiet, that early stillness before the noise creeps in. I can already tell the bed's empty. The sheets are pushed back, body heat fading fast. My fingers find the spot where he was. It's not cold yet.

I sit up slowly, every part of me aching with questions I shouldn't still have. Hair falls over my face, which I move away and gaze up, and there he is.

Zane, standing by the kitchen counter.

Shirtless. Just a pair of low-slung boxers hanging off his hips, the waistband riding too low, toeing the line of indecent without giving a single fuck. His back's to me. He's moving like he doesn't know I'm watching, shoulders flexing, every muscle carved and tight, veins running down his arms.

But it's not the way he moves that knots my stomach.

It's the bruises.

Purple and blue and fucking brutal. One rides high on his ribs, another lower down, near his spine. His knuckles are red and look split. Dried blood crusted along one. There's a mark on his shoulder blade, red and angry. One that landed with intention.

He shifts slightly, reaches for a mug, and I see more.

And still he's just standing there. Making coffee. Completely calm.

My mouth goes dry. I swallow the lump that's rising. Part of me wants to crawl out of bed and run my hands over every one of those marks, count them, kiss them, curse whoever left them. The other part wants to scream at him until my voice breaks.

I stare, breath snagged halfway in my throat, chest tight around it.

He reaches past the kettle to grab a second mug, and that's when I see the rest of him.

The bruises across his front make the ones on his back look like nothing.

A mess of deep purples and sickly yellows blooming across his ribs. There's a cut under one pec. The skin around it's inflamed, the kind of swelling that fucking hurts to move.

And then there's the outline of his cock beneath the worn cotton of his boxers. Hanging to the left, thick, even though he's soft. He's not hard, not even close. But fuck, I feel the heat crawl up my spine, anyway.

I swallow hard, and my mouth suddenly dries.

Zane doesn't know I'm awake. His jaw tenses like it always does when he's trying to hold something in.

"Zane?"

My voice cracks. I clear my throat and repeat it, louder this time, trying to steady it.

He glances over his shoulder, casual as fuck, as if I haven't just woken up to a battlefield mapped across his body. He grabs the mug from the counter and walks toward the bed.

"Morning," he says, too fucking casual. Handing me a coffee, as if he didn't come back torn apart.

I wrap my fingers around the mug, more to keep my hands from shaking than anything else.

"What happened?"

He shrugs, and the motion makes him wince, before he covers it with another bullshit line.

"Got into it with some guy. It wasn't a big deal."

The fuck it wasn't.

I narrow my eyes, searching his face for something. A twitch. A crack. Anything that proves this is hitting deeper than he's letting on.

"You got jumped?"

"Sort of. Doesn't really matter."

"Zane—"

He cuts me off with a stare. Cold. Exhausted. A silent warning to drop it. His silence feels sharper than any words, as if saying it out loud would make it too fucking real.

"I handled it."

"That's not what I asked."

He takes a long sip of coffee. Eyes forward. Mouth shut.

And I sit there, heart breaking, because he's right here and I still can't fucking reach him.

I sip mine too, the mug heavy in my hands. My eyes stay on him, watching over the rim, watching every goddamn detail. The stiffness in his shoulders. The way he avoids looking at me.

There's something he's not telling me.

"Did you go looking for it?" I ask, voice low, almost afraid of the answer. "For the fight?"

He smirks. It's not amusement. It's defense. Deflection. A mask.

"Is that what you think of me?"

"I don't know what to fucking think, Zane." My heart thuds hard enough that I can feel it in my throat. "You disappear all night. You won't tell me where you were, and now you look like someone used you as a fucking punching bag."

His gaze lifts, finally meeting mine. There's no warmth in it. Just something hard, a wall I can't climb, no matter how hard I try.

"I said I handled it," he mutters, sharper now.

I set the mug down on the old stool beside the bed. My hands are shaking, fingers curling into fists against the blankets.

"I'm not stupid."

The words hang in the air, heavier than they should be. I lean back against the headboard, pull my knees up, and wrap my arms around them. My chest is too tight.

"If you want to shut me out, fine. Do that. But don't stand there and feed me bullshit."

His jaw ticks. A muscle jumps near his temple.

"I'm not lying."

"You're not telling me the truth either." I scoff under my breath.

His eyes stay on the floor, on a crack in the wood that doesn't matter. He doesn't move. Doesn't even blink.

And that's what fucking kills me.

"Are you in trouble?" I ask, voice quieter than I mean it to be. My heart is thudding with something I don't want to name.

He finally looks up. Just for a second. "No."

But it's not the kind of no that settles anything.

"But you can't tell me where you were?"

He drags in a breath through his nose, eyes already gone cold again. He doesn't even try to lie. Instead, he turns. Walks back to the sink and drops his mug in it. That's the end of the fucking conversation, apparently.

I sit there frozen, knees tucked under my chin, arms still wrapped tight around myself like that'll hold me together.

He pulls on his jeans, shirt, and boots by the door. Every move is silent. He walks to the door, opens it without a word, and leaves.

The door shuts behind him with a soft click.

I stare at the spot he just left. There's a weight pressing down on my chest, crawling beneath my ribs, settling in.

Something's happening—something I'm not allowed to know about.

He's slipping through my fingers, inch by inch, and I don't know how to stop it without breaking us or myself.

But I can feel it coming—one crack at a time.

Chapter 28

ZANE

I've fought twice now. Two wins. Ten grand in cash. They call it easy money, but there's nothing easy about standing inside a cage while a crowd howls for blood. The air there tastes of sweat and iron, and the noise digs under your skin until it's all you can hear. They cheer when bones crack, when a man's head hits the concrete, when someone stops moving. They feed on it.

The rich ones stand closest to the cage, suits too clean for a place like that. Cigars hanging from their mouths, whiskey glasses half full. They clap slowly when someone goes down, all smug smiles and cold eyes, pretending they're better than the rest. They are not. They're just the filthiest bastards in the room.

Between rounds, I stare at them. Their watches glitter; their laughter cuts through the roar. The conversation revolves around odds, how long we'll last. They don't see fighters. They see flesh they can bet on. Collateral they will forget by the next night.

My ribs ache. My knuckles are raw. Blood seeps through the tape and stains the floor. The crowd loves it. They always do.

Last night almost killed me.

The guy was bigger, meaner. Didn't stop when the bell rang. Didn't care about rules that never existed in the first place. I took a hit to the jaw that made the world blur. I could feel my heartbeat pounding at the back of my throat. Still, I swung back. Harder. Kept going until he dropped.

When they raised my hand, there was no victory. Only emptiness.

The money's good. The rush is better. But the come down after... It's a different kind of pain. The kind that crawls inside your head and whispers that this is all you'll ever be.

Now it's morning. My body's a mess. My hands are shaking. Ten grand in an envelope and not a single part of me feels alive.

I tell myself it's worth it. That it's for her. That I'm doing this to fix what's broken.

But deep down I know I'm lying.

I'm not fighting for Skylar. I'm fighting to punish myself for every part of me she keeps trying to save.

I couldn't go home last night. Not looking like this. Not with my eye swollen shut and the taste of blood still thick at the back of my throat. Every breath burns down my side. Ribs screaming, lungs tight. Skylar would see through it in seconds. She'd press those soft hands against the bruises and then ask the questions I'm not ready to answer.

And Rainer — he wouldn't even need to ask. He'd take one glance and see it. Hell, he already did, that day I showed up at the garage after my first fight. I fed him a bullshit story about tripping while I was working on the car he gave me, said it was late and I was tired, and lost my balance. He didn't call me out on my bullshit, but I saw it in his eyes. That flicker of disappointment. He gave me that long, quiet stare and handed me the wrench.

He knows I'm falling.

Mason though... that fucker knows.

I caught the smirk on his face that morning in the workshop, stiff and aching after my first fight. He didn't say much. He didn't need to as he leaned against the hood of the beat-up Chevelle he's been working on with Rainer, arms crossed, mouth twitching with whatever smug bullshit he was choking back.

That's when he said it. Called it a "hobby." That one word, thrown out there with a little too much bite, a little too much knowing behind it.

It means he was there.

In the crowd watching. Probably one of the fuckers in the back corner placing bets, sipping beer, laughing with his boys.

And if he fucking says one word to Skylar or Rainer with that cocky mouth of his, I'll end him.

Ten grand in cash. Stacked in a rubber-banded roll in my backpack, tucked between a busted charger and a half-empty bottle of painkillers. More money than I've ever touched in my entire fucking life. It's heavy in all the wrong ways. Stained before I've even touched it. Blood money.

I crashed at a piss-stained motel off the highway. A place where people go to disappear. The walls reeked of mold and cigarettes. The mattress sagged in the middle. The sheets were stiff. The air con kept rattling, stuttering, before choking out warm air. I lay there all night, eyes on the ceiling, with a sick weight crawling under my skin as I thought about her.

Skylar.

She deserves better than a guy who comes home with busted knuckles and a bag full of dirty money.

For the first time in my life, I want something clean.

Not easy, or perfect—just clean. I want mornings where the sheets are tangled around her legs, where her hair's a fucking mess and she's half-asleep, grinning at me through the sunlight. I want her voice to be the first thing I hear when I open my eyes. I want her laugh, that low, raspy one she only uses when she forgets the weight she carries.

I know now that I want a fucking future with her.

I love her.

God, I fucking love her.

It's not a gentle love. It's brutal, consuming, and bigger than anything I've ever had inside me. It takes up all the space in my chest and still doesn't fit. She's everything... chaos and calm, fire and softness, and she doesn't even realize it.

She smiles at me sometimes when she thinks I'm not watching, when Skylar forgets she's supposed to keep those walls up. That smile tears straight through me, because I know what she's giving me in those moments. Trust. Hope. A glimpse of what life could be if I were someone else.

And it kills me. Every fucking time.

But the world I come from doesn't hand out shit like that. It fucks you up early and teaches you to stop hoping. It dangles the good stuff close enough so you can taste it, and when you reach for it... it rips it away before you get your fingers on it.

Happy endings aren't for people like me.

All I'm doing is trying to hold on long enough to pretend this story isn't already over.

I sit on the edge of the motel bed, jeans still sticking to skin that hasn't stopped throbbing since noon.

I should go home. I can't keep her waiting forever.

By the time the sun dips low enough to set the sky on fire, I've made up my mind. I have to go.

I stop at the shitty Chinese joint on the corner. Grease-stained windows, neon buzzing above the door like it's trying to warn me off. I order noodles—her favorite—plus extra spring rolls and fried rice, because she always steals mine even when she says she's not hungry. The woman behind the counter doesn't meet my eyes. Only swipes the crumpled bills from my hand and slides the plastic bag across the counter.

When I reach the workshop, climb the steps to the apartment, and reach the landing, something tightens low in my gut. It's that deeper kind of knowing, the one that creeps in before the truth lands. Before it rips the ground out from under you.

I press my hand to the door and push it open.

She's there.

Skylar, by the bed, frozen mid-movement, hair tangled, face wet with tears she probably tried to wipe away before I got here. But they're still there, shining on her cheeks in the low light. Her mouth's pressed tight. A half-packed duffel sits on the bed, zipper gaping, shirts and jeans spilling out in a mess that looks too final.

It hits me harder than any punch I've ever taken.

My throat closes, heart pounding against bruised ribs, because this isn't a fight I can win. This is her walking away. And I see it for what it is—I fucking did this.

She doesn't look at me as she keeps folding. Her hands tremble around the fabric, fingers clenched too tight as she shoves another shirt into the bag.

I drop the takeout on the table and take a step toward her.

"Don't," she says. Voice thin. Shaking. Cracked straight through the middle. "Don't say a fucking word."

But silence has never been something I'm good at. Not when the girl I love is standing in front of me packing her fucking life into a duffel bag.

My chest is thudding hard, ribs screaming every time I breathe. "What are you doing?"

She doesn't answer. Just grabs another shirt, folds it fast as if she needs the motion to hold herself together.

I watch her hands. The way they twitch. The way her breath catches in her throat. And I understand that if she walks out that door, I'll tear apart every fucked-up thing I've built to bring her back.

"Skylar. Answer me," I say, stepping closer. "What the fuck are you doing?"

She whirls around, eyes blazing, face streaked with fresh tears. "What does it fucking look like? I'm done, Zane. I'm not doing this anymore."

Something tears through my chest. "What the fuck do you mean, done?"

"You disappear and then lie to me. You shut me out and act like I'm too stupid to notice." Her voice breaks, but she doesn't stop. "Was I just some pussy you didn't have to chase? Just something easy, someone already in your bed, so you didn't have to go looking for it."

Her eyes flick to my face, before dropping to the split skin on my knuckles.

"You think I don't see the way you come home half-alive and won't look me in the fucking eye? Please tell me," she whispers. "Tell me you fucked someone else instead of leading me along. Have the fucking guts to say it."

She zips the bag. The sound rips through the air, and she slings it over her shoulder. That's when it hits.

She's really walking out.

I take a step toward her. "Don't."

She turns, eyes blazing. "Don't what?"

"Don't walk out that door."

Her chin tips up, defiant. "Why not?"

Because I'll fucking fall apart, that's why. Because I've spent my whole life keeping people at arm's length, and now you're the only thing that makes me want to stay. That's why.

I swallow, trying to force the words past my lips. I've taken punches that left me gasping. Seen my own blood hit the floor. But none of it comes close to this.

"Skylar," I rasp. "Stop."

She stills. Just for a second. But it's enough. That tiny pause, that flicker makes me reach for her wrist.

My fingers wrap around her skin. Her pulse beats hard beneath my thumb. I feel it. Every rapid thud.

I lower my voice. "Don't go. Please. I can't figure out how to do this shit," I say, words cracking apart as they come out. "I don't understand how to be the guy who talks about feelings or does things right. I don't know how not to fuck everything up."

She doesn't move. "You could start by telling me the truth. Tell me who you've been fucking."

I flinch, jaw clenched, heart thudding. "You want the truth?"

"Yes."

I drag a hand down my face. "I fought."

She blinks. The seconds that follow are dead silent. A heartbeat later: "You what?"

"I've been fighting," I say, eyes locked on hers. "Underground. For cash."

She stares at me, trying to make sense of it, as if she looks hard enough, the words will rearrange themselves into something easier to understand. Her shoulders drop. "Jesus Christ, Zane."

"I didn't plan it," I blurt out. "It just happened. Griff, this guy who was in one of my homes knew some guys who run fights. Said they'd pay good money. And I needed it. We needed it."

She blinks. Her mouth opens, but she's too stunned to speak. She shakes her head, takes a step back, and another. "I needed it. You think I asked you to do that, Zane?"

"No," I say, voice rising, my frustration boiling. "I'm trying to give you something better. Something stable."

"You think I give a shit about money? You think I care about some fucking stable future if it means losing you in the process?"

"Then, tell me what it is," I shout, the words ripping out of me. "Because I'm standing here fucking bleeding for you, Skylar!"

Her eyes burn into me. "No, you're bleeding because you can't stop fighting ghosts that aren't even chasing you anymore."

That one lands deeper than I expect. Cuts right to the bone.

I drag a hand through my hair, wincing when my fingers graze the bruise on my temple.

"You don't get it," I bite out. "Every time I step into that ring, I win. For once, I fucking win at something. It means I'm not some useless fuck-up who only ever drags everyone down."

Her arms cross tightly over her chest. Her eyes glisten. "I didn't ask you to fight for me. I wanted you to tell me the truth." She swallows. "I just wanted you."

The space between us hums, thick with all the words we've never said. The entire world feels too small to hold everything that's happening here. I take a step forward until we're face to face. My hands itch to touch her, but I force them to stay at my sides. I have to get this out first. I have to tell her how I fucking feel before she walks away for good.

Swallowing, I drag up the words from deep down. I'm scared of saying too much, but I push through.

"I've never fucking loved anything in my life," I say, voice rough. "Nothing ever felt worth it."

Her eyes stay locked on mine, but I don't stop.

"But I love you." The words tear out of me. "I fucking love you, Skylar." My voice cracks, but I keep going. "I didn't mean to. Hell, I didn't even know it was happening until it already had. But it's here." I tap my chest. "In my fucking heart. You're in my head every second of every day. When I'm lying in bed beside you staring at the ceiling, trying not to drown in everything I can't say."

Her lips part, but nothing comes out. A stray tear slides down her cheek, catching the light as it falls.

I press on, even though my throat's closing around the words.

"I wake up and you're the only thing that makes sense in this fucked-up world. I tried not to love you. God, I fucking tried. I did everything to push it down. Buried it under anger, distraction, pain. But you... you crawled under my fucking skin and made a home there."

I step closer, eyes locked on hers.

"I have no fucking idea how to be me anymore without you. You've got my heart, Sky, and I don't even think you fucking meant to take it. But it's yours.

All the broken, fucked-up pieces of it. You own me in a way no one ever has. I don't have the right words, not the sweet ones you deserve. I'm not built for that shit. But this... me standing here, telling you this, it's everything I've got."

I grab her face, my thumbs catching the tears on her cheeks. "You want the truth?" My voice scrapes out of me. "I'm fucking terrified of needing anyone. Of what that does to a person. But I need you, Sky."

"You could get killed, Zane," she says, her voice quieter now.

"Yeah," I rasp. "But I won't."

"You don't know that."

"I don't need to," I say, leaning in, forehead pressing to hers. "I've got something to fight for now."

Her hand lifts, palm flattening over my chest, right over the heart I pretend doesn't beat for anyone.

"You're such an idiot," she whispers.

"Yeah," I breathe. "But I'm your idiot."

She exhales. Her eyes don't move from mine. And then she says, "I love you too, Zane."

The words land and for a second, I forget how to fucking breathe.

No one's ever said that to me before. It wraps around my ribs, wedges between the cracks I didn't know were still bleeding.

"You mean it?" I ask, and fuck, I hate how broken I sound.

She nods, eyes glistening. "Yeah. I mean-"

I don't let her finish. I kiss her like I've been crawling through glass, and she's the first breath I've had in weeks. It's not soft. It's fucking brutal. All teeth and heat and need. Her bag hits the floor with a thud, and I grip her hips, yanking her against me. My hands find the dip of her spine, the curve of her ass.

She moans into my mouth, fingers in my hair as if she's anchoring herself to something solid. I bite her bottom lip, and she gasps. Every bruise on my body disappears under the press of her body against mine.

I pull back, but only just.

"You're mine, Skylar," I rasp, voice strained.

With calloused fingers, I slip my hands under her shirt, causing her breath to hitch. Pressing my hard cock against her, she lets out a sexy moan that always ignites my desire for her.

Chapter 29

SKYLAR

His hands are on the hem of my shirt, chest rising with that storm I've only ever seen when he's about to fuck or fight. He yanks it off, taking my bra with it. My breath stutters when his mouth closes around my nipple, sucking until my spine bows. I'm already shaking, every nerve igniting.

He pulls back just enough to yank off his own shirt, and my breath snags. His chest is a map of bruises, purple, swollen and raw. I trace one with my fingers, barely touching it, but he flinches anyway.

I press my lips to one bruise, then another, until he's growling under his breath. I trace one near his ribs without thinking. His hands grip my waist and he flips us onto the bed, so that I am straddling him.

"Christ," he whispers, voice rough, eyes burning with a hunger that knocks the air out of me.

His fingers skim the slope of my breast, trailing down my side until they settle at the curve of my hip. His thumb moves in slow, lazy circles.

"You're so fucking perfect," he says, voice lower now, edged with something tender that makes my chest ache.

The words melt into me. He sees me. All of me. And still he wants more.

I reach down, grip the waistband of his jeans and tug. "I want these off. Now."

His grin is wicked, that signature bad-boy smirk creeping across his mouth. "Can't get enough of my cock now, huh?" he teases, eyes gleaming with heat.

My fingers work fast. I pop the button on his jeans and drag the zipper down.

"Lift," I tell him, my hands gentle even though my body's begging to go faster. I know he's bruised, broken in places I can't see.

He lifts his hips, and I ease the jeans down along with his boxers. His cock springs free, thick and hard, brushing against his lower stomach, and my mouth goes dry at the sight of him.

He stretches out on the bed, hands folded behind his head, his body on full display, the bruises painted on his skin. My gaze drags over him, tracing every line, every mark, until it lands on the ink over his chest. Black and bold, curling over the left side and disappearing up over his shoulder. A reminder that even in pain, something beautiful can live.

I reach out, tracing it with my fingers. His skin reacts beneath my touch, goosebumps rising in the wake of my hand. This boy, bruised and so fucking stubborn, tough enough to survive anything, still shivers when I touch him.

He watches me, eyes soft in a way that suggests he doesn't care how broken I am underneath.

He loves me.

That thought hits with the force of something I didn't know I was waiting for. I'd hoped. God, I'd prayed in every silent second that he'd meet my eyes and carry the same weight in his chest that I'd been dragging around for weeks. That I wasn't loving him alone in the dark.

And for the first time in forever, I don't feel unloved. I am seen. Wanted. Held.

I undress quickly, then move forward. I trace my fingers up the underside of his cock, tracing the thick vein that pulses beneath my touch.

He watches me through half-lidded eyes. I lean forward, tongue tracing the length of that vein, tasting the heat of him.

"Fuck," he groans, voice hoarse. His arms fall from behind his head, fists curling tight in the sheets beside him like the urge to take control is killing him.

I do it again, slower this time. My lips glide over the thick ridge, my tongue flicking at the tip, and the restraint coming off him vibrates through the air. His stomach tightens, every muscle coiled, shaking with the need to touch, to fuck me.

His nostrils flare. "Skylar."

He says my name like it's some sort of prayer and a curse at the same time. I look up at him, our eyes locking, and I see it written all over his face. He'd burn the whole fucking world down if I asked him to.

A startled squeal slips before I can stop it as he yanks me into him, crashing his mouth to mine. It's not soft. It's not sweet. It's wild... desperate. His lips devour mine like he's starved and I'm the only thing that's ever made sense.

I sink my teeth into his bottom lip, hard enough to make him growl, needing more. His tongue strokes over the seam of my lips with a hunger that borders on feral, tasting, claiming, demanding. I give in, opening for him, letting him in, and his control shatters completely.

He groans as one hand comes up to cradle the front of my throat. While his other hand grips my hip.

The kiss deepens. Becomes something else. My whole body aches with the intensity of it. My skin burns under his hands, every cell tuned to him. I can't breathe. I can't think, can't do anything but whimper into his mouth, high from the taste of him.

His fingers pinch my nipple, and I gasp, hips grinding down before I can stop myself. It sets something off in me. A switch, a fucking explosion. I'm desperate, my body burning with the need that makes my skin pull too tight.

I tear my mouth from his, panting, tasting him still on my lips. "I want you to fuck me."

His eyes darken. That cocky grin slips, replaced by something hungrier. He drags me closer with both hands on my hips, grinding me down until the thick head of his cock slides through the wet mess between my thighs. I shudder, every nerve in my body lighting up as I feel the shape of him hot against me.

"You don't need to fucking ask, Sky. Get off on my cock any time you want."

The way he says it, goes straight to my core. I roll my hips, dragging my soaked cunt over his length. My thighs tremble from how fucking good it is. Every ridge, every vein, every goddamn inch of him is built to please me.

My stomach coils, heat building fast. His cock moves on my clit, and I nearly cry out from how fucking sensitive I am. "Oh my god... Zane."

"Christ," he breathes out, voice rough and ragged as I glide over him again. "Your pretty pussy's drenching my cock."

The heat in his eyes darkens, that edge of hunger sharpening as his hand wraps around the base of his cock. "Rub it on your clit."

I don't hesitate. I curl my fingers around him, guiding him where I need him most.

His gaze drops, locked on every stroke I make. "That's it," he mutters through gritted teeth, the muscle in his jaw twitching as I drag the thick head against my sensitive bundle of nerves. "Fuck."

A low moan slips out of me before I can stop it, hips already chasing more. The drag of him against me—firm, perfect, soaked in everything I'm giving—is almost too much.

"Feels good, huh?" he says, voice hoarse.

"So good," I whisper, breath catching. But it's not just the pressure or the friction that's got me unraveling. It's him. It's the way he looks at me, like I'm something sacred and filthy all at once. He makes me believe I'm fucking beautiful.

Zane's lips part, chest rising and falling as if he's barely holding himself together. That raw need burns in his eyes, and I know he wants every piece of this.

I moan again, louder this time, as I pick up the pace. The tip of his cock drags across my clit with every stroke, slick and steady, and my thighs tremble from how close I am.

"Fuck, I can feel you throbbing on my cock," he groans, head tipping back, jaw clenched, hands digging into my hips as if he's trying to keep it together. "You're so close."

I am. Every part of me is lit up, begging for more, and his voice only fans the fire. "I need you inside me when I come," I breathe out, desperate and aching.

His eyes snap open.

That look hits me straight in the chest.

He sits upright, pulling me closer. One hand wraps around my lower back, dragging me in with a possessive grip. "I want my cock buried inside you too."

Goosebumps race over my skin; my breath stalls in my throat. His words are a promise. A threat. A fucking prayer.

Our eyes lock as he slowly enters me.

"Fuck, you take me so good," he mutters, voice tight.

I grind against him, the pressure so intense it blurs the world. Every roll of my hips makes him hiss through his teeth. His mouth finds mine again—messy, claiming, tongue sliding in deep and filthy—and it sets something off in me.

My moans turn frantic, fingers digging into his shoulders as I ride him harder, chasing every ounce of friction. His thumb slips down and works my clit while his cock fills me, and I swear I could shatter from how good it is.

Each thrust has me unraveling, pleasure climbing fast and ruthless.

"Oh my God," I gasp, head thrown back. "I'm... fuck... I'm coming—"

A deep growl tears from his throat as my pussy clenches around him, every pulse of pleasure dragging me further over the edge. His cock jerks, and I swear I feel the tremor roll through his whole body, chest rising and falling hard against mine. His forehead presses to mine, skin damp, breaths ragged, like he just fell apart with me.

I don't move. I can't.

My limbs are heavy, my thoughts slow, and all I can do is melt into him, head tipped against his, eyes fluttering closed with the tiny splutters of pleasure still hitting my body.

His arms wrap around me tighter, pulling me in until there's nothing left but skin and breath and the steady thrum of our hearts. I catch his pulse against my ribs. The way his chest presses against mine.

His breath ghosts against my lips as he whispers my name. His voice is quieter than before. He tilts his head, resting his forehead against mine again. There's restraint in him, a need to make sense of whatever this is, but instead, he threads his fingers through my hair and stares at me.

Zane Rivera. All grit and chaos. And right now? He's holding me like I'm the only fucking thing keeping him steady.

My heart quickens as I take in every sharp line of his jaw, every flicker of emotion behind his eyes, riddled with a hunger that borders on pain. His chest heaves, muscles tight, every part of him straining to stay still while he's still buried deep inside me. But he doesn't move. Not yet.

I lean in, lips brushing the shell of his ear, my voice nothing but a desperate breath.

"I need you to fuck me and make me yours."

His whole body goes rigid. For a second, he doesn't move, just stares down at me like he's trying to decide if he should ruin me completely or worship every inch of me until I fall apart beneath him.

Then his hands clamp down on my ass, fingers digging in, his restraint snapping under the weight of everything I just said.

The second he pulls out, I feel it. Emptiness so sudden it makes my whole body ache. The loss cuts deep, but before I can even think to protest, he flips me onto my back. Onto the bed.

The look in his eyes is lethal. All rough edges and bad intentions. He looms over me, muscles coiled, the predator in him fully awake now, and I am nothing but prey spread beneath him, begging to be devoured.

"You already belong to me, Sky." His voice is rough, low, dangerous. "Every fucking part of you."

Then he drops to his knees.

"Now fucking spread those legs."

As soon as I do, he dives in. His tongue slides through my folds, every movement practiced, precise, devastating. He flicks, circles, and sucks, working me over with such filthy talent that I can't stop the breathy moans spilling out of me. It's fucking obscene how good it feels. My fingers claw into the sheets as his mouth claims every inch, like he's trying to undo me from the inside out.

Then his hand slides up my body until he finds my breast and pinches my nipple just hard enough to make my back arch off the bed. My gasp rips through the room. His mouth doesn't stop. He groans into me; the sound vibrating straight through my clit. It's too much. It's not enough. I swear I'm going to lose my mind.

He switches it up, tongue flattening against me while two fingers join the game. My thighs tremble. My hips jerk. I roll against his face, needing more, chasing it.

"Zane," I gasp, breath hitching. "Please... fuck... just fuck me already."

He pulls back, lips swollen, chin soaked in me, cocky grin spread wide as if he's proud of the mess he's made.

"Fuck, look at you," he murmurs. "Soaked and desperate. Just for me."

I groan, half in frustration, half because he looks so goddamn good kneeling there with that arrogant smirk and the evidence of my slick, glistening on his skin. He's an asshole. A gorgeous, dangerous asshole who likes to tease the fuck out of me.

He leans over, voice a low rasp that scrapes across my stomach. "How badly do you crave my cock?"

That cocky smirk curves his mouth—fuck, he knows exactly what he's doing.

He wants the words.

Wants to hear me beg.

"I asked you a question, baby," he murmurs, voice thick with that dangerous edge that always does something to me. "How badly do you want my cock?"

"What do you think, asshole?" I snap, fisting one hand in his hair and yanking his face back between my thighs.

His low laugh rumbles against my pussy, lips brushing over me in a kiss that's pure sin. The sound, the feel of it, sends a jolt straight through my spine.

"You want it that bad, huh?" he murmurs, mouth slick, eyes burning.

I bite down on my bottom lip, breath caught, heart thudding against my ribs. All I can do is nod as his thumb presses in soft circles over my clit.

"You're so fucking wet," he groans, pulling his head away and grabbing his cock, putting the head to my opening. He doesn't rush. Just lines it up and lowers his mouth to my stomach, kissing a path along my skin while I tremble beneath him.

"Take a deep breath," he whispers.

Then he pushes in.

My back arches, mouth falling open.

"Oh, fuck," I gasp. It's more than a stretch. It's a possessive, punishing claim that leaves no doubt I belong to him.

He doesn't stop. He pulls back and drives deeper until he's buried to the base, cock pulsing inside me, his hips flush against mine.

"Fuck," he groans, the sound dragging from deep in his chest. "You're so fucking tight, Sky."

His head drops for a second, jaw clenched, breath ragged as he tries to hold it together. Rising onto his knees, he holds my hips, pulling me hard against him. His grip is brutal. I know I'll wear the bruises tomorrow, and the thought only turns me on more.

He pulls back slowly, then slams into me, the slap of skin-on-skin echoing through the room.

Again, and again.

My thighs shake, the bed jerking beneath us, but he doesn't ease up. He pounds into me, eating every moan I give like it fuels him.

"You feel that?" he grits out, slamming deep. "That's me owning this pussy."

The pleasure is too much. My legs tremble. My vision blurs. He fucks me until I can't remember my name. Until all I know is him... his cock, his voice as he ruins me all over again.

"Zane," I whisper, voice trembling, my hand reaching for him, like he's the only thing anchoring me to this world. The need within me is wild. Bigger than anything I've ever known. It claws at my insides, consuming me until there's nothing left but the ache of wanting him.

His gaze is full of fire. It pins me in place, steals the air from my lungs. There's no hiding under that stare. He sees everything. All my craving, the desperation. All of me.

"I love you," he says, so quiet it nearly shatters me.

His hips slow, rolling into me with a deliberate grind that makes my spine arch. It's different now. More than just heat and skin. Each thrust sinks deeper, steadier. He's not rushing. He's giving it to me as if it means something.

And fuck, it's so good; it makes my toes curl, my breath stutter and my chest tighten with every filthy, perfect movement.

I lift my hips to meet him, matching his rhythm, feeding that fire between us.

"Zane," I moan again, but it's not just his name anymore. It's a plea. A prayer. A promise.

Because whatever this is... whatever we've become, I don't want it to end.

Every time he thrusts into me, I come apart a little more. He doesn't just fuck me, he buries himself so deep it's as if he's trying to live inside my skin.

He's never taken me like this before.

There's hunger in every move, desperation carved into every breath.

And then it hits me.

This isn't just about the sex. He's tearing down every wall between us, brick by brutal brick, until there's nothing left but this.

He wants me to see him. All of him.

My fingers trace his jaw, lingering on the rough stubble, careful not to press too hard against the bruise blooming along the bone. He's fucking beautiful. All scars and silence. And at this moment, he's mine.

His eyes find mine, and the look there guts me. It's worship. It's a vow.

He holds me tighter, moving slower now as if memorizing the way our bodies fit together.

He's not just inside me. He's etched into every breath, moan, every fucking heartbeat.

Zane Rivera doesn't just fuck me. He worships me.

As our fingers tangle together, Zane raises one of my hands above my head, pinning it there. The other trails between us, his touch unrelenting as his fingers find my clit. He knows exactly what he's doing. How to drive me wild, to strip me bare with nothing but a touch. Every deep, punishing thrust tears a whimper from my throat, dragging me closer and closer to the edge.

I part my lips, meaning to beg for mercy, for just a second to breathe, but all that escapes is a moan. I bite down on my lip, trying to quiet the sounds, but it's no use. My body betrays me.

"Fucking hell," he mutters, voice strained.

His next thrust knocks the breath from my lungs. It shatters something inside me. My orgasm crashes over me in a sudden, overwhelming wave, a cry ripping from my throat as every muscle locks up tight. I come with a force that steals my voice, leaving my body trembling beneath him.

Zane stills.

His eyes search mine, and for a second, all the cocky bravado slips away. "Are you okay?" he asks.

I exhale shakily, a lazy smile tugging at the corner of my mouth.

"Better than okay," I whisper, my body still thrumming with aftershocks.

He fucks me hard, rough and relentless, chasing his own pleasure with a need that borders on desperation. His thrusts are deep, punishing, making the bed creak beneath us. The muscles in his arms flex with every movement, that filthy mouth drops open as he groans, head tipping forward, eyes half-lidded with the kind of bliss that looks obscene on someone that beautiful.

I watch his face contort as he finally loses control. His body jerks against mine as he comes with a ragged moan, cock pulsing inside me, as he fucks me through his orgasm.

He stills, breath coming in short, uneven gasps. I feel the aftershocks of him coming ripple through his body as he unravels piece by piece. My fingers find his hair, and I thread them through the damp strands, gently pulling him closer until his cheek is pressed against my breast. He holds me, one arm wrapped tightly around my waist, the other splayed across my stomach.

When he finally lifts his head, there's a softness in his expression. His gaze drags across my face.

"Fucking hell," he breathes, voice low. A crooked grin tugs at his mouth, cocky as fuck and everything him. "I've fucked no one like that before."

His hand slides up, slow and steady, fingers brushing over my ribs, skimming the underside of my breast, before resting right above my heart, where it thunders, loud beneath his palm.

His eyes meet mine, that signature arrogance fading into something real.

"You know what this is," he says. He leans in, forehead brushing mine, breath ghosting over my lips. "You're mine now, and I'm fucking yours. Every fucked-up, broken, bleeding piece of me, you've got it. No one else gets to touch you or this pussy. No one else gets to see me like this."

His thumb strokes over that scar above my brow, his mouth inches from mine. "Say something before I lose my fucking mind."

I stare at him. That brutal beauty wrapped around a heart he swears doesn't know how to love. But I've seen it.

"I love you," I whisper, the words trembling in the quiet.

His eyes close, lashes lowering... like the sound of those three words are too much to bear. I watch it hit him—the bad boy who's spent his whole life pretending he doesn't have a heart.

When he opens his eyes again, they're wet, sad with something I've never seen in him before. His voice comes out rough, almost broken. "You are the only person who has ever said that to me."

I reach up, fingers slipping through his hair, and I press a soft kiss to his lips.

"I mean it, Zane," I whisper against his mouth. "Every fucking word."

Chapter 30

ZANE

I told Skylar I was done. No more fights. Told her she didn't have to worry anymore.

But I've got one more fucking fight I can't get out of. I couldn't tell her that. I didn't want to see the disappointment on her face.

The deal is already locked in. Blood money changing hands before I even step into that cage. Cash is already in circulation, names signed, bets stacked higher than the bruises I've been collecting. This isn't some local tournament I can walk away from. Pulling out now won't just burn bridges. It'll light a fucking match and drop on everything.

And I know the type of people I'm fighting for, they'd come for me if I don't show up.

If they can't find me... Then they'll likely come for her to make sure I feel the punishment.

The one person I swore I'd protect with everything I had.

I should never have fucking got involved in this shit because those sick rich bastards got their hooks in me the second I took that envelope full of cash.

I'm in the shop with Rainer. My jaw's still swollen, ribs tender as fuck when I twist too fast. He doesn't say shit at first, just hands me a wrench and nods toward the busted-up Dodge Neon that smells like someone died in the backseat. I don't miss the way his eyes flick to the bruises blooming across my cheek, sticking out like a confession.

Skylar notices them, too. Pretends she doesn't, but when she thinks I'm asleep, her fingers skim over them, featherlight and careful, as if touching them might somehow make them hurt less.

She's been talking more to Rainer lately. I hear her laugh from the front of the shop when she comes home from school. Rainer's not much of a talker, but with her, he tries, and I appreciate that.

Mason packs up and bails for the night, the sound of his boots fading, the door slamming shut behind him. Rainer doesn't follow. He stays exactly where he is, arms folded, shoulders hunched. He leans against the bench, eyes on me, jaw set, face carved out of stone and silence. That same tired look I've seen on him a hundred times.

He's not mad, just worn the fuck down from caring too long about someone who never gave him a reason to.

I keep my head down, pretending I don't feel the weight of his stare, or the heaviness of everything unsaid pressing down with his gaze. I focus on the Dodge in front of me, grab the wrench, and twist hard. My ribs bark in protest, but I don't stop.

He waits. Silent, steady. Then, finally, he speaks.

"You gonna tell me?"

I don't lift my head. If I meet his eyes, he'll see every fucking thing I've been hiding. So I don't.

I dig the wrench into the bolt harder than necessary. It slips, scrapes my knuckles raw, but I don't flinch.

"Tell you what?" My voice is sharper than I mean it to be.

"Don't play dumb with me, Zane. You've got a shiner and a busted lip. Thought you were past all that."

My shoulders tense. The wrench in my hand stills against the carburetor. I don't meet his eyes.

Rainer's boots sound against the concrete as he steps closer.

"I thought you didn't have to fight anymore," he says.

I stare at the rusted metal in front of me, tracing the cracks in the casing. "I didn't mean to."

"You didn't mean to?" His tone sharpens. "Zane, you're not some lost fucking kid anymore."

The words burn. I clench my jaw. "Maybe I still feel like one."

Silence stretches with all the things I can't say. It's been there for years. All the nights I spent with blood in my mouth from fights in alleys, the sting of bone meeting skin, the way pain reminded me I was still alive. Every swing was a prayer, every bruise proof I hadn't disappeared yet. And the mornings, lying on a mattress, counting the seconds before the world started demanding something from me again. Wondering if anyone would ever see me and find something other than a body built to take hits.

Rainer goes quiet for a while. He stands there, the hum of the light above catching the silver in his hair. When he finally moves, he steps closer and sets one hand on the edge of the hood of the car.

"You've been nothing your whole life. Is that what you think?" His voice cuts through the noise in my head.

I shrug, but my chest twists so tight I can barely breathe. "Feels that way sometimes."

"Bullshit." His tone sharpens. "You're something to me. You're—fuck, Zane." He blows out a rough breath, shaking his head. "You're the closest thing I've got to a son."

The words land deep, somewhere I don't let anyone touch. I keep my eyes on the engine, on the bolts and grease, as my throat burns.

He keeps going. "And you sure as shit mean something to that girl."

My heart stutters. Skylar.

"She needs you," Rainer says, voice low. "Whether or not you see it. She needs you just like I do. For fuck sake, Zane, you don't have to keep fighting. You don't have to do it all alone anymore."

That's the part that gets to me. The way he gives a fuck when he doesn't have to. This man isn't blood, but he's stood in every place my father should've been. He's patched me up, yelled at me, and fed me. My own fucking mother couldn't give two shits if I lived or died, and for the life of me, I can't figure out why he sees something worth saving. Why Skylar does. Maybe they're both blind, or perhaps they see something in me I've never been able to find.

Rainer doesn't just care; he sees me. Not the fists, not the temper, not the fuck-ups. Me.

The kid who didn't get a chance to be anything else.

I drag my hand across my mouth, the split in my lip pulling, a sting that feels earned. I stare at the floor because I owe him the truth. Especially after everything he's done for me, the least I can do is not lie to his face.

"I've got one more," I mumble.

He blinks, confusion flickering in his eyes. "One more what?"

"Fight."

Rainer's face goes still. His eyes lock on mine, and I can see the disappointment flicker there before he masks it. "Are you serious?"

I nod once. "Yeah."

Rainer exhales through his nose.

"You sure it's just one?" he asks finally, voice low.

"Yeah," I mutter. "It's just one."

"Have you told them that?"

"I told them."

He studies me for a long time, rubbing a hand over the back of his neck. "Sometimes it's hard to get out," he says, almost to himself.

"I'll get out."

Rainer's stare doesn't waver. "Better be for real. You've got more to lose now. Do you love her?" he asks.

I hesitate because standing here talking about this leaves me too exposed.

Rainer's eyes narrow. "It's not a trick question, Zane."

I swallow, the lump in my throat, it's almost painful. "Yeah. I do."

He doesn't speak; he waits, with that steady silence that always pulls more out of me than I mean to give.

"I can't imagine my life without her," I say, voice low. The truth scrapes out of me like gravel. "She's the only thing that makes any sense in all of this."

He nods. "Then give it up for her," he says. "She deserves better than this. Better than some guy who keeps choosing pain over peace."

I know he's right. I look down at my hands. Scabbed. Bruised. Torn across the knuckles where skin split open hours ago. They're the hands that were built to destroy, not to hold something soft. Skylar deserves hands that don't carry blood beneath the nails or tremble with anger they can't bury. She deserves something clean. Something I've never been.

"Yeah," I say, voice low. "She does."

Rainer lets out a slow breath, something that sounds a lot like relief. "Then make it right."

"I'll make it right."

For a moment, he doesn't answer. He studies me, his eyes running over everything I try to hide.

"You will," he says finally, putting his hand on my shoulder, before walking away.

I stare down at my hands again, flexing them until the knuckles ache. They've only ever known how to fight, but maybe, if I try hard enough, they can learn how to hold on.

Chapter 31

Skylar

I run my fingers through my hair, trying to fix it in the smeared, grimy window of Lou's Diner. It's barely ten, but the air already reeks of burned grease, stale bacon, and broken fucking dreams.

A flickering "Help Wanted" sign hums in the corner, buzzing like it's half a second from giving up on life. Still, it's a job. And I need it. If Zane's out there breaking himself to make money, then I need to step the fuck up. If he's fighting to keep us afloat, the least I can do is stop watching him bleed for it.

"One small step for minimum wage," Cassie mutters, pushing the door open with her hip. "One giant leap for future grease fires and deep-fried dignity."

I shoot her a look. "You promised you'd be supportive."

"I am," she says, all sugar-sweet and full of shit. She leans against the counter like she's posing for some fuck-you fashion campaign, all legs and attitude. "But I'm also not gonna lie to you. You're gonna smell like onions and regret for the rest of your life."

"You're such a bitch."

She grins. "Only to the people I love."

The guy at the counter doesn't bother to glance up. He's too busy filling his oversized cup with Coke from the self-serve fountain. He's wearing a uniform, so I know he works here, but he's moving slow as shit.

Someone in the back yells something about frozen patties, voice hoarse and pissed off, and another guy's jamming a butter knife into the side of the milkshake machine, swearing under his breath while he smears something across his apron.

It's chaos. Greasy, low-budget chaos.

The office door opens, and a man with a stomach too big for his shirt and a name tag that reads "Derek" waddles out, adjusting his belt.

Classy.

"You're the one who called about the job?"

I nod. "Yeah. Skylar."

He gives me the once-over. A bored, dead-inside look that says he's sizing me up to see if I'll quit before my first shift or make it long enough to wipe down a few tables.

"Have you ever worked in food service before?" he asks, already sounding tired.

"No," I say, lifting my chin. "But I'm a fast learner and I'm really good with people."

Cassie chokes on her gum behind me.

I swing my elbow back and catch her in the ribs. Hard enough to shut her up.

Derek scratches the back of his head. "Pays fifteen an hour. Shifts are when we need you, mostly afternoons, weekends, and whenever someone fucks off without notice. We clean our own shit, and some customers are a special brand of asshole. You think you can handle that?"

I nod. "Yeah. I can handle it."

He stares for a second longer, then shrugs, tired and over it. "You're hired. We're desperate."

Not exactly the dream scenario. No handshake, no welcome aboard, no laminated training manual. Just a man in a sweat-stained polo admitting they'll take whoever shows up and doesn't puke at the smell of old grease.

But fuck it, it's a job, a start. It's something that might keep Zane out of that ring a little longer.

"Thanks," I say, and I mean it. My voice is low but solid.

"Can you start Monday?"

I nod again. "Yeah. Monday's good."

"Bring sneakers," he mutters, already turning away. "And don't be late."

He turns away, muttering something under his breath about fryers and teenagers, and Cassie nudges my shoulder with a smirk that's already loaded.

"Well," she says, popping her gum, "dreams do come true. Next stop: Employee of the fucking month."

I snort, shaking my head. "Shut up."

She widens her eyes. "No, seriously, I can already see your picture on the wall. Holding a mop with tears in your eyes."

As we head to the door, I roll my eyes, but then I spot the table by the window. Liam.

Of fucking course.

There he is, all varsity swagger and leftover ego, camped out with his two brain-dead shadows—Connor and Bryce. Same matching haircuts, like their barber gave them all the group discount for douchebags.

Cassie follows my gaze. "Jesus. I didn't realize rats came with the fries."

Liam grins, too wide, teeth flashing as if he thinks he's charming. "Hey, Sky."

I don't answer.

"I didn't know you were applying here." His voice carries loud enough for the whole place to hear. "You planning on getting my order all nice and wet for me?"

I keep walking.

Bryce wheezes with laughter, already halfway to choking on his fries. Connor mumbles something crude, probably about my mouth or my ass.

Cassie flips him off without hesitation, her middle finger standing proud. "Your face looks like a sunburned scrotum, Liam."

I grab Cassie's wrist before she can say more.

"Don't. Not today."

She turns, fire blazing in her eyes, jaw tight. "He can't keep getting away with talking to you like that."

I push open the door and step out. I keep walking, head held high, every step measured, refusing to give those assholes the satisfaction of knowing they got to me.

I can still feel their eyes on me. The way they stare isn't curious. It's ownership. The kind that makes your stomach twist and your skin crawl.

Cassie falls into step beside me.

"You know they're not gonna let up," she says after a few blocks.

"I don't care."

"Well, I do. They are obsessed with you. It's fucking gross."

"They're just assholes," I say, voice clipped.

"No, they are the assholes who think "no" means try harder."

I don't answer because she's right.

Everyone knows what they do at parties.

How they corner girls when the music's too loud and the lights are too dim.

How they wait until someone's too dizzy to stand straight.

When a girl says no, they laugh, as if it's a joke.

They run in a pack, feeding off each other's arrogance, untouchable because their dads play golf with the sheriff and their moms host charity brunches.

Cassie sighs, dramatic as hell, then perks up like someone just handed her a shot of tequila.

"Okay, but real talk now. Are we celebrating your rise to burger royalty with fries or ice cream? I vote for fries. With cheese. And bacon. And zero shame."

"Zane," I say, before I even realize I'm thinking it out loud.

She pauses mid-stride. "Huh?"

"I want to tell Zane first."

Her brows lift. "Oh?"

I shrug, trying to play it off. But the truth is, he's the first person I want to tell.

Cassie's expression softens instantly. All that sass melts off her face like butter on a hot plate.

"He'll be proud of you, too, Sky. Even if he just grunts and walks off, that's Zane-speak for I'm fucking proud."

"I hope so." A smile tugs at my lips.

"You know what else I hope?" Cassie says, grinning. "That I get to be there the first time he walks in and sees you in a paper hat and apron while flipping patties."

"Shut up." I laugh, shaking my head.

"No, seriously. It's gonna be the highlight of my entire year. I might film it. Could put it on TikTok. Caption it "bad boy gets emotionally wrecked over girl in food service uniform.""

I roll my eyes, but my cheeks ache from smiling.

For the first time in a while, things don't feel so impossible.

We turn down a quieter street with empty lots and boarded-up windows. Cassie's in the middle of some wild rant about how soft serve machines are government-controlled sabotage when I hear footsteps behind us.

Then a voice.

"Well, well. If it isn't Skylar."

My stomach drops hard.

I don't need to turn around to know who it is. Liam. That smug tone is carved into my bones from years of ignoring it.

Cassie goes rigid beside me. "Ignore them."

I try. But the footsteps keep coming. Louder. Closer. Fast enough to make my pulse pound in my ears.

"Keep walking," Cassie mutters.

I do.

"Not gonna say hi?" Liam calls out, with that fake fucking charm, the one he puts on when there's an audience. "Hey, don't walk away from us. So, you're gonna act all stuck-up now that you're flipping patties?"

Then another voice sounds behind me.

Bryce, the guy who'd laugh at his own dick pic, is trying to outgross the rest. "Heard they're making her wear a tight little uniform. Bet she bends real easy over the fryer."

Laughter follows. Not the kind that fades quickly, it's cruel.

I grab Cassie's hand without thinking, fingers clenched tight around hers as we pick up the pace. Our sneakers slap against the concrete, rhythm quickens, hearts thudding harder in our chests with every footfall behind us.

We cross the street without checking for traffic, instincts kicking in. Fast walk turns into a half-run. We pass a chain-link fence, a smashed phone booth, a dumpster that reeks of rot. But the street's too still. The houses on this stretch are ghosted. Windows boarded up, yards overgrown, fences leaning as if they had given up a long time ago.

Despite that, they're not stopping.

If anything, they are getting closer.

Cassie squeezes my fingers.

"Fucking hell," she hisses. "They're still coming."

I don't look back because I can sense them.

The weight of their stares presses against my spine. The sound of their boots behind us is haunting.

"Should we run?" Cassie's voice is low.

"No," I mutter. "Don't let them think we're scared."

But I am. I'm fucking scared shitless and my heartbeat is pounding like a fucking war drum.

"Skylar," Liam calls again, dragging my name out with that smug cockiness that always makes my skin crawl. "Don't be rude, Baby," he adds. "We're just being friendly."

Cassie hisses beside me, "Fuck. I swear to God, I'm buying pepper spray and a taser the size of my dildo."

"Walk faster," I murmur, eyes locked ahead.

The echo of their boots picks up behind us.

Liam's voice slides down my spine. "Where are you two headed in such a hurry, huh? Got somewhere better to be than with us?"

I don't answer. Neither does Cassie.

"Oh, come on, Slut," Liam drawls. "No need to act all shy now. You're always strutting around school in those tight little jeans. Thought you were begging for the attention."

Cassie stiffens, her fingers locking around mine, knuckles white. I can feel the fury vibrating through her skin, the kind that comes from years of swallowing it down. She's five seconds from snapping, from turning around and telling them to fuck off, even if it gets her hurt.

Bryce laughs, that low, cruel sound. "She's got those good-girl eyes, but you just know she fucks dirty."

Something ugly twists in my chest.

Cassie goes to whip around, fury written all over her, but I catch her arm fast.

"Don't." My voice is cold, a warning.

Then fast footsteps hit the pavement.

Bryce cuts us off, sliding in front of me with that smug, dead-eyed grin he always wears when he's about to be a piece of shit.

Connor drifts in on the other side, close enough that I catch the sour stench of his body spray. "She's got that face. The kind you wanna wreck. Bet she cries real pretty."

Liam's behind us now. I catch the shift of his weight, his breath too close. "Nah. She's got a mouth I wanna have choking on my cock."

Cassie stiffens beside me. She shifts, rage pouring off her in waves. She's about to swing, and fuck, I don't blame her. But I step in front of her, my shoulders squared.

"Get the fuck out of our way." My voice is stern, sharp, nothing at all like how I feel on the inside.

Bryce leans in, too close, breath hot with that rotten smell of teeth that don't get brushed. "Don't be a fucking bitch. You'd be real sweet if you dropped the act. Bet you're soaked just being near us."

I move to push past Bryce, but he shifts again, blocking me as if it's a game.

Liam laughs. "I heard you let that shit heap Zane get between those pretty lips. Or are you still out here pretending your pussy is some untouched fucking shrine? I bet it isn't. I bet you spread real easy once someone says the right thing. Girls like you always do."

I don't give him the satisfaction of a reply. Just hold his stare. It's all I've got left that doesn't shake.

He reaches out, fingers aimed at my cheek. I twist away before he can touch me, jaw clenched so tight it hurts. My skin crawls just being this close.

Cassie has had enough.

"Touch her again and I'll rip your dick off and feed it to my dog." She cracks her knuckles. "He eats trash."

"Shit. She's mouthy," Connor snorts. "You into that, Bryce?"

Bryce drops his gaze to my tits. "Only when they're crying and begging for me to stop. That's when they are at their hottest."

The bile in my throat rises. They are not just assholes. They are fucking monsters.

I need to get the fuck out of here with Cassie. Now. Every instinct is screaming. I'm wracking my brain for a way out, for anything. A distraction, any fucking gap in their formation I can shove us through.

But they are closing in.

And suddenly I'm boxed in. My back hits something solid... Liam. His chest presses against me.

"Don't fucking touch me," I snap, voice cracking through the tension.

He laughs, close to my ear.

"Relax, Sky. You should be flattered."

Bryce runs a hand through his greasy hair, his eyes crawling down my body. "That mouth's gonna get you in trouble, sweetheart."

"She's already in trouble," Liam mutters, his breath near my neck. "Walking around town dressed like she's begging for a good fucking."

I spin around and shove at his chest, but he barely moves. My skin burns when he gets too close.

Connor steps in, grin spreading, eyes flicking between me and his asshole buddies. "You ever had three guys at once?" he asks, voice dripping filth. "Bet you'd love it."

"Say that again, you limp-dick piece of shit," Cassie snaps.

She shoves forward, but Bryce blocks her with an arm across her chest. He smirks, all teeth and arrogance.

"Easy, Princess," he taunts. "You'll get your turn."

Cassie swings anyway, catching him off guard. She tries to reach for me again, but it only makes things worse.

Liam laughs, darker this time, his hand snaking around my waist before he pulls me against him. I almost vomit when I feel his hard cock against my ass. I slam my elbow back; he grunts, but he doesn't let go.

"Get the fuck off me!" My heart's pounding so loud I can barely hear my voice.

He leans closer, his lips ghosting my ear. "Keep fighting, baby. It just makes it more fun."

And that's when I know this isn't just some joke gone too far. This is fucking real. And if I don't find a way out soon, we're fucked.

I twist hard, my shoulder slamming against Liam's chest, but he only presses closer, his body a wall of heat. His breath hits the side of my face.

"I bet your pussy's tight as fuck," he hisses, voice low. "Probably warm and dripping already."

"Get the fuck off me!" I shove, nails scraping across his arm, but he doesn't budge. He laughs, the sound of it thick and cruel in my ear.

Out of the corner of my eye, I spot Cassie. Her face is pale; her hand trembles as she presses the phone tight against her ear.

My pulse spikes. Smart girl. She's calling someone. The Police. Zane maybe. I don't care who, as long as someone fucking comes and makes them stop.

But then Bryce notices. His smirk dies, eyes cutting toward her. He steps in fast, blocking my view. "What the fuck do you think you are doing?"

Chapter 32

ZANE

The engine purrs like a fucking dream. Raw power under the hood, finally running smooth after months of hard work. Every bolt, every wire, every late night spent in this workshop has built to this.

I've been pouring myself into this car for months. Not because I care about torque or horsepower. I fixed her because it's the only thing I could control in my life. It's about putting something back together when the rest of my life is a fucking mess beyond recognition. Every time I look in the mirror, I see a kid chasing ghosts and trying to outrun the parts of himself that won't fucking die.

And now I've got one more fight, and I pray to God I don't fuck everything up by not telling Skylar about it. It sits heavy on my chest, the weight of that secret, pressing harder with every hour that passes. She trusts me. And I've already walked that line too close—between keeping her safe and keeping her in the dark.

Rainer's no idiot. He took one glance at me and saw through the silence. Just stared me down like he'd already seen how this ends. That stare in his eyes wasn't curiosity. It was history. The knowing that only comes from being knee-deep in shit and barely crawling out alive.

When he told me to make sure I get out clean, it wasn't some throwaway line. It was a warning.

I knew at that moment he wasn't talking about the fight. He was talking about her. About Skylar. About the girl who walked into my mess and didn't run.

He was telling me not to drag her down with me and become the man who ruins the one good thing he ever had.

I toss the wrench back into the toolbox; the clang echoes through the garage. My shoulders roll with a low crack, muscles pulled taut. A reminder of every hit I didn't dodge, every punch I took to stay standing.

But pain I can handle; I've had it all my fucking life.

The phone buzzes in my back pocket.

I almost don't check it.

No one calls me unless they want something. And if it's Griff again, trying to line up another fight or shove some dirty cash in my hands, he can fuck right off. I'm done with this shit. No more cage bloodbaths or shady deals with men who smile with perfect teeth and promise you glory before tossing you to the wolves.

I let the phone ring once.

Twice.

But when I pull it out and see the name lit up on the screen, my heart stutters.

Cassie.

What the fuck does she want?

She never calls me. The only time she did was when she told me Skylar needed me. That was the night everything changed.

If Cassie's calling, something's wrong.

Something's happened to Skylar.

I answer. "What's wrong?"

All I hear is breathing... fast, panicked, broken, and a string of fucks tangled in it.

"Cassie," I bark, already moving toward the door. "Breathe. Calm the fuck down and tell me."

"It's Skylar," she chokes out, her voice cracked and shaking. "They've got her cornered near the alley behind Sanders Street. It's Liam. And those two dickheads he hangs with. They...fuck, Zane...they're surrounding her and I...I can't get to her—"

My vision tunnels. Every instinct in me snaps awake like a fuse lit under gasoline.

I don't wait. I don't even register the rest of what Cassie's trying to say. My body moves before my thoughts can catch up. I'm out the door, heart pounding, legs already eating up the pavement.

I swear to God, if one of them lays a finger on her, if they even breathe the wrong way, I'll break bones without blinking. I'll make sure they remember the name Zane Rivera every time they look in the mirror and see what's left of their fucking face.

Every footstep pounds with one word.

Skylar.

Skylar.

Skylar.

The name beats through me harder than my pulse. Every muscle in my body burns, but I don't slow down. Gravel spits out from under my boots. I need to fucking get there now.

I can see them in my head—Liam with that smug, shit-eating grin, Connor with his slow, poisonous stare, Bryce leaning back as if he already owns whatever he wants.

They have always viewed her as something they could use and discard. The things they said to her in school corridors and classrooms made my gut curl in rage. I remember those nights when I wanted to find them and make them pay for every stare, every filthy word they said to her.

Now they have got her exactly where they want her. If they've fucking put their hands on the one person I would move heaven and hell for, I swear to God, I'll kill them.

I hit the corner of Sanders Street, lungs burning, heart punching against my ribs like it's trying to rip through bone. The street's dead quiet. Too fucking quiet.

My boots skid as I cut down the alley, and that's when I see them.

Three bodies.

Two flank her, blocking any exit. One in front pressed too close.

Bryce.

That smug motherfuckers got his hand up Skylar's shirt, his mouth twisted in that sleazy grin I've wanted to smash off his face since sophomore year. His lips move. No doubt saying shit I don't need to hear to know it's filthy. The poison he always spews.

Skylar's face is drained of color, eyes wide, locked on him. Her fists are small and trembling against his chest as she tries to push back, but he doesn't move. Her whole body is shaking. Trying to hold him off, and fuck, that kills me.

Cassie is behind them, screaming, shoving, trying to claw past Connor's arm as he blocks her path. None of them are listening. They're too far gone on their own power trip.

My vision goes red.

I don't think.

I move.

The second Bryce turns, my fist connects with his jaw. The impact snaps through the air, a hard, clean crack that bounces off the alley walls.

His head jerks to the side, spit and blood flying as his body stumbles backward. He tries to steady himself, one hand reaching out, but I'm already moving. I grab his shirt, yank him forward, and drive my knuckles into his cheekbone. The blow lands deep, and the sound of it hits harder than the punch itself. His knees buckle, boots scraping across the concrete before he collapses to the ground.

The other two rush at me, trying to drag me off Bryce, but they're slow, sloppy. I twist out of their grip and swing hard, knuckles crashing into Connor's jaw. His head snaps sideways, and he drops without a sound, crumpling onto the concrete.

Liam comes next, face twisted, fists flying. One punch clips my shoulder, but I don't flinch. I step in close, grab the front of his shirt, and drive my elbow straight into his face. The force sends him backward, spine slamming against the wall before he drops to his knees, hands clutching his nose as blood pours through his fingers.

Bryce tries to crawl away, elbows digging into the gravel as he drags himself through the dirt, but he's slow, way too fucking slow. I catch his ankle and yank him back. My boot slams into his side once. He curls in on himself with a broken sound. I hit him again, harder this time. His body jolts, then goes still.

The only sound left in the alley is the three of them groaning.

My pulse is pounding. My vision swims; my chest rises too fast, too hard.

They are done—all three of them.

I stand over Bryce, fists still clenched, blood dripping from my knuckles. My arms shake, not from fear, but from the weight of everything I've been holding back.

When I finally lift my head, I see her.

Skylar.

Cassie is at her side, gripping her arm, tugging, whispering something I can't make out. Skylar isn't moving. Her face is pale, eyes locked on me, wide and glassy.

I take one step toward her—just one.

And she flinches. Just the slightest jerk of her shoulders, barely a step back. And I fucking hate it.

"Sky," I breathe.

She doesn't speak. Just launches herself at me, as if her legs can't hold her anymore, and then she's in my arms.

Her face presses into my chest, her breath hitched and uneven. I wrap my arms around her, crushing her against me, holding her so fucking tight my ribs scream.

Cassie stands beside us, chest heaving, eyes wide. Her jaw clenches when she sees Bryce on his ass with his phone out, blood smeared across his face like war paint.

"Fucking asshole," she snaps, stepping closer. "What's wrong, Bryce? Not so fucking tough now? You've been running your mouth at Skylar for months—guess it's hard to talk shit when your teeth are loose." Cassie tilts her head, eyes glinting. "You know, I've waited a long time to see one of you idiots eat shit. Guess karma's got a mean right hook."

Cassie turns back to us, fire still burning in her eyes. "Come on," she says, voice low but urgent now. "We have to go. Before some nosy fuck calls the cops and starts asking why there are three pricks bleeding in the street."

I nod before turning back to Skylar. She's trembling under my arm. I pull her in tighter, press a kiss to her hair. Cassie moves ahead, checking the street. I don't look back.

When we finally reach the workshop Cassie yanks the door open, and the harsh light spills over us. The world slams back into color—concrete floors, rusted tool chests, oil-soaked air that's familiar. But nothing inside me settles. Not with Skylar still glued to my side, her body trembling against mine.

She hasn't let go. Not once.

Rainer's by the back bench. The second he sees us, his whole face changes. Brows crash down. Jaw tightens. That calm he always wears vanishes.

"What the fuck happened?" His voice is sharp, clipped, as he strides toward us.

His eyes move fast. He takes in Skylar's face; the dirt smeared along her cheek, the ripped shirt, the panic still swimming in her eyes.

Without waiting for an answer, he pulls a stool over and taps it. "Sit here." Then, barking over his shoulder, "Get her a glass of water."

Cassie nods once, then bolts for the sink. She grabs one of the chipped mugs sitting next to the wrench set. The tap squeals as it runs, water splashing over her hand while she mutters something sharp under her breath. Her movements are jerky and fast, fueled by adrenaline and rage. She's barely holding it together.

Skylar lowers herself onto the stool. Her arms wrap around her middle, and she curls in on herself. Small. Shaking. Trying like hell not to fall apart, even though I can see the tears building in her eyes.

"Who did this?" Rainer asks.

Cassie shoots a glare over her shoulder, her voice sharp enough to cut steel.

"Those fucking assholes with Bryce? Yeah, real tough when it's three against two girls in an alley."

Rainer's jaw locks. The lines around his mouth deepen. "Bryce who?"

"Anders."

His expression shifts

"Bryce Anders," he says. "His father's Bryan Anders. That lawyer who gets every drunk driver, wife beater, and rich asshole off clean." He swears again, louder this time. "Fucking hell. Of course it's that piece of shit's kid."

Cassie returns, mug in hand. She sets it down on the bench in front of Skylar, then looks at Rainer. "What do we do?"

Rainer doesn't answer. Not yet. His eyes are still on Skylar. On the way, she's shaking. Then they shift to me.

And I know what he's thinking.

It's the same thing as I am.

This isn't over. Not even close.

Rainer studies me for a long second, his eyes unreadable, before dropping to my hands. The second he sees the fresh blood on my knuckles, his expression shifts. He expected better. He hoped I'd learned something from all the times he told me to think before I swing.

"Zane," he mutters, voice low and strained. "Tell me you fucking didn't."

I hold his stare. My chest is still heaving, but my voice comes out calm.

"He had his fucking hands on her."

Cassie kneels in front of Skylar, offering her the mug.

Rainer lets out a long, exhausted sigh and scrubs a hand down his face. "You should've called the cops."

Cassie stands, her arms folded across her chest, her chin lifted in a challenge. "Which is exactly why I called Zane."

"Yeah," he mutters finally, rubbing the back of his neck, "and now the cops are gonna do what they have to."

Silence stretches. The workshop hums faintly with the buzz of overhead lights, the tick of the clock on the far wall the only thing keeping time. Everything else feels suspended, caught in the aftermath.

And I want to burn the whole fucking town to the ground.

For letting this happen, for raising boys like Bryce and letting them grow into monsters.

Rainer's voice finally cuts through the silence. "You need to clean your hands."

I glance down to see that the blood is already drying. Proof of what I did and what I'd do again in a heartbeat.

Then there's a sound.

Faint at first, like a whisper.

A siren.

It slices through the stillness, building fast, shrieking louder with every breath. The high-pitched whine ricochets off the steel beams and oil-stained walls until it feels like the workshop itself is holding its breath, waiting for impact.

Cassie's head snaps up. Her mouth opens, but no words come—just the fire in her eyes. The weight of the moment etched across her face.

Beside me, Skylar stiffens. Her fingers clamp around the mug.

The red and blue lights creep through the windows, washing the walls in short, pulsing flashes.

Rainer rushes to the window, his boots heavy against the floor. He doesn't look at me when he speaks.

"They're here for you, Zane."

And fuck, if that doesn't feel like the end of something.

I glance down at Skylar. I reach out, slow and careful, and tilt her chin up with two fingers.

"Are you okay?" I ask, even though I know the answer.

She nods, barely. Her eyes shine, and when they meet mine, something inside me snaps clean. Just a hollow crack down the middle of my chest.

Rainer steps forward. "I'll handle what I can," he says, eyes flicking to the flashing lights outside. "But you need to know, kid…" He pauses, jaw tight. "You went after the wrong man's son."

I don't care. Not one fucking bit. I'd do it again. Every swing. Because no one fucking touches Skyler and walks away breathing.

Rainer's already moving. He throws a look over his shoulder at me, sharp and full of warning.

"Not a word, Zane. You let me handle it, you hear me?"

I nod.

He reaches the door, pauses just long enough to square his shoulders, then pulls it open in one smooth motion.

"Evening, officers," he says, calm as ever. Polite. That easy going tone he uses when he's chatting shit with the parts supplier or playing nice with customers who don't know better.

Two cops stand just outside. Badges gleaming. Their expressions are tight, unreadable, but there's judgment in the set of their jaws.

One of them flips open a notepad. Scans something scribbled across the page.

"Zane Rivera?"

I lift my chin. "Yeah."

The other one steps forward, voice flat. "You're under arrest for assault."

Skylar gasps beside me. Cassie swears under her breath.

And I stand there and let it hit, let it settle.

Because deep down, I knew this was years in the making. Every fight I picked. Every time I let my fists speak louder than my mouth. All the warnings Rainer gave me, I shrugged off. It was always leading here to this moment.

So I don't argue. Don't resist.

I just let them cuff me. Let them forcefully load me into the back seat, the door slamming shut behind me.

Skylar's face flashes in my mind.

I press my head back against the seat, heart thudding.

Fuck.

I should have kissed her one last time.

Chapter 33

SKYLAR

The hard vinyl bench clings to the backs of my thighs. My cheek's pressed against something solid and warm, and for a second, I can't figure out what it is.

Then I catch the smell. Grease and I know.

Rainer.

His shirt smells like the workshop he's spent most of his life working in. It's grounding, holding me there for a moment when everything else keeps trying to rip me out of my skin.

I shift a little, my neck screaming from the angle I slept in, spine cracking one vertebra at a time.

The lights above us buzz like they're short-circuiting, flickering against the pale green linoleum that covers the floor.

The police station feels sterile in a way that makes me itch. Everything has been wiped clean, but it still stinks of stale coffee and the men who'd rather ask what I was wearing than what Bryce Anders did.

The clock on the wall blinks 4:42 AM. We've been here all night.

I peel myself off Rainer's shoulder slowly. He doesn't move. Only sits there, arms folded, stare fixed ahead. That same look on his face he's had since the second they cuffed Zane.

When I glance up at him, he finally looks down and gives me a slight nod.

"Are you okay?" His voice is rough.

I nod. But I'm the opposite of fucking okay.

"Sorry," I murmur, voice cracking on the word. "I didn't mean to fall asleep."

"It's fine, Skylar. You didn't miss anything." His voice is flat, tired. "Bet these assholes are keeping us waiting. Dragging it out because they can."

After they arrested Zane and took him away, I told Rainer everything. What those assholes did to me and what they tried to do.

What Zane did to stop it.

Rainer didn't interrupt. He listened with clenched fists and a locked jaw. And when I got to the part where Zane showed up and everything went red, he closed his eyes and sighed.

And we both knew at that moment that Zane's fucked.

Rainer leans forward, elbows resting heavily on his knees, shoulders hunched as if the weight of it all is finally settling in.

"He's not walking away from this, is he?" I ask.

He doesn't speak right away. He sits there, staring at the floor, like he's trying to find the words that will soften the blow.

Then after a long pause he turns his head towards me. "No. Not with who we're up against."

Bryan fucking Anders.

Rainer told me about him last night. Bryce's father, the smug, polished bastard who shows up in courtrooms with thousand-dollar shoes. A man who drinks scotch with judges, plays golf with cops, and slithers through the system as if it was built to serve him.

He doesn't lose. Not when his kid's on the line.

Zane won't walk from this; he'll be made an example of. To remind people that the law often favours those with money.

A door creaks open to the left of us. Two people stride through, footsteps heavy. One of them, I recognize, is the officer who cuffed Zane. The other one is dressed to impress. Pressed shirt, expensive tie, sleeves rolled just enough to show off a gold watch. Tan skin, slicked-back hair. Arrogant and entitled. A man who's never heard the word no in his life.

"That's the asshole's father. Bryan Anders," Rainer mutters beside me.

They stop near the front desk, their voices carrying across the quiet space.

"That kid's going down," Bryce's father says to the officer beside him, loud enough for everyone to hear. "Broke my son's jaw in two places. Can you believe that shit?" he scoffs. "My sources tell me he's some underground fighter. Real lowlife. The kid's been in and out of the system for years. What else can you expect?"

I'm on my feet before I even realize I've moved. The fact that he was in the foster system doesn't make him worthless, and it sure as shit doesn't make him disposable.

Rainer reaches out, hand gripping my arm.

"That's bullshit," I snap. My voice cracks, but I don't care.

Bryan turns. His eyes drag over me from head to toe, taking his time, and I swear I feel every inch like a violation.

"This must be the girl," he says, lips curling around the words as if I'm nothing but a case file. A thing. A problem to dismiss. "The one he's saying he was protecting. Sweetheart, you don't want to tie yourself to someone like that. Trash stays trash."

Before I can open my mouth to tell him to go fuck himself and that he doesn't know shit about Zane or anything we've lived through, Rainer steps forward.

"His background has nothing to do with his character."

Rainer's staring straight at him, his eyes like stone. The tension bleeds off him in waves, all tight shoulders.

The lawyer laughs. "Character? Don't start preaching morality to me. My son's in the hospital with a broken jaw. Your guy's got a record longer than this precinct's hallway. Let's be clear. This asshole is doing time. You should figure out how to say goodbye."

The cop says nothing, simply shifts awkwardly beside him.

I feel Rainer's hand on my arm again, holding me in place before I can throw something or scream in his face.

I fucking hate this. The waiting. Hate that Zane's sitting somewhere behind those walls—probably pacing that shitty concrete floor with blood still crusted on his hands, and still, we do not know a damn thing.

No one is telling us shit. No updates. What he's been charged with.

Just silence.

The kind that makes your skin itch. That presses against your chest until you can't tell if you're about to scream or throw up.

• • • • • • • • • •

The courtroom hums with noise. The kind that doesn't stay in your ears, but sinks into your skin and writhes there. Whispers. Pages flipping. The occasional fake cough from someone who's only here because they want to see blood spilled without punches.

Rainer sits on my right, shoulders set, spine straight. He has said little since we walked in, but I can feel the tension rolling off him. His shirt's white, crisp. Clean jeans. His hair is even combed. It's the first time I've seen him without grease under his nails and oil smudged down his forearms. Guess this is one of those moments when you've got to clean yourself up to be taken seriously.

Cassie's on my left, legs crossed tight, a crumpled tissue balled in her fist, which she hasn't touched. Her eyes are red. Raw. She's been crying for both of us. Guilt's carved deep into her face, sharp at the edges. She keeps blaming herself, whispering that she should've called the cops. That maybe if she had, none of this would be happening.

But I get it.

People like us don't trust systems.

We don't believe the cops or, even, in this case, judges will give a damn about our side.

We believe in each other. That's all we've ever had.

I haven't cried since the night they took him. Not because it didn't break me. Fuck, it did. But I've spent years teaching myself how to keep my tears locked down, how to bite down hard and breathe through it. Crying changes nothing. And if I cry now, I'm scared I won't be able to stop.

The door at the side of the courtroom opens and everything stops.

Then, suddenly he's there.

Zane.

The chain between his wrists rattles as the officer leads him in. His hair's messy, strands falling into his face. The bruising still shadows his jaw and cheekbone from the underground fight; it still looks ugly and raw. And I know what everyone else in this room is going to see.

They will see a kid who looks like trouble. The person their daughters shouldn't talk to. The kind judges look at once and throw away.

But it's his eyes that knock the air out of my lungs. They don't flick around the gallery searching for us; they don't scan the benches. They stare straight ahead. Blank and detached, as if he's already accepted that no one in this room's going to give him a way out.

The officer leads him to the table before Zane is forced into a chair. He sits there, eyes locked on the table in front of him. The lawyer Rainer organized for him leans in and whispers something, and still he doesn't look up.

That's when I catch it.

The murmurs. Soft at first. Barely there whispers curling around the room, slithering between the rows. But they grow. Words crawl through the courtroom like insects. Ugly. Itchy.

All here to watch a boy burn.

They don't even try to lower their voices.

My skin crawls. Heat rises under it, boiling up my spine.

I want to stand. I want to fucking scream. Tell them all to shut the fuck up because they don't know him. They don't know a goddamn thing about what happened in that alley. Don't know the soft boy who gave up his bed, so I didn't have to sleep on the floor. They don't know that everything he did to them was to protect me.

But I don't move. I sit there, fists clenched in my lap, nails biting into skin, teeth grinding down the words building in my throat.

Because I already know the truth.

None of them wants to listen.

Not the people watching with their smug little smirks, or the cops who refused to write my full statement.

When Rainer and I sat down to tell them every fucking detail of what those three assholes did to me, they didn't ask questions. They looked tired, uninterested, as if they had already decided I was just a kid from the system, causing problems again.

Zane doesn't seem right sitting there. He doesn't seem like the boy who made me laugh until I couldn't breathe. The one who stood in the kitchen at midnight, making me cheese melts because I couldn't sleep. The boy who pulled me into his arms and told me he fucking loved me, his voice shaking when he said it.

Now he sits there, shoulders heavy, eyes empty. The spark that always burned in him is gone. It's as if they had already taken everything from him before the judge even arrived.

Bryce's old man stands, smooth as ever, as if he's not a lawyer but the fucking director of this whole mess. He scans the courtroom with a calm detachment, eyes skating over the rows until they land on someone.

I follow his gaze.

And there they are.

The three assholes.

Bryce, Liam, and Connor. All sitting in the front row, right behind the partition.

Bryce has a metal contraption strapped across his jaw, locking his mouth in place.

Connor has a bandage across his cheekbone, barely clinging to skin that's not even bleeding.

Liam's got his arm in a sling, but he's still using it to scroll on his phone.

It's a goddamn courtroom performance written and staged to twist the truth into something else.

I shift my eyes back to the man orchestrating it all. Bryce's father adjusts his tie, calm as ever, as he leans in close and says something to his son. Then there's a smug smile that curves across the man's face, the kind of expression you want to slap off with a crowbar.

Rainer shifts beside me.

"It's stacked against him," he mutters. "Poor kid never had a chance. You don't win against assholes like that. Not when their daddies can buy the ending."

Cassie's fingers slip into mine before the words have even finished hanging in the air. She grips my hand tight. I feel her shaking, but I don't glance at her.

I can't.

All I can see is Zane.

Sitting there, cuffed and silent, while they script his future from across the aisle.

Someone in the courtroom tells us to stand as the judge enters the room, but it barely registers—another command echoing through the fog in my head. Everything blurs around the edges. I feel Cassie's hands grip my arms, pulling me to my feet. My legs don't want to move, but somehow, now I'm standing.

Then we are sitting again.

The bailiff reads something official, and the charges hit.

Assault.

Battery.

Intent to cause harm.

Each word lands hard. One blow after another.

They read them out like a grocery list. Stripped of the truth.

Each charge is another chain they wrap around Zane's neck. Another stone added to the pile they're building on his chest.

They say intent to cause harm. But no one mentions the hands that grabbed me. No one mentions the fear that froze me in place.

They say assault, but they're only talking about the bruises on them. Not the ones that landed on me.

Bryce's father stands.

And now the real show begins.

He steps into the space in front of the table with the calm swagger of a man who's never lost a fight he couldn't buy his way out of. His voice is smooth, slick with charm. Every word is rehearsed. Every sentence lands with precision. He doesn't give anyone the chance to question his version of the truth.

He starts by naming Zane. He calls him aggressive.

Lets it hang in the air long enough to stain.

He calls him unstable. Says the kid has issues, a history, a reputation that speaks for itself. That he's dangerous to those around him, that he cannot be trusted to walk free.

Then come the buzzwords.

Violent tendencies. Criminal past. Uncontrolled rage.

He tells them that Zane fights underground, part of an illegal circuit, using his fists for money. He paints a picture of a boy born broken. Says he lashes out. Says he doesn't know how to control himself.

He says it proves everything they need to know.

He never mentions me or what Bryce and the others were doing. He strips me out of the story entirely because my existence ruins his version of events.

And I sit here, teeth clenched, fists white-knuckled in my lap, watching the court nod along.

Everything around me slips into a haze that keeps pulling further away. Voices blur. Movement blurs. Nothing touches me.

I don't register the questions. I miss the muttered comments. It all fades beneath the weight pressing in behind my eyes and the ringing in my ears that won't let up.

Rainer told me yesterday. He sat me down with the unwavering gaze in his eyes and told me the truth like he couldn't bear to dress it up.

There is no way out for him.

Not with Bryan Anders pulling the strings. Not with his money or his connections. He said Anders has too many people in his pocket, too many judges and officers who owe him favors.

He told me the best we could hope for was a reduced sentence. That the lawyer he found— the one Rainer paid for with his life savings—might be able to keep Zane from being swallowed whole.

That was the win in all of this. We're aiming for less time rather than no time at all.

He told me the night after Zane was arrested that I could stay in the apartment for as long as I need to. Said Zane would want that and so did he.

The gavel hits wood, and the crack of it snaps through the courtroom like a gunshot, causing me to jump, breath catching in my throat, fingers clutching the edge of the bench.

A pause. Then the words: "Guilty on all counts."

It hits like a blow to the chest.

Cassie gasps beside me. Her hand flies to her mouth, but it's too late. Rainer mutters something under his breath, a curse carved from disbelief and fury. His fist slams once against his knee, jaw clenched so tight it might snap.

The asshole, Bryan Anders, smirks, all fake teeth and bullshit lies.

The judge speaks, voice steady, almost emotionless. Legal terms. Formal phrasing that turns what happened into a procedure. But then I hear it.

"Seven years."

The words hang in the air. Heavy. Final.

"Seven years," repeats the judge, like the first time wasn't enough to crush whatever was left standing inside me.

Seven fucking years.

Seven years for saving me.

I can't breathe. The air's thick and sharp, clawing at my throat. My chest aches, not from the pain, but from the emptiness suddenly sitting there.

The officer steps forward and grabs Zane's arm.

Zane doesn't fight. He doesn't look at us, just lets them lead him away, his silence louder than anything in this room.

I want to throw myself forward and wrap my arms around him, grab his face in my hands and force him to look at me. I want him to see that I'm still here. That I'm not leaving. That I'll fucking wait, however long it takes.

But my legs won't move.

My body won't listen.

My hands grip the edge of the bench, knuckles white, nails digging into wood, trying to hold on to something before I completely fall apart.

Because this isn't fucking justice.

This is punishment for loving someone the world decided wasn't worth saving.

Then he's gone.

The door swings shut behind him with a dull thud, and that sound settles in my chest heavier than any sentence ever could.

The courtroom clears out, row by row. Spectators rise, having witnessed a performance. They got their resolution. Now, their hushed conversations dissipate, their footsteps reverberate, fading into silence.

It's just me, Rainer, and Cassie left sitting in the middle of it all.

Cassie remains silent. Rainer leans forward, elbows on his knees, head down. And I'm still frozen in place.

For the first time since Zane found me outside that library, I have no idea of what comes next.

• • • • • • • • • •

I'm sitting in the visiting room of the prison, and everything about it makes my skin crawl. The overhead lights buzz constantly, too bright, too white, casting shadows under the eyes of every person waiting here. The tables and chairs are bolted to the floor, arranged in straight lines. Each one is waiting for some version of heartbreak.

I sit at one of them, hands folded in my lap, heart pounding so loud it's all I can hear. Other people wait too. Mothers with tired eyes, girlfriends with fresh makeup, kids shifting in their seats, not fully understanding what this place is. It's not a place built for comfort.

I don't know how Zane breathes in here.

It's been a week.

Seven long, dragging days since Zane was sentenced. Since they told me the next chapter of our lives would be written behind these bars.

This is the first time he has been allowed to have visitors. And only one person can come.

Rainer told me to go. Said he'd see Zane in a few days, that this one needed to be mine. I'm not sure I believe that.

Not after the way he wouldn't meet my gaze at the courthouse.

So now I'm here. Positioned at one of the cheap-ass tables. Elbows on the surface. Heart in my throat.

Waiting for him.

And praying to every fucking thing out there that he's still him when he walks through that door.

My knee bounces beneath the table. I try to stop it but fail.

Every second stretches like a wire pulled too tight.

The door at the far end sounds with a loud metal click that draws everyone's eyes.

There's a pause, a thick stretch of silence, and then the inmates file in one by one.

The visitors around me shift. Two kids sitting at the table closest to the wall gasp when they spot their father—both jump as they want to run to him, but stay locked in place. The rules are clear here. No one moves until the guards give the order.

A woman at the end of the row clutches her toddler in her lap, pressing kisses to the top of his head while tears slip down her cheeks. She wipes them away quickly and puts on a smile.

It's a quiet heartbreak in here. The kind no one talks about but everyone wears in their eyes.

I watch it all, heart kicking inside my ribs, but my eyes never leave the doorway.

And before long, I see him.

Zane.

The jumpsuit looks wrong on him. He doesn't belong in it. There's a fresh cut on his right cheek, skin swollen around the edge, already healing into something that'll scar—signs of a fight, or perhaps a struggle for survival.

He enters silently, saying nothing. He avoids everyone's gaze, including mine.

His eyes stay low as he walks forward. He lowers himself into the seat opposite me. Spine straight. Shoulders set. But nothing about him feels steady.

He doesn't speak.

The boy who once pulled me into his arms, who held my face in his hands and kissed me with the desperation that made it hard to breathe, who whispered he loved me, won't even lift his eyes to meet mine.

I feel my heart tear in half. All the hope I carried into this room, all the weight I held onto, is gone.

But I'm still here. I came, I waited for him. In fact, I haven't stopped waiting. Every second of every day since they took him.

And now he sits across from me, empty and distant, a wall where there used to be warmth. They didn't just take his freedom. They took us too. Everything we were was taken away the second they closed that cell door behind him.

"I thought you'd at least... I don't know, say hi."

My voice wavers and I hate how small it sounds.

Zane's gaze finally shifts. It brushes over my face for half a second, but it's enough to make my breath hitch. But it isn't the look I need. It isn't soft or the boy I remember. It's cold. Detached.

"You shouldn't be here," he says.

The words land hard, cutting deeper than I'm ready for. I try to keep my chin up, even as the crack opens wider in my chest.

"Well, I am," I snap, swallowing the sting.

He leans back, arms folded across his chest. His stare sharpens, all steel and silence. Every inch of him is locked down, closed off.

But I press on, because I didn't come here to sit in silence.

"Cassie's okay," I say, voice thinner now. "Still shaken, but she's alright. She wanted to come, but they only allow one person to see you. She blames herself, you know. Keeps saying she should've called the cops first. That maybe then—"

Nothing. Not a twitch.

He sits still, as if he is frozen in place.

"Rainer's working on something," I try again, clutching at words, hoping one of them will reach him. "I mean, he's busy in the workshop. He got rid of Mason—"

"Skylar."

His voice sounds over mine.

"Stop."

It's one word, but it shuts everything down.

And all I can do is sit here, heart bleeding out across the table, wondering if the boy I love is still somewhere inside the man in front of me.

I blink, the words catching in my throat before I can find the next breath. "I thought you'd want to hear—"

"I don't."

He says it without hesitation.

I stare at him. "I'm just trying to keep you in the loop."

"There's no loop to keep me in," he says, voice steady. "I'm in here. You're out there. That's how it is now."

My throat tightens until it's hard to swallow. "I don't want it to be."

"Yeah, well, no one gets what they want, do they?"

I bite down hard, willing the tears to stay where they are. "You can't shut me out."

"I'm not shutting you out." His voice dips, quiet at first. There's a softness in it, just for a second, enough to give me hope, but then it hardens. "I'm setting you free."

"I don't want to be free of you."

"Then you're fucking stupid."

Zane leans forward, elbows on the table, shoulders tight. His eyes lock onto mine and don't waver.

"You think I want you coming in here every week?" he spits. "Being here, wasting your life on someone who's already been written off? I'm a fucking inmate now, Sky. A number. A mistake someone's already boxed up and filed away."

His voice cracks, just enough to bleed.

"And you—" He cuts off, jaw clenched so tight his neck strains with the pressure. He shakes his head, breathing hard through his nose. "You're not meant for this shit, Sky."

My hands tremble under the table, but I keep my voice steady. "You don't get to decide that for me."

"I already did."

I reach across the table, desperate to close the space between us, but he jerks back as if my touch might poison him.

"Zane, please don't do this."

"I don't want you here."

"You don't mean that."

"I do."

The words hit bone. Tears press against the back of my eyes, stinging, but I refuse to let them fall. I shake my head, heart cracking open in my chest.

"You said you loved me."

His mouth tightens, the muscle in his jaw ticking. His fists curl on the table, tight enough that his knuckles go white.

"That night," I whisper, "you said it to me and you meant it."

He leans forward. "I lied. I said it so I could fuck you. Get it through your fucking head that I don't love you," he snaps. "I never have. You were just a fuck. That's all. Easy pussy."

My whole body goes still, every part of me frozen in place. My ears ring. My skin burns.

He stands and turns his back, as if I'm invisible, and heads toward the guard stationed by the door—the same one he walked through moments before.

I sit there, stunned, watching the boy I love walk away with pieces of me still in his hands, knowing that there's nothing left to hold on to.

Chapter 34

ZANE

The door clangs shut behind me. I swear that sound is gonna haunt me for the rest of my fucking life.

The cell's small. Ten steps from one end to the other if I push it. Thin-ass mattress on a slab of metal that barely qualifies as a bed. No pillow. A steel toilet in the corner reeking worse than it looks. The walls are stained with a hundred lives that passed through before me. The light above flickers with a kind of desperate rhythm.

This is it.

Home. For the next seven fucking years.

I walk straight to the bed and drop down.

Fuck.

I can still see it. The second it landed. The way her eyes went wide, stunned and full of tears she refused to let fall. The way her lips parted to survive the hit.

And I fucking broke her.

With the one thing she trusted.

Me.

My voice. The same mouth, once telling her she was the only goddamn thing that ever made sense.

I told her she was nothing. Called her an easy fuck. Told her I never loved her.

And I watched it crush her.

Watched her pull into herself, small and shaking, trying to hold it together in a room full of strangers while I sat there pretending it didn't kill me to do it.

But it did.

It felt like driving a fucking sledgehammer into my own chest. Blow after blow, straight to the ribs. I wanted to throw the table across the room and pull her into my arms and tell her the truth.

That she is everything. That I fucking love her with a force strong enough to burn this place to the ground.

That I see her when I close my eyes. Hear her voice when this place gets too quiet.

But I can't let her ruin her life for me.

She doesn't belong in this world.

Not during visiting hours and scheduled phone calls.

She deserves more than the walls closing in around me. She deserves more than a boy who's nothing but a record and a number now.

So I did the only thing I could.

I pushed her away hard enough to make sure she wouldn't come back.

And it fucking hurts. God, it's fucking killing me. Every breath. Every second since I walked out of that room.

But the pain is easier to carry than the thought of her throwing her entire future away for a broken boy with blood on his hands.

I'll take this punishment.

I'll take the sentence.

But I won't take her down with me.

My shoulders shake. My chest caves in on itself until it feels like the air's been stripped right out of me. My throat burns. I try to swallow it down, bury it deep where everything else lives, but it's no good.

I cry.

For the first time in my life, I fucking cry.

The sound ripping out of me doesn't even sound human.

Through all the foster homes. The cracked walls and cold floors. The fists, the belts. The nights I lay in bed hungry because someone else got the last piece of bread. Through every bruise that faded. Every rib that healed crooked. Every social worker who said, "You'll be okay" and then left me to rot.

I never cried.

Not once.

But now, sitting in this cell with her name still breaking through my teeth, I can't stop.

Because losing Skylar isn't another hit to survive.

I know that it'll be the one that fucking ends me.

This is only the beginning.
Zane and Skylar's story concludes in Forgetting You.

ISBN 9781923416246 – Broken Pieces

Also by Eve

Rockstar Romance Series

Five Summers
Sixty Days of Summer
Seven Lost Summers

School Bully Romance Series

Cruel Intentions
Cruel Truths
Cruel Promises

Mafia Romance Series

The Lies We Lived
The Scars We Keep

Love This Story?
Don't miss what is coming next.
Join the chaos—books, news, and sneak peeks all in one place:
https://linktr.ee/evecampbell.author

www.ingramcontent.com/pod-product-compliance
Lightning Source LLC
Chambersburg PA
CBHW071234190726
48292CB00007B/2278